THE WAITING ROOMS

PRAISE FOR *THE WAITING ROOMS*

'Stunning and terrifying ... *The Waiting Rooms* wrenches your heart in every way possible, but written with such humanity and emotion' Miranda Dickinson

'If you're the kind of person who watches *Contagion* during a pandemic, you'll love *The Waiting Rooms* ... Chillingly close to reality, this gripping thriller brims with authenticity. A captivating, accomplished and timely debut from an author to watch' Adam Hamdy

'I galloped through this gripping and disturbing story of a world in which antibiotic resistance has become a reality. It feels especially prescient in the time of COVID-19, when discrimination against the over-seventies is already a reality. The medical research is convincing, the scenarios plausible, and the story is emotionally engaging. This is an incredible debut!' Gill Paul

'If the themes are dark and topical, the writing is exquisite ... A superb and satisfying novel' Louise Beech

'*The Waiting Rooms* is engrossing and eye-opening ... with heart-stopping plot twists, showing what everyday life would be like in a world wherein medicine no longer cures even the simplest infections ... *The Waiting Rooms* is a stunning medical thriller set in a terrifying possible future' *Foreword Reviews*

'*The Waiting Rooms* will certainly distract us from the real world for a few hours and this is the immeasurable value of fiction. It gives hope that, as in Eve Smith's fictitious world, the possibility of a happy ending still exists' *Die Burger*

'*The Waiting Rooms* is thoroughly engaging and it's clear that an enormous amount of research was done to craft a convincing story. That it's firmly based in facts ironically makes for a reassuring, albeit eye-opening read' Crime Fiction Lover

'This is THE book of our time. Literally unputdownable and unforgettable!' Phillipa's Quick Book Review Podcast

'*The Waiting Rooms* is a captivating, if slightly scary, read ... With realistic characters and an evocative storyline' On-the-Shelf Reviews

'This is very much a novel of our times and a thought-provoking story' Trip Fiction

'My emotions ranged from horror to compassion to sadness while reading this gripping, well-told story ... while this was an enjoyable read, it's also uncomfortable and illuminating' Suidi's Book Reviews

'*The Waiting Rooms* is a superbly written novel ... it shocked me, it sobered me and it gave me all the goosebumps that great books always do ... one of the best dystopian books that I have had the pleasure of reading, this book is going to be huge' The Reading Closet

'Eve Smith is a name I will definitely be looking out for when her next novel is published, and so should you. Her work captures the essence of Margaret Atwood and George Orwell … two of my favourite authors. If Smith's next novels are of the same calibre I can imagine her name being added to that list' Number 9 Reviews

'Before the COVID-19 pandemic we were already aware that antimicrobial resistance was becoming a problem, and this thriller provides plenty of thought-provoking material about that … a somewhat dark read, but with plenty of interesting details about what the future could look like alongside an exciting storyline' Emma B Books

'This book drew me in from the very first page and didn't let go until the final page had been turned. A shocking but scarily relevant read, this is a stunning debut' Cal Turner Book Reviews

'Hard-hitting, thought-provoking and scarily realistic, *The Waiting Rooms* should be on everyone's bookshelf' The Book Magnet

ABOUT THE AUTHOR

Eve Smith writes speculative fiction, mainly about the things that scare her. She attributes her love of all things dark and dystopian to a childhood watching *Tales of the Unexpected* and black-and-white Edgar Allen Poe double bills. In this world of questionable facts, stats and news, she believes storytelling is more important than ever to engage people in real life issues.

Set twenty years after an antibiotic crisis, her debut novel *The Waiting Rooms* was shortlisted for the Bridport Prize First Novel Award. Her flash fiction has been shortlisted for the Bath Flash Fiction Award and highly commended for The Brighton Prize.

When she's not writing she's racing across fields after her dog, trying to organise herself and her family, or off exploring somewhere new.

Follow Eve on Twitter @evecsmith and on her website: evesmithauthor.com

THE WAITING ROOMS

For Patricia

It is not difficult to make microbes resistant to penicillin...

The time may come when penicillin can be bought by anyone in the shops. Then there is the danger that the ignorant man may easily underdose himself and by exposing his microbes to non-lethal quantities of the drug, make them resistant.

—Sir Alexander Fleming, Nobel Lecture, 11th December 1945

There are already widespread resistance mechanisms in nature to drugs we haven't invented yet ... When we dump a new antibiotic into the environment, we apply selective pressure and resistance grows. We need to be smart about this. Bacteria use antibiotics judiciously. Humans do not.

—Brad Spellberg, MD, November 2019
Dr Spellberg is Chief Medical Officer at Los Angeles County – University of Southern California Medical Center and Associate Dean for Clinical Affairs at USC's Keck School of Medicine.

CHAPTER 1

Twenty years post-Crisis

KATE

'Kate? We've got a problem. Bed fourteen. Daughter's just pitched up with hubby and now she's raising merry hell.'

I glance up. Angie's at the end of the bed, face screwed tight. 'The usual?' I ask.

'You got it. Notification was sent this morning.'

My eyes flick back to the monitor. Why do they always have to arrive at the end of a shift? For once I wanted to get off on time, get things ready for tomorrow.

Angie starts drumming on the bedrail. It makes a soft padding sound through her gloves. 'I'm sorry, Katie,' she says. 'It's just ... well, she's pretty worked up.'

It pulls at me, the same old quandary. I could ask one of the others, but these AD meetings aren't easy. There was a time when they used to upset me; now they're just part of the daily routine.

'What time?'

'Two o'clock.'

I check my watch and sigh. 'OK. I'll just finish up here. Give me fifteen.'

A smile breaks out behind her mask. I'm a sucker for saying yes and she knows it.

'Thanks. I owe you.'

I check my patient's pulse as his chest teeters up and down. Grey whiskers straggle across cheeks that look like they're folding in on themselves. Aspiration pneumonia. One bite of food went down the wrong way and he ended up here. If he lasts the night, I'll ask Angie to give him a shave tomorrow.

I gently mop his face, change the drip and reset the monitor. As I roll him onto his side he mewls like a kitten.

'Sorry, Mr Harrison,' I say. 'I'll be quick.' I scan under his gown for bedsores. 'There, all done.' I pull the sheets back up and tuck them in. He stares at the floor, mouth clamped shut, but I can still hear that wheezy rattle. I've not had one word from him since he arrived. There's nothing wrong with his cognitive functions. This is a protest. Dying is an undignified business. And he hasn't signed a directive, so there's precious little else he can do.

I lean over and touch his hand. Ridged blue veins run across it like rivers. 'Just rest,' I whisper. 'Rest is good.'

His fingers curl away from mine but he shuts his eyes. I wait until his breathing slows a little, until I know the next dose is kicking in. I wonder what he dreams about. What memories he summons. They tried to trace a relative, but couldn't find one. Looks like no one's coming to his farewell.

I rip off my coverall and gloves, and scrub my hands, soaping each finger in turn. The lift whines towards me. I key in the code to the sanitation floor, and the metal doors shudder shut. Thoughts of tomorrow creep into my head, bleeding the breath from my lungs. I focus on the numbers, count down each floor until the lift bounces and grinds to a stop.

I turn left to the women's section and place my feet on the circle. A red light slithers over my eyes. There's a click as the lock releases. Strange. Never usually works first time. I grab my kit from the locker, dump my scrubs in the laundry and turn the shower on full blast. Jets of tepid water spill over my head. I remember when I used to turn that temperature dial up to scalding: now they're all pre-set. Another lesson we learned the hard way. Not a good idea to let your pores open up, when you've done time on these wards.

Soap fizzes on my skin: bursts of lemon overwhelmed by antiseptic. I press my hands against the tiles and rest my head on my arms. Let the water pummel my neck until it's numb. You don't just wash off the germs, you leave the rest behind too. So you can become that other person: wife, mother, friend. But today my work isn't quite done.

I step into the scanner and hold out my arms. A violet beam sweeps over my skin as water crawls down my back. The green circle flashes and the dryer clicks on: I am clean. I pull on my regulation green trousers and white shirt, turn my back to the mirror and scrape the brush through my hair. Reflections are best avoided. After a ten-hour shift, I barely recognise myself.

On my way to the public building, I rehearse what I'm going to say. They'll ask the impossible, they always do. The next shift is clocking on, and some of the nurses nod at me as they file past. I head into the lobby and press the button for the lift. Just as the doors are closing a middle-aged man prises himself in. His eyes meet mine for a second and drop to the floor. He takes off his glasses with tremulous hands and starts to polish them. He rubs the same lens over and over. As if it might make the difference he needs.

I step out onto plush oatmeal carpet: sheer luxury after all those hours on cold tiles. The man follows me and turns right, down a different corridor. A hint of lavender softens the clinical white walls; wooden-framed prints hang at respectful intervals.

Trees, lakes and waterfalls. Moss, rocks and flowers. It's all been meticulously planned. This is, after all, the family floor. The place where we are judged.

Room 15.

My fingers hover over the handle. There's no noise from within, only the faint hum of air filters. I push my hair back behind my ears and adjust my collar. I take one more breath. And go in.

There's just the two of them. He's by the sofa and she's by the window. The room smells of perfume and sweat. She's late forties I'd say, maybe a little older. All kitted out in designer skirt, jacket and heels, her hair scraped back in a tight bun.

'Mr and Mrs Atkinson? I'm Kate Connelly, ward sister.' I raise my palm, the now-customary greeting. 'Pleased to meet you.'

No one touches each other's hands anymore. Not unless they're intimate.

She dabs at her swollen grey eyes with a white cotton handkerchief that is clenched in one fist. She doesn't return the greeting.

The husband steps forward, sneaking his phone back into his pocket. His thick brown hair is just about keeping the grey at bay around the edges. 'Roy. Roy Atkinson.' He nods his head as if he's at some kind of business meeting.

'Sorry to keep you waiting,' I say. 'I'm sure you understand, we have to put the patients first.'

She gives a strangled snort. He shoots her a look. It's the sort of look I get from Mark sometimes.

'Before we get started, would you like another drink?' I say. 'I could organise more coffee? Or something cold perhaps—'

She reels round. 'I'm here for an assisted dying, not bloody afternoon tea!'

I don't respond. It's best to leave the anger there, hanging. Let them enjoy it or regret it before you move on.

'Sorry,' he whispers, his eyes scurrying past my face. 'She's just, you know ... very upset.'

'Of course, I understand.' I indicate the sofa. 'Shall we sit?' I'm praying he says yes.

He hesitates and takes a seat. She remains standing. A painted thumbnail digs into the web of skin between her left thumb and forefinger. It's already raw. Soon it will start to bleed.

'I'm here to answer your questions.' I address her first and then him. 'To support you in any way I can, while respecting your father's wishes. I understand you received the notification this morning?'

He looks at her but she is silent. He runs his tongue over his lips. 'Yes. That's right.'

He has nice eyes, I think, a deep turquoise, like the Alboran Sea. Our last holiday before they shut the borders.

He stares at his feet and frowns, as if he's just trodden in something. 'My wife and I, we don't want ... I mean, we don't believe it's necessary. To make that level of decision. At this stage.'

She is watching me. Waiting for me to speak. I don't.

'What I'm trying to say is ... well, we feel this is all very sudden. There must be options.' He sighs, his pockets of words already dwindling. 'I mean, he must still be in shock; he can't be thinking straight.'

I make my move. 'Mr and Mrs Atkinson,' I keep my voice soft and slow, 'I understand how difficult this is. But your father *has* thought this through. It's not an impulsive reaction to his latest results. He's in pain. A lot of pain. He's been preparing for this for a long time.'

She erupts. 'It's his prostate, for Christ's sake! He's only seventy-three. Surely there's something you can do?'

She has broken the skin. A dark line of blood gathers in the crease.

I turn to her. 'Your father's cancer is advanced. His tumour is what we call T4. That means it has spread beyond the prostate and is affecting his other organs. His Gleason score is nine, which means it is a high-grade, fast-growing cancer.' Her eyes are fixed on me, jaw clenched tight, as if she's battling to hold her tongue. 'He's no longer responding to hormone therapy. The longer we leave it, the further it will spread.'

'I don't understand,' says the husband. 'What about radiotherapy? Or at least a blast of chemo? I thought they were still eligible for some procedures.'

'Even a mild course of chemotherapy would have serious consequences.'

He looks at me like a confused child, mouth agape. People just don't get it, no matter how many times they're told. It's as if they think we're making it up.

'All cancer treatments increase the risk of infection,' I say, trying to be kind. 'Chemotherapy depresses the immune system. Radiotherapy kills healthy cells as well as bad ones. Surgery opens up patients to all kinds of bacteria. Your father would end up going through considerable pain and discomfort, including some highly unpleasant side-effects for no benefit. Without effective antibiotics, these treatments simply won't work.'

Tears spill onto her cheeks and carve their way down to her chin. I think of Pen and my chest constricts. This is too soon, much too soon; I shouldn't have agreed to come.

'I understand how hard this is,' I say. 'But your father doesn't want things to be drawn out.' I swallow. 'You have to let him make his choice.'

She buries her face in her hands. The husband tentatively wraps his arms around her, as if she might break. I feel sorry for her, of course I do, but these people mistake their passionate pleas for love. It isn't. It's their own grief, getting in the way.

'You were aware of his intentions?' I say to them. 'You were both witnesses to his directive?'

'Yes, yes, we were.' He gives me a desperate look. 'But that was a long time ago. And, well, we never thought that ... We never imagined that he'd actually ever have to...' His voice trails off. It's like a swear word, dying. Some people just can't say it.

She steps away from her husband. A wisp of hair has escaped from her bun. She claws it back behind her ear. 'Convenient, isn't it?' At first I think it's her husband she's speaking to. 'Patients shipping themselves off. Unblocking those beds.' Her words sound swollen. 'You have targets, I suppose?'

'Helen. Please.' He draws in a long, staggered breath. I glance at the clock and brace myself for the next stage of this meeting.

Mrs Atkinson casts her eyes around the room. She gazes at me with an intensity that's all too familiar. 'We're wealthy, you know,' she whispers. 'We have money—'

He shakes his head. 'Helen, don't!'

She thrusts her hand in her bag and starts tearing through it. 'We can pay!' She brandishes a burgundy leather purse with gold buckles. 'We can give you whatever it takes!'

'Stop it!' Her husband snatches it from her. 'You're just making things worse.'

'Mrs Atkinson,' I say, stepping back. 'I'm sorry. That's not only illegal, it's not even possible—'

'I know it happens! You look after your own, don't you?' Her voice slices through the room. 'I've read the stories. I'll bet you'd do it if it was your own father—'

'I don't know what you've read, but the truth is that the drugs simply aren't available.' I slow things right down, as we've been taught. 'We don't have access to them in this sort of hospital. None of them do.'

'You're lying!' she shouts. 'Why won't you help us? What is it? Don't we fit your criteria? Aren't we the right kind of people?'

I'm about to respond, but she cuts in.

'Is it you? Do you do it?' Her breathing is quick and shallow; she has composed herself now, channelled her anger.

'I'm sorry?'

'Do you kill them? Or does someone else?'

I hold her gaze. My pulse sounds amplified, like Sasha's heartbeat, all those years ago when I had my prenatal scans.

My eyes flick up to the security camera and back again. 'If you're asking me whether I assist patients to end their lives, then the answer is yes.'

She recoils with a suck of air as if I've just bitten her. They're prepared to put their pets to sleep but not their parents. I wish I could show them the horrors of the alternative, but we're not allowed to interfere.

'How many? How many have you done?'

I pause, weighing honesty against diplomacy. Almost twenty years since the act was passed. It must be thousands.

'I'm not sure,' I say, eventually. 'I don't keep count.'

Her eyes widen as her husband darts between us. She shoves him aside. 'They should lock you up! Murder, that's what it is. You can dress it up with your fancy names but it doesn't change what you're doing.'

'Helen, that's enough!' He grabs her by the arm. I can hear the feet already, running down the corridor. 'She didn't mean that,' he says, flushes of pink breaking out across his face. 'I'm so sorry, it's the grief talking.'

I swallow. 'Mrs Atkinson. I know this is difficult. But if you wish to be present, you'll have to compose yourself.'

She breaks away from him and thrusts her finger in my face. 'You know where you're going? You're going to hell!'

What do you call this? I think. I look at her red, screwed-up face, the mascara running down her cheeks. I used to rant like her. I used to beat my fists. But it doesn't do anyone any good. It doesn't change anything.

The door bursts open and two security officers march in. They move him aside and seize her. She squirms like a feral cat. One of them yanks out the restraints.

'It's OK,' I say, raising both hands. 'That won't be necessary. Mrs Atkinson just needs a moment.'

The officer's tongue pushes round his mouth as if he's about to spit. He doesn't loosen his grip. There's a reason we have the cameras and security up here.

I check the clock and sweat prickles up my neck. 'Please. Just give her five minutes. Then you can escort them both to the Peace Chamber.'

His eyes fix on mine. 'OK. But that's your call. Not mine.'

I hurry along the carpet to the large double doors at the end. I key in the code and the doors sigh open. The Peace Chamber is a beautiful room, a bit like a lounge in a show home: pleasing to the eye but not entirely welcoming. Because it's never lived in. Plump cushions recline on low sofas with bleached-beech arms; parcels of light stream through white wooden slats onto the walls. A slender-leafed plant arcs towards the window. The only imposter is a stubby brown bottle waiting patiently on the side.

I press the remote and violins glide into the room. 'The Lark Ascending': one of my favourites. You get to know them all, in time.

I check the volume on the camera and adjust the blinds. Just in time. The lock clicks and an elderly man in a pale-grey suit is wheeled in by two porters. His jacket hangs off him; a starched white collar gapes at his throat. I picture him as he would have been: at a business meeting or perhaps the cricket, his MCC Member's tie curled snugly around his neck. The porters lift him carefully onto the sofa. One could do it: he must weigh barely more than a child.

'Good afternoon, Mr Casey.' I give him my best smile. 'I'm here to assist you with your directive. Make you as comfortable as I can.'

Watery blue eyes focus through a film of pain. 'Hello, Sister. That's very kind. You've all been very kind.' He nods at each of us, the bones pushing out of his face. The porters incline their heads and leave.

'Is my daughter here?'

'She's just coming.'

His eyes drop to his hands. He sinks a little. 'She doesn't approve, you know. She refused to see the soul midwife.'

I take a breath. 'I know. But this is your decision.'

He taps his thigh. 'She lost her mother, you see. Two years ago.' The wrinkles on his forehead deepen. 'It's hard for her. To have no parents. To be no one's child.'

My chest tightens. His eyes slide to the brown bottle. 'Dying is the easy bit.'

I touch his shoulder. 'We all have to leave our children. I

know it's difficult, but this is about you now. You need to prepare yourself.'

I pick up the bottle and scan the label. 'Whisky flavour, eh?' He smiles. I give it a good shake.

'The water of life. Ironic, don't you think?' He presses his knuckles together. 'Does it taste anything like it?'

'Apparently it's pretty good.'

They used to give patients chocolate, before. To mask the drug's bitterness. Now you can take your poison in any flavour or colour you like.

I break the seal and pour the golden liquid into a glass, tapping out every last drop.

He watches me. 'Well, it certainly *looks* like whisky.' Perspiration beads his brow. 'Got any ice?'

We both laugh just as the doors open. Mrs Atkinson glares at me, but when she sees her father her face collapses. She drops to her knees in front of him and sinks her head into his lap.

'What're you doing down there, Helen?' he says, stroking her hair. He pats the cushion, his eyes glistening. 'Come on. It may not be up to your usual standards but the sofa really isn't that bad.'

Her husband goes to help her up, but she shakes him off.

Mr Casey smiles. 'Stubborn one, eh, Roy? Always was.' He pulls a handkerchief out of his pocket and gently dabs her cheeks. 'There, there. Don't cry. Come on, love.'

Mrs Atkinson heaves out a sigh. 'You're sure, Daddy? Really sure?'

'Yes, Helen. I'm sure.'

The second hand ticks round. I say it as softly as I can. 'It's time.'

She hauls herself up beside her father, and he hugs her close.

I clear my throat and face the camera. 'Are you James Robert Casey?'

'I am.'

'Do you want to die?'

'I do.'

'If you drink this liquid, you will die. Your breathing will stop and then your heart.'

Mrs Atkinson makes a choking sound. His face tightens. 'I understand. That is my wish.'

I give him the glass. 'Go in peace.' He cradles it in his palm, swirling the liquid round.

Mrs Atkinson's eyes lock on to her father's, as if the sheer force of her stare might stay his hand. I wish I could tell her that he's going to a better place. That all this suffering means something. But this is the best I can do.

One second passes, two. Just as I think she's succeeded he raises the glass as if he's making a toast and knocks it straight back.

'Not bad!' He coughs. He puts the glass down and coughs again. 'Not quite a Speyside, but better than some.'

She seizes his hand, squeezing the blood out of his fingers. 'Stop it, Dad. I know what you're doing. Please, don't. Not now.'

'I'm sorry, Helen.' The tenderness in his face makes my throat swell. 'Forgive me.'

Tears spill down her cheeks. She nods. Mr Atkinson hovers by the blinds, looking the most lost.

Mr Casey takes a deep breath. 'Well. I guess this is it.' He turns to his son-in-law. 'Thanks, Roy. For all you've done.' He swallows. 'Look after her, won't you?'

Mr Atkinson lurches forward. For a terrible moment I think

he's going to shake the old man's hand. Instead he grips his father-in-law's shoulder, spasms flickering across his face.

Mr Casey kisses his daughter's head. 'Remember how much I love you, Helen. How much your mother loved you.' His voice cracks.

Mrs Atkinson sinks into her father, their fingers still intertwined. 'I love you too, Daddy.'

The lark swoops and climbs. The woodwind joins the strings, and the music builds.

Mr Casey's eyes flit around the room as if they are searching for something. His breathing deepens.

'Daddy?' Her brow creases. 'Daddy?'

'Dizzy...' he mumbles.

I step closer. 'It's alright, Mr Casey. You should begin to feel sleepy. Just close your eyes.' The numbers on the monitor start to drop. His gaze wanders back to his daughter, but it's already distant. His eyelids flutter. I see her jaw tremble.

The monitor flashes. His head slumps onto his chest.

I lean over and feel for a pulse. Her eyes meet mine. I nod.

Life is extinct.

She utters something between a roar and a wail. Her husband stands behind her, one hand outstretched. Not quite touching.

I switch off the monitor and the camera as quietly as I can. I whisper to Mr Atkinson: 'Take as long as you want.'

He blinks at me. 'How? How did it come to this?'

I have a sudden urge to put my arms around him, to tell him how sorry I really am. But I don't. Because I haven't the energy to explain.

And even if I did, it wouldn't make him feel any better.

CHAPTER 2

LILY

48.

My stomach churns. It's a Pavlovian response; it happens every time I look at my calendar. Those white paper squares are like a game of Sudoku. Each day has a number at the bottom written in the same black felt-tip pen: the one with a rubber tube around its middle, like those used by infants who are struggling to write.

Forty-eight days until my birthday. The big seven-o.

This is no childish anticipation. Quite the opposite. Cut-off. That's the expression they like to use. Rolls off the tongue a bit quicker than 'no longer eligible for treatment'. Elaine used to say that if octogenarians were a classified species they'd be almost extinct. Poor Elaine. She never made eighty. It started with a common cold, and the next thing, she'd got pneumonia. 'Old man's friend', wasn't that what they used to call it? Or, in her case, old woman's. I suppose there are worse ways to go. But I miss her. She was the closest thing I had to a friend here. She was the only one who ever got the joke.

'You're dead right, Lily,' she said to me one afternoon, as she contemplated my rows of little white squares. 'Our days are most definitely numbered.'

I press the pen back into its clip, slip my wrists into the clamps and wheel my frame out in front of me. I slide my right foot forward, my left foot, and stop. I repeat this pattern, again, and again, edging along the carpet. It's an effort, even at this woeful pace, and I can feel the damp spreading under my arms. Eleven shuffles and I make it to the door. I raise my wrist and the sensor flashes. The lock thuds across. Freedom.

I head left, getting into my own slow rhythm: push, shuffle, push, shuffle. Before my cartilage started crumbling I rushed everywhere. I never walked, I marched. It took some adjusting. At first I ignored it, pushed on, despite the pain. I took a few falls. But now I've had to accept my limitations. If I have another break, they won't operate: I'm too close to cut-off. And I've seen what can happen, even with minor fractures. Bone infections are bad. They don't go away. Not without treatment.

A wall dispenser puffs out a chemical waft of jasmine. It doesn't disguise the acrid stench of disinfectant. I glance at the nameplates as I move past: *Dr Elizabeth Miles (Edin). Dr Bill Jackson (Camb)*. I don't know why they bother putting up your letters. Must be some marketing gimmick. *Professor Harriet Weatherly (Oxf)*. I knew her: medical sciences, I think. A real pioneer in oncology. Now she's got Alzheimer's. See what becomes of these once-great minds? They're either losing their marbles, or trapped in failing bodies, like mine. None of our knowledge can save us now.

I hear someone coming up fast behind me.

'Off for a stroll, Lily?'

It's only Anne, in a hurry, as usual. She's a good one, Anne; I could have done a lot worse. Carers must be a bit like keyworkers at nursery. You get a bad one, you might not live to regret it.

'That's right,' I say. 'Fancied a bit of fresh air.'

She cocks her head to one side like a bird. 'What about the

grand quiz? Aren't they about to start?' Her eyebrows arch. 'Thought you liked testing the old grey matter?'

I pause just long enough. 'I do.'

She shakes her head, but I see the crease of a smile as she turns. My rebellion, as always, is subtle: it has to be. But Anne can take it. And sometimes, it's a relief to be me.

The eye of a camera swivels round above me and back again. I've reached Auden. Everything is green here, like the Emerald City. The colours are supposed to help us, in case we get confused. Betjeman is Tuscan orange, Donne is rose pink, and my dorm, Carroll, is jaundice yellow. The San's plain white, so I've been told. That's where we all end up, eventually.

I press on, battling hot spikes of pain in my fingers. It may be a little further, but Auden has my favourite garden. It's south-facing, and there's a bench tucked away in an arbour next to a Boscobel rose bush that gives out the most glorious scent. I stare at the lurid green walls and think of those little pastel strips they used to have, to test your urine. As if we need reminding. I remember when it used to be heart disease or cancer. Now, for women my age, there's a new number one: UTIs. The infection passes into your blood and knocks out your organs. I've taken to drinking cranberry juice. I'm surprised my pee isn't pink, the amount I put away.

I slump over my frame and flash my wrist. The lock releases and the doors swing open. They tell us all this security is for our own safety, to stop the bad guys getting in. But we know better.

I wheel onto the ramp, digging my frame into the grooves. A warm breeze blows the white wisps of hair around my head like a dandelion clock. I edge along the path, pausing to admire a white gardenia. Mauve and indigo asters nestle amongst feathered daisies; hollyhocks tower over lupins that are peppered with bees. Nature continues, despite all. It's a comforting thought.

I pause by a clump of lavender. My knotted fingers sneak around a stem and claw a few buds loose. We're not supposed to touch the plants but flowers don't frighten me. In any case, they've all been neutered: genetic variants with no spikes or thorns. I lift the lavender to my nose, and a childhood memory sparks: Grandmother's furrowed hands, flour and aprons. Sanctuary.

I tuck the lavender into my pocket and gear myself up for the final sprint.

As I lift my frame I hear the crunch of tyres on gravel. I freeze. The other side of that fence is what my grandmother used to call the tradesmen's entrance, round the back. These days it's a different kind of trade.

One door slams, and another. I hear talking. Sounds like male voices, but they're muffled, indistinct. Another door opens and something slides out. My stomach clenches. I flip back to yesterday and run through the faces, using my mnemonic to work my way around the room. It can't be anyone from Carroll. They were all there. Weren't they? My hips protest, but I push on, past the arbour, and stab my frame into the lawn.

Footsteps march up the drive and stop. I try to hurry, but my feet keep catching on the grass. I rest a moment, conscious of my heart hammering beneath my patch. It's about the only thing we're good for, generating data; there must be terabytes of it, streaming through the ether. As soon as your profile wavers, they send in the heavies. But data has its limits.

I reach the fence. I take my arms out of the clamps and squash my face up against the fake willow mesh that covers the bars. I'm only just in time.

Two men emerge from the San with a stretcher; they're all suited up in coveralls, masks and goggles. A still body lies strapped under the regulation grey blanket. They head towards the ambulance. I say ambulance, but it's more of a taxi: most of the equipment has been removed. As they come closer, a pale face I don't recognise lolls towards me and stares with glassy eyes. My heart flutters in my chest like a trapped bird.

The men slide the stretcher into the back, secure it and slam the doors. As they amble back round, one of them starts to whistle. I squeeze my frame so hard that my knuckle bones stick out, a chalky white beneath my skin.

Dr Barrows appears, wearing her trademark white suit and black boots. She takes off her mask and I feel an absurd rush of hope.

'Stage two: severe sepsis,' she barks at them. 'I've administered a sedative.' She hands one of the men a small black screen.

'Another day-tripper, then,' he mutters. He scribbles something and hands it back. 'Forms completed?'

'They'll come up when you scan her.'

Both men hop into the front. They drive off, small cuts of gravel flying out behind. The rear windows of the ambulance gaze back at me like skeletal sockets absent of their eyes.

I say the words in my head like a prayer:

I hope Dr Barrows pumped her full of Valium.

I hope she reaches stage three.

I hope her heart gives out before she arrives.

I want to turn and run, run like I used to, the wind screaming past my ears. But instead I push myself up, hook my wrists into the clamps and shuffle back to the path.

When I reach the arbour I do not stop.

And I do not smell the roses.

CHAPTER 3

KATE

'You alright, Mum?'

The room slides into focus. Sasha is peering at me, her eyes inscrutable behind their long, thick lashes.

'Yes, love. I'm fine.' I gaze at my wine glass. Surprisingly, it is still full. 'It went OK, didn't it?'

Sasha picks at the tablecloth. 'Yeah.' She sucks in her lips. 'Gran would've loved it.'

Someone breaks out into high-pitched laughter, which reverberates around the room. It all feels too sharp, too loud. A bit like I'm stoned.

I reach across and stroke Sasha's cheek. It's still slightly damp. 'You read beautifully.' My hand betrays me with a tremble, and I snatch it back. 'Have you eaten anything?'

Sasha's lip curls. 'Buffets aren't exactly my thing. What about you?'

I contemplate the remnants of sandwiches encased in cellophane wrappers, scattered over platters like fallen soldiers. 'I think your dad got me a plate, but I haven't really had a moment. People want to talk, you know. Anyway, I'm not that hungry.'

She shakes her head at me and tuts. 'Not a good idea to skip meals, Mum.' Sasha loves to mock my many cautionary sayings. At least I glimpse the hint of a smile.

She folds her arm into mine and steers me back to our table.

It still amazes me how she's managed to get so tall. My daughter looks down on me these days; I shall never get used to it. At least her eyes haven't changed. They're the same startling blue they were when they first squinted out at the world.

'Look who I found,' Sasha says triumphantly, as if I've been caught playing truant.

Mark pats the chair next to him. 'Get over here,' he says. 'I bagged you two vol-au-vents and three chocolate brownies before the vultures swooped in.'

Their kindness strips me bare. I stare hard at the food until my eyes behave. My plate looks like an advert for bad parenting.

'Funeral diet.' Mark nods at me. 'Scientifically proven. The body craves sugars and saturated fats.'

A smile breaks through and I unclench, just a little. I drop into the chair and wonder if I'll ever be able to get up. Mark leans over and kisses me on the cheek. I breathe him in: that wonderful scent of soap and skin that makes me feel safe.

'Well, everyone seems to be enjoying themselves, as per the brief,' he says, running his fingers slowly up and down my back. 'In fact, I'd say the bar is getting a pretty good hammering.'

I take in the white linen, the polished cutlery and glass. Strange, how these fripperies still convey a semblance of order.

One of the waiting staff approaches our table.

'I'm sorry to bother you, Mrs Connelly. But some of your guests were enquiring about where they should send the donations.'

I stifle a sigh. Why can't people follow simple instructions? 'The details were on the order of service,' I say, trying not to snap. 'It's the Antimicrobial Research Fund.'

Mark pushes back his chair. 'You stay put and finish your food.' He squeezes my shoulder. 'I'll take over duties from here.'

I press my hand over his. I can't quite bring myself to let it go. He eases out of my grasp. I watch him walk across the room and feel a twist of love.

I bite into a pastry and survey my guests. Women glide past in radiant dresses and heels; men huddle in herds of striped shirts and jackets. You'd think we were all off to the races. There's just one couple in black, by the buffet, looking uncomfortable. I listen to the buzz of conversation and inhale a heady mix of wine and perfume. Pen would have approved. But something is starting to nag. Something's not right.

As I reach for my wine a woman in a turquoise maxi dress swoops onto the seat next to me. It's my old school mate, Jess.

'Dear Kate,' she says. 'How are you?' Silver hoops shudder in her ears.

'Jess. Thanks for coming.'

She holds out her arms. 'May I?'

'Of course.' She clamps me between them, and I try not to stiffen. How long is it since I've seen her? Funny to think we used to be close.

'I thought the service was amazing. You did your mum proud. And as for Sasha, she did such a good job, didn't she? I can't believe how grown up she is! What can I say? The apple doesn't fall far from the tree!'

My mouth stretches into a smile. If only Jess knew.

She leans closer and lowers her voice. 'Mark told me what happened. He said you were at work when you got the call.'

I feel the familiar swerve in my chest. 'Yes. Yes, I was.'

'So good she didn't suffer. But still, I can't begin to imagine.' She chews her lip, and I know what's coming. 'What was it like? Do you mind me asking? You know, when she went...'

An image of Pen drifts into my mind, her hand cupped in

mine. Those intelligent eyes fading, her jaw going slack. I don't know how long I stayed, after. Long enough for her cheek to feel cool when I kissed it. The warmth in her fingers fed by my blood, not hers.

I clasp my palms together. 'Peaceful.' I look down. 'It was what she wanted. Before things ... deteriorated.'

Jess gives a solemn nod. 'Christ, it's hard. Guess I've got all that ahead of me.' She sighs. 'Still, she knew what she was doing. Thank heavens Mum's already signed. I tell you, I'm going to scrawl my name across those papers the moment I hit seventy.'

I don't say anything. It's a bit like having children. Until you go through it yourself, you have no idea.

'Hey, I loved that one you told about Pen dancing. What a lady! Did so well, didn't she? Seventy-nine!'

I take a long, slow breath. Jess is an intelligent woman: a secondary-school teacher, and a good one at that. But it's as if she's forgotten. How things used to be. I deal with death's grim reality for a living, but I still feel robbed. Pen was healthy enough: as sharp as a pin before the pneumonia set in.

She clocks my face and her smile wilts. 'You must be exhausted, Katie,' she says quickly. 'Shall I get you a coffee?'

I nod. I have a sudden, overwhelming urge to lie down, as if she's cast some kind of spell. I let my lids close, just for a second. When I open them, Jess is halfway to the bar, stilettos stabbing the parquet floor. And that's when I get it. I realise what's wrong.

When I was a child, the sending off of the departed was a big family occasion. Hordes of elderly relatives and friends would emerge in a flurry of hats and pearls, ferried like royalty from car to church to pub. I remember them reminiscing with watery eyes, conjuring ancestral names and discussing each other's ailments with glee. Like some ancient court ritual, Pen would parade me in front of them, as cigarette smoke swirled around our heads. A wrinkled hand would reach through the haze and ruffle my hair, or a wavering voice might ask about school.

I look around this room, with its disinfected surfaces and purified air. There are no elderly hordes here. No reminiscing huddles.

No one in the room is over seventy.

■ ■ ■

I'm sprawled across the sofa, watching something mindless. We only got back a couple of hours ago. Mark made me a good old-fashioned shepherd's pie: that man knows how to spoil me. With the price of real meat these days, even your basic mince is a wallet-buster.

'There you go,' he says, handing me a fresh glass of pinot grigio. 'Get that down the hatch.' He slumps down next to me, and I stretch my legs out over his lap. God, it's good to be home.

I swirl the wine around the glass. 'You know who was missing today?' Mark gives me a blank look. 'Lucy.' I smile. 'Pen used to call Luce her other daughter. She was so good to her. Always let her stay, no questions asked.' My smile fades.

Mark squeezes my foot. 'Not sure how Lucy would have gone down with the bridge crowd, though.' I chuckle. Luce would have ambushed that reception.

We sit in silence for a while. 'So, then,' he says. 'Have you given it any more thought?'

I gaze at Mark, bleary-eyed. 'What?'

'You know.' He traces his fingers over the sofa. 'What Pen said.'

It takes me a moment. 'Oh. That.'

I stare at the painting above Mark's head. It's a Dorset seascape: rich curls of green and silver crashing into cobbled walls. How many summers did Pen and I spend on those beaches? Sasha wasn't allowed near a beach until she was six. Even then, the sea air couldn't entirely be trusted. I paid through the nose for a spotty pink mask so at least her swimsuit would match.

'Or is it none of my sodding business?' He raises an eyebrow, a smile playing around his lips.

'Don't be so daft,' I say, pushing my foot into his ribs. I try to think how I can stave off this conversation, but my brain's too frazzled. I press my fingers against the cool glass; loops and whorls materialise and vanish. 'I'm not sure. I mean, it seems … disloyal, somehow.'

Mark peers at me over the rim of his glass. 'Disloyal? But Pen was the one who suggested it.'

I notice the dark circles under his eyes. He loved Pen; it's taken its toll on him too.

'I know, but that's Pen. It's exactly the kind of thing she would say, worrying about us all, right up to the last. It doesn't mean it's what she really wanted.'

Mark doesn't say anything. I foolishly think we're done.

He takes a breath. 'Maybe Pen knew something.' I take another swig. 'She said it would be a good thing, Kate. A kind thing. Before it's too late.'

'Look, Mark, I just don't know if it's a good idea. Let sleeping dogs lie and all that.' My toes stretch and contract as if they're limbering up for something. 'I mean, even if she's still alive, I doubt she wants me turning up on her doorstep, not after all this time.'

'Sorry, babe.' He touches my arm. 'Typical me, storming in as usual. It's your decision, of course it is. It's just...' He swallows.

'Just what?' It's not like Mark to tiptoe around.

'Well, if it were me...' He risks a glance. 'If I'd had a child, and I'd had to give it up for whatever reason ... I think I'd like to make my peace.'

'What are you two talking about?'

My head shoots round. Sasha is standing in the doorway.

I wrestle myself into a sitting position. 'How long have you been there?' The words spill out, sharp and shrill.

'Long enough.'

My eyes squeeze shut.

Mark jumps up. 'Your mum and I are having a little chat. Just the two of us, OK?'

I can't see behind the sofa but I imagine Mark giving her the wide-eyed 'come on, love, play along' look.

'There's some wine in the fridge, if you fancy it,' he adds: a sure sign of desperation.

Sasha ignores him. 'Mum?' Just the one word.

This is my fault: I should have told her I was adopted years ago; I don't know why I didn't. I never lied, it just didn't come up. I won't ever lie to my daughter again, no matter how hard it is. That's the rule I set myself, after Ellie – the first of her friends who died.

Mark catches my eye. I shake my head, ever so slightly.

'Let's not do this now,' he says, hands outstretched as if he's refereeing. 'It's been a long day. We're all exhausted.'

Sasha doesn't move. Her pale forehead creases into a frown, and I glimpse the six-year-old Sasha, thumping the kitchen table, asking me why.

She's back to school tomorrow. But still I hesitate. I don't want this to change things, the way she sees Pen. Or worse, force me into a decision I don't want to make. Pen was always there, from my earliest memories, and before, right from the start. As far as I'm concerned, she is my mother. My heart clenches. Was. God, I wish Mark had never brought it up.

Sasha's lips tighten. 'Do I have a sister?'

I stare at her, mouth open, like an imbecile. 'I'm sorry, I—'

'You were talking about a child,' she says. 'About giving up a child.'

It hits me then. I mean, really hits me.

I remember how I felt after I got pregnant with Sasha. How Mark and I agonised over that decision: how careful we had to be. Even if you survived the TB, all those other infections were just lying in wait. Metritis, peritonitis, septicaemia. It's hard to believe how cavalier mothers used to be. As if having children were a right, not a gift.

I would have killed anyone who tried to take Sasha away.

'No, love.' My voice splinters. I heave myself up. 'Mark, go and get that wine, will you?' I grasp my daughter's hands in mine. 'Sit down, Sasha. There's something I need to tell you.'

CHAPTER 4

LILY

'Morning, Lily!'

I hear words, but they are distant. I am running. Running as fast as I can.

'Wakey, wakey!'

The layers of sleep fall away as I shift from that world to this one. The thumping in my chest subsides. I peel back my eyelids. A fuzzy outline moves past the window. The curtains open, and I blink back the light.

'Alright, Lily?' It's Anne. 'You were having a right old moan. Bad dream?'

I lift my hand to my face. It is wet. I stare at the wallpaper and focus on the flowers. There are four species in this pattern: common daisy, English lavender, wood forget-me-not, and an English rose I can't be sure of. I suspect they've made it up.

Anne presses the remote and the bed whines into action, pushing me upright. 'How are you feeling? Everything back to normal?'

'I'm fine,' I say, fingering my chest. 'Probably just a bit too much sun.'

They checked my patch yesterday, after my little episode. That's the price you pay for 24/7 real-time analysis.

'Well, make sure you wear your hat next time. Don't want to take any chances, do we?'

No. We do not.

I adopt a benign smile as the bed completes its moves. Anne whisks back the duvet and I haul my legs over the side. I don't look down; the sight of my limbs appals me. Anne wheels my frame over and fits my slippers onto my feet.

'Ready?'

I nod and place my hands up on the bar like a gymnast. Or rather what pass for my hands these days. Fingers should be straight and slender, with smooth pink skin; oval nails with little white moons. Mine resemble something a child might draw: swollen and crooked, with knotty lumps like the growths you see on trees. I still can't believe they're mine. Perhaps it is my punishment.

'One, two, three.' She helps me to my feet. There, I am standing.

'Right then. Shall we commence morning rituals?' She pulls on her gloves; they snap around her wrists like a slap. 'Morning rituals'. That's my expression; Anne's adopted it. I've invented my own vernacular for the daily humiliations of ageing. It occupies the mind, and the carers seem to like it.

I fit my wrists into the clamps and hobble towards the bathroom. As I wheel onto the linoleum I can see she's already got the bedpan ready. I manoeuvre myself round, lift my nightdress and start to pull at my pants.

'Here, Lily, let me help.'

Anne reaches forward and, with one professional yank, sends them careering down my legs to my ankles. She helps me lower myself onto the seat.

'Ooh, that's cold,' I say.

'Would you like me to warm it up for you next time?'

'That would be nice.' Our little joke.

She leaves me to it. That's Anne for you. Some of the others, they stand there, watching, as if you've waived all rights to privacy. They expect us to perform like battery hens, so they can get on with their day. I make sure I take an age when they do that. I refuse to pee on demand.

'Finished?' she asks, outside the door.

'All done.'

She comes back in and helps me up. I shuffle to the basin and rub soap into each finger. Anne has a kind face, I think, not that I can see much of it right now: broad cheekbones, hazel eyes. At least she takes off her mask after the all-clear. You entrust these people with your life, but I have no idea what some of them look like: you only ever see their eyes.

'Who was it yesterday?' My thought escapes before I can censor it.

Anne screws the lid on the specimen pot, a scowl pulling at her cheek. 'Are you asking what I think you're asking, Lily?' She rips off her gloves and drops them in the bin.

I swallow. 'I heard them come. When I was in the garden.'

Her breath catches. She shakes her head. 'Lily, you know I can't.'

I offer my hands up to the sanitiser and smooth the gel over my lumps. 'Sorry, it's just, I was wondering ... you know...' As my voice trails off we both know what I'm really asking.

Her mouth makes a clicking sound. She walks over and whispers in my ear: 'NC. But you didn't hear that from me, understood?'

I nod, despising myself for the relief I feel. NC: not contagious. Whatever infection carted that poor woman off to the Waiting Rooms isn't coming for me yet.

'Right then, onto the next one,' says Anne, trying to muster some cheer.

I shuffle past the walnut credenza that belonged to my grandmother. They still haven't fixed the crack in the glass. I turn myself round and reverse into the chair, inching backwards until my calves touch the seat. I wave my hands out behind, feeling for the arms, and lower myself down. Anne watches me, close by. I grunt a little just before my bottom hits the cushion.

'Bullseye!' She snaps on another pair of gloves and wheels the trolley over. She takes my left hand and uncurls my forefinger. 'Shall we use this one today?'

'Why not?'

She slips a heat pad on it for a couple of seconds and picks up the lancet. 'Ready?' I nod. The lancet punctures my skin like a stapler. Anne holds the tube underneath, gently squeezing my finger. My blood drips out, a deep crimson. When it reaches halfway she releases the pressure. 'There we are, all done.' She sticks a label on the tube and slots it into the tray next to the other one, ready to go up to the lab.

'I've got some news for you,' she says.

My stomach thumps. Please, don't let her be leaving; I won't get another like Anne.

'We've a new one starting next week. Her name's Natalie. She's going to be working with me on Carroll.'

I'm almost giddy with relief. 'Oh. What's she like?'

'Seems nice enough. A little quiet, maybe. Don't worry, we'll have her trained up in no time.'

I eye the specimen tray and decide to risk it. 'Well, as long as she isn't another Pam...'

Anne frowns at me as if I'm a child who's just said something mildly amusing but naughty. 'Now, now, Lily. She's alright really. Got a lot going on, that's all.' She sighs. 'What with her mother and everything ... The poor woman's in a terrible state.'

'Oh. I'm sorry.' It's easy to forget that our carers have their own elderly relatives to contend with. 'How long has she been ill?'

'She's not ill.' Anne purses her lips. 'Not yet, at any rate. But the place she's living...' She shakes her head. 'She's moved to one of those apartment complexes, you know.' She glances at me. 'For the elderly.' That's code for over seventy. 'They're really not nice.'

I've heard about these places. I even visited one, once. They market themselves as affordable retirement villages, but they're really just holding pens for the Waiting Rooms: cheap, soulless flats with precious little in the way of health services or infection control. But cracking surveillance. The moment a profile dips, or somebody's chip goes off grid, security's there like a shot.

'Don't say anything, will you, Lily?'

'Of course not.' I wonder why Pam's mother isn't living with her. I'm about to ask but I check myself. One step too far.

Anne wheels the trolley to the door. 'I'll see you later. Try and eat *some* of your breakfast.'

I watch the door close behind her. The lock thuds across. We have to stay in our rooms until we get the all-clear. I don't mind, it's quite nice having breakfast in your nightie. It's just the waiting. They carry a heavy responsibility, those little samples. No wonder we struggle to get our eggs down.

I pull my tray round and use the pen to tap the control. A blue screen lights up on the wall. 'Radio.' I enunciate each syllable. Lots of people predicted the demise of radio, but, like me, it has endured. The list of stations appears. 'BBC Radio Four.' I hear the familiar pips and think back to a world long gone where things seemed to be under control. The illusion won't last. It's the news.

'The opposition has launched a scathing attack on the government after yesterday's figures on the economy were released.'

'Here we go,' I say. I often talk to the radio. It's a lot more rewarding than most of my conversations.

'The report showed that the slump is set to continue, with the budget deficit at its highest point since the Antibiotic Crisis. The government defended its position, arguing that any reductions in healthcare spending or arbitrary policy changes would be "highly irresponsible" and that recovery would be "a long-term process".'

I brace myself as they cut to an interview with the prime minister.

'We live in a time when we have had to make some extremely tough choices.'

'Indeed we have, Mr Prime Minister.' I dig my nails into the chair. 'Tougher for some than for others.'

'This government pledged that we would subsidise investment in new antibiotics and diagnostic tools. We promised to enforce responsible usage and rigorous infection control. We have kept those promises and we will continue to do so. Because we owe it to our children.' There's a rehearsed pause that makes my blood boil. 'We must never allow another antibiotic crisis.'

I give a contemptuous snort. Too little, too late. How many warnings did they ignore? For all their bluster, it took a global TB pandemic to finally spur Westminster into action.

The door unlocks, and a whiff of eggs permeates the room. Pam slouches in with that surly look that spells trouble, so I mute the radio and keep my mouth shut. I try to think of something nice to say, but she slaps the tray down with such force that a stream of cranberry juice squirts out of the beaker's spout.

'So, what's on the menu today?' I ask, attempting to sound jolly. The hardening yolk of a boiled egg glares at me, like a gammy eye.

She makes a sucking noise, as if she's got something stuck in her teeth. 'Pancakes.' The way she says it sounds like a swear word. And I have a shameful thought. Maybe this is why Pam's mother isn't living with her.

Pam turns to go. 'Oh,' she says, digging in her pocket. 'This came for you.' She thrusts a small white envelope on my tray.

My birthday's still a few weeks away, but I suppose someone might have got confused. A tide of cranberry juice advances towards the envelope, so I flick it to one side. Part of me is tempted to rip it open straight away, but if I don't eat while the food's at least warm, I won't stand a chance.

I stare at my plate. The pancakes look like mottled flaps of skin, oozing honey. I hook my fingers around the fork's plastic handle. After a couple of attempts I spear a slither and raise it to my lips. My stomach loops. I put it down and pick up the beaker. I drink the juice down to the last drop, savouring the tartness on my tongue. As I steel myself to attack the egg my eyes wander back to the envelope.

The address is printed: black, Times New Roman, I'd say twelve point. London postmark. I rub my thumb along the edge and think of the diminishing straggle of cards bearing increasingly illegible scrawls. It's probably just another begging letter. A ginger cat with big eyes and amputated claws, or a child with a swollen stomach. Either that or funeral insurance. I slip the fork under the flap and tear. After a couple of attempts, I prize it out.

It's as if I've been slapped.

I scan every detail: the broad, square lips, the conical ears, the ridges of skin that are like plates of armour.

My fingers stumble as I turn the postcard over. It's blank. Just a few empty lines where the message should be.

A high-pitched whine sears through my head. This could only have been sent by one person.

But they died, nineteen years ago.

CHAPTER 5

Twenty-seven years pre-Crisis

MARY

I part the thorny branches and search for those tell-tale strips of green at the ends. They've had a right old feast on this one: acacia's always a favourite. I hold a snapped stem and reach for my callipers. Looks like a pair of pruning clippers has been at it. I measure the length and the diameter and take a GPS reading. As I scribble in my field book a hornbill swoops onto the tree next to me. I take off my hat and mop the sweat. I'll never get used to this heat.

That's when I spot it, behind the acacia. I feel a pulse of excitement. The three toenails are quite distinct: the large one at the front, the two smaller ones either side. The track is round, about twenty centimetres across with no indentation at the back. I can't believe my luck, they're incredibly rare: it's a black. I reach for my camera and snap away: click, click, click.

The first thing I hear is the snort. I freeze. I lower the camera, my eyes darting between the bushes. I don't see anything, not yet. The hornbill cackles above me, impossibly loud. There's another snort, followed by a stamp. I train all of my senses on the acacia. And I see them: two massive horns swaying through the scrub. Blood abandons my guts for my limbs. The animal trots forward a few steps and swings its huge nostrils round. It hasn't spotted me yet, but it can smell me alright. The ears are in perpetual motion, twisting one way then the other.

A single bead of sweat trickles down my cheek. I have to use all my strength to override it: the urge to run. I tell myself, if I stay where I am, I'll be OK; I just need to keep still. Seconds pass. They could be hours. My arms, neck, head grow heavy. Other sounds rush in: the warning bark of a baboon, the pulse of veins, the rubbing of a thousand crickets' wings.

A fly lands on my face. I let it crawl over my skin and drink the sweat.

Then the camera switches itself off. Only a little noise, just the lens pulling back into the frame. It's enough. The creature spins round and starts to pant. I see the thick folds of skin on its chest, the enormous front legs. A smaller shape presses in underneath. And that's when I know I'm in trouble.

I drop the camera and run. All the training, all the guidance evaporates, and something else takes over. I tear across the scrub, zigzagging, because I know the mother will outrun me on the straight. Her hooves thunder behind me, the heavy rhythm of her panting drawing closer until I'm sure it's her breath I feel on the backs of my legs. Thorns rip at my ankles. I take quick, ragged gasps, my eyes swivelling, desperate for something to climb. Then I hear a different noise. A man, shouting. His arms wave at me in the distance. He's pointing at something. A marula tree. Fifty metres to my left.

A gunshot echoes and I run faster than I have ever run. The ground vibrates under the tempo of her feet. I throw myself at the tree, haul myself up, hands scrabbling, thighs scraping bark. She thumps into the trunk and the whole tree judders. I heave myself along a branch, arms and legs clenched tight. The man's still shouting, clapping his hands. I dig my nails into the bark and bury my face in the leaves. I count the passing of each breath.

An eerie silence descends.

'*Wat de fok is jy?*'

I peer through the branches. There is no sign of the rhino. Instead, a tall man with sun-bleached hair is bent over, hands on knees, gasping. His damp shirt clings to his skin, exposing the curve of muscle underneath. A rifle is slung over one shoulder, but he doesn't look like a ranger. After a couple more gasps he stands up. His eyes are the colour of a monsoon sky, before the rain falls.

'*Is jy fokken stupid?*'

I blink at him. My cheeks flush a furious red. I don't need Afrikaans for that one.

'No. I am not.' I inch my way back along the branch. My hands won't stop shaking. He doesn't offer any help.

'English. *Ek moes geraai het*,' he mutters. 'What do you think you are doing?' He sounds out each syllable in his thick, guttural accent, as if I'm an idiot. 'You could've got that animal killed!'

'*That animal?*' The bark bites into my palms. 'What about me?'

He gives me a cursory glance. 'Plenty more like you. Not so many like her.'

My anger makes me careless and I skid down the last bit of trunk, gouging my leg. Warm blood trickles down my thigh.

He tosses his head. 'You shouldn't be out here on your own.'

He's right, I shouldn't. 'I have a research permit,' I say, with as much authority as I can muster.

'Really?'

He arches his eyebrows, and for a ridiculous moment, I imagine he is impressed.

'What are you researching? How fast rhinos can run?'

My chest swells. I want to slap his arrogant Boer face. I want to shout at him that it's work like mine that'll save his precious rhinos.

But my fury morphs into something totally unexpected, and I start to laugh.

CHAPTER 6

London Prepares for Mass Protests on Anniversary of Medication Act

Security has been doubled in the capital ahead of the nineteenth anniversary of the introduction of the Medication Act. Large-scale demonstrations are expected across the country, in support of the over-seventies' right to antibiotics. Last year, more than a million protestors staged die-ins outside hospitals, transport hubs and government buildings, bringing some cities to a halt.

The controversial Medication Act, which was passed under emergency measures during the Crisis, was intended to stem the growth of antibiotic resistance and extend the shelf lives of new drugs. It was based on evidence from a mass screening programme that indicated elderly patients are more prone to antimicrobial resistance because of their longer history of antibiotic usage and increased vulnerability to disease. Campaigners refute this evidence, claiming it is no longer valid and nothing more than a scientific smokescreen. They maintain the real motives were, and still are, financial.

'The genocide of the elderly has to stop,' says sixty-eight-year-old protest organiser Tessa Beecham. 'We all have a right to treatment, no matter what our age. The drugs are available, the government just doesn't want to pay for them. We will not rest until they abolish this inhumane and unnecessary Act.'

KATE

My finger hovers over the mouse. I've completed the form as best I can, although a few beige boxes are still bereft. The cursor blinks, daring me. All I have to do is click on 'submit'. Submit the page, submit to Pen, submit to whatever comes next. It's only a bit of paper, I tell myself. I'm lying. It's much, much more than that.

It's the fifth time I've visited the General Register Office website. I make life-and-death decisions every day, but here I am, still deliberating, as the minutes tick by. A little voice whispers that even if I get my birth certificate, I don't have to take things any further. I run my hand through my hair and think of Pen; agonise over the unknown one more time. *You should look.* I can still see her, nodding at me between breaths. Tears threaten as I feel the same raw ache inside. Why am I even contemplating this? She could be anyone, my birth mother.

A nebulous face floats into my mind, like the greyed-out silhouette of an absent profile picture. I think of her as young: late teens, the spiky aura of some unknown tragedy rippling at her edges. She has visited me ever since Pen's funeral, like a genie released from its lamp. Something must have happened. Something terrible. Why else would you give your baby away?

Lunch break's nearly over. *Come on, Kate, make a bloody decision.* I drum the desk, weigh up the pros and cons one last time. I might spend months, even years, trying to find her, and never succeed. And even if I did, why would she want to see me – the unwanted product of some vicious history? But one biological fact trumps them all.

Because she's your mother.

It stirs, every time, this faint flutter. Buried deep, beside childhood dreams of flying governesses with parrot-handled umbrellas, and good witches who glide in with a swoosh of satin and make it all better. I can't quite bring myself to crush it. Not yet.

I keep thinking about my own pregnancy. How all-consuming it was: a fierce, desperate love for the tiny life inside me, coupled with the nightly fears of all that could go wrong. Before the Crisis, most women, in this country at least, just assumed that they would get pregnant and carry their babies to term, that both mother and child would survive the birth and their newborns would grow into healthy toddlers. Whereas Mark and I couldn't assume anything. Modern medicine had failed us, as it had been failing other mothers in less fortunate parts of the world for years, robbing us of the joy of pregnancy, robbing our babies of an infection-free start.

It was like a miracle when Sasha was born.

Brisk footsteps march down the corridor. My heart skitters in my chest. I click 'submit' and scrabble to close the page, as if I've been trawling for porn.

'Sister, do you have a moment?'

I swing my chair round. The ward manager's voice is extra calm. A sure sign that some emergency has arisen.

'Of course.' I brush invisible crumbs off my trousers.

'We have a situation. Major incident declared.' He allows me a moment to adjust. 'Westbourne Centre, Afro-Caribbean male; they're not sure what he's carrying.' Our eyes meet. 'Assume it's airborne.'

The breath squeezes out of me. It's much less frequent, but it still happens. Some lunatic gets themselves infected with the latest strain and decides to make a statement.

'Have they contained him?'

'Being tested as we speak. I suppose we should be grateful he drove. At least it's only the centre we've got to worry about.'

My stomach tightens. Only the centre? That place is huge. No matter how many purifiers they put in, it's never enough; they'll need all the isolation chambers they can get.

'How many are we talking?'

'Not sure yet.' His face darkens. 'They were running some kind of promotion. And he waited till lunchtime.'

Bastard. I manage not to say it. Just. So much for glittery wands and satin dresses. It's never the good witch who comes.

He swallows. 'I've organised extra shifts.' His eyes flick to mine and away again. 'I feel bad for asking; I know you're dealing with a lot right now. It's just, well, we're a bit thin on the ground.'

I look wistfully at the clock as the tiredness claws my insides. I'm not sure I'm up to another shift, let alone one on the isolation ward. He doesn't have to ask, he could just tell me, but he's smart enough to know that he needs me on side. I'm one of only seven staff here who nursed during the Crisis. We thought that nothing could touch us, but it was too many, too fast. Of the few staff that made it, most either quit or chose to work in the other kinds of hospitals: the normal ones. Where people get well.

A memory surfaces. Rows of beds crammed together, hardly enough room to squeeze in between. The endless hacking and coughing. That rasping chorus never ceased; I still hear it in my sleep.

He taps the desk, trying not to hurry me. I think of all those families happily browsing. The workers who'd popped in for lunch.

I take a breath. 'Don't worry, Boss. I get it. Time to suit up.'

His face softens, as if the creases have been ironed out. 'Thanks, Kate. I really appreciate it.'

I'm about to head for the lift when it clicks like a trigger: Westbourne Centre.

Lunchtime.

Sasha.

'My daughter. I have to call her.' My words erupt, in no particular order: the first of the magma gushing up inside. 'She might be...' I baulk at saying it, as if by giving voice to the thought I somehow make it true. 'She goes there, sometimes. For lunch.'

'Oh. Of course. Use my office, if you like.' He holds out his arm in a curiously old-fashioned gesture as I hurtle past.

I can see them already: swarms of bacteria spiralling through that greenhouse, sneaking up noses and down throats.

The ward manager strides up behind me, a little breathless. 'I seriously hope you don't need it. But we should get the list soon.'

My heart thuds. I cannot contemplate the possibility of Sasha's name being on there. I imagine her rummaging for tops. Bolting a forkful of sushi from a bamboo tray as some new contagion floats past.

'Let me know if you need anything,' says the ward manager, and eases the door shut.

I punch Sasha's number into the phone and check the time: nearly half-one. It goes straight to voicemail. I clench the handset. 'Hello, Sasha. Mum here.' I use every skill I possess to sound normal. 'Could you give me a call when you get this? As soon as you can.' My thumb lingers over the end button. I listen to the clatter of my breathing. 'Love you.'

I dial the school. She'd have to be back from lunch now, wouldn't she? Unless she had a free period. I try to summon her timetable as my fingers tremble over the keys. Friday. Does she have a free on Fridays?

'Bridfield Academy, how can I—'

'It's Sasha Connelly's mum; there's been an incident at the Westbourne Centre.' My words tumble out. 'Is Sasha there?'

'Hello, Mrs Connelly, it's Vivienne. We've just seen the alert.' She sounds far too calm to have seen anything. 'We're about to take the regis—'

'She's not answering her phone.' My professional veneer is thinning. I don't care. 'Please. I need you to check.'

Vivienne tries again. 'They're doing registration now. Are you alright to hold?'

What do you bloody think? I swallow. 'Yes.'

Some classical tune starts simpering at me. My nails dig into my palm. I see Sasha stepping off the bus, smoothing that gold curtain of hair behind her ears. The doors of the centre sliding open for her like a trap.

Please, God. Please. Don't let her be there.

'Mrs Connelly? It's Vivienne.' There's a pause that makes my heart leap. 'Sasha's name isn't on the register, but please don't be alarmed.' A gasp escapes my lips. 'She has a free period. And she hasn't signed out, so she must still be on the premises.'

I sink my teeth into a knuckle. Sasha never signs out; she's always getting in trouble for it. And I'll bet she hasn't taken her mask.

'We're trying the sixth-form centre and the library. Do you want to continue holding? Or would you like me to call you back?'

'I'll hold.' My voice sounds like ash falling.

The ward manager twists his head round the door. 'Sorry to interrupt, but your husband's trying to reach you. He hasn't been able to contact your daughter. Any news?'

I slump forward. 'She's not on the register.' I try to remember if he's a father, if he has any idea. 'Have they ID'ed it yet?' I search his face for clues but he just shakes his head.

'Looks like a new one, I'm afraid.'

I grip the phone as if it's Sasha's lifeline, the safety rope that will bring her back to shore. Twenty minutes. That's all it takes for a whole new generation of bacteria to birth. While we scrabble around with our drugs, trying to play catch-up.

He runs his tongue over his lips. 'No one's claimed it.' His eyes lift to mine. 'But they think he's EAA.'

My whole body stiffens. EAA: Equality Above All. The catalysts of the Crisis, the fanatics who tipped us over the edge. Just as I dare to hope they've perished, another cell pops up, finding new targets, new ways to attack. I want to slam my fist into the wall.

'Try not to think the worst,' he adds quickly. 'You don't know for sure that she's there. And the mortality rate so far's not too bad.'

As if that's meant to reassure me. Why? Why do they keep doing it? These idiots don't value their own lives or anyone else's. Babies or priests. Nurses. Friends. My fist clenches as I think of Lucy. They're all fair game.

I pull up the news on the monitor. Five hundred shoppers quarantined in the central atrium. Another two thousand in the cinema complex. It's a total lock-down.

'Mrs Connelly?'

I flinch. I have a sudden urge to hang up. I can't hear her say it. I cannot have her make it true.

'We've found her.' The breath spills out of me. 'She's on the other line. I'll put you through now.'

I hear a slight rustle: 'Mum?'

My hand flies up to my mouth. 'Hello, baby,' I say, forgetting she's a teenager, forgetting everything apart from the fact that she's safe.

'What's going on? Miss Granger said there'd been another attack. No one's allowed out.'

'That's right.' I try to steady my breathing. 'At the Westbourne Centre. Are you OK?'

'I'm fine. Are you alright? You sound terrible.'

I bark out a laugh: that's my girl. 'I was just worried, that's all. You didn't answer your phone.'

'Oh, Mum. It was BakeFest, remember?' The desk shimmers slightly. 'I was one of the judges. All I've done for the past hour is shovel down cake. I thought I'd told you. Sorry.'

I press the heel of my hand into my forehead as my adrenaline fizzes out. This is normal to her, quite normal. While she's been eating cake, a few miles down the road a terrorist with a lethal disease has walked into a shopping centre and infected hundreds, possibly thousands of people. Should I feel relieved that it bothers her so little, or terrified?

'You're awfully quiet, Mum. Are you sure you're OK?'

A wave of exhaustion hits. 'Yes, I ... I'm just a little tired.' I grapple behind for a chair.

She sucks the air through her teeth. 'OK. Well, I suppose I'd better get back. See you later, yeah?'

'Assuming the curfew lifts. You will come straight home, Sasha, won't you?'

'Yes,' she says in a drawl that tells me I shouldn't have asked.

'And you've got your mask?'

'Mum, really?'

'OK, OK.' I clench my hands. 'Love you. A lot.'

'You too.'

I hold on to the phone, unable to put it down. Never forget. Never forget how precious she is. Because the world can change, and you can lose everything, in an instant.

'All OK?'

I look up. The ward manager's still clutching the door: I'd forgotten. 'I think so,' I say, although I'm really not sure. 'She's safe.'

He breaks into a smile. 'Thank goodness.' He glances at his phone. 'The results are in. It's another flu mutation. They're sending us fifty.' He pauses. 'Look, I completely understand if you'd rather—'

'I'll be there. Just give me five minutes. I need to call Mark.'

I take a deep breath and dial. As the phone rings I think about all those people destined to die because of one misguided man, and all the staff who will put their lives at risk trying to save them.

We just keep going round and round in the same futile circles.

I wonder if it will ever end.

CHAPTER 7

LILY

'Enjoying the music, Lily?' Anne leans over and fills my cup. I say cup but it's actually a beaker: orange plastic with two handles.

I eye the man who is sweating into his microphone, chubby legs spread wide astride the stool. He's cranking up for the finale, hammering away on that keyboard with his fat little hands.

'It's certainly a change,' I say, as the electric drum throbs inside my head. They look like sausages, his fingers. Bangers, that's what my grandmother used to call them. Nice with a bit of mash. Not that I can talk, of course. My twisted fingers look more crustacean than human. They curl into my palms, as if even they're embarrassed.

Anne bends towards me, her gloved hands at the ready. 'Here you go.'

I open my mouth like a baby bird. She puts two capsules on my tongue. I lift the water to my lips and swallow. 'Down the hatch!' That's what I always say. She smiles, even though she must have heard it a thousand times. It's what we do, these little rituals: the carers know what to expect, and we do what's expected.

'All gone?' Anne asks. I nod as the singer disembowels another refrain. Beads of moisture glisten on his forehead. 'Good girl. Well done.'

Anne moves on to George, who is slumped in the armchair next to me. She's waving at him to get his attention, but his rheumy eyes are far away, in some better place. Right now I wish I could join him. Music therapy is the latest addition to our activities schedule. They play us songs from our youth; it's supposed to jumpstart our neural pathways. The trouble is, they've hired someone whose musical talents would be better utilised calling the numbers at bingo. But it's either this or the solitude of my room. And solitude doesn't feel as good as it used to.

I wait until Anne's moved on to Vivienne and Pam's busy with the tea trolley. I force a cough and tug my lace hanky out of my sleeve. My tongue dislodges the capsule and on my next cough I spit it into the hanky. I check on Anne. She's still hovering in front of Vivienne with a smile that's becoming strained. I fold the hanky over and slip it into my pocket.

'Let's slow things down, shall we?' shouts the man. A couple of frail heads nod politely. 'Remember this? Bet you all had a few smooches to this one!'

It stabs me after a couple of notes, even though this version is pitiful. My eyes snap shut. I see the emerald butterfly leaves fluttering above us. I feel his hands around my waist, the dust between my toes. His fingers were slim and tanned, their hairs burned blonde in the sun. Sometimes he'd get calluses and they'd catch like sandpaper against my skin.

A piercing wail drags me back. Vivienne is crumpled over her tray.

'My legs! My poor legs!' She rocks back and forth, making little whimpering sounds, her hands clawing the air. I notice an ominous stain on her skirt. 'Please, do something!'

The musician falters and stops. The organ carries on playing without him.

Anne rushes over. 'Oh, Viv, what happened?'

'My tea ... it, it scalded me!'

Only now do I see the cup on the floor. My heart sinks. They're not supposed to serve the drinks too hot; someone's going to get it in the neck for that.

'It's alright, Viv,' says Anne. 'Just try and keep still.' Anne carefully lifts Vivienne's skirt, revealing a glimpse of tan support stockings. I ought to turn away but I can't. Angry puce rages across translucent skin. Anne turns to Pam and lowers her voice. 'Call Dr Barrows. And bring me a chair, quick.'

Vivienne stares at her thighs, hands clenching and unclenching, her narrow chest pulsating like a tiny sparrow's.

'We need to get your skirt off, Viv, get some cold water on them right away,' says Anne.

Vivienne's eyes brim. 'Is it bad?' she whispers.

Anne runs her tongue over her lips. 'Don't worry. It looks much worse than it is.'

We all know she's lying. Burns are notorious: they take ages to heal. It's only a matter of time before infection sets in.

Anne pulls on a fresh set of gloves. 'We'll run your legs under the tap for a bit and wrap them up in cling film; that should do the trick.' Her smile is so forced I have to look away.

The performer manages to switch off his machine. He clasps his hands together, eyes fixed on the carpet. George starts picking at his sleeve, whispering words I cannot hear. The rest of us watch in silence. When Pam brings the wheelchair they take great pains to be gentle, but Vivienne screams when they lift her in. As Anne wheels her out, the back of Vivienne's head gets smaller and smaller until they turn a corner and she disappears.

Pam whispers to the music man. He fiddles with some buttons and a ballad bursts into the room. Pam squats down on her haunches and starts mopping up the tea. I shuffle my bottom to the edge of the chair, kick the tray contraption away with my feet and scrabble for my walker. My elbows dig into the arms as I hoist myself up. I manage to get an inch clear before collapsing back on the seat.

'What *are* you doing, Lily?'

I don't answer. *What does it bloody look like?*

'You know you're not supposed to,' Pam says, and slams Vivienne's cup back on its tray. 'Not after your little episode. What if you have another fall?'

I want to shout at her that I don't care. But the trouble is, I do. All the scenarios race through my brain unbidden: a catalogue of disasters waiting to unfold.

'Need the loo again?' she asks.

I nod, even though I don't. Might make her hurry up and help me if she thinks I'm going to piss on the chair. 'Come on, then.' She grabs me under the arms and hauls me up.

I twist my wrists into the clamps and shove my frame forward. My feet refuse to move, as if they've come out in protest; I have to haul them across the carpet. No one looks up, no one speaks. I know what they're thinking. Just one slip of a teacup. Is that all it comes down to, in the end?

By the time I get back to my room, my head is pounding; the tinny electric beat still pulses between my ears. I shuffle to my wardrobe and creak the door open. Cloth sachets seesaw above me, withered notes of rose and lavender infusing the must. I grope behind the hangers for the ledge. My fingers close around a small, steel tube. After a couple of attempts I manage to unscrew the lid. I deposit the pill from my hanky safely inside. I think of the postcard and my grip tightens. Just a couple more should do.

As I wedge the tube back my hand brushes something else: hard, wooden. The idea circles like a wary fox. I lift the box out, sending dust motes spinning through the air. My heart races beneath the patch. I balance the box on my frame and slide over to the dressing table. I rummage around the disused make-up brushes and ageing pots of age-defying creams until I find it: a green metal tin. I prise it open. Nestled amidst a tangle of brown kirby grips is a small silver key.

I ease myself into the chair and catch my breath. I have learned how to do this over the years, one sense at a time. I slot the key into the hole and close my eyes. There's a grating noise as the lock turns. I flip the lid. It's still there, but much fainter now. A smell of otherness. Another place. Another life.

The first thing I see is the velvet pouch. I tug the drawstring loose. Spirals of gold dance across the walls as the bracelet tips into my palm. Unlike me, it has not dulled. I rub the cool metal with my thumb, press my fingers into its grooves. Memories beckon: meticulous but frayed. That's the trouble with memories: the more they're summoned, the faster the originals fade, until only the edits remain. It's like those old music cassettes that you used to play over and over. You learned the words off by heart, but the spool of tape wore perilously thin.

I slip the bracelet back into its pouch. I sift through yellowing papers and bundles of creased envelopes. My hand halts at a folded newspaper cutting, and I feel the familiar lurch. That bit of paper finds me every time. I make myself pass on, keep looking, until eventually I find it: a small rectangular envelope, no writing on the front. A bitter taste fills my mouth. It has never been opened, not in twenty years. I had hoped it never would be.

I slip my thumb into a corner and tear. Inside is a crisp, white business card with three oval green leaves embossed at the top. They're so lustrous and fine, they might have been printed just yesterday. I swallow and turn the card over. My fingers won't be still, as if they're itching to stuff the damn thing straight back. I focus on the handwritten letters. The blood whines in my ears.

I hesitate. But I have no choice. I reach for my tablet.

He's the only one who can help.

CHAPTER 8

Twenty-seven years pre-Crisis

MARY

I squint at the oblong grey packets with funny names. You'd think the pharmacy section would at least have some English brands. I select a box with a bald orange head that looks as if it has been set on fire and scan the shop for someone to ask. Pink-faced tourists huddle by fridges, enjoying a brief respite from the heat. Two little girls in lacy shorts shunt a freezer lid back and forth while their parents load burgers and chicken wings into their trollies. The next aisle along, a woman is on her knees, stacking shelves. I'm about to head over to her when I spot a tanned guy in khaki shorts at the till. My breath stops.

It's him.

My eyes swerve back to the painkillers. I tuck in my shirt and drag my fingers through my hair. He hasn't clocked me yet. Too busy chatting with that girl behind the counter, all eyelashes and teeth. When he does eventually turn, I hold up one hand in a hesitant wave. He frowns, and for a terrible moment I think he's forgotten. But then he ambles over.

'Raced any more rhinos, recently?' A smile plays around his lips.

'Actually,' I say, jutting out my chin, 'I decided to stick to plants. They don't run as fast.'

He throws back his head and laughs. Something inside me leaps.

He nods at the tablets. 'Hurt yourself?'

'Oh, just a bit of back pain.' I twist the packet round, squeezing it between my fingers. 'Too much crouching over bushes.'

'Ah.' His mouth makes a clicking sound. 'Professional hazard.'

I wonder again what exactly it is he does. He wasn't very forthcoming the last time we met, although I did glean that he used to be a ranger. When I asked one of the other researchers about him, they told me he's bioprospecting for medicinal compounds from plants.

'So, how long are you down for?' he asks.

I manage to meet his gaze for a second. Jesus. I want to give myself a good slap. 'Just the day. Replenishing supplies, picking up post, that sort of thing. I may even attempt a couple of calls. How about you?'

'Same. Need to restock. Then it's back to the field.'

My eyes scurry over his face, lingering on a small white scar on his left cheek. It looks like an inverse beauty spot. I try to think what to say, but words have abandoned me.

'So.' He claps his hands together. 'This is the only place in the park that sells half-decent coffee. Want to grab one?'

I check my watch, as if I'm not entirely certain my schedule can permit it. As if. 'Sure.' A blush burns in my cheeks. 'Why not?'

I follow him out onto a stone veranda. A cluster of white plastic tables have been impaled with canvas umbrellas. He chooses one right by the railings, overlooking the dam. Three crocodiles cruise the murky waters below, just the tops of their eyes and the uppermost ridge of scales visible. There's a pungent smell of animals and damp vegetation.

The waitress takes our order and he starts firing questions at me about my research. I'm flattered by his interest, only too happy to talk. Research can be a lonely business. I pull out my field book, even show him some of my precious data. He listens attentively, nodding.

'So then,' I say, suddenly aware how long I've been talking. Something about his expression suggests he may have stopped listening a few data points back. I tug a strand of hair behind my ear. 'What do you think?'

A muscle in his arm twitches. 'I think that all sounds quite interesting.'

The heat rushes into my face. *Quite interesting?* I'm doing a PhD at Oxford. My papers will be published in leading scientific journals.

'Don't get me wrong,' he adds, 'you're doing great work.' He rests his elbows on the table. 'But I think your talents could be put to better use.'

My hand tightens around my field book. I glare past his shoulder to the dam. A pair of waterbuck are wandering down the bank. They stamp their hooves, tails swishing, summoning the courage to drink.

He fixes me with his gaze. 'Half of all prescribed drugs are derived from plants. You probably know that. Quinine, morphine, codeine: the list goes on. But here's the thing: none of them are antibiotics. Even though many plants are rich in antimicrobial compounds. And that's just the ones we know about.' He leans forward, and I catch a pulse of perfumed sweat: sharp and fragrant, like the zest of lemon.

I arch my fingers in a show of calm. 'Which is why we need

more research. To catalogue and conserve the species. Before they disappear.'

His lips slide back, revealing a blaze of teeth. 'Oh, I couldn't agree more.'

Patronising as well as arrogant. My eyes veer back to the dam. The male waterbuck moves cautiously to the edge. He splays his front legs and lowers his head, his spiralled horns reflected in the water. I think of my camera, trapped in my bag.

'Antibiotic resistance is growing, Mary. Skin and gut infections. Sexually transmitted diseases. TB. Some of them are becoming practically untreatable.' His elbow brushes mine. 'Have you heard of an American drug called Taxol?'

I shake my head. A fat bead of sweat slopes down my back. I start fanning myself with the menu.

'Cancer drug. A report was published last year on the results from phase-two trials on patients with ovarian cancer.' He pauses. 'Taxol had a response rate of thirty percent. We're talking one of the biggest ever breakthroughs in cancer treatment.'

The sun arcs under the umbrella, blinding me. He cups one hand over his eyes. 'Do you know where Taxol comes from?'

My thighs make a sucking sound as I peel them off the plastic and scrape my chair into the shade. 'No.' I'm an intelligent woman but this man has the knack of making me feel stupid.

'Taxus brevifolia.'

At last. Familiar territory. 'The Pacific yew,' I say. He smiles.

Now the female waterbuck steps down, her pale haunches twitching. After a prolonged scan of the bank, she dips her dainty mouth in the water.

'Taxol is the name given to the active compound they isolated from its bark. Which is what inhibited the cancer's progress. And do you know how they found it?'

I swat the air between us with the menu. 'No, but I have a feeling you're going to tell me.' Most people would be discouraged by that. But not him.

'Back in the sixties, the National Cancer Institute commissioned a plant-screening programme. American botanists were paid to collect a thousand samples a year. Taxol was the result of that programme.' Trickles of sweat seep into golden curls beneath his collar. 'The Americans have just launched another one, focussing on HIV. But antibiotics aren't even on their radar.'

Suddenly there's a loud splash. One of the larger crocs launches out of the water and lunges towards the female. She leaps back just in time; her lithe body twists through the air as the creature plummets back into the depths.

The corner of his mouth twitches. 'Lucky...' His eyes dart back to mine. 'Mary, we know at least ten percent of South Africa's plants are already used in traditional medicine. Many with positive results.' He stabs my field book with his finger. 'Some of them are listed in here. So why not put all that knowledge to use?'

I feel myself flush. What the hell is he implying? That what I do now isn't of use? 'Isn't that your job?' I swipe some hair back off my forehead. 'You're the pharmacologist, not me.'

He shakes his head. 'I work with what we already know. There are thousands more plants out there. We need people like you, Mary – experienced botanists – to help discover the next generation of drugs.'

I shift in my seat. I can't argue with what he's saying, but this is my life he's speculating with, and I'm tired of being preached at. My hackles are up.

'Species are going extinct before we've even identified them,'

I say, brushing crumbs of earth off my shorts. 'If that happens there won't be any plants left to supply drugs, food or anything else for that matter.' I hold his gaze. 'Frankly, I see the conservation agenda as more pressing.'

His lips tighten. 'Really?' The r rolls slowly off his tongue. He looks almost as angry as he did the first time.

'Look,' he says, sitting back, 'I know I get a bit carried away. Sometimes things don't come across quite the way I mean.'

They come across exactly how you mean, I think. But in a weird way, that's part of the attraction: his absence of filter, his raw passion.

'Come out with me tomorrow,' he says then. 'I'd like to show you something. Perhaps it will change your mind.'

I look past him, to the dam. The waterbuck have disappeared, leaving the crocodiles to prowl alone. Until the next time.

I could say no, and we could go our separate ways. I could tell him where to shove it.

I deliberate one, two, three seconds at most. They might as well be infinity.

'OK.'

CHAPTER 9

Are you over seventy and suffering from an illness or injury caused by someone else?

Broken purifier? Sick shop assistant? A neighbour's dog?
Then we're here to help.
If your infection is due to someone else's negligence,
claim the compensation you're legally entitled to
and contact REESE-LEIGH PERSONAL INFECTION SOLICITORS today.
Don't delay! Free initial consultation. No win, no fee.

We can't work miracles but we can ease life
for the loved ones you leave behind.

■ ■ ■

KATE

'Kate? What are you doing? We should have left twenty minutes ago!'

Mark's voice is a distant wail as I dash around upstairs. I check Sasha's room first and then ours: windows shut, air purifiers on. I hit the bathroom for taps. Just as well, the cold one's been left running; I'll bet it was Mark, although he always denies it. I skid through the kitchen and grab my bag.

Mask. Gloves. Resus bags. OK. I can leave.

As I slide into my seat Mark glances up from his phone. 'The invitation did say seven-thirty not eight-thirty, right?'

I ignore him and flip down the sun visor. I scowl at the mirror and navigate a smear of lipstick as Mark speed-reverses down the drive.

We've been going about ten minutes when I remember: 'You did pick up the present, didn't you?'

He runs his tongue over his teeth and hits the brake.

'Oh, Mark!' I curse myself for not checking earlier.

He gives me a smug grin and accelerates. 'In the boot.'

My eyes narrow. 'Funny.'

'Relax, woman! You're off duty.'

Relax. Relaxing. Now there's a concept. We're off to celebrate his brother's birthday at some extortionate restaurant that's bloody miles away. While disinfecting the cutlery, I'll have to stop myself tallying up all the things we should have spent the money on instead.

Mark mutters something about the driver in front and pulls onto the dual carriageway. 'So, how was your day?'

My stomach loops. I think of the envelope with the GRO postmark that came this morning. I snaffled it into my handbag like a shoplifter on my way out the door.

'Oh, you know. The usual.' I feel a twinge of guilt, but now's not the time to tell him. I daren't derail myself before the alcohol starts flowing. 'A woman was admitted with septicaemia who'd been scratched by her cat.'

He frowns. 'Another one? I just don't get it.' Mark was no cat-lover even before the Crisis. 'Why risk it when there are so many clawless varieties to choose from?'

'She'd had it fifteen years. Probably a stray. One of those "liberated" pets that escaped the culls.' I think of the poor woman's mottled cheeks, the sweat rolling down onto the pillows. 'She kept asking me where it was. I didn't have the heart to tell her.'

Mark shakes his head and accelerates into the fast lane. As he overtakes a hatchback, a young girl with dark, frizzy hair and a pink-and-purple mask glares at me from her child seat.

'So why didn't she get it declawed?' Mark isn't giving up on this. 'It's a free service.'

I glance at him. 'Apparently it's like having the ends of your fingers amputated. Some people think it's cruel.'

'Not as cruel as giving someone septicaemia,' he mutters. 'I'm amazed some ambulance chaser didn't show up at her bedside and try and get her to sue.' He sighs. 'Did you see that one, by the way? About the man who's suing his daughter? Because her Jack Russell gave him a nip?' He shakes his head. 'Bloody lawyers. They're the only ones profiting from this mess.'

He's right: the litigation is relentless. Families and neighbours turning on each other. People scared of being in the same room as a seventy-year-old, let alone talking to one. It's hardly surprising that so many end up sequestered away in those awful retirement flats or, if they're lucky, a care home.

'I know it's hard, love. But try not to let them get to you.'

'Who? The lawyers?'

'No, your patients.'

Easier said than done. I twist the handle of my bag around my fingers. At least the woman got to talk to a soul midwife. Prepared herself for what's to come.

My thoughts drift back to my birth certificate. It was lime yellow with a swirling watermark that reminded me of a William Morris design. When I looked more closely I could see the circles of crowns surrounding the letters 'GRO': General Register Office England.

Mark does one of his noisy throat-clears. 'Kate? You're awfully quiet. Is there something else going on?'

It's no good, I can't keep a thing from him. I take a deep breath. 'It arrived today.'

His head swivels round. 'What? Why didn't you say?'

'I don't know...' I shrug out a sigh. 'I wasn't holding out on you, it's just all a bit...' I rummage for the right words but succumb to a cliché. 'I'm still trying to process it myself.'

Mark doesn't say anything. He keeps his eyes on the road, sneaking glances at me when he thinks I'm not looking.

I squirreled myself away in the ladies and stared at that envelope for what seemed like hours. When I finally drummed up the courage to open it, my eyes scrambled across the paper as if they were afraid the words might disappear, just as she had.

All of a sudden, Mark indicates and starts to brake. We turn into a desolate layby.

'We don't have to go, you know.' He reaches for my hand. 'I can take us home. Right now.' A lorry tears past, making the car quiver. 'I'll tell Bill I've eaten a dodgy sandwich. Make barfing noises down the phone.'

I shake my head. 'No, Mark. We should go.' I give him a weak smile. 'I'm fine, honestly.'

I remember the feeling I had as my eyes moved down the page. I used to have the same feeling on fairground rides, just before they started.

The engine ticks. A pigeon pecks morosely at a crisp packet on the verge. I inhale and say the words like a spell: 'Mary Sommers. Mary Kate Sommers.'

Saying it out loud unlocks something, and I have to look away. It's the only thing she gave me, my name. I lean back and feel the tiredness pulling at me.

'Nice name,' Mark says, nodding. He squeezes my fingers. 'Not sure about the middle one, though.'

I smile. He is one decision I got right. This man seems able to navigate even the most difficult paths.

'Was she young?' he asks.

'Not especially.' My voice sounds all high and whiny, not like mine at all. 'Twenty-five.' My chest tightens. 'Just two years younger than me when I had Sasha.'

I know it's unfair, but it feels like a betrayal. I didn't think she'd be that old.

I remember all the arguments Mark and I had about bringing a child into this world. How hard it was to persuade him, because of the risks to the baby and to me. The delivery suite felt more like A&E. I'll never forget the sound from the next cubicle. At first I thought the woman must still be in labour. I'd heard plenty of mothers scream before, but this was different. It was a primal sound: a howling wail, more animal than human. And then the midwife walked past with that silent, still bundle. And I knew.

Mark sighs. 'We have to remember. Things were so different then.'

Yes. Yes, they were. No armed guards outside maternity wards. No police escorts on the way home. No matter how many times they told me to lay her in her cot, I kept Sasha tucked in tight to my belly, her little mask on. I couldn't sleep. I was convinced that if I did, when I woke up, she'd either be dead or gone.

'So that makes her, what, sixty-nine?'

'Yup.' Something spiky pricks inside. 'Just as well I got started. If she's not already died, she soon will.'

'Hey, come on.' Mark pulls me into a hug.

I rest my head against his shoulder, his sweater bristling my cheek. A few weeks ago, I couldn't have cared less about this woman.

Mark kisses the top of my head. 'Where did it say the birth was registered?'

'West London somewhere. I didn't recognise the hospital – must have been private.' I wait a couple of seconds. 'No mention of a father.'

It shouldn't make a difference, really it shouldn't. But when I saw that empty box it threw me. I'd been so focussed on my birth mother, I hadn't really given him much thought. I felt strangely bereft. As if I'd been abandoned not once, but twice.

Mark runs his fingers slowly through my hair. 'Well, at least you've got a trail to follow now. That is, if you want to.'

I dig my nails into the seat. I thought that getting this information would help, would make me feel more certain. But part of me just wants to rip up that damned certificate. Send it spiralling skywards, like an errant meteor, to collide with some other planet.

Cars stream past, tail-lights winking, as the sky fades to a silky grey. My head feels woolly, as if I'm coming down with something. I imagine dozing off, snuggled into Mark, here, in this layby. Drifting back to a time before any of this had been set loose.

Mark's chest presses against my face as he inhales. 'You could always make an appointment with one of those adoption advisors. I'm sure they could give you some guidance.'

Typical Mark. He's probably done more research into this whole process than I have.

'Maybe. I'll give it some thought.' My words are swallowed by a yawn. 'Anyway, look, we'd better get moving. We're going to be obscenely late, even by my standards.'

Mark doesn't stir. He frowns at me. 'You're sure?'

I arch my back and give him an emphatic nod. 'Sure.'

He looks at me a moment longer, and starts the engine. I rest back and close my eyes.

Honi soit qui mal y pense.

After I'd read all the boxes on my birth certificate, I found myself staring at that motto, on the royal coat of arms.

'Shame be to him who evil thinks'.

Who are you, Mary Sommers? Are you still with us?

And then comes the darker thought.

Why? Why did you give me away?

CHAPTER 10

LILY

'There you are! I've been all over, looking for you.'

I drag my eyes away from my book. Pam's face is a volcanic red, and she's puffing enough to blow. They did their research, those architects; they created these little nooks and crannies to encourage the antisocial ones out of their rooms. Unless someone looks behind this particular stack in the library, they haven't a clue you're there.

'I've been in here twice already,' she adds, just to be clear it's my fault. 'You've got a visitor.'

My adrenaline spikes. Despite the email, I wasn't convinced he'd come.

'Room four.'

How fitting. Four is an unlucky number in many Asian languages. Because it sounds like the word for death.

Pam heaves me up. Reluctantly, I hand her the novel for the sterilisation rack. It's such a treat, having a real book between my fingers. Sometimes I'll hold one up to my nose and try to catch the smell of a bygone age.

Like everything else, printing stopped during the Crisis. Even though the risk of infection was minimal. Book stores went first and libraries followed. By the time the new drugs came along, people had got used to touch-free audio and screens. Second-hand books became a titillating rarity, a bit like mercury-laden barometers or old medicine jars. Until someone invented a page steriliser that didn't melt the print. I suppose we're lucky, really. It's only homes like ours that can afford them.

Pam scuttles off ahead as I begin my slow trek to the visitor wing. I wheel past wooden tables with red-shaded lamps and wood-panelled walls. A couple of the residents look up, their faces a mixture of envy and surprise. I know what they're thinking: I never get visitors. Most of us don't. I see how it gets to some of them when, week after week, nobody comes. I suppose I should feel honoured. But this is no family visit.

A dispenser puffs out more chemical jasmine as I shuffle past. Beyond the library, the decor changes to pastels with magnolia, and insipid landscape prints start to colonise the walls. My heart is leaping around as if it's forgotten how old it is, and I stop a moment to rest. I wonder how much he's changed. Probably weathered better than I have. He won't be holed up in some tightly regulated care home. Oh, no. It'll be the good life for him.

Eventually I reach the carpeted area that signals I've made it to the border crossing: that closely guarded place where they let the outside in. Pictures are replaced with notices that shout in capitals about screening protocols and penalties. I pay no attention to them and step straight onto the circle. A violet beam hovers over my eyes. There's a beep and the security doors slide open.

This side of the curtain it's black leather sofas and cream carpets, artificial flowers in glass vases. The stern warnings have all but disappeared. A large screen flashes mute images of crowds brandishing signs outside Westminster:

Stop the Genocide!

Don't Cut Me Off!

I follow the headlines scrolling along the bottom:

More clashes between protestors and police as pressure mounts for abolition of the Medication Act...

I think of poor Vivienne. No amount of protests can help her now.

I shuffle along the carpet, marshalling my questions, as the blood races through my veins. It's me that's asked him here. I must remember that. But memories keep closing in, like hungry sharks. It's as if I'm living in two parallel worlds: the one that existed before I got the postcard, and a new, uncertain world that reaches back into my past and throws out questions I cannot answer.

I contemplate the large silver '4' on the door. Perhaps it was deliberate: Graham's idea of a joke. I have a ridiculous impulse to knock. I ignore it.

He is sitting with his back to me, staring at a picture on the wall. My eyes swerve to the painting. It's a typical Oxford scene, all Cotswold stone and cobbles, bicycles lined up outside a college gate. It brings no comfort.

He grips the chair with lean, manicured fingers and manoeuvres himself round. His hair has greyed, and he's thinner than I remember. I expected the wrinkles, but not the bones pushing out as if his skin's preparing to shed.

'Ah, Lily.' He rolls his tongue over the ls, just to put me on edge. I resist the urge to walk back out. 'How long has it been?'

He knows the answer – he knows everything about me. But I tell him anyway.

'Nineteen years.'

His sharp grey eyes flit over my invalid's frame, my hunched body, my crab claws. His mouth puckers. I can't tell whether it's in amusement or disgust. I must look like an old hag to him. But the real monster in the room is right there.

'Well, I have to say, your email came as something of a surprise.' He smiles. His teeth look too big for his mouth. 'I never expected to hear from you. But I kept the account open. Just in case.'

His voice hasn't changed: the same silky-smooth charm, which, like everything else, is false.

I lower myself into one of the chairs and tug my sleeves over my hands. He watches every painstaking move. I try to remember what my first question was.

He sniffs. 'Not a bad place to end up.'

Easy for him to say. Although I could be rotting away in one of those flats, like Pam's mother. Or those detention centres they converted and called care homes, where they send pensioners with no money when their families eventually kick them out.

His gaze shifts to the camera mounted in the corner. They're not supposed to record the sound, but you never know. 'They treat you well?'

'Well enough.'

He nods. 'So, this must be your big year, then?' Another smile flickers. 'I suppose you've seen the protests.'

I haven't asked him here to make small talk, but I don't have much choice. 'Yes.'

'Not that they'll make any difference.' He sighs. 'There's no way this government will entertain any watering down of the Act. Not while shelf lives are still struggling to get beyond a year. Apart from anything else, they could never afford the drugs.'

He's right, of course. Usage would go through the ceiling. "Reservoirs of resistance": that's what care homes like this were called. And, even with all the price caps and subsidies, antibiotics are still exorbitant. I remember the days when doctors used to hand them out like sweets, even for viral infections like coughs and colds. When, in some countries, you could buy them over the counter. One pill at a time.

'I thought they'd raised the possibility of an extension, though?' I say, indulging him. 'Making cut-off seventy-five?'

He snorts. 'Delay tactics. No minister in his right mind would extend cut-off. You know how quickly things could slide.' He flaps his hand. 'All those weakened immune systems and repeat medications. Don't forget, it was our age group that wreaked the most havoc. The over-seventies used to account for a quarter of all antibiotic prescriptions before resistance screening came in.' He shakes his head. 'Those old buggers can protest all they like. The truth is, the only reason things are just about functioning is because the seventy- and eighty-year-olds keep dying.'

It suddenly occurs to me that this is the reason he thinks I've brought him here. To beg for an exception. Ask him to pull one of his many strings.

His lids hover over his eyes. 'Of course, they'll have to do something eventually. But not until we've weaned ourselves off this absurd reliance on drugs.' He wags his finger at me. 'Gene editing: that's the future.' He nods. 'We'll eliminate disease by playing the microbes at their own game. The Chinese have already bred HIV-resistant mice, so it won't be long before they're meddling with humans. Smart, eh? But that'll be too late for the likes of you and me.'

A slow grin stretches across his face. 'Does it worry you at all? This dying business? Or are you ready to meet your maker, Lily?'

My heart hammers in my chest but I hold his gaze. 'You know what, Graham? I've been ready for years.'

He wheezes with laughter. 'That's more like the woman I remember. So, then.' He spreads his palms out in front of him, as if he has all the time in the world. 'What exactly was it that you wanted to discuss?'

I steel myself. Even now, asking him for anything feels like treason. 'I was sent something. A postcard.'

One eyebrow arches. 'How quaint.'

'The photo on the front...' I swallow. 'It was a rhino. A white rhino.'

His face betrays nothing more than mild curiosity. 'Any message?'

'No, it was blank.' I clasp my fingers, letting the pain scream around my joints. 'Only one person could have sent it.' I stare at him. 'Think about it. Only the team knew. This has to be him.'

A small laugh escapes. 'You don't mean...? You're not serious?'

'Well, who else could it be?'

'There's just one problem. He died, remember?' Graham slides his tongue over his teeth. 'Nineteen years ago, to be precise.'

I know how it sounds but I can't lose him on this. I lean forward and whisper, even though the camera should be muted and there's no one else here. 'What if he didn't? What if he did some kind of deal? With your lot or ... or EAA?'

'For goodness sake, he—'

'I wasn't there when it happened. Nor were you. The whole thing could have been some elaborate sham.'

He throws his hands up in the air. 'The man was cremated, for God's sake! All that's left of him are ashes.' Graham turns his back to the camera. 'Anyone could have sent this. There could still be relatives out there with an axe to grind. Not forgetting the press. They can't resist dredging up an old scandal.'

His words slice right through me.

'After all this time? How would they even find me?'

He gives me a disparaging look. 'Anyone can find anyone, if they have the right technology.'

I feel the room spinning away from me. 'But ... but you promised! You guaranteed I'd be safe.'

'That was two decades ago. We were careful, very careful. But with the kit they've got nowadays, frankly anything is possible.'

I clench my jaw, hot shards of panic coursing through me. 'You have to swear, Graham. Swear to me he's dead. Because if he isn't, I'm not the only person he'd come for—'

'You've been watching too many films, Lily.' His lip curls. 'What proof do you need? An affidavit from the prison doctor? The x-ray of his lungs? Look, at the end of the day, it's just a postcard. You've had worse.'

I scan his face but it offers no clues. I never could tell when he was lying.

He gives an elaborate sigh. 'Look, I'll make some enquiries. Run a few checks.' His voice has a weariness that shows just how futile he thinks it is. 'But I'm telling you, whoever's doing this, it isn't Bekker. Not unless he's figured out how to come back from the grave.'

With some effort, he pushes himself up to standing. 'Now, I'm afraid I really must be going.' I notice a sheen of sweat on his forehead. Maybe he's not doing so well after all. As he moves towards me I stiffen. 'Goodbye, Lily.' He holds out his hand. It looks like a relic I once saw in the vault of an Italian church:

small, brown and shrivelled. 'Don't worry,' he smiles. 'I used the sanitiser.'

I force myself to take it. 'Goodbye, Graham.'

'I'll be in touch.' He moves past me, trailing some fancy cologne that smells like fruit on the turn. 'And do stop worrying. At your age, it really isn't good for you.'

I sink back against the wall. He thinks I'm overreacting, that what I said doesn't make sense. A lot of things don't make sense. It hasn't stopped them happening, though.

By the time I reach my room it's all I can do to lift my wrist for the sensor. But as the door swings open I hear a rustling sound. Something's trapped underneath, on the carpet.

I peer over my frame. It's an article, torn from a newspaper. The photo's faded but you can still see them.

'Kill Not Cure...'

Some of the children appear to be sleeping. Others stare with fixed, glassy eyes, like the ones they used to put in dolls. They look as though they are searching for something. Something that never comes.

The walls swoop in, crushing me between them like the boards of a flower press.

I don't have to read it, I know every word.

It's exactly the same cutting as the one in my box.

CHAPTER 11

Twenty-seven years pre-Crisis

'Urgent Action Required' Warns WHO as TB Deaths Continue To Rise

The World Health Organisation gave a sharp message to governments this week about the dangers of tuberculosis, which has risen to become the fifth leading cause of death globally. WHO estimates that there were 7.5 million new cases of TB last year, which caused 2.5 million fatalities. 1.7 billion people globally are thought to be infected.

'We are facing an extremely serious problem,' commented a spokesperson. 'The number of people infected is growing each year. We urgently need more investment in the development of new vaccines and new drugs so that we can roll out simpler, shorter treatment regimens. Doing nothing is no longer an option.'

■ ■ ■

MARY

The boy lies curled on the bed, shivering, although it must be nearly forty degrees. He looks maybe seven or eight. Probably older. He's thrown off the sheets, exposing his thighs: more bone than flesh. Sweat streams down his face, seeping into the surgical mask that covers his nose and mouth. The mask must have been white once, like mine; now it is patterned with ominous stains. He stares, transfixed, at the ceiling fan; the circling blades do little more than stir the air.

All of a sudden, he convulses with a wet, rasping cough; his tiny body heaves and heaves. The boy tries to lever himself up, get his head over the side, but he hasn't the strength. He claws at his mask as a red jet of sputum erupts onto the pillow. My hand flies to my mask. I snatch it away, praying Piet didn't notice. The boy rolls over, draws his knees up to his chest and shuts his eyes.

'He's one of the lucky ones,' mutters Piet. His expression is blank, but I sense the anger coiled inside. 'At least he's got a bed.'

I look at the men, women and children, all sandwiched together in this fetid room. More patients are slumped against the peeling corridor walls, spilling onto the street outside. The stench of bodies is overwhelming. This clinic is just fifty miles from the park border: is this the best they can do?

'Pulmonary tuberculosis,' he says, eyes still glued to the boy. 'There are no symptoms for the first two or three months, while the infection incubates. It starts with the cough. Most people dismiss it, wait for it to go away. But every day that passes, it gets worse. With each cough or sneeze, it spreads. Which, of course, is why it's such an effective pathogen.' He turns to me. 'TB doesn't announce its presence. Like the best killers, it moves quietly. Catching its victims unawares.'

Tuberculosis? I think of history books with grainy black-and-white photos of children lying in hospital beds outside. Victorian ladies coughing into lace hankies. Surely this is a disease of the past?

'After the cough comes the chest pain. Then the night sweats. Exhaustion sets in.' His voice is monotone. 'Body weight plummets as the fever intensifies. Then they start coughing up blood. That's because cavities are developing in the tissue of their lungs.'

A strange rattling noise makes us both look round. It's a woman in one of the adjacent beds: her teeth are chattering.

'Without treatment, the bacteria progress to other parts of the body. Eventually the patients start haemorrhaging and their organs fail.' He doesn't take his fierce blue gaze off the boy. 'There's a reason this disease used to be called consumption. It consumes you.'

My eyes seek refuge outside. Corrugated iron huts line the road, holes cut in the sides to make windows and doors. Some have been painted bright colours, others are held together by planks of wood, *Shoe Repairs* or *Barber* scrawled across the front. Coils of barbed wire stretch across the top of concrete walls painted with garish slogans for things most people will never be able to afford.

'I don't understand.' I swallow. 'I thought TB had been wiped out.'

He gives a dry laugh. 'Maybe in countries like yours.' Something inside me shrivels. 'TB's been in Africa since the Ancient Egyptians. We like to kid ourselves that it's under control, but it always finds a way back. And this time, it's back with a vengeance.'

I wipe my forehead with my sleeve and adjust my mask. I'm finding it hard to breathe, but the last thing I'm going to do is faint.

'HIV's triggered an explosion of new cases. TB usually targets weaker immune systems: the old, the young and the sick. In most healthy adults, the TB bacilli can lie dormant for years. But with HIV all that changes.' His chest swells with a sigh. 'The virus targets and destroys the very cells responsible for immunity, laying patients wide open. It's a lethal combination.'

'But what about the vaccine?' I ask. 'Why aren't they protected?'

He makes a noise like a punctured tyre. 'You mean the BCG?' He shakes his head. 'It's not effective against pulmonary TB, not in adults. In any case, vaccination programmes out here are sketchy at best.' His gaze moves to the window. 'TB spreads through prolonged contact in a confined space. With HIV on the rampage, townships like these are a perfect breeding ground. The infection rate has climbed to one in a hundred. For children it's double.'

On the street outside a skeletal dog is licking a cardboard box. Slouched against one of the shacks is a man in a filthy brown shirt and tattered trousers. His sodden shirt clings to him, outlining each of his ribs. He reminds me of one of those Holocaust pictures.

'But, if so many people are ill,' I say, 'surely there must be another vaccine in development?'

'You'd think so, wouldn't you? If all things were equal.' His mask creases with a smile but it's the kind that makes me shiver. 'TB's simply not a priority for the West. In fact a lot of countries have stopped using the BCG altogether. So, why bother investing in a new vaccine? No money to be made there.'

A slow burn starts in my stomach and creeps all the way up to my cheeks. I want to rip off my branded shirt and designer sunglasses, kick off my trainers. I think of all the cash we waste back home on things we don't need, while people out here are dying of a disease that should have been consigned to history.

I clench my hands. 'Surely there must be *some* kind of treatment?'

A man on the other side of the room slumps forward and retches into a bowl.

'Most people aren't even diagnosed, let alone treated. It's only when the headache and fever creep in, when they start bringing up blood, that they seek help. By then their diagnosis is immaterial. The nearest hospital's too far away and they can't afford the antibiotics themselves. Their families are the only ones left to care for them.'

My eyes wander to another bed, near the window. A little girl lies on her back, clutching a toy rabbit. She stares at me with misted eyes, her chest rising and falling impossibly fast.

'Even if they can get to a doctor, many don't. They've been put off by stories about the number of tablets they'll have to take and all the side-effects. Sometimes, the drugs don't work. So they go without. Or they turn to other forms of medicine.'

Does he mean traditional remedies? Is that where all this is leading? I think of my ignorant rebuttals at the dam, and my insides roil.

A nurse brushes past with a trolley. Piet asks her something in Zulu. I notice the deep hollows under her eyes. I wonder how many of the staff end up getting sick too.

'I thought so,' Piet mutters. He nods at the woman in the bed next to the little girl. 'That's the girl's mother. She was treated for TB about a year ago. They thought she'd made a full recovery, but now it's back. She wasn't going to come. But then her daughter got sick so they made the journey.'

The nurse lifts the girl into a sitting position and hunkers down next to her. The girl looks tiny against her pillow, still clasping the threadbare rabbit. The nurse gently takes the rabbit's paw and pretends to put something in it. She raises the paw to its mouth, smiling and nodding. The girl shakes her head. The nurse repeats the pantomime, but the tablets remain in their dish.

'She says she's not responding to treatment,' Piet continues. 'Nor is her mother. They're seeing cases like this more and more. New strains are emerging that have developed resistance. It's not surprising really. Even if patients agree to take the pills, many don't finish them. They're supposed to take them for six months. Imagine. There just aren't the resources to follow up.'

And there it is. I consider myself an educated woman, a graduate of one of the most renowned institutions in the world. But before this moment, I'd never even heard of drug-resistant TB.

Piet swipes a sleeve across his forehead. The sweat has bled into his shirt; dark patches glue to his skin. 'Some strains aren't resistant to just one drug, either. To stand any chance of recovery, patients will have to take more pills for even longer.' He shakes his head. 'I just don't see that happening. I'm telling you, it's a ticking time-bomb.'

The anger rushes up inside me. 'Why don't we know about any of this? Why the hell aren't the government doing something?'

He gives me a look that brings me up short, that reminds me we're in the realm of apartheid and the rules simply don't apply. The feeling I had earlier returns: shame about the colour of my skin, shame about the fact I will earn more money in a week than these people earn in a year, shame about my healthy lungs and the ease with which I breathe. Which is why I find myself saying: 'How can I help?'

He smiles. This time his eyes wrinkle with a proper smile. It banishes the fear of what he will ask next.

'If we're going to eradicate this disease, we're going to have to find the solutions ourselves.' He points out of the window. 'Local healers are widely consulted. Not just in townships, either. Because some of these traditional remedies do work. The trouble is, we don't always understand why.' He turns to me. 'Knowledge is handed down by word of mouth. It's rarely documented.'

I know what's coming and my brain is screaming that I can't do this, I can't just switch horses mid-race, it would be career suicide. But I am cornered prey.

'You remember Taxol?' I nod. 'Well, we're setting up our own screening programme, here, in South Africa. A joint venture between two universities and a local pharma firm.' His eyes bore into me. 'We've already recruited some brilliant botanists, but I think we'd benefit from having more international players on our team.' He pauses. 'People with contacts as well as skills.'

My gaze returns to the little girl. I think of my rooms waiting for me back in Oxford. The safe, respectable path I have chosen. My colleagues and my friends.

I consider stalling, telling him I need more time.

He takes a breath. 'You know how much diversity we have out here, Mary. How much potential.' He touches my arm. 'Thousands of years of medicine can't be wrong.'

I dig my nails into my palms. His words shimmer with tantalising possibilities. The fan blades circle slowly round.

I'd like to say that I made my decision on moral grounds. I'd like to say it seemed the right thing to do. These were factors, of course they were.

But the real reason was, if I didn't say yes, I probably wouldn't ever see him again.

CHAPTER 12

KATE

I tap my pen against my cheek, scroll through yet another profile. There must be dozens of Mary Sommers cluttering my screen. I swore I wouldn't, but here I am, doing exactly what the guidance tells you not to: flitting through random pages of women who almost certainly are not my birth mother. They grin at me, these women, teeth bared; some have grey hair, some brown, some curly red. A few are suited and stern, dressed to impress; others look half-cut, lipstick smeared across their mouths. I know this is crazy, but something inside me has stirred. Like a small, wild creature, it gnaws at me, sends irrational thoughts scampering through my head.

I've set my filters for the decade after I was born. I figure if I'm going to find anything, better go pre-Crisis. No death has been registered, so, according to the records, she's definitely still alive. She'd have been fighting her way up the career ladder back then, assuming she had one. Falling in love. Maybe starting a family. One she wanted to keep.

I click on another profile. A busty brunette smoulders astride a stool, cerise shirt splayed, advertising her ample cleavage. I am shocked at how much people used to reveal of themselves and their lives. All those intimate photos of parties and pets. I have to keep reminding myself that this was the time of plenty, for the West at least: everyone whooping it up like revellers on the *Titanic*, oblivious to the silent cooperation of microbes. Reading it now makes me feel quite nauseous. Like the morning after a heavy night.

The doorbell rings, making me start. I close the laptop and cast a critical eye over the room, even though I've dusted every object and surface at least twice. I spot the recycling box in the hallway and tuck last night's wine bottle under a carton of juice. It feels as if I'm about to take an exam. Why am I so nervous? This is about her, not me. That's what I keep telling myself.

I smooth my hand over my skirt, take a deep breath and open the door. On my doorstep is a woman in a mottled-green raincoat with dyed-blonde hair and designer glasses. Her face erupts in a smile.

'Hello. Kate, I presume?' She holds up her hand. She looks my age, but could be younger. 'I'm Janet. From the agency.'

I swallow and raise my palm.

'You'll be wanting to check this.' She flashes her medi-profile dashboard. Verified this morning: a blaze of green. 'I'm good to go.'

'Thank you. Please, come in.'

I notice the scruffy leather briefcase clutched in her palm and try not to think about how many germs it's culturing. As she walks past, I catch a trail of scent: one of those cheap, flowery ones they sell in the chemists.

'Lovely place you've got here.' She clocks the photos in the hallway, the framed prints. Taking everything in.

'Thanks,' I say, trying not to mind. She's the professional here now, not me. 'You found me OK, then?'

'Oh yes. Your directions were spot on.'

I lead her into the sitting room. 'Please. Take a seat.'

'Thank you.' She lifts her briefcase in both hands and places it carefully on the table between us, like a baby being settled in its cot. She takes out a small notebook. I notice her roots are starting to show: a furrow of brown across blonde.

'Can I get you a drink?' My eyes linger on the case.

'Just a glass of water, please.'

I fetch us both one. She takes a couple of sips, sits back and smiles. I'm about to suggest we get started when she takes a breath.

'So, Kate. You probably want to understand what my role is in all this.' She nods at me. 'I'm your caseworker. I'm here to help you and your family. To provide you with whatever support you need during this process.'

I manage a small smile. I wonder how many times a week she says that.

'It's very important you take your time over this. That you're clear about why you want to find your birth mother.' She runs a chipped pearlescent nail along the spine of her book. 'Is there a reason why you've waited until now?'

She's studying me closely, but I've got my work face on. I don't answer. I'm still deciding how much to say.

'I understand your mother passed away quite recently.'

Our eyes meet. Someone's been busy with their own research.

'I'm very sorry for your loss.' She pauses. 'We find that it's quite common for adopted children to approach us after their adoptive parents pass on.'

Pass on. Pass away. I wonder how many more of these euphemisms she's going to use.

'Some people feel that making that first step is somehow … easier. That it removes any issues they might have about loyalty.'

My throat tightens. She's tiptoeing around the sinkholes. I should say something, make it easier for her.

'Have you thought about what you actually want to achieve

through this process, Kate? Are you looking for answers?' Her small eyes blink at me. 'Do you want to develop an ongoing relationship with your birth mother?'

I take a breath and dive in. 'The truth is, I'm not sure. My parents told me I was adopted when I was ten. It didn't bother me then, it never has. They're the only parents I ever knew, and I couldn't have wished for better.' I'm gabbling; I need to slow it down. 'But when my mum got ill ... when things started to deteriorate, well...' I squeeze my fingers. 'She was the one who suggested it, not me.'

Janet nods, her eyebrows knitted with concern. 'And how did that make you feel?'

I shift in my seat and swallow. It's not much fun being this side of the couch.

'I don't know. Sad, I guess. A little conflicted.'

She does more nodding. 'Of course. That's entirely normal.'

I suppress a sigh. I'm beginning to see how irritating conversations like this must be for my patients' families.

She wets her lips. 'I have to warn you that a search can be a slow and frustrating process. While a lot of information is in the public domain, a lot was lost during the Crisis. There are no guarantees you'll find your birth mother. And even if you do, there's a risk she may not respond. As you're aware, she's quite elderly now; she might not be in the best of health.'

Janet waits for a reaction. I manage a brittle smile.

'Then again, many families do find each other. And, eventually, some meet. But even then, not everyone likes what they find.'

Is she trying to put me off? Or is this some kind of risk-management exercise in case it all goes tits up?

'Of course,' she continues, 'I realise in your profession you're used to dealing with challenging situations. But from my own experience, I can tell you, it doesn't make it any easier when you're the one in the frame.'

What she doesn't realise is that I've already been through the scenarios. Violence, drugs, alcohol. Mental illness, religion. It's the not knowing that's killing me.

She gives me another of her smiles. 'That's why I'm here. To help you think through the implications, not just for you, but for your whole family. Because this is going to affect them too.'

My heart skips a little as I think of Sasha. I've boxed that one off. For now.

'But, before we go any further, Kate, there is something I need to tell you.'

I glance up. The smile has faltered. Her pearly nails tap the page.

'Quite soon after your adoption, the laws changed to make it easier for adopted children and birth parents to find each other. The Adoption Contact Register was set up.' Her eyes flick to the case. 'Your birth mother emailed the register, during the Crisis.' She pauses. 'She made a request for no contact.'

My palms press into my thighs. My face has just about held, but if she's any good, she'll have noticed.

'I know this must be upsetting for you, Kate.' Janet's eyes brim with sympathy. 'But giving up a child for adoption is an incredibly complex decision. Sometimes, there are situations ... pressures, which prevent mothers from revealing their true motives. That compel them to protect their privacy.'

It's true, then. She really didn't want me. I have a sudden urge to snatch the case off the table. Rip it open.

Janet leans closer. 'As I'm sure you're aware, life was very different. Before the Crisis.'

'Yes. I was there.'

I push myself up. This was a mistake: I knew it. 'So, I guess that's it, then.' I want this woman out of my house.

'No, Kate. It's not. Not unless you want it to be.' Her hand moves to the case. 'No one can stop you searching, if you still want to. I have your original adoption records with me, and you're entitled to see them.' The buckles on the case snap open. 'All this means is that our agency can't pass on any personal information that might assist you in locating your birth mother.'

I stand there, frozen. Unable to decide.

'Please, Kate.' She pats the seat beside her. 'You've come this far. Won't you sit down?'

She gazes up at me, and I notice the lines around her eyes. I shouldn't take it out on her. She's only doing her job.

I slump into the chair. It makes a noise like it's been winded.

Janet takes out a blue plastic wallet that looks ominously thin. She removes two sheets of paper. 'Would you like me to leave you alone, for a little while?'

I shake my head. 'That's not necessary.' My voice sounds arid, parched. I take the pages from her. I try to hold them still as my eyes pick over loops of black ink.

Mother was working abroad ...

... living alone ...

... no relationship with the father ...

I put the papers face down on the table. In the garden, three sparrows are clamped to the birdfeeder, chucking out the bits they don't want onto the grass.

I squeeze my palms together.

The mother does not feel able to support her child.

That's all I amounted to. Just that one statement. No booze

problem or heroin habit. No bruises or nervous breakdown. My adoption appears to have been quite a simple transaction: less than two sides of A4.

'I realise how difficult this is, Kate,' says Janet, her doe eyes boring into me. 'It can feel very clinical, just reading the bare facts like that. Particularly when there isn't a lot of information.'

'It's fine,' I say, forcing some levity into my words. Tears threaten and I furiously blink them back. 'I wasn't expecting *War and Peace*.' My quip jars like a drunkard in church.

Janet touches my arm. 'Just because her reasons aren't recorded in that file doesn't mean your mother didn't agonise over her decision. There could be all kinds of circumstances, which had nothing to do with her feelings for you...'

She carries on in her soft, consoling voice, but I'm no longer listening. I don't want sympathy or sanitary excuses. I am besieged by a whirl of emotions, each vying for my attention. If I meant that little, then why bother? If all I'm going to find at the end of this is a woman who couldn't care less, then what's the point?

Janet is still blathering on about agencies and intermediaries as my thoughts begin to settle, solidify, like milk in a churn.

Honi soit qui mal y pense...

My jaw stiffens. And I make the call.

I don't give a stuff about your privacy, Mary Sommers. You're my mother.

I'm going to do whatever it takes to track you down.

CHAPTER 13

LILY

'Miss Alice de Rothschild was passionate about the manor's spectacular gardens and was always seen with a weeding tool in hand...'

My tablet sags in my lap. I recognise the words but they've lost their meaning; they're just a stream of letters floating past my eyes. I'd actually been looking forward to this trip until yesterday. The gardens are very well stocked. But now the shadow of that news cutting taints everything. Whoever left it must be close. Close enough to try again.

'Are we leaving soon?' I ask Anne on her way past. I'm sweating like a horse in this cashmere. We're all kitted out in our posh clothes, the ones they don't let us wear very often because they're difficult to clean.

'In a few minutes,' she says, which is what she said half an hour ago. She looks like she's sweating too.

Behind me there's a queue of wheelchairs and behind them are the semi-mobile ones, hunched over frames and walking sticks, all lined up like decrepit cars on the start grid. Only this race takes hours to get going. Any respite from here is good, but it's always the same, these interminable waits. Not that we get many outings these days. Most places won't take groups our age, and those that do charge a pretty penny, what with all the infection controls, and the insurance. Even so, lots of residents, like Jean, refuse to go. All it takes is one dirty surface. One scratch or sneeze. We aren't visitors anymore, we are targets. Targets for contagion.

I scroll down another page, try to focus on the flowers. There's no mistaking Gazania rigens. Definitely a Strelitzia, possibly the reginae. Which Canna is it, though? As I rake through the possibilities a news alert flashes up on my screen.

'World's Oldest Person Dies'.

My skin prickles. There are gasps behind and a growing murmur, as if someone's just poked a stick into a hive.

'Australian Diane Seymour died peacefully in her bed at 2.21 this morning, aged ninety-four years, seven months and fifteen days. Her son, Michael, told reporters that she had been suffering from pneumonia for some time.'

My body sinks deeper into the chair. It can only be a matter of months since she took up the mantle; the record keeps dropping every year. I remember when they predicted that everyone would live to a hundred. When the Queen needed a whole team of people to help send out her royal congratulations. This king hasn't sent one.

'Have you seen this?' I say to Anne. Every resident is pinned to their screen.

The corners of her mouth fold in. 'Pam just told me. So sad.'

Someone muffles a sob. None of us knows this woman from Eve, but we still mourn her. As if her death somehow brings all of ours closer.

The news feed switches to a live link inside a hospital for the elderly. A woman in a suit steps up to a podium and leans into the microphone. 'As Diane's family are still coming to terms with their loss, Diane's son, Michael, has asked me to say a few words on the family's behalf.'

She unfolds a piece of paper and clears her throat.

'Our family would like to express their thanks to all the people who have sent such comforting messages of support. Their kindness is much appreciated during this difficult time.'

About twenty cameras fire off rounds of flashes. Somehow, she manages not to blink.

'Our mother, Diane, was an amazing woman. Selfless. Stoic. And kind. We are lucky to have had her in our lives and in the lives of our children for so many years.' She swallows. 'We know that we have enjoyed more time with her than most families get to spend together. But it does not make her loss any less grievous.' She looks straight at the cameras. 'Had she been permitted one course of antibiotics, she would still be alive today. Her death was completely avoidable. I speak for my mother and for all of us when I say: it is time we put an end to this heinous policy.'

The screen flares with light as the room erupts, the reporters shouting over each other. The woman steps off the podium.

Well. Good on you, Michael. Things are seriously going to kick off now.

Sure enough, reports stream in of crowds already gathering in Sydney and Adelaide, waving their placards and white flags. I click on a photo. A drugs company's name has been scrawled across a sheet in dripping red letters. Another banner has an elderly woman's face, with the slogan: *Your Turn Next*. She looks vaguely familiar. It's the Australian prime minister. Well, a version of her. Someone's done a bit of Photoshopping: quite effective, really. I hope they do one of ours. This should certainly step up the anniversary protests.

Another alert jumps onto the screen:

'Diane Seymour Assisted with Death, Source Reveals'.

Pictures start flooding in of hordes of protestors outside the hospital gates. One group appear to be wearing surgical coats and masks: they're brandishing some sort of stick. At their feet are sprawled rows of men and women, face down on the pavement. I enlarge the picture. The banner reads: *Murdered at 94. Repeal the Devil's Act.*

The Devil's Act: that's what the pro-lifers call the Assisted Dying Act. And I see I was mistaken. The protestors aren't holding sticks. They're scythes.

Anne peers over my shoulder and frowns. 'Goodness me.'

I shake my head. 'What a circus. I'll bet they set the whole thing up before the poor woman even died.'

The images switch to Diane Seymour's home: a small white bungalow with a picket fence and a magnificent Jacaranda mimosifolia with indigo flowers. Campaigners jostle outside with news teams, making the fence quiver.

Choice in Life Not Death.

Kill Pain Not Patients.

Stop Doctor Deaths.

Anne tuts. 'They shouldn't harass the poor family like that. They're in mourning. And it was her right to choose.'

Some choice, I think. 'People like having someone to blame.'

Anne sighs. 'Won't be long before the unrest spreads. It's already going off in Asia. Mark my words, we'll be next.'

I think about what Graham said. Whether any of it will make the slightest difference. But, right now, I have more pressing concerns close to home. I close the screen and return to the safety of flowers.

Mrs Downing marches up, looking rather flushed. Her spectacles are slightly askew. 'Right, then,' she says to Anne. 'I think we're there. I'll take the meds box if you start loading them on.'

She opens the door but none of us moves. Surely she must have heard?

Her fingers tighten around the handle. 'Come on, then. Chop! Chop! We don't want to be late, do we?' She clutches her collar around her vulturine neck as the residents stare. Death itself won't obstruct her schedule.

'We'd better get going,' whispers Anne. She wheels me outside, and I suck cool air into my lungs. Out here, all appears to be normal. The same weary-looking drivers slouched up against their minibuses, the same manicured bushes trying to liven up the drive. But the day is already spoiled. Like a wedding reception that still goes ahead even though the bride never showed up.

'Morning, Ted,' says Anne to a large, red-faced man who is bent over the ramp. 'Ready for the onslaught?'

'Aye, just about,' he says, in a thick accent. Yorkshire, I think. 'We're twelve on here, right?'

'I believe so.' Anne drops her voice. 'Unless she-who-must-be-obeyed has changed it all again.' They exchange smirks. The man called Ted wheels me on and fastens the latches. I try not to think about the dirt trapped underneath his fingernails or the wheeze in his chest. Surely he must qualify for some kind of respiratory medication. Although, these days, even if you are under seventy, they still make you go through a dozen hoops.

The ramp starts to rise. I keep my eyes down, neck hunched into my coat like a turtle.

'Alright, love?' he shouts. I wince. Why must they always assume we're deaf? 'Looking forward to your big day out?'

My nose wrinkles. Even from behind a mask, his breath still smells. I give him my best withering look, but he doesn't seem to notice. Perhaps he assumes it's my normal expression. He pats my arm with his grubby hand and lumbers off to get the next one.

It takes nearly forty-five minutes to load everyone on, by which time I am approaching frantic. I used to be able to manage these trips on my frame, but with cut-off looming, I can't take the risk. So now I'm trapped in a chair, dependent on people who treat me as though it's my brain that's wasting away, not my cartilage. Thankfully, there isn't much traffic, and after an hour we arrive. The house looks like a fairy-tale French castle with its golden stone towers and silver domes, but it holds no spell for me today. They park us out front and split us into two groups: one for the house, one for the gardens. There's a brisk breeze, but at least the weather has held.

I scour the long gravel driveway as the previous visitors hurry out. We barely mix with the younger generations these days, apart from staff. Any amenities that do actually allow us in have age-specific rotas that are strictly enforced. With all the lawsuits flying around, I don't blame them. But it's like we're living in some kind of ageist apartheid.

Someone grips my chair, making me start. I look up. It's that new carer. I wanted Anne. Where's Anne?

'Hello. You're Lily, aren't you?' She smiles. 'I'm Natalie.' Her skin is rather sallow but she has nice teeth: white and even, like mine used to be.

'Oh. Hello. Looks like you've drawn the short straw.'

'Oh, I wouldn't say that. Anne's told me all about you. Says you've quite the sense of humour.'

I notice her vowels are very slightly clipped. I should ask her where she's from.

'Apparently you're very knowledgeable about flowers,' she says. 'You'll have to educate me. I'm hopeless, I'm afraid.'

I smooth out a crease in my skirt. I don't say anything, just smile. Better to be humble about one's past, particularly with the carers.

'Shall we get going, Lily?'

'Yes. Let's.'

She pushes me past conflagrations of roses towards the place they call the parterre. Silver jets spiral out of stone fountains. The spray fizzes across my cheek like a kiss.

'Are there any specific gardens you'd like to visit, Lily?'

My head swivels round. I notice her eyes. They are an unusual fawn colour, but there are deep wrinkles around them. She must be older than I thought.

'The Tropical Mound. It's not far, you just turn right down that path.' I glance behind. 'Perhaps we could get a head start.'

She takes the hint and propels me forward. To my irritation, some of the others start to follow, their wheelchairs churning up the gravel. 'Don't worry,' whispers Natalie in my ear, tightening my belt. 'I've got arms like Popeye. We'll leave them for dust.'

She ups the pace, and a small smile creeps onto my face. Perhaps the day might be rescued after all. 'Do I detect an accent?' There, I remembered. My memory isn't failing me yet. She doesn't reply at first and I wonder if she's heard.

'You're very observant,' she says, as we pound along the path. 'Hardly anyone notices.'

Oh dear, I've offended her: not a good move. 'Sorry,' I say quickly. 'It's the kind of thing I pick up on.'

'It's OK. I've been here so long now, I guess I think of myself as a Brit. My parents moved over from Australia when I was young.'

As the path climbs her pace slows a little. We pause to admire a topiary hedge: undulating leaves stretch along a border like waves.

'So, Lily, what got you interested in plants, then?'

You can tell she's new. Normally they switch off straight away.

'I used to do a bit of gardening.'

There are a lot of things I used to do. I used to dance. I used to discover things. I used to make men's heads turn.

'Really? My mother was into all that. Didn't rub off on me, I'm sorry to say. Perhaps you can tell me what everything is.'

Is she just being polite or does she really want to know? It's not often I get an audience these days. Like toddlers, we are tended to but rarely heard. It doesn't matter though: we've arrived.

A pink-and-orange star extends towards us like a tropical sea-creature, composed entirely of dahlias. Riotous palms tower over gazania treasure flowers; red and yellow canna lilies flaunt their leaves like cabaret dancers. There must be a dozen strelitzias: their orange and purple spikes soar above the blue agapanthus like exotic birds. I want to clap my hands. It's been so long. So very long.

'Goodness,' says Natalie. 'Just look at all those colours!'

'Would you mind taking some pictures for me?' I hand her my tablet.

'Of course.'

She snaps away as I point out the different flowers and, for a few moments, the pressure lifts. And then I see it. An explosion of scarlet crowning glossy green leaves. The blood rushes to my cheeks.

'What's that one, over there? With those tiny petals?' Natalie is staring at the same plant. 'They look like feathers. Such a gorgeous red.'

The breath sticks in my throat. Scadoxus puniceus...

'A lily.' I swallow. 'A blood lily. We're lucky, they only bloom once a year.'

I see the clay pot on the table. He is standing behind me, his lips on my neck.

Happy Birthday...

A forgotten heat stirs.

It changes. The petals fade and drop. A purple-spotted stem pokes up through the leaves, obscene.

'Lily?'

Two red lines.

'Are you alright?'

Two bloody stumps.

'Lily, look at me!'

I solemnly and sincerely declare...

Something touches my arm. I flinch. Natalie is crouched in front of me, eyes boring into my face.

'Are you OK?' Her grip tightens. 'Did something just happen?'

I realise I'm panting. 'Sorry, the garden, it...' I catch myself before I say too much.

She clamps her fingers over my wrist; they feel cool against my skin. 'Hmm...' She unzips my coat. 'Can you try and raise both arms for me?'

I heave them up. She bites her lip. A frown settles into her face. 'I think we'd better get you back.'

We speed past the flowerbeds, past the hedges, my arms bouncing at my sides like a rag doll's. The other residents stare at us, fear breaking out across their faces.

'I'll ask Dr Barrows to check you over,' says Natalie, breathing hard. 'Take a look at your profile. Just to be safe.'

I clench my chair as the gravel spits out behind us, my heart throbbing beneath my patch.

I am here, in this garden, in an English stately home.

So why is it I can still hear him?

Why can I hear his voice?

CHAPTER 14

Twenty-seven years pre-Crisis

MARY

People say that you can't choose who you love. I never used to believe them. I thought it was a convenient excuse for the ones who made bad choices or had affairs. Everything I'd seen indicated that love was a fluctuating series of responses to sex, charisma or power. But nothing about nature is random. Evolutionary mechanisms are at play, driving us to find our optimal partner. It's quite simple really: we are biologically programmed to find our most genetically compatible mate. But sometimes the most compatible is the most deadly.

I dab my mouth with the napkin as alcohol-infused banter barrels round the room. An untouched slab of chocolate torte glares at me. My eyes stray to the adjacent table where Piet is holding court. He looks different out of field gear: all dapper in chinos and a crisp blue shirt. He sweeps one hand through the air like a conductor and delivers his punchline. His audience toss their heads with laughter. I lift my glass to my lips, let the wine linger on my tongue. I've resigned myself to the fact he's unavailable. I've heard all about his cute daughter, how happily married he is. It doesn't stop me wanting him.

The lab rat on my left leans over and slurs something; he's stuck to me like a wad of chewing gum all night. There's a whoop and a cheer from another table, and someone smashes a glass. My table companion breathes another waft of garlic in my face. I think he just asked if I want to go outside. I give him an icy smile and edge away. He's not the only one who'll have a sore head tomorrow. Let's hope Terminalia sericea can cure hangovers as well as AIDS.

After beavering away for months, the lab teams have finally hit the jackpot: they've chemically characterised the molecule responsible for attacking HIV-1. Suddenly the university thinks my career change is a wonderful idea, and the money's flooding in. Of course the politics are with me, too. As the end of apartheid draws closer, my colleagues are keen to cosy up to the more liberal academics here. Piet hasn't let up the pressure, though. The TB count is escalating, with an alarming increase in multidrug-resistant strains. And, thanks to HIV, this is no longer just Africa's problem. Large-scale, highly lethal epidemics of MDR-TB have broken out in New York, Miami, Rio de Janeiro and Bangkok. London could be next.

As for the job itself, like any research, it's meticulous. I have to detail which parts of the plant are used for what, record their traditional preparation and dosage, and then deliver samples to the labs. Every part of the plant has potential: leaves, stems, bark. Flowers, roots and seeds. One part may be beneficial and another extremely toxic. The method of preparation is also critical. You need the right amount, added to the right solvent, mashed, burned or boiled in the right way. These plants can kill as well as cure. Precision is the key.

I see Piet fold his napkin and push back his chair. He walks briskly towards the exit. My insides stretch as tight as a wire.

'Excuse me.' Before the lab rat can assemble his words I stand up and pad across the thick, patterned carpet towards the double doors. Cool-blue silk pulls taut on my thighs, my slingbacks slip-slapping against my heels. I follow Piet out onto the terrace. He leans over the balcony rail and sips his beer, unaware I'm there. I watch him for a second. It's as if the very air around him is charged.

I tuck in a curl of hair that's escaped from my chignon. 'Taking a breather?'

Piet turns. He doesn't seem surprised to see me. But his expression does not convey celebration. 'Look.' He gestures at the sprawl below. 'We're up here getting pissed. Down there it's carnage.' He takes another swig; his eyes are a steely blue. 'As if we don't have enough sickness and death to contend with, without this slaughter.'

I've been immersed in South Africa's politics ever since I arrived. I've learned the hard way that, sometimes, it's better to keep your mouth shut.

He shakes his head. 'I tell you, it can't go on like this much longer.'

I follow his gaze to the towers of concrete and glass rising up through the haze. They look innocent enough from here: just another huddle of office blocks. Nothing could be further from the truth. I decide to risk it. 'I hear the central district is like a warzone.'

He rubs his thumb over the bottle; tiny beads of condensation slide down the glass. 'There's been so much violence.' He sighs. 'This government has to stop fighting the inevitable.' He pushes back from the railings, and I catch a fresh, soapy scent, a fleeting triumph over the city's perennial stench of sewers. 'Trouble is, some people will sacrifice anything to hang on to power. No matter how much suffering they cause.' His jaw stiffens. 'You don't see animals behaving that way.'

I've never seen him like this; perhaps it's the drink. 'I

thought lots of species killed for power,' I say, twisting my necklace round. 'But I guess you'd know more about that than me.'

He looks up, and it's as though he sees me for the first time. 'Yes. Some do.' He nods slowly. 'When I was a ranger, I witnessed many fights for territory. I saw animals pick off the old, the young and the weak. But even then, there was always a balance.' He frowns. 'That's something we've lost along the way.'

His honesty is electrifying; I don't want him to stop. 'Do you miss it? Being a ranger, I mean?'

He smiles and for a moment his face lifts. 'Sometimes.' He stares into the bottle. 'Don't get me wrong, I love what I do, but there's something about being alone in the wilderness, seeing nature in the raw. Although there were bad times too, of course. When the rains didn't come. And the fires. Huge areas of smoking black earth. One burnt carcass after another.' He grimaces. 'The stench. It never leaves you.'

The sun trails a fiery line across the horizon. In this light, his hair looks a burnished gold.

He takes another drink. 'Often, the only way to slow the spread was to start another fire. Starve the flames.' His gaze moves back to the sky. 'You knew animals would get caught. You had to sacrifice some to save the others.'

I stare at him and try to imagine what it must have been like to make those decisions.

'Would you ever go back to it?'

He hesitates and slowly shakes his head. 'No, I don't think so. I'm committed to another cause now. And it's not a great life for a young family. I'd be away from them even more than I am now, and I miss them when I'm gone, especially my little Cara.'

My eyes return to the high rises. A few windows have lit up; the rest remain ominously dark.

He takes a breath. 'Anyway, enough of me. How are things with you? Any regrets?'

I look up at him and smile. 'Actually, I've never been happier.'

'Really?'

'I've learned so much. Met so many interesting people. Traditional healers, community elders. Even the herbarium guys.' He smiles. 'And I get to spend loads of time in the field doing the thing I love most. It's beautiful out there. Really beautiful.' I press my palms against the rails. 'I'm beginning to think I'll never leave.' I feel Piet's eyes on me, and my face grows warm.

'Well, I've been hearing lots of good reports. You're certainly keeping the boys in the labs busy: our inventory's building up nicely.'

'Just a matter of time.' I edge closer. 'First stop, HIV. Next stop, TB.'

He downs the rest of his beer. 'Let's hope so. For all our sakes.'

A light breeze pushes my dress against my legs. The rush of distant traffic rolls in like waves across shingle.

He takes a breath. 'I'm glad you came with me that day to the hospital. Glad I was able to change your mind.'

A pulse of perfume floats between us. It is me that finally looks away.

'I have this bolthole,' he says, as the sky softens from purple to grey. 'An old ranger's hut. Near the Letaba River. Before I left, I persuaded them to let me rent it.' He twists the bottle round in his fingers. 'Sometimes, I just take myself off there for a day or two. Forget all about the human race.'

A lock of hair caresses my neck. Breath ebbs and flows.

'It's next to a waterhole. I've seen all sorts down there: rhino, leopard. Herds of elephant. You just wander down and watch the animals come to drink.'

Silence builds like a force of gravity between us. I will not be the one to break it.

There's a click in his throat and my heart leaps. 'Next time you're up that way, let me know.'

I tell myself afterwards that it doesn't mean anything; that nothing will come of it. It's just the drink talking; tomorrow, he won't even remember.

Now, when I look back, I see that I knew all along.

I knew that he meant it. I knew that I'd go there. And I knew what the consequences would be.

But I did not know how it would end.

CHAPTER 15

Steri-Swim™: the safe new swimming experience.

Now you can enjoy all the pleasures of the water with none of the risks!

As the weather heats up, you may think a quick dip in your local approved river or chemically treated swimming pool might be refreshing, but think again.

A recent UK study has shown that recreational water activities were responsible for almost ten million infections last year, including ear, skin and respiratory illnesses as well as some nasty gastro-intestinal bugs. Some of these water-borne infections proved fatal, even after treatment. The primary culprit? Swimming.

Cryptosporidium, norovirus and E.coli are just a few of the pathogens lurking in our pools, rivers and beaches. And because these microbes are carried in by other swimmers, chlorination and pollution control measures won't work.

Which is why we have developed Steri-Swim™: your own, personal swimming experience using freshly sterilised water every time. Our patented water treatment and filtration process ensures our swim vats harbour no nasty surprises. You and your children can relax in safety and concentrate on your strokes without fear of bringing home anything other than your towel!

To find your nearest centre, visit SteriSwim.com or call us now on our toll-free number.

KATE

My finger darts over the phone, summoning agency success rates and prices. I click on Archway Investigations and scan the reviews one more time. I've pored over countless testimonials, but I'm not fool enough to believe these sugary endings come to us all. For every marketed reunion there's probably at least one miss and three horror stories. Let's face it, things haven't got off to the most promising start.

I've narrowed it down to two out of the list Janet gave me: the tracing agencies that she deemed reputable. The industry's much better regulated these days, but you still have to be careful. After the Crisis, cowboy operators flooded in to profit from the misery of others. With communications down, many families had become separated, with no way of knowing if relatives were still alive. The tracing market boomed. Desperate people make easy prey.

The cursor flashes at me, urging me to decide. Janet warned against rushing into this, but, to her credit, she still helped. I told her I just wanted closure, that I'd keep my expectations in check. I didn't tell her that those two bits of paper have afflicted me like a virus: breaking down my defences and consuming my thoughts. Each morning, I wake with the same suffocating tautness in my chest.

The bus lurches to a stop. Through rain-spattered panes loom two hulking grey towers: shit, we're here. I stumble down the gangway and jump onto the pavement, narrowly missing a large puddle. The bus pulls away, spraying my trousers with filthy water. I curse under my breath, bend my umbrella into the wind and stomp towards the crossing. It's only when I get there that I see them: a swarm of protestors jostling by the security fence, brandishing their placards like weapons.

Assisted Living, Not Dying!

Stop the Slaughter!

Damn it. I should have checked after all the Diane Seymour business. Only yesterday, another doctor was attacked in North London. Someone injected him with a lethal dose of painkillers. Left him to die on the pavement. Those suits in Westminster are the ones who passed the laws. But it's us that take the rap.

People shove past, spiking my umbrella, flicking cold spears of rain into my face. Surely if it was serious they would've warned us, sent a secure bus to the meeting point. I consider calling, just to check. Instead I hunch my neck into my coat and stride onto the crossing. But, as I reach the other side, my heart sinks. A film crew are lurking behind the campaigners, right outside the gates. I turn and march the other way, barging into people, my brolly clenched in both hands. There's a shout behind; I tell myself not to look. My neck spins round regardless. It's a reporter; he must have clocked my regulation green trousers. He grabs the cameraman, and they sprint after me like bloodhounds on a scent.

'Hey! Hey you!' shouts the reporter. 'We'd like to hear your thoughts on legalised killing!'

I step off the kerb into the traffic, looking for a chance to cross. Car after car thunders past. Another bus pulls in, forcing me back onto the pavement. Commuters stream out, cutting me off. I glance round. The newsman's at my heels, flushed with the chase; the rest of the mob are surging up behind. I sneak my mobile into my pocket and press the emergency key.

'Do you support the proposed changes to the Medication Act?' he says, panting. He shoves a sodden mic towards me.

'No comment.' I swivel my head, try to spot a way through. The newsman and his cameraman track me, step for step. A wet poster is rammed in my face. It's a gun with a syringe in its butt. *HOSPITALS FOR LIFE NOT DEATH!*

'Let's face it, we all know the drugs are available,' the newsman continues, oblivious to the water spooling down his cheeks. 'Isn't it immoral, what you're doing? Why should some people get them and not others? Why should someone's age determine whether they live or die?'

I swallow. 'No comment.'

The protestors push closer, buffeting me dangerously close to the kerb. I scan the morass of bodies for any sudden lunges or darting hands. Hot prickles of sweat creep over my skin.

Stay calm. Follow procedure. They'll be here soon.

'Is she one of those "nurses"?' gasps a corpulent lady with a black golf umbrella. Her efforts to catch up have clearly taken their toll. She jabs her finger at me. 'Shame on you. You're supposed to care for people. Not help them die!'

'I do the best that I can for my patients,' I say, although I know it's a mistake to engage.

'"Patients"?' she snorts. 'I remember when this used to be a proper hospital, not a slaughterhouse!'

I remember it too: I worked there. After they passed the Medication Act, they converted forty percent of the hospitals into hospitals for the elderly. The government refused to call them hospices. Then they had to build some more.

I take a breath. 'The people who come to us are in a critical condition. We provide them with the best care we can.'

'Have you even read the Hippocratic Oath?' She thrusts a sopping bit of paper at me and starts to read out loud like some kind of preacher. The cameraman elbows the others aside to get a clear shot. 'I will exercise my art solely for the benefit of my patients, the relief of suffering, the prevention of disease and promotion of health, and I will give no drug and perform no act for an immoral pur—'

'Firstly, I'm not a doctor,' I say. 'And secondly, I am obliged to operate within the letter of the law—'

'Are you aware of the latest victim?' interrupts the newsman, eyes flashing. 'Seventy-year-old man in Devon got the flu. Bit of a temperature and a runny nose. His daughter couldn't wait for her inheritance so she convinced him to sign the forms.' He leans closer. 'He was "assisted" alright. Hardly voluntary, though. In fact I'd call that murder, wouldn't you?'

I shake my head. These people warp the truth and it doesn't help anybody. The flu that man caught was a mutated strain, a particularly vicious one: his death was a mercy. But I am aware of more doubtful cases.

'Travesties like this happen every day.' He nods at the camera. 'You know what they call you? "Angels of death". This level of abuse can't go on.'

'"Thou shalt not kill." What about that law?' shouts another lady in a beige mackintosh who's clawed her way to the front. 'I don't suppose you remember me?' she says, with glittering eyes. 'But I remember you.'

They should lock you up...

All the hairs on the back of my neck stand up. It's Mr Casey's daughter: the woman with the bleeding hand. Has she orchestrated this? Is there someone here with a syringe for me?

She turns to the crowd. 'This woman calls herself a nurse, but she's a serial killer. In fact, she's killed so many people she's lost count. I know, because she murdered my father.' She juts out her thumb behind her. 'In that death camp they call a hospital.'

She pulls back her head and spits at me. It slicks down my cheek, mixing with the rain. The mob start chanting: 'Murderer! Murderer!'

I'm jostled back and forth, trapped in a blur of wild eyes and angry mouths. There's a stench of wet bodies; stale breath in my face. Barbs of fear prick up and down my spine. I'm so hemmed in that I can't grab my mask or gel. There must be other staff caught up in this. Why the hell weren't we warned?

'Looks like you aren't too popular,' says the newsman, watching me squirm.

I manage to yank one hand free and shove it over the camera. 'You need to take this to Downing Street,' I hiss. The cameraman bats my hand away. 'We're just doing our jobs.'

'Isn't that what the Nazis said?' replies the newsman, struggling against the surge. 'Too many old people and not enough money to take care of them. Isn't this another Final Solution?'

His words rock me to the core. A placard thumps into my back, propelling me forward. My head slams into the camera and for a moment everything goes black. I hang there, propped against my accusers, as the chanting echoes and warps. When I come to, the reporter's lips are still moving but his words are lost in a fog of static. A searing pain presses behind my eyes.

Suddenly, the pressure relents. I have to grab someone to stop my fall. Shrill whistles pierce my skull; I'm not sure if they're real or some kind of defence mechanism going off in my brain. The cameraman checks his lens and swivels away from me at last.

'Miss! Miss, over here!' A man in a black helmet is parting the crowd like Moses. Behind him I can just make out a line of security officers in full protection gear wielding batons. Some are holding up cameras. I feel strangely distant, as if I am behind one of those cameras, watching, not in front.

A black glove seizes my arm. I stare up into eyes that move everywhere at once: me, the protestors, his men.

'Did they use anything? Syringes? Needles?' His gaze moves over me like a laser as his officers encircle me in a human shield.

'I...' My voice dissolves; I try again. 'I don't think so...'

'Any puncture wounds?' Muscled fingers clamp onto my pulse.

I swallow. 'Not that I saw.'

'What about that cut on your forehead?'

What cut? 'I ... My head ... hit the camera.'

And only then, in that moment, does the full horror of what might have happened register.

He catches me just as my legs buckle. It's as if someone's pulled out the plug.

'OK, we're going to get you back inside, right away.' He grips my waist. 'Lean against me. That's it. Don't say anything, don't do anything, don't even look at those pieces of shit, you understand? Everything's going to be OK.'

We all start moving towards the gates, steps synchronised, as if we're different parts of the same organism. One massive centipede. He waves his baton out in front like an antenna as I drag my feet forward, keeping my eyes on the ground. They're still shouting things, horrible things. I start my own chant in my head and try to picture Pen saying the words:

It'll be fine. It'll be fine.

By the time we get through the hospital doors he's virtually carrying me.

'Here you are.' He leads me into a small room I've never been in before. I collapse onto a seat. 'The doctor should be here any minute. She'll run all the checks.' He touches my shoulder. 'You did really well. I'll be back later to take some details.' His eyes narrow. 'They won't get away with it, I promise you. We got them all on film.'

Hot tears sting behind my eyes. Before I can muster my thanks, he's gone. A female officer in black uniform appears and wraps a blanket around me.

'Hey, honey. How about a nice hot drink? Tea, coffee?'

I just nod. She brings me a coffee. I hold out both hands to take it: they're spotted with blood. It takes me a while to figure out that it's dripping from my forehead. The coffee is loaded with sugar and tastes awful, but I drink it anyway.

She reappears with a first-aid kit. 'Close your eyes,' she says, wielding a can of antiseptic. When she sprays the cut I can't help but wince.

'Sorry. I'm no nurse, I'm afraid.'

No kidding, I think as she tapes on a wad of dressing.

'That should stem the bleeding for now. Do you think you can hold this for me?' She jams a cold compress against my forehead. 'I'll be right back. Just going to chase up that doctor.'

I feel a series of vibrations in my pocket. Three missed calls: all of them from Mark. It rings again; my fingers fumble over the keys but I catch it: 'Hello?'

'Kate, thank God.' His words race out in a rush of breath. Just hearing them makes me crumple. 'Are you alright?'

I try to answer but it's as if a bandage has wedged in my throat.

His tone becomes more urgent. 'Are you hurt? Did they hurt you?'

Tears squeeze down my cheeks as my head pounds. 'I ... I'm OK. Just a couple of knocks.'

'Have they checked you over yet? You're still at the hospital, right?'

I wipe my nose on my sleeve. 'Yeah.' I swallow. 'The doctor's on her way.'

His voice shatters. 'Idiots. Stupid fucking idiots! These people haven't a clue, how hard you work. How much you care.'

The throbbing in my head steps up a notch. Now I'm seeing flashes of light. Not a good sign.

'Why the hell weren't you warned? What are those imbeciles in security paid for? Why did they take so long?'

And that's when I realise: he's seen it. They must have uploaded it live.

'Oh God, it's out, isn't it? You don't think Sasha saw, do you?' Just the thought of it makes me want to howl.

'Don't worry about that, I'll deal with it,' he says. 'It's already been taken down. The most important thing is you're safe.' A horn blasts in the background. 'I'm at the Tube now, I should be with you in two hours, max. Call me as soon as they've seen you, OK?'

'OK.'

'And don't you even think about going to work or anything stupid like that. Promise?'

'Promise.'

I hear his breathing, deep and ragged. 'I love you, Kate Connelly.'

I have to gulp down a sob. 'You too.'

I squint at my phone, blinking back a wash of colours. Nothing from Sasha yet. Even though I know Mark will do it, I text her anyway. Just in case she thinks he's covering for something worse.

'The doctor's here to see you now,' says the security officer. 'Are you OK to walk?'

'I think so.' I stand up. The room spins violently, and I pitch to the left.

She grasps me firmly around the shoulders. 'Feeling dizzy?'

'Just a little.'

Her eyebrows arch. 'Don't play the saint, Kate. It won't help you or us if you keel over.' She slips one arm around my waist and grasps my arm with the other. 'Come on. Let's take this one step at a time.'

We shuffle towards a cubicle like decrepit dance partners. I glance at her. 'Why weren't we warned?'

She puckers her mouth in a way that tells me she's probably not meant to say. 'They hacked the emergency plan. Took down the back-up as well as the operating system.' Her jaw tightens. 'But keep that to yourself.'

She helps me onto the bed. I slump into the pillows as the pale-blue curtain panels sway back and forth. I think about the reporter and that preacher lady. Mr Casey's daughter. There was a time when I would have been executed for what I do.

You know what they call you? 'Angels of death'.

You're supposed to care for people, not help them die.

We all have to take our share of the blame for what happened. For the laws that followed. For the whole damned shitty lot.

But if I look into my heart, if I strip away the 'for all the right reasons', a doubt still lingers.

Can what I do, day in, day out, ever really be justified?

CHAPTER 16

LILY

The security lights filter through the curtains, casting a sickly glimmer across the room. My eyes flick over the walls. I can't see the flowers, but I know they're there. It's a curse, this sleeping thing. Recent events haven't exactly helped. You'd think the home would have a schedule for our insomnia, organise late-night film clubs or something, but Mrs Downing refuses, in case we keep the other residents awake. Ironic, really, because here we all are, fighting our demons, ticking off the slow, silent hours before morning. Wondering who's up for the Waiting Rooms next.

The clock flashes four. I hear the mournful cries of two tawny owls, calling to each other as they hunt. I imagine their soft, brown bodies gliding through the dark like spirits. Last night, I woke to the sound of screaming. I froze in my bed, unable to breathe. Then I remembered: foxes. It's been a while since I've heard that haunting bark. Not since the last culls. They call it the vixen's scream, but believe me, males can scream too.

I lever myself up on my elbows and switch on the light.

But the wicked are like the troubled sea, when it cannot rest, whose waters cast up mire and dirt...

I see Mother, belting out those verses with a glint in her eye. She was particularly fond of the prophet Isaiah. She used to march me up that hill and deliver me into the bleak clutches of a pathological Presbyterian. I don't think she actually believed in God. But she believed in discipline. And if she couldn't beat it into me, then that minister certainly could.

I glance at the wardrobe, circling the same old questions. And I reach for my tablet. Maybe Graham has insomnia too.

No messages.

I type another chaser. I have to edit it twice for diplomacy's sake. I thought the press cutting would make him take this more seriously. But then, it's not Graham who's getting the notes. Perhaps he thinks he's untouchable. But I know things. I'm not going down alone.

I open the spreadsheet. The cursor circles as the cells spill into view. The residents' names read like some memorial to the fallen, a presage of things to come. It took me nearly a week to collect them all, shuffling past every damned door in this place. One of Graham's minions should be doing this, not me. He's the one with access to all the information. Or so he claims.

Elspeth Hartley, Oxf.

I tap her name into the search box. A few blue names appear. I scroll through, checking dates and locations, but none of them amount to anything. I try the alumni site. Nothing. Probably her married name; the women always make it harder. I expel a long, slow breath. The hours I've spent on this already. And the sum total of my achievement? Eleven unknowns, twenty-two rejects and no suspects. Ninety-one to go.

My eyes skulk back to the wardrobe. It pulls at me, the thought, like a dangerous old friend. A craving I have learned to ignore. I push it away, but my ghosts crowd in, whispering with their sweet, velveteen tongues, urging me on. I glance at the calendar. On yesterday's square is scribbled the number *24*.

I picture myself unscrewing the tube. The capsules dropping like petals into my palm.

Down the hatch!

A beeping noise rips through the room. It's Graham. My fingers scrabble with the stylus.

'My. You are the night owl.'

His voice creeps over my skin like a spider. Thank God it's only on audio. Although, with him, I can't entirely be sure. I clear my throat. 'I was beginning to think you'd forgotten about me.'

I hear a suck of breath. 'Been offline for a couple of days. Little procedure. You know how it is.'

Not for much longer, I think. Even though he must be pushing eighty, I'll bet Graham still gets all the procedures he needs.

'So, anything to report?' he asks, as if I'm about to reel off the latest set of figures.

I drag my nail along the quilt; it makes a ripping sound. I don't tell him about my abortive research efforts. Or that I only have twenty-three days until cut-off. I don't tell him how close I am to other escapes. How very close.

'I was rather hoping you might be the one reporting,' I say, eventually.

'Well, as it happens, I have managed to do a little digging.' He pauses for effect. It works. The dread in my gut uncoils. Lifts its head.

'You definitely don't need to worry about Piet Bekker.'

I sense the flicker of a tongue.

'His ashes were taken back to South Africa. By his daughter. There's a discreet memorial on the family's estate.'

I hold on to his words like the gospel. I want to believe, but I don't. 'You're sure?'

'I checked the crematorium, customs, the whole works. It's

all legit.' He takes a breath. 'His wife's ashes were interred next to his.'

His wife's?

'Suicide. Her family hushed it up, of course,' he adds, casually. 'Kept it out of the papers. They made it look like an accident.'

I splay my fingers over the wallpaper and press down hard. He just had to throw that in. Graham has no shame. No shame at all.

I swallow. 'So, what about the postcard?' My voice is tinny, echoing in his mic. 'That information was never released.'

'Someone on the team must have blabbed. Tongues tend to loosen when people get scared.'

I carve my nail across a rose. *And you'd know all about that, wouldn't you?*

'Anyway,' he continues, 'I ran a little check on your housemates. It's as I thought: you should be looking closer to home.'

Fear slides its cool scales deeper. I think of my list. So: it is a resident, after all.

'Do you know a woman called Margaret Benn?'

A memory glimmers as my brain fires off searches: *Margaret Jenning, Maggie Tatum, Meg, Meg, wasn't there a Meg?* 'It rings a bell, but I can't quite place it,' I say, bringing up the spreadsheet.

'Same age as you.' I hear a slight wheeze. 'Came to the home about a year ago.'

I scroll down. 'Hang on a minute...' My heart thuds. Betjeman, typical. I hadn't got to her yet. 'She's in one of the other dorms. Why, what have you found?'

'She had a daughter, called Emily. Her only child.' He pauses and I know what's coming. 'Emily moved to South Africa. Just before the Crisis.'

My eyes squeeze shut.

For your hands are defiled with blood, and your fingers with iniquity; your lips have spoken lies, your tongue hath muttered perverseness...

'How old?' I whisper.

'Pardon?'

'How old was she?'

He hesitates. 'Twenty-six.'

I do the maths. I can't stop myself doing it, even if I wanted to. Forty-three years less than me.

Graham sighs. 'How many times did we go over this? She'd have died anyway. They all would.'

It rears up inside me: 'Just because you never gave a shit, Graham, doesn't mean the rest of us shouldn't.'

Silence. He won't even acknowledge it. As if it's some infant's outburst.

He gives a little cough. 'As you might imagine, her mother didn't take it too well. Kicked up one hell of a fuss. Went after the directors, led campaigns for compensation, that sort of thing. Frankly, it's just as well you disappeared.'

And there it is, the return smash, just to remind me how grateful I should be. I hate having to rely on him. I hate being put in this position, all over again.

I swallow. 'How did she trace me here?' There's a faint rustling. I have a sudden image of Graham propped up in bed, his bony body languishing beneath the sheets.

'As I said, technology's moved on. Lots of attempts have been made to find you over the years. None have been successful. Possibly until now.'

I laugh: a short, sharp bark. 'Is that supposed to reassure me?' I'll bet he's loving this, being back in the saddle.

'We've no actual proof that she's the one who sent your little missives. But the history fits. I think the best thing is for us to keep an eye on her. Wait and see what she does next.'

Is that the royal we, I wonder, or is he going to put some muscle behind it?

'What exactly are you proposing?'

'Don't worry about the details. Leave that with me. But don't confront her. Not until we're sure.' There's an intake of breath which sounds like a poorly disguised yawn. 'Now, if you don't mind, I'm going to try and get some sleep. I suggest you do the same. I'll be back in touch when I have news.'

The first tentative notes of birdsong trill outside, as if it's just another day. I stare at the name on my screen and try to picture this mother who has sought me out. But it's not Margaret Benn's face I see. It's my mother's.

Her mouth looms over me, spittle flying from her lips.

There is no peace, saith my God, to the wicked.

CHAPTER 17

Twenty-six years pre-Crisis

MARY

We lean over the railing, spotting tracks in the river bed, the metal clanking as the bridge heats up. A pied kingfisher perches a little further along, beak poised for the strike. Piet's elbow stretches towards mine, not quite touching, but I can sense his warmth. I plot the slow trudge of elephant feet: circular wells in the silt. The hooves of kudu, or some other antelope, that look like mangos cut in half. And the long, sandy furrows that criss-cross down to the water like a giant game of snakes and ladders. I grip the rail a little tighter and nudge Piet.

'Check those out.' Either side of the furrows are the twisted imprints of heavy toes splayed wide, deep points at the end where the claws have sunk in.

Piet grins. The sun is making him squint; his eyes are slits of cobalt blue. 'Wouldn't fancy getting stuck on a sandbank with him.'

A cloud of swallows swoops up over our heads and back under the bridge. 'How big, d'you reckon?'

Piet shrugs; his shirtsleeve pulls tight around his arm. 'Five metres?'

My neck prickles. Those furrows weren't made by snakes, they were made by tails. The tails of one of Africa's most patient predators: the Nile crocodile.

I swipe at a fly and scan the cluster of trees on the river bank; it's habit now, whether I'm working or not. Ebony jackalberry, tamboti, sycamore fig. The glossy green leaves of a Natal mahogany. I've harvested practically every part of that tree; we've got a dozen saplings in the nursery. I recognise the distinctive red flowers of a weeping boer bean: another one that's showing promise. Its bark is rich in tannins, although they haven't isolated any activity yet.

Piet lifts his binoculars. 'Have you seen your saddle-billed?'

My head swivels round. 'Where?' Of all the storks, this is my favourite; I always try to spot them first.

'Handsome fellow. On that rock, by the left bank.'

I clamp the binoculars to my eyes and adjust the focus. A large wader with magnificent black-and-white plumage is staccato-stepping over a boulder. It always amazes me how their legs bend the other way, like arms. It dips its red bill in the water, showing off the yellow saddle-shaped shield that gives it its name.

'You know those dangly yellow lobes, either side of the bill?' I say. 'Is it just the males that have them?'

He lowers his binoculars. 'The wattles, you mean? Yes. Just the males.'

'"Wattles"?' I laugh and take a step closer. I draw one finger slowly across his cheek. 'So, where do you keep your wattles?'

His mouth curls into a smile. I slide my arms around his waist and pull his body into mine.

His eyes dart behind. 'Not here...' he murmurs. I sink my fingers into the hair at the nape of his neck, tugging the roots. His stubble grazes my chin. I press my lips hard against his as a delicious heat swells through me.

After a few seconds I pull away. I note the flush in his face, the pant in his breath. I have power. Albeit temporary. But I've learned how to use it.

He runs his thumb along the curve of my jaw. 'You're trouble, Mary Sommers. You know that?'

'It's you they call the honey badger.'

Piet's company nickname. Which he loves. Honey badgers are renowned for having no fear. If hungry or provoked, they'll attack anything, from big cats to venomous snakes. Their unrelenting grip deters would-be predators twice their size.

'Honey badgers have a soft side, you know,' he says. I arch an eyebrow. 'So what do they call you, then?'

'Mary.'

He smiles. 'And what does Mary mean?'

I take his hand and press it to my breast. 'Beloved...' I slide it up, over my throat to my lips. 'Wished for...' My eyes do not waver. 'And rebellious.' I slip his thumb into my mouth and gently squeeze my teeth, resisting the urge to bite down harder.

'Better be careful, then.' I hear a push of breath as I release him. 'I don't know how much rebellion a honey badger can take.'

We swing ourselves into the jeep and take off. I feel light, almost dizzy. The cool wind is a welcome relief after the sultry heat on the bridge. The road stretches ahead of us, shimmering; white pillows of cloud drape across a vast blue canvas. There's a pungent odour of animals and fresh branches tossed in the road. Piet slows, and, sure enough, the bulbous heads of four young bull elephants materialise between the trees, slow-fanning themselves with their ears. They deftly curl their trunks around the thorny branches and strip leaves as if they're shucking corn.

Piet steers the jeep over to the other side of the road. The constant rustling is punctuated with occasional snaps. One of the males eyes us warily, pulverising his leafy debris in slow chomps. He turns his head, displaying his tusks, and flaps his ears. We crawl forward. The bull raises his trunk and takes a purposeful step towards us.

'What is it with you and animals?' says Piet, eyes fixed on the approaching elephant.

'I'm not sure.' My fingers tighten around the grab handle. 'But I'm beginning to think they don't like me.'

As if in response, the elephant ups his pace to a trot, trunk swinging like a rope that's come loose.

'Hold on.' Piet shoves his foot down. As we accelerate past, the young bull gives a thunderous trumpet that makes my heart leap, before wheeling back into the bush.

Piet grins at me, his cheeks streaked with dirt that the tyres kicked up. 'You see?' He wags his finger. 'He knows you're trouble, too.'

I burst out laughing as the rush of adrenaline subsides. So this is it then: happiness. I shuffle across and run my tongue over the lobe of his ear. It tastes of salt. 'Nice wattle.'

The wind barrels into my face, sending my hair streaming out behind. Piet veers sharp left onto a gravel road and I have to clutch my seat. I try to remember the last time I felt so alive. When I was eighteen, maybe: after I slammed the front door for the last time. Finally able to leave.

I sneak glances at Piet, studying each detail, as I would with one of my specimens, to get me through until our next time. His arm, hanging effortlessly across the wheel. The jut of bone in his cheek. The fold of muscle in his thigh when he changes gear. It pulls at me, this incessant longing, even during the little time he's with me.

'Piet?' I have to shout over the drone of tyres.

'Yeah?'

I touch his arm. 'You know, tonight...?'

He keeps his eyes on the road. His face stiffens. 'Please, Mary. Don't ask.'

The same old battle commences inside me: a clash of want and judgement.

'But, why?' I sound like some whiny child. 'It's not as if you go home.'

He always leaves early, just as the first streaks of gold colour the sky. That's when the guilt comes knocking, but it's his betrayal, not mine. When I feel the sleep pulling at me, I wrap myself into him, curl my arms and legs tight around his, as if my body can somehow confine him. He always escapes. Each morning, I roll over into a cold, empty space, red dust on the pillow.

Piet takes a breath. 'You know why. We've been over it a hundred times.' He presses his lips together as if that's it, he's shutting up shop: no more kisses for me. 'I always call her, first thing. Before she goes to school. Sometimes Cara calls me. I have to get back to the flat.'

I dig my nails into the seat and mutter under my breath: 'Well, it still sounds like bullshit to me.'

He slips his hand onto my knee. The sun reflects off the golden band around his finger, just to spite me. 'Hey, come on. Don't spoil it.'

You're the one who's spoiling it, I think. I should slip that damned ring off when he's asleep; drop it down a ravine. I'll bet he'd stay a bit longer then.

Even as I think the words I regret them. That's exactly the kind of thing Mother would say. And I recall the other meaning of my name: the one I didn't tell Piet. In Hebrew, Mary means: 'sea of bitterness'. No wonder my mother chose it.

I clasp Piet's arm and resolve to be nice.

He smiles at me. 'I have high hopes, you know.' My heart flutters. 'Dodonaea viscosa. I really think we could be onto something.' The flutter hardens into something still and unyielding. Like a fossilised insect. 'What do you reckon?'

Not only do I have to compete with his family, I have to compete with his work, too. It's exhausting. I focus on the hills in the distance and imagine a lone leopardess stalking those rocks, sun gleaming on golden fur. 'Maybe.'

He tuts. 'More than "maybe".' His hand slides up to my thigh. 'You did a great job, bringing that one back to the lab.'

I shift my leg. His hand slips off. 'I can hardly claim any credit there. Communities have been using those leaves for decades.' I'm not *that* desperate for his praise. 'Their medicinal use was documented back in the sixties.'

A frown clouds his face. His grip tightens around the wheel. 'Yes, but they didn't understand *why* it worked. They didn't isolate the flavonoids.' It was a mistake to contradict him. 'That plant is inhibiting the growth of some TB strains. Which is a lot more than can be said for any other drugs out there. Hardly surprising, given the big firms aren't even bothering to look.'

Piet's ambition never wavers. Part of me is impressed by such determination, but I hope he's not another Captain Ahab, pursuing his whale at any expense. Me included.

Piet scowls at the road. 'I mean, it's criminal.' Great. Now he's working himself up into one. 'All those billions of dollars they're making, flogging the same old antibiotics, which don't even work anymore. Well, most of them. Millions are dying and there's still no investment in TB. When untapped sources like this are just sitting there.' He shakes his head. 'And where has it got us? MDR-TB, that's where.' He swallows. 'Well, now their chickens are coming home to roost.'

The wind whips into my eyes. He's driving a little faster than he should, no doubt anxious to get back.

'While the pharma boys merrily blast more and more drugs at them, those bacteria are busy cooperating. Transferring resistant DNA between strains.'

We round a corner, startling a herd of impalas. They scatter, their hooves kicking up the dust. I try to think of something to say before what little time we have left is ruined. I wonder if he'll ever have this much passion for me.

'Those Joburg outbreaks ... be glad you never saw them. Whole hospital wards going down.' A dung beetle makes a sharp crack as it bounces off the windscreen. 'I tell you, for all our superior intelligence, there's only one winner in this war right now, and that's Myobacterium tuberculosis.' He swipes his sleeve across his forehead. 'A single-celled microbe four millionths of a metre long that takes nearly a day to divide.'

I slide my hand across to his seat. 'Well, to be fair, those snaking little rods have had time on their side.' I edge a little closer. 'Let's face it, anything that can flourish for three million years must be pretty adept at survival.'

He snorts. 'True. When it comes to evolution, they've certainly seized the advantage.'

I dance my fingers over his thigh and risk a smile. 'I think part of you secretly admires them.'

His eyes narrow. 'Who? The bacteria?' He shakes his head. 'I don't admire them. I want to conquer them.'

I cast him a sideways glance. His choice of words is

unexpected. 'Well, as you say, the Americans need help with this one too. And you've already felt the depth of their pockets.'

I lean back in my seat and wait.

Piet bares his teeth in a slow smile.

CHAPTER 18

KATE

The lights lower and the screens go blank. A hush settles across the cavernous space. I can feel the heat steaming from all those bodies as tension builds. There's a crash of drums and everyone's wristbands start to flash. Lucy squeals. Her face is flushed, blonde strands of hair stuck to her forehead. Mascara creeps down from her eyes like black tears.

She squeezes my hand. 'Oh my God, this is it! Katie, I owe you big time!'

The screens flare, a blinding white, then erupt in a blaze of kaleidoscopic patterns: hundreds of fluorescent cells divide and merge, synchronised to the beat. The arena echoes with whistles and cheers.

I scan the rows in front and behind. All eyes are on the stage. Security men slouch at the exits, arms crossed. Lucy seems oblivious too, clapping and stamping her feet. But something's not right here. I can feel it. Like a dark shadow hovering at the edge of my mind.

Canons blast fire across the front of the stage, making me jump. The cheers become screams. The band walks on and my body stiffens. As the bass picks out the first notes, the lead singer leaps whirling onto the stage. I feel a sickening lurch. He looks like a Renaissance angel: bright-blue eyes and golden hair.

I grab Lucy. 'We have to go.'

She grins and pushes me away.

'No, really, Luce. I'm serious.'

The singer sprints down the runway and snatches the mic. An acrid taste creeps into my mouth. I seize Lucy's wrist and haul her along behind me, as lasers sweep the hall.

'Kate, you lunatic!' She yanks her arm, tries to shake me off. 'What the fuck are you doing?'

I tighten my grip. 'You have to trust me! No time to explain.'

People swear at me as I push past them, trampling hot-dog wrappers and kicking over drinks. Some try to shove me back but I hold my ground, the sweat already dripping down my back.

'Have you taken something, Kate?' Lucy clings to a seat, desperately trying to wrestle free.

I fix my eyes on hers. 'Listen to me. He's contagious.'

Her jaw drops. She stops struggling.

I've almost got us to the aisle when a woman in a beige raincoat blocks my path. 'Where exactly do you think you're going?'

'Please...' I'm panting now even though every breath fills me with terror. 'We have to leave. Everyone needs to get out.'

Her lip curls back in a sneer. 'Murderer. They should lock you up.'

She punches me in the face. Lucy's hand flies out of mine as I topple over the seats. My head smashes onto the concrete floor, and I feel a warm trickle of blood down my neck. I scrabble to the aisle on all fours, but she's there, with her foot ready; she kicks me so hard I fall backwards, slamming into one step after another, plummeting down towards the stage. The music surges, louder and louder, one discordant song crashing into the next.

Suddenly I'm at the bottom. The band has stopped playing.

Silence fills the arena. A spotlight encircles the singer as he walks towards me, to the edge of the stage. I kick my legs out, try to push away from him, heaving my body back across the floor. He looks down at me with pity in his eyes, like Jesus on the cross.

'Kate?'

As he opens his mouth thousands of dark droplets stream out like tiny flies. I smother my face with my hands but they shoot past my fingers, cramming into my throat. I start to gag.

'Kate, it's me.'

My blood roars as the pressure builds in my chest.

'It's OK, baby. I'm here.'

There's a rustle. It sounds unnaturally loud, swooping into my ears and out again. The singer disappears. I manage to suck in some air and breathe.

I lift my lids, just a fraction. Too bright. I try again. There's a dark shape framed by a square of light. Gradually, it slides into focus.

'Well, hello there.'

Mark. It's my husband, Mark.

He kisses me on the cheek. 'How are you feeling?'

I try to anchor myself in our room: Mark's shirt impaled on the wardrobe door, the turquoise-and-gold wallpaper we chose from that extortionate shop. One arm of a sweater making a break for it out of my drawer.

His smile wanes. 'Bad dream?'

I rub my eyes as the horror slowly dissipates. 'Yeah.' I am left with a hollow sadness as Lucy's face fades.

'Hardly surprising after what you've been through. My poor love.' He strokes my arm. 'How's the head?'

I take another breath. 'A bit woozy. What time is it?'

'Four-thirty.'

'Jesus!' I try to push myself up but Mark stops me.

'Oh no you don't. You aren't going anywhere. You took a serious blow to the head, Kate.'

I want to protest but I don't have the strength. 'Can I at least sit up?'

Mark manhandles my pillows and gently lifts me up. 'Was it the same dream?'

'Pretty much.' It's already creeping back to its lair but I can summon some fragments. 'With a few extras thrown in.' I chew my lip. That woman in the raincoat was a nice touch. Is she going to start haunting me too?

'I'd like to take Lucy some flowers.' I glance at him. 'We haven't been for a while.'

'Sure.' Mark clasps my hand. 'We can go any time.'

I tentatively prod my bandage. My head feels as if it's been stuffed with bubble wrap.

'That's quite a golf ball you've got there.' He smiles. 'No need to worry: the scan came back clear. And the cut cleaned up just fine.'

I was lucky. I think of that doctor in London and rewind to the moment I crossed the road. Stupid. So stupid.

I pick at the sheet. 'How long was it up? The film, I mean.'

'Oh, barely twenty minutes. It cut out just as you head-butted the camera.' He grins. 'They'll be rueing the day they picked on you. Some idiot may try to post it again, but believe me, security are onto it.'

'Had a few words, did you?'

'Just a few.' His thumb circles the back of my hand. 'One of the officers will be over later. Apparently the police have already ID'ed a couple of them from the security footage.' His thumb slows to a stop. 'I don't want that ever happening again.' He lifts his eyes. 'Next time, you don't get off that bus.'

It's his way of saying 'be careful, you need to be more careful'.

I fold my hand over his and squeeze. 'I know.'

As he leans forward to kiss me his head bumps my bandage. 'Ow!'

'God, sorry!'

I burst out laughing. 'Well, it was almost romantic.'

His phone beeps and he frowns. 'Bugger. I'm supposed to be on a call in five.'

I flap my hand at him. 'Go on. You've done your Florence bit. Off you go.'

He exhales. 'I don't know ... You're sure?'

'I don't think we'd better risk any more contact. In any case, won't Sasha be back soon?'

'True.' He points his finger at me. 'But no emails, you hear? Doctor's orders. Get some more rest.'

I hold up my hand in a mock salute and obediently shut my eyes. I'm not going to sleep, though. I have a powerful urge to see Sasha. As if it's her that's been hurt, not me.

I rearrange my pillows and settle back down. A few minutes later, the front door bangs. There's a brief exchange of voices and then the familiar thump up the stairs. I quickly run my fingers through my hair. The door flies open.

'Hi, Mum!' As Sasha steps in her face tells me all I need to know about mine. She swallows. 'Gosh. How are you feeling?'

'Apparently much better than I look.' I hadn't thought to check. 'It's not that bad, is it?'

'Umm ... well, put it this way, you might be needing a touch more foundation.'

I thrust out a hand. 'Mirror.'

She hesitates and fetches my hand mirror. Lord. The bandage covers most of my forehead, but I can still see the bulge where the lump is. My eyes peer out like some nocturnal creature's: small and puffy, dark circles underneath.

'Oh, hell.' I sigh. 'I look like an extra from a low-budget disaster movie.'

Sasha chuckles and kicks off her shoes. She arranges herself next to me, on Mark's side of the bed. She leans over and scrutinises my dressing. 'Ouch.' The freckles on her nose wrinkle. 'Does it hurt?'

'Only a bit.'

'Really?' She gives me a doubtful look. 'You're not just being brave?'

I smile. 'No, love. I'm fine. A bit battered and bruised, that's all. But I could do with a hug.'

As she snuggles into me I inhale her smell: a medley of shampoo, body spray and sanitiser gel. I hug her a little tighter.

'Those people...' She shakes her head. 'What are they on?' She sits up and wags her finger at me. '"Thou shalt not kill..." I mean, really?'

My face drops. Mark didn't warn me. So she did see it, after all.

'And as for that news guy ... What a loser!' Her blue eyes flash. 'You should have told him where to get off, Mum. You were far too nice. I'd have let rip.'

I swallow. It's always the same with Sasha. She thinks bravado makes you invincible. As if.

'Did any of your friends see it?' I try to make it sound casual.

'Mum, we *all* saw it. It was everywhere.' She grins. 'You caused quite a stir. It's not every mother that gets compared to the Nazis.'

Something inside me sinks. She thinks it's funny. I'd hoped for more.

'Did they say anything?' I ask, although I know I shouldn't. My head gives a cautionary throb. 'You know, about my job?'

She calls herself a nurse, but she's a serial killer ...

Sasha frowns at me and starts picking at her nails. 'They all know what you do, Mum. It's no big deal.'

My chest swells. 'You know, it's not easy, Sasha,' I say, my voice already hardening. 'For the patients or their families.' She doesn't look up. 'We all thought the law would change after a couple of years. But two turned into ten. And ten's turned into twenty. They've a right to be angry.'

'Yes, Mum,' she says, half speaking, half sighing. 'So you keep telling me.'

I stare at my daughter. I have a sudden need to burst her smug balloon.

'So how do you reckon you'll feel, then?' I say to her. 'When someone has to help me die?'

'Mum!' Her hands drop to the bed. Finally, she looks up. 'What kind of question is that?'

'A real one, Sasha.' The words feel strong and mealy in my mouth. 'Because it doesn't seem to have occurred to you.'

She glares at me. 'Actually, *Mother*, it has.' Only Sasha can make that word sound like an expletive. She juts out her chin. 'When Gran died. And it felt like shit, if you really want to know.'

Touché.

I close my eyes. Why do I do this, let myself bite? I'm supposed to be the adult here.

I slide my hand across the sheet. 'Sorry, I ... I shouldn't have said that. I'm just a bit ... done in.'

Her shoulders stay hunched, but I wait, resisting the temptation to say more.

Eventually her face softens. 'I miss her, you know. A lot.' She leans on those last two words and my heart aches.

'I know, love.' I sigh. Your own grief is bad enough, but watching those you love suffer is worse. 'When the phone rings, in the evening, I think: that'll be her. There are so many things that remind me. That I miss.' Sasha yanks at a loose thread on the blanket. 'Just the other day, in the supermarket, I picked up a packet of those biscuits she liked. Then I remembered. I couldn't bring myself to put them back.'

Sasha's brow furrows. I squeeze her hand.

'Mum?' she says, after a while.

'Yes?'

'Can I ask you something?'

'Sure.'

She glances at me. 'Did you call her Pen because you were adopted?'

I study Sasha's face. Where did that come from?

'No. I used to call her Mum when I was little. But when I was about thirteen, I started calling her Pen. I don't know why.' I hazard a smile. 'I suppose I thought it was cool. It had nothing to do with being adopted. And Pen being Pen, didn't seem to mind. Why do you ask?'

She pushes her hair back behind her ears. 'I don't know. I was just wondering.'

I run my tongue over my lips. This is new territory. For both of us. 'Does it worry you, Sasha? The fact that I was adopted?'

Her mouth tightens. 'Lots of kids in my class are adopted. It doesn't seem to bother them.'

There was a surge in adoption rates, after the Crisis. So many babies never made their fifth birthday, not to mention all those deaths in childbirth. Then came the rising infertility caused by resistant STDs. Amongst those who survived, there was no shortage of orphans or would-be parents.

Sasha winds the loose thread round and round her finger. 'Should it worry me?'

'No. It's just...' I take great care over my next words: there could be a mine underneath any one of them. 'Well, it must have been quite a shock, I suppose. Particularly now we know my birth mother is still alive.'

The thread breaks.

I falter, unsure where to go next.

'You know,' I say, 'it's weird. I've always known I was adopted, and it never bothered me either. Although it was more unusual, back then. To me, it was just another fact. Like having brown hair or blue eyes. In fact, the only time I really thought about it was after I had you.' I glance at Sasha. Her eyes are riveted on the blanket. 'Other new mums used to love pointing out family traits they thought their babies had inherited. You know, whether they looked more like the mum's side or the dad's. But with you, there was only your father's side to go on. And me.' I give a nervous laugh. 'Pen was always so good about that. I used to wonder if she felt a bit cheated, but if she did, she never let on. She loved me unconditionally, the same way she loved you: as if we were her own.'

Sasha's cheek twitches, but she doesn't speak. I plough on. 'But since I made the decision to look for her – my birth mother, I mean – well, it's taken on this impetus of its own.'

Sasha drags her hands through her hair and sighs. 'If it's what you want, Mum. I've already told you – it's fine by me.'

The way she says it sounds the exact opposite. This isn't just my birth mother I'm looking for, it's her grandmother. A grandmother she never knew existed. Until now.

'You know, this won't change anything, Sasha.'

But even as I say it, the doubts crawl back. Is this some selfish whim of mine? Some knee-jerk reaction to losing Pen? I think of those two bits of paper. Of all the caveats and cautions stacked behind Janet's soft words.

The reality is, I have no idea who I might be bringing into our lives.

So how can I promise Sasha, or any of my family, that things won't change?

CHAPTER 19

'UK Borders To Stay Closed'
Says Home Secretary

Twenty years after they were imposed, emergency border controls and trade embargos will remain in place for the thirteen countries who do not yet meet the international health-risk standards, despite international aid agencies' claims that they are 'deeply unethical' and should be lifted.

A spokesperson for one agency commented: 'These emergency measures were introduced when the UK was in crisis. They should have been abolished years ago. Not only do they condemn helpless nations to failure, but they perpetuate the continued loss of innocent lives.'

The home secretary has rebuffed such claims, maintaining that UK policy is in line with fellow Health Alliance member states, and that his first duty is to 'keep British citizens safe'.

■ ■ ■

LILY

The words leap out at me, razor sharp. As if they were written just yesterday.

'Mother's fight for justice continues...'

I must have read more than sixty articles inspired by this woman. They each slice the scab off the same raw wound. In this one, she's standing outside a courthouse, her head tipped back, displaying a defiant jaw. A short brown bob frames a face I don't recognise here. Either age has had its way with her, as it has with me, or she's one of those that never comes out of their room. No wonder the name rang a bell. Margaret Benn didn't just fight a campaign. She waged a war.

She used to be a physicist. Quite a renowned one, by all accounts. But she gave it all up: career, marriage; she sacrificed the lot. She didn't give up fighting, though. It takes a lot of courage to take on the kind of people she did. I should know.

The door opens and Anne bustles in. 'Right then, Lily. It's all run. You're first on today.' She winks. 'As usual.' She brandishes a fluffy white bathrobe and sinks into a mock curtsey. 'Your bath awaits, my lady.'

Of course. It's Thursday: bath day. Maybe a good soak is what I need: one of the few indulgences my body can still permit. Although part of me wants to shuffle straight over to Betjeman and get it over with, once and for all.

Anne helps me up. 'How are you feeling? No more episodes?'

I wish they'd stop fussing. 'Oh, no. All back to normal,' I lie. I have no idea what normal is, anymore.

'Didn't Dr Barrows reckon it was some kind of panic attack?' She takes off my nightie and scoops me into the robe. 'I wouldn't have put you and panic in the same sentence.'

If only you knew.

I take a breath. 'Actually, my mother suffered from them. But in those days, they were dismissed as "funny turns".' When she started throwing knives, they took her a little more seriously.

Anne's mouth drops. 'Oh. I'm so sorry, Lily, I didn't know.' She hands me my frame, and I start shuffling to the door. 'Do you have any idea what triggered it?'

'Dr Barrows asked me if I was worried about my birthday. She said cut-off sometimes affects people that way.'

Anne looks at me. Her expression is unreadable. 'And what was your answer?'

'"No more than usual". Which didn't seem to satisfy her.'

She sighs. 'Well, you certainly gave Natalie a fright. Terrified, she was, poor woman. Thought you were about to meet your maker on her first watch.' She grins. 'I told her you were made of tougher stuff than that.' She wags her finger at me. 'All the same, we'll be keeping an extra eye out.'

I wheel into the bathroom and am blinded by all the chrome and white. There's a smell of tea tree and something else I can never remember that's supposed to help. I wait a couple of beats before I ask. 'Have you ever worked on any of the other dorms here, Anne?'

She swings the bath seat round and locks it into place. 'Oh, yes. Quite a few, over the years. Covering holidays and sick leave, that kind of thing.' Steam rises from the bath and a perfumed mist clouds around our heads.

My eyes sidle to the floor. 'Did you ever work on Betjeman?'

She glances at me. 'Why, are you putting in for a move?' She unties my belt. 'Trying to get shot of me?'

'Anne, you're the *last* person I'd want to get rid of.'

She chuckles and carefully slips off my robe. There was a time when I took pleasure in being undressed. Gave pleasure, even. Now I feel like a wrinkly old turtle that's been yanked out of its shell.

'Let's see ... Yes, I covered for Eloise just a few months back. She had to take some time off to be with her father.' She lowers me onto the seat. My skin looks a ghostly grey against the glare of clinical white. She grabs the remote. 'Ready?'

'Ready.'

The chair starts to rise. My toes lift off: I am airborne.

'Why do you ask?'

'I recognised a name on a door. It's probably just coincidence.' I pause. 'Margaret Benn.' Just saying those two words makes my pulse quicken. 'I used to work with a Margaret Benn. At the university.'

'Margaret? Hmm. There might have been a Margaret...' She tuts. 'My memory, honestly. It's going to the dogs.' My legs clear the side of the bath and she swings me round. 'I'll check with Eloise. It'd be nice for you to make a new friend.'

'I don't want any fuss,' I say quickly. 'It was a long time ago. It might not be her.'

Anne hits the button and I begin my descent.

'Well, why don't I have a quiet word? Eloise can point her out to you. Don't worry, she's very discreet.'

The tips of my toes brush the water, sending goose bumps up my legs. Suddenly the chair grinds to a stop.

'Uh, oh.' Anne stabs the button. Nothing happens. She tries again. 'I don't believe it. This infernal machine was playing up yesterday. I thought they'd fixed it.' She shakes her head and tries a different button. There's a small whirring sound. I think I hear Anne swear.

I'm beginning to get cold, but I don't say anything. The hairs on my skin lift up like hackles. Anne tries again and frowns. 'I'm sorry, Lily. Looks like it isn't going to play ball. We may have to abandon this.'

I gaze at the water beneath me as coils of steam curl around my ankles. 'But it seems such a waste,' I say. 'And this is my only perk.'

Only medical conditions such as mine warrant a bath.

Normal practice is showers: less time, less hassle for the carers, and much easier to sterilise.

I attempt a coquettish smile. 'Couldn't I just, you know, slip in?'

Anne stands back and folds her arms. 'And how exactly are you going to "slip in"? Or out, for that matter?' She shakes her head. 'Come on, let's get you off that contraption. Before you catch a chill.'

She unlocks the arm, but I'm not giving up that easily. That cushioning warmth of water is one of the highlights of my week.

'Please, Anne...' As she swings me back round, I touch her arm. 'My joints have been giving me hell. I know how busy you all are; I didn't want to make a fuss.'

She gives me a long hard stare. 'Lily Taylor, you push me to the limit, you really do.'

I do my best to look contrite. She leans in and puts one arm under my knees, the other under my arms.

'You'd better not breathe a word of this, you hear? Just as well there's nothing of you.' I fold my arms around her neck. 'Hang on tight. On three.'

'OK.'

'One, two, three...'

She lifts me over the side of the bath. My body slides out of her grip with an ungainly splash. I spin over and get a face full of water.

'Whoa, you OK?' She catches my arm and pulls me back round. I'd forgotten how slippery it is, without the seat. 'And that is exactly why we shouldn't do what we just did,' she says, breathing hard.

I pat the water playfully with one hand. 'Most fun I've had in ages.'

I hook my wrists over the handrails and glide back down. My skin tingles as the water covers my ears. It's a delight, being weightless: no creaking limbs or stiff moves. Anne is still remonstrating; I watch her lips, just the odd word breaking through. I have a sudden flashback to myself as a young girl in the bath, my mother raging silently above me.

Anne pulls me back up. 'Lily, what on earth do you think you—?'

The buzz of a phone cuts her off. She wipes her hands on a towel. 'This really is turning into one of those mornings,' she mutters. She scans the screen and her face hardens. 'I have to go, Lily. Right away.' I don't say anything. 'I'm sorry, but you know I can't leave you. We'll have to get you out.'

I roll my eyes. 'But I've only just got in! You're not going to be long, are you?'

'That's not the point, and you know it.' She spreads the bathmat out. 'Now please don't be difficult. What if you slip? Or have another episode?'

'I won't. I'll hold on, I promise.'

Her phone buzzes again. 'Alright, alright!' She glares at it, her cheeks colouring.

I point at the red plastic emergency cord dangling over my head. 'If I get into trouble, I can always pull that. Say I got in without you.'

She eyes me warily and sighs. 'Five minutes. I'm relying on you, Lily. No silly business. This kind of thing could cost me my job.'

She scurries out, and the door clicks shut. I count to five and sink back down. I am on my own in the bath for the first time in nearly five years. I feel a pulse of excitement, like a teenager who has bunked off school.

I close my eyes. The water lifts me, massaging my hips and shoulders, tickling the back of my neck. A soothing warmth seeps into my joints. I scull my arms, sending ripples across my stomach, and, like the Tin Man, feel myself start to unlock. I listen to my heartbeat, drumming its own gentle rhythm, and imagine I am floating in a turquoise sea, waves lapping my body, fish nibbling my toes. Memories flicker. The heat of sun on flesh. The lick of salt on skin. Sand, pushing against my back.

The water caresses my skin. I drift, weightless, as the shadow of a cloud passes overhead.

My mind stirs, sleepy but insistent.

There can be no clouds. Because that is a ceiling, not a sky.

I open my eyes just as my face goes under. My hands flail for the rails. I strain to lift my head, but it's too heavy, as if someone is pressing it down. I swing my arms up, claw at the sides, but I can't get a grip. I force my eyes to stay open; all I see is a stinging blur of light. I wedge my feet against the edge, try to lever myself up, grab the cord. My legs thrash against the porcelain as the pressure mounts in my chest. On reflex I inhale; minty water burns down my throat. I cough out my breath in a blast of bubbles.

Someone hauls me up. They drag me over the side and my body hits the deck like a speared fish. Pain ricochets up my spine. They roll me onto my side and slap my back as I hack the water out of my lungs. I hear muffled words, but I can't make sense of them. I gulp some air and explode in a fit of coughing.

'Sweet Jesus. Bring it up, that's it. Get it all out.'

Anne's olive face presses up to mine; her voice sounds miles away. She rubs my back and I heave again. The room swims in and out of focus.

'I'm so sorry, Lily. I should never have left you. To think what might have ... If I'd been a minute later...'

My eyes dart behind her, but no one else is there.

'Lord in heaven, what happened? Did you have another attack?'

I see the fright in her eyes but I cannot answer. It's all I can do to breathe.

'It's OK, Lily, take your time, take your time.' She gives my back quick little pats. 'Are you OK to sit up now, do you think?'

I nod. She props me up against the wall and swaddles me in the bathrobe like a baby. My head sags down over my knees. I can't stop shaking.

'Were you holding on to the rails, Lily? Were you? Now tell me the truth.' Anne is so close I can see the pucker lines around her mouth.

'I don't...' Each word stings like acid. I try to swallow. 'I was just lying there, when...' I hesitate.

She stops rubbing. 'What?'

'I saw something.'

'What do you mean?'

'Like a shadow. In the room.'

She sits back on her ankles. 'What kind of shadow?' I notice the damp patches I've made all over her uniform. She frowns. 'What exactly are you saying, Lily?'

'I ... I don't know.' I stare at the tiles. 'It was just before my head went under.'

Anne takes a deep breath. 'There was no one here.' Her voice is a little gentler. 'The corridor was empty. Are you sure?'

There was something. I saw it, didn't I? And that pressure on my head...

'Perhaps you dropped off? Just for a second?' she says. 'Or maybe it was a trick of the light?' I shake my head and sigh. She squeezes my arm. 'You've had a horrible shock, you poor thing.

No wonder you're at sixes and sevens.' She stands up. 'Come on, let's get you back to your room. I need to give you a proper check over. Then I'll bring you a nice cup of tea.'

Anne fetches the wheelchair and helps me in. As she fusses over me I don't say a word.

Could Anne be right? Did I drift off and slip under? Or has Margaret Benn tired of paper?

I rewind over and over, but it's like an old radio that won't tune in.

The truth is, I really can't be sure.

CHAPTER 20

Twenty-six years pre-Crisis

MARY

'That's it. Just a few more steps.'

He steers me to the right, his knees pressing into the backs of my thighs. I bang into something sharp and my eyes flick open. All I see are slits of pinkish light.

He tuts. 'No cheating.'

My lashes sweep back down. Amidst the salted scent of him I detect a new smell: faint but sweet, like nectar. My face grows sticky under his palms. For some reason, I'm finding it hard to breathe. I fight the urge to prize off his fingers.

He releases me. 'OK, you can look.'

It's a blaze of colour. Hundreds of delicate tendrils curl out from their stems, each a slightly different shade: carmine, vermilion, scarlet. As if all the reds in the world have blossomed in these feathery petals, here, on this table.

His breath blows into my neck. 'Do you like them?'

'I ... They're stunning.' I scrutinise the green, spotted stems, the undulating glossy leaves. They must be some kind of lily, but I haven't come across this species before. 'What are they?'

'A South African treasure.' His lips graze my hair. 'Scadoxus puniceus.'

Scadoxus...? My brain attempts to place it as his fingers climb down the thin cotton of my dress.

'We call them *Rooikwas*. Means "red brush".' My spine arches as he snakes round another vertebra. 'But they have several names.' He skirts the small of my back, damp where the sweat has gathered. 'The paintbrush lily. The snake lily.' His tongue probes my ear as he circles my coccyx. 'But I prefer their other name.' His hand slides down, under my dress. 'The African blood lily.' My eyes close as words melt into flesh. 'They only bloom once a year.'

I press my hands against the table, moving with him, breaths drawing short and quick. The lilies tremble in their pot as he reaches deeper, his lips covering my face, my throat. Colours streak behind my eyes as the petals, the room, the constant dread of him leaving fade. All that remains is the pant of breath, the pulse of blood that quickens until the heat swells through my body and I surrender to that sweet, sweet release.

'Happy Birthday,' he whispers. I bury my head in his chest, listen to his heart. In moments like this, I can believe he is mine.

My breathing slows as the room folds back into view. My dress clings to me like a second skin.

He rubs his thumb over my lips. 'Thirsty?' He reaches into a cool box and lifts out a fat-bottomed bottle. My eyes widen. Iced droplets glisten on emerald glass.

I laugh. 'Now *that* is smooth.' I brush my hair off my face. 'How on earth did you get hold of it?'

He twists off the wire and grasps the cork. 'I have connections, you know.'

We sit on the veranda and watch the sun drop out of the sky as the creamy lime petals of a bushwillow pulse out their scent. I let each mouthful of champagne linger, popping fruit on my tongue.

Piet empties the last few drops into my glass. 'Fancy a stroll to the hide? It's almost a full moon.'

I peer up at him, the alcohol trickling through my veins. 'Actually, I had other plans.' I tug at his belt. My words are sluggish, bordering on slurred.

Piet smiles and takes my hand. 'Come on. The light will be perfect.'

I let him haul me up. We wander across the grass, the air cooling at last. As the light wanes, the trees recede to silhouettes, and hundreds of male frogs commence their evening chorus of courtship. We climb the steps of the hide and I wait while Piet flicks on his torch and checks for less welcome visitors. We settle on the wooden bench and open the viewing slats. A bulbous moon ripples across the water.

Gradually, the greys distinguish themselves and shapes materialise on the banks. None of them are animals. I hold myself rigid, as if stilling my own body might encourage others to come. All around us frogs compete with the chirps of bush crickets rubbing their wings to attract a mate. Something stirs in the water, spreading slow circles across its surface, but whatever made them remains invisible below. I glance at Piet. I can just make out his sharp nose and the firm, unrelenting jaw. My fingers itch to touch him. I resist.

Minutes pass. I recognise the purring chant of a nightjar followed by a scops owl's clipped trill. My eyes start to play tricks on me, summoning creatures out of bushes, but still nothing comes. It's stifling in the hide, as if all the day's heat has been sealed into this little wooden box. A moth batters past my face, and I flinch. Piet doesn't stir. I lean forward to adjust my weight and the bench creaks.

All of a sudden, Piet holds up one hand. He tilts his head.

I try to blank out the other sounds and train my senses on whatever it is he just heard. Another second and I have it: a strange rasping noise, like someone sawing wood. Piet puts one finger to his lips and claws the air. He doesn't need to. I know what it is. I can hardly believe it. He's told me about her before.

We wait two, maybe three minutes. It feels like thirty. And then, through the trees, I see her. I've seen pictures, watched programmes, but nothing has prepared me for such muscled grace. Her golden fur gleams a silvery pearl in the moonlight, amplifying intricate black patterns of rosettes. She takes four strides along the bank and stops. I glimpse pale-amber eyes perfectly outlined in black. She sniffs the air and her body tenses. She backs up against a bush and lifts her tail.

'She's marking,' Piet whispers, eyes fixed straight ahead. 'She must be in season. That was her. Calling to a male.'

My first leopard. These are highly elusive, solitary creatures. And there she is, all forty kilos of her, just the other side of these planks.

She pads towards the waterhole, her huge paws sinking into the mud. As she turns I catch a gleam of white behind her ears. She lowers her head and laps the water, eyes constantly on alert.

'Adults only come together for courtship and mating. Even then it's just for a few days.' His eyes glitter. 'It's the females who initiate it. They'll mate every five or ten minutes. Then they go their separate ways.'

I'm tempted to say something but don't. The leopardess licks her mouth and whiskers, revealing a flash of murderous teeth. She lifts her head, and my eyes meet hers. I feel something powerful, unnameable, akin to yearning. This female is perfectly adapted to her life in solitude. A supreme hunter and a devoted mother. She needs no mate by her side to make her feel whole.

We watch her wander back along the bank: deliberate but unhurried, the pronounced bone and muscles in each shoulder sliding up with every step. When she reaches the trees she stops. Her tail flicks up behind her, a splash of white at its tip. She gives a cursory glance back towards us and, like a spell, she is gone.

'Well,' says Piet, 'you couldn't get a better birthday gift than that. Pretty damn special.'

I exhale, unaware I'd been holding my breath. I imagine her stalking through the undergrowth, seeking out her quarry. Marking her scent in places I will never know.

He slips his hand through mine. 'Magnificent, isn't she?'

'Yes.' I stiffen. 'Absolutely in her prime.'

We don't talk much on the way back. It's still sweltering inside, so Piet drags the mattress out onto the veranda while I light the mosquito coils. We lie on our backs and stare up at the sky. It is something to behold, an African night: a blaze of stars as far as you can see. But despite the stars and the leopard and all the trouble Piet's gone to, this heaviness in me won't budge.

Piet lifts his finger. 'Orion. Can you see it?' I don't respond. 'Go to the Milky Way, then across.' I squint up at the night sky like a reluctant child. 'Look for the three belt stars first: the really bright ones.' A curl of smoke encircles his hand and floats up into the ether. 'The Ancient Egyptians believed Osiris descended from those stars. That's why the pyramids at Giza are aligned to Orion's Belt.'

There is no end to Piet's knowledge, it seems. Normally I'm all ears.

'Got them? Good. Now look for the hunter.' He traces a shape in the air as a soft breeze rattles the leaves. 'Follow his arm out to the bow.'

Out of the morass of stars, a distinct figure appears. I frown. 'Where did you learn all this stuff?'

'My dad taught me. When I was young. We used to camp out.'

My ears prick up. Piet rarely talks about his family. It's one of those subjects that's off limits, that rips open the curtain he must draw across his betrayal to enjoy it. All I've been able to gather is that his dad left Piet's mother for another woman when Piet was in his teens, and died some years after.

I risk a question. 'What was he like? Your father?'

Piet's eyes remain locked on the firmament. Just as I think he won't answer he takes a breath. 'He was the kind of man who was happiest outdoors. In the bush.'

I watch Piet's chest rise and fall. 'Were you close?'

He glances at me. There's a scurrying, snuffling sound underneath the veranda: some small creature foraging. Piet's eyes sweep back to the sky. 'We had different views about things. Politics especially.' He pauses. 'And he made my mother very unhappy.'

An unhappy mother: that's something I can relate to. But I don't want to think about that now. I press on. 'You never told me how he died.'

Piet's chest stills. The change in his expression makes me want to scoop the words back into my mouth.

He turns to me. His eyes are indecipherable, dark pools. 'Haven't you guessed?'

The blood rushes to my cheeks. 'Oh. I'm sorry ... So they couldn't...?' I bite my lip. 'The treatment didn't work?'

'No.' I roll over and rest my head on his chest. 'He didn't go for treatment.' I listen to the breath sigh out of him. 'My father wanted to die. Nobody knows, apart from me.'

I lift myself up on my elbows and cup Piet's face in my hand. 'I'm so sorry.' My lips brush the smooth, white circle of scar tissue.

'Don't be.' His body tenses. 'He was a quitter.' Piet spits out the word like a bite of rotten fruit. 'In death as in life.'

Something inside me shifts. I was mistaken.

This isn't grief. It's rage.

CHAPTER 21

KATE

I run my hand over the wood, press my thumb into the grain. My kitchen table is a faithful old piece that, like me, has survived the years, but bears the marks to prove it. I gingerly prod my forehead. The bandage is off, and the cut's healing nicely. Should be back to work tomorrow. I walk over to the sink, humming one of Sasha's favourites as the kettle fills. A memory of the protest surfaces and I freeze. Stale breath. Hot, damp bodies. Water splashes over the rim and pours down my sleeve.

Listen to the tick of the clock. The dishwasher's hum. The wind stirring the branches outside.

I turn off the tap, dry myself with a tea towel and place the kettle carefully on its stand. Just as I reach for a mug the phone rips into the room. My pulse leaps. I could just ignore it. The thought mushrooms, gathering strength. But all the what-ifs kick in: Sasha. Mark. Work.

I pick up. 'Hello?'

'Hi, Mrs Connelly. It's Harry. From Archway Investigations.'

I exhale. 'Hi, Harry, how's it going?'

Harry's proved to be a welcome distraction. He's only had the case a couple of days and he's already getting stuck in. After my conversation with Sasha, I began to have second thoughts. But Harry reassured me. I can stop this investigation any time I want to. The reality, of course, is that every clod he unearths only lures me in further.

'Good, very good,' he says, sounding rather pleased with himself. 'Actually I've had an idea. I'd like you to try something.'

'What is it?' I drop a teabag into my mug.

'Potential short-cut. AKA the alumni team at your mother's uni. When it comes to record-keeping, those guys could give the GRO a run for their money.'

It turns out Mary Sommers is no dunce: she got a first from Oxford. Stayed on to do a PhD.

'You see, they like tapping up their old students for cash,' he continues. 'So they may have an address for her post-Crisis. It could save us a lot of time, particularly if she went overseas. They won't release the information to us, but they might to you.'

I stir my tea in slow circles. 'Really? Universities are normally right sticklers about their data.'

'Well, technically they shouldn't ... but if you get the right person, pull at the old heartstrings...' I raise my eyebrows. 'Other outfits pretend to be the clients and do it themselves. But we don't operate that way.'

Harry appears to be at pains to establish his credentials. Given his line of business, it seems rather quaint.

'I don't mean to sound insensitive, Mrs Connelly, but you need to ham it up a bit. Give them a sob story. Even if they don't release her details, they might offer to send her a message.'

Harry spends another five minutes coaching me on what I should say, how to play it. I don't have the heart to tell him I've engaged in many such conversations before. The amount of time we spend trying to track down patients' relatives, I'm virtually a sleuth myself. But the tightness in my gut suggests my own family investigations might not be quite as straightforward.

After I hang up I sit at the table, squinting at the number

he's given me, rehearsing what I'm going to say. I take a breath and dial. It rings and rings. Part of me begins to hope no one picks up.

'Alumni Relations, Jayne speaking.'

I feel a rush as the adrenaline kicks in. 'Ah, hello, this is Kate Connelly. Ward sister at the Marston Hospital for the Elderly. Can I speak to the alumni officer, please?'

'Speaking. How can I help you?'

The handset's already feeling a little sweaty. 'Well, I should start by saying I'm not on hospital business. This is a personal matter.' I hesitate, just long enough to demonstrate vulnerability. 'The thing is, I'm trying to locate my birth mother, Mary Sommers. She was at Oxford back in the eighties.'

'I see.' Jayne sounds rather officious. 'Well, normal procedure for enquiries is to send us the person's name and date of birth, and we'll respond within forty-eight hours, confirming whether they studied here or—'

'Her name was published in the class lists. I know she did.' There's a pause. Probably not a good idea to interrupt. 'I'm sorry, it's just, well, she turns seventy this year. I've not had any contact with her since I was born so ... I was hoping you might have a forwarding address—'

'I'm sorry, we can't give out that kind of information. There are procedures we have to follow. Data protection laws.'

'Of course, of course.' Time to ramp it up. 'You see, my mother – my adoptive mother that is – died very recently.' I swallow. 'My father died five years ago. So my birth mother is all the family I have left.'

Just saying those words unplugs an unexpected well of emotion. Conjured for effect, the truth of them strikes home.

'Oh. I'm very sorry for your loss,' she says, as if she really means it. 'I know how difficult it is.' She sighs. 'I lost my own father last year.'

'I'm sorry.' I pause. 'That's why ... It would be such a relief to know where she is. To have a chance to meet her, before ... Well, I'm sure you understand. Those last years are so precious.'

I clamp my mouth shut and let the silence between us grow.

'I suppose it can't do any harm...' Her voice lowers. 'Do you want to give me the dates she was here?'

I reel them off. 'Thank you. Thank you so much.'

'Of course, if we do have any contact details, I won't be able to divulge them. But I can send her a message on your behalf.'

'That would be wonderful.' I listen to her tapping the keys, willing her to go faster.

The typing stops. 'Oh.'

The way she says it isn't good. 'Is something the matter?'

'I'm sorry, I'm going to have to put you on hold.' She speaks quickly, as if she can't wait to get me off the phone. There's a click and a recorded voice starts wheedling in my ear about bequests.

'Hello? Who is this?'

A different woman: Jayne must have palmed me off on someone else. I start again, keeping it friendly. 'My name's Kate Connelly, I'm a ward sister at the Marston Hospital for the Elderly—'

'Oh, please. Credit me with some intelligence. I thought I'd made myself clear.'

'I'm sorry?'

'You've got a nerve, trying it again. The lies you people tell!'

My brain rebounds. Did Harry call them already? Is that what's pissed her off?

'I ... I think there's been some mistake.' I swallow. 'This is the first time I've rung—'

'What you're doing is against the law. Impersonating others. Trying to extract personal information through deceit. I have your number right here; do you want me to call the police?'

My heart is pounding, but I manage to keep my voice calm. 'I'm sorry but I honestly don't know what you're talking about. I'm just trying to locate my birth mother, that's not a—'

'OK, that's it. If you call again, I'll report you. Go trawl along the bottom of some other ocean.'

The line goes dead.

I blink at the phone. What the hell? I should make a formal complaint.

I punch the first three digits of Harry's number and stop. I run through the conversation again. She thought I was someone who'd rung before. By the sounds of it, some rogue operator. The question is, why? Who else would be looking for my birth mother?

I grab my laptop and log on; my fingers tear across the keys. This time I set my date filter later – to capture more recent entries. A rash of blue headlines appears. Suddenly my tongue feels too large for my mouth.

I drag the cursor slowly down. My finger hovers over one of the headlines and falls, like a guillotine.

'Scientist Investigated over TB Drug Scandal'

A scientist who worked for the drugs company, Pharmaplanta, has been summoned to give evidence after the health secretary launched an official investigation into the use of Brotanol in South African hospitals.

The experimental TB drug caused multiple organ failure, leading to over six hundred deaths…

I stare at the words as the second hand on my watch stomps round. Somewhere outside a dog barks.

I tell myself that it might not be the same woman. That there's no actual proof it's her. But I feel it already, like a force of gravity, pressing me down. The grim, irrevocable certainty that it is.

I hunt through the other results but they're all variations of the same story. I search another year, and another, but there are no more mentions.

Mary Sommers has disappeared.

CHAPTER 22

LILY

Every time I look at her the palpitations quicken in my chest. She's there. Just the other side of the table. Head bent, her grey bob draped like a shroud over her face. She ties and knots the cloth with a dexterity I can only dream of. Are those really the hands that pushed me? I can still taste that minty burn. I imagine her, stalking into the bathroom, her shadow passing over my face. My eyes move to the soft, pale skin at the nape of her neck. Even murderers have their weak spot.

She puts her Abayomi doll down and squints in my direction. But it's not me she's looking at, it's the sewing box. Her eyes peer out behind silver-framed glasses, like dark beads. She rummages around the box, lips puckered as if in disapproval, picking at ribbons like a crow. My scissors have stuck mid-cut, the plastic handles wedged tight around my knuckles. My fingers are already bulging: fiery-red and swelling fast. I try to force the blades apart. They fly open, stabbing my doll in the face. Now she has scars, too.

'Careful, Lily. Here, let me.' Eloise gently frees me of the scissors and slices briskly through the cloth. All I've managed to accomplish so far is one twisted skirt. I sneak another glance at Margaret. She's still absorbed with her ribbons.

'There you are.' Eloise slides her glasses back up her nose. 'Just say if you want help, Lily.' She leans closer: 'Why don't you try saying hello?'

I shake my head. 'She's not who I thought she was.'

Eloise's mouth droops. 'Oh. Are you sure?' A thin crest of hair quivers on her lip.

'I'm afraid so.' I give her a tight smile. 'Must be a coincidence after all.'

Eloise tuts. 'What a shame. I think it would have done her good to see an old friend.' She unspools more lengths of wool. 'Mind you, there's nothing to stop you two having a chat.'

I don't dignify that with a reply. Chatting isn't exactly on the agenda. I busy myself with the doll's turban until Eloise moves on. The voices of the other residents merge into an insect-like murmur, punctuated with the occasional scissor snip. There's a pleasant smell of lavender and rose, tainted with the ever-present sting of disinfectant. I wind one more piece of cloth around the wooden peg and slip the scissors into my pocket.

'There we are,' says a woman in a purple cardigan, brandishing her work.

'Oh, that's lovely, Heather,' gushes Eloise. 'Goodness me, is that your fourth? Those children will be pleased. You're a proper little production line today, aren't you, ladies?'

Laughter tinkles through the room. Eloise bustles round the table, sweeping fabric ends into a pink plastic tub with one meaty hand. I wait until her back is turned. I reach for my frame and shuffle as fast as I can to the door.

'Going already, Lily?'

Damn it. I swivel round. Fortunately, Margaret is still bent over her doll.

'Sorry.' I hold up a hand. 'They're really playing up. I think I need to give them a rest.'

Before she has a chance to respond I head left towards Betjeman and try to pick up some pace. By my calculations I have thirty minutes at best. As I reach the Tuscan-orange walls I feel a flutter of trepidation. Just because I don't have a relationship with my cleaner, doesn't mean Margaret doesn't have one with hers.

I scour the corridor for the sanitation trolley but it's nowhere to be seen. I wheel slowly past each door, pausing to listen, my insides stretched as tight as a wire. When I reach the seventh door, I hear it: the Hoover's bellow and whine. I pass another three rooms and stop.

Margaret Benn (Oxf)

The witch's lair.

I wait outside, praying nobody else comes. Eventually a door opens and a small, wiry woman emerges, trailing the vacuum cleaner behind her like a dog. I try to catch her eye but she disappears back inside. She returns with the trolley and rattles it along the carpet towards me. All I can see of her behind the brushes and mops are her feet. Her scuffed brown lace-ups remind me of the shoes they made us wear at school.

I clear my throat. 'Excuse me?'

The trolley's making such a racket that she doesn't hear. I try a little louder.

'Excuse me? Hello?'

She pokes her head round. It looks as though the bones in her face have shrunk. The poor woman must be nearly as old as me.

'Ah, I think there's a problem.' I hold up my arm. 'With my chip.'

She stares through me, as if I'm invisible.

I point at my arm and then at Margaret Benn's door. 'It won't open.' I flash her an apologetic smile. She doesn't smile back. Either she doesn't understand or she doesn't care. 'Can you help me?'

Her jaw sets. She gives one shake of her head, firm and slow.

I clench my abdomen with both hands. 'Please. I'm desperate.'

She mutters something to herself and sighs. 'Not allow.' She gives the trolley a good shove.

OK, then. It's going to have to be the full monty.

I scoop up my dress and yank at my tights with one claw, grunting. She turns. Her eyes widen.

'No, no, no!' She flaps her hands and scuttles forward. She grabs her lanyard and waves the metal card at the door. It beeps.

She sticks one bony finger in my face. 'Not say, OK?'

I nod. 'OK.' I shuffle past her.

I'm in.

■ ■ ■

I stand in the middle of the room, heart racing. It's a good size, bigger than mine, but doesn't look it. Every corner is crammed with furniture and knick-knacks, as if she's emptied her entire house into one room. There must be at least twenty photo frames strewn over the surfaces and walls. I pick one from the window sill. It's a younger Margaret, the one I recognise from the news articles. She has the same short bob and serious expression, but her hair is brown, not grey, and her eyes look bigger, less shrew-like. She's in formal college dress: mortar board and gown.

I head towards a large gold frame mounted above the sideboard. Some instinct warns me, even before I look. I see now, just how pretty her daughter was. The press photos didn't do her justice. Peach-coloured skin and oval brown eyes, a cascade of long, chestnut hair. As I look at the other photos I realise that, apart from a couple, all of them are of her. The first day at primary: stiff collar, white socks. A concert at secondary. Sprawling teenager and triumphant graduate. I follow her daughter's life around the room until I reach the one just before it ends.

She beams at the camera, golden freckles dusting her cheeks, one arm flung loosely around some guy. My chest burns. She radiates happiness. Everything ahead of her. So much promise, commemorated in that smile.

What am I doing here, in this woman's room? All I can offer her are apologies. I cannot change what happened, God knows, I've wished I could. Maybe I should just let Margaret get on with it: whatever's next on her list. Tell Graham to leave it be.

I hear a click and the lock thuds back.

The door swings open.

A faint hope glimmers that it's the cleaner, come to check I haven't made a mess on the floor.

I glimpse the shoes.

It's not.

CHAPTER 23

Twenty-six years pre-Crisis

Clinicians Sound the Alarm as MRSA Outbreaks Spread

The New York State Department of Health has released figures that show a sharp rise in hospital infection rates of Methicillin-resistant Staphylococcus aureus (MRSA). According to the report, there has been a dramatic increase in the number of resistant infections, which mirrors similar increases in other cities, both in the US and abroad. 'We have already seen fatalities from MRSA sepsis and pneumonia,' said one doctor in a New York hospital. 'We're not alone. Our medical practice is now reliant on a few costly antibiotics that are still efficient in treating these infections. But if MRSA continues to expand the scope of its resistance then we will be in a very dark place indeed.

■ ■ ■

MARY

I lean over the wooden rail and gaze at the vast riverbed below. The silvered veins of the mighty Olifants flow nearly six hundred kilometres through South Africa into Mozambique, nourishing a catchment area over twice the size of Wales.

Sprinklings of waterbuck and impala graze its banks: grey and gold flecks against the grass. The river's rush is accompanied by a refrain of hippo honks and puffs that sounds like someone learning to play the tuba. Their glossy backs plunge out of sight and minutes later resurface, as if they're playing a game of hide and seek; their bulging eyes keep watch above the water.

I have ventured north in search of an elusive woody shrub. Luckily for me, this necessitates a stay at one of the most scenic camps in the park. The bush savanna is denser here, with the usual proliferation of mopane, red bushwillow and leadwood; from this high up, on the balcony, the trees look like stubble covering the ground. In the distance, a baobab's ancient trunk thrusts skyward, its gnarled branches straggling out like roots, as though some toddler giant plucked it from the earth and, for a laugh, put it back upside down. It's easy to imagine how it was, five million years ago, when the hippos' ancestors, the mega-herbivores, roamed these lands.

I feel a hand on my shoulder. I spin round. 'I ... You made it!' I remember where I am and just manage not to throw my arms around Piet's neck.

He grins. 'Couldn't pass up an opportunity for this view.'

It's a hell of a journey; I never thought he'd come. I gaze at him, skin prickling as the air charges between us.

'How long did it take?'

'Seven hours.' It should take at least eight. My eyebrows rise. '*Ja*, I tanked it.'

I allow myself a discreet brush of his arm. I can't stop smiling. 'Come on. I think I owe you a coffee.'

We take a seat by the edge. A vervet monkey scampers past, eyeing up the plates on a recently vacated table. Just as it's about to strike a waiter strides over and shoos it away. The animal scowls at him and takes refuge under a cactus, its fur shimmering like silver in the sun.

'So,' says Piet. 'How's it been? Any luck?'

I tap my seat. 'Not yet. But I have it on good authority where to look.'

The plant I seek only inhabits the dry mountain slopes in the north. Aptly named the resurrection plant, it can survive extreme dehydration until, with the onset of rain, its seemingly dead brown leaves unfurl and turn a dazzling green.

'Like you said, the oil from its leaves is highly prized,' I continue. 'It's not only used to cure respiratory and urinary infections. It's also used by local tribes to dress burns and wounds.'

'Encouraging.' He nods. 'The records did suggest there could be antimicrobial activity.' He rubs his eyes. 'Let's hope one of them comes good soon.'

Piet looks exhausted. It could be the drive, but I suspect there's more to it. As we order our coffees, a little girl with wavy blonde hair runs up to the railing, clutching a small furry giraffe. The hippos erupt in another tuneful blast, and she squeals with laughter.

I keep my voice neutral. 'So, how are things back at the ranch?'

'Oh, you know, the usual. Some good, some bad. Making progress with the antivirals.' His mouth pinches. 'Still being given the run-around by our friend. Even Dodonaea viscosa can't handle the resistant TB strains.'

His eyes move past me, to the river. I follow his gaze. On a far bank I spot movement: the slow, purposeful lumber of an elephant navigating the rocks, one of thousands that come here to drink.

'On the plus side, we're getting some traction with it against Streptococcus pneumoniae. Which is something, at least.'

'That's good.' I hesitate. 'And MRSA?'

His expression darkens. 'Nothing. Despite all the money we've thrown at it.' He shakes his head. 'God, the things I've seen … you wouldn't believe it. Like a battleground.' He heaves out a sigh. 'I saw this one kid in the hospital, thigh bandaged up. He'd trodden on some glass, cut his foot. The infection hadn't responded to treatment. They'd taken half his leg off, for Christ's sake: there was nothing else they could do. It's like we've gone back a hundred years.'

I don't know what to say. I remember those horror stories my grandmother told me. About soldiers in the First World War. How many of them died, not just in combat, but afterwards, from infected wounds and disease.

The young girl dances her giraffe along the rail, chattering away and singing to it. Piet's face lifts. She looks a little like that photo of his daughter: the one he carries round in his wallet. He didn't show me it, of course. I suppose you could say I was curious.

I curl a strand of hair round my finger. 'Cute, isn't she?'

His eyes follow her along the balcony. 'At that age, they usually are.'

My chest tightens. No one ever said that about me.

Piet reaches under the table and gently squeezes my hand. He leans closer. 'I've missed you.'

I study the arch of his lips; inhale his salty tang. The longing pulls at me, reeling me back in. 'I've missed you too,' I whisper, as my fingers curl over his palm.

All of a sudden there's a scream. I'm out of my chair without even registering what's happened. It's the girl: she's somehow managed to heave herself up onto the rail and is dangling towards the electric perimeter fence, her little legs kicking out furiously behind. I lunge forward, seize her under the arms and yank her back onto the balcony.

Tears bubble from her blue doll eyes. She's trying to tell me something but her words are strangled by sobs. 'It's OK,' I say, as her tiny body presses against me. 'Ssh. I've got you now.'

'Jesus, Susie!' A woman dashes over and snatches her up, eyes wide with fright. 'How many times have I told you to stay away from the edge?'

The little girl points at the fence and wails, her face all blotchy and red. The woman clutches her to her chest, kissing her hair. 'There, there,' she whispers, rocking the child gently. 'It's OK, baby. You're safe.' She takes a long slow breath and mouths at me: 'Thank you.'

I nod. Her daughter doesn't stop crying.

A cluster of staff appear on the balcony and start talking to Piet; there seems to be a lot of gesticulating. It's only when I join him by the railing that I realise why. Piet points at something lying in the dirt on the other side. The amber eyes of a small, furry giraffe peer up at me.

'Ah. So *that's* it,' I say.

'Yeah. I think she might have been attempting her own rescue operation.'

I smile and shake my head. 'All in the name of love.'

One of the waiters fetches a rake. Piet slings it over the rail, inches from the fence.

'Careful.' I frown at the electric wire, which is buzzing slightly. 'I wouldn't want such a long journey to go to waste.'

Piet grins and deftly hooks the toy with the rake. As he hoists it up, the giraffe's neck flops sideways and it topples to the ground. He quickly scoops it up again. An African starling flits onto the emerald spike of a candelabra tree. It cocks its head and regards the levitating giraffe with one glassy eye.

The rake reaches the top of the railing. As Piet pulls it closer, the head tilts and the animal slips off. Piet mutters something under his breath. I think of that arcade game, with the soft toys and the claw. The odds aren't good.

On his next attempt, Piet has to lean right over the rails to reach it. I grip the back of my chair. I'm beginning to hope that damned toy plummets over the edge.

'Gerry!' The little girl breaks free from her mother and races over just as the giraffe falls a third time. By now the entire restaurant is watching.

Piet adjusts his grip on the handle and spears the animal with two of the rake's teeth. The girl sucks in her breath but doesn't protest. He flips the rake, cradling the toy in its head, and, in one swift movement, swings it over the rail. The onlookers burst into applause.

Piet squats down in front of her and eases the giraffe off the prongs. 'Look who's back from his big adventure.'

She eyes Piet for a second and grabs the toy. She squeezes it into her chest. 'Naughty Gerry!' she scolds, with a wag of her finger. 'I told you not to play on the rails.'

After much thanking and hugging we eventually return to our table. Our coffees have gone cold so they bring us some more. I smile at Piet and clench my hands together in mock-adulation. 'My hero!'

Piet rolls his eyes. 'I hooked a stuffed animal. It was you who saved the girl.' He takes a sip. 'That was impressive, you know. It's like you acted on instinct. A mother's instinct.'

I pick at my shorts. 'Oh, I wouldn't go that far.' My smile hardens. 'Not if my own mother's instinct is anything to go by.'

Piet puts down his cup. 'Listen to me, Mary.' He takes my face in his hands. 'We may be the product of our parents, but we are not bound by the same thread of their mistakes.' He gazes at me. 'You'll make an excellent mother.'

The blood rushes to my cheeks. *Don't be absurd*, I think. *In what dimension of reality would that ever happen?*

But then I meet his gaze and, just for a second, dare to imagine. A soft-skinned baby, jiggling on my knee.

Golden curls.

Pudgy toes.

Saucer eyes. The colour of a monsoon sky. Before the rain falls.

Something inside me unfurls, like a flower.

I smile. 'Maybe.'

CHAPTER 24

KATE

'Tell me again: exactly what did that tracer guy say?' Mark sucks in his cheeks, eyes riveted to the article. As if, unobserved, the words might explode.

I slump deeper into the cushions. I've just put in a ten-hour shift. 'It's definitely her: the Brotanol woman.' My voice is brittle; it could crack any moment. 'At least now I understand why that terrier at the alumni office chewed my ears off.'

Mark frowns. 'But how does he know? For certain?'

My fingers peck at a loose thread on the sofa. 'Oh, he found some insurance records or something. Matched up her NR number.'

Mark's eyes widen. 'Is that even legal?'

'I didn't ask. I've moved to a need-to-know basis. And right now, I need to know who she is. Or was.'

The familiar crease creeps into his cheek: it always betrays him. He gets up and starts to pace. 'Jesus, Kate. This is a lot to take in. I mean, that drug poisoned people. A lot of people. Many of them children...'

I feel an uncomfortable tightening in my chest. 'I know. No wonder she didn't want any contact.'

I remember the day this leaked. Who could forget those terrible pictures? They had to put the directors under police protection.

Hundreds Alleged To Have Died in South Africa after Being Given TB 'Miracle Cure'...

Shocking as this discovery is, a small part of me is reassured. It might explain why she shut me out.

Mark sighs. 'Wasn't she the scientist who was supposed to have discovered it? That plant?'

I expel a long, slow breath. 'That's what the investigation said.'

He shakes his head. 'Imagine working with Piet Bekker. That must have taken some guts, to testify against him.'

I stare at the grainy black-and-white photo that Harry sent me from the news archive. The picture's been enlarged and the quality isn't great, but I can still make out her features. She has what Pen would have called an intelligent face: aquiline nose, strong cheekbones, high forehead. I can't tell what colour her eyes are, though. They're fixed on Bekker as he is led up the steps.

Mark halts at the sideboard. 'They reckoned he was in with the top guys at EAA. That he helped mastermind the attacks.'

'So they claimed.'

He fixes me with a stare. 'So, what's your take on it?'

I bide my time before answering. For some reason, I'm wary. I'm never wary, in front of Mark.

'Well, I guess Janet was right. This birth-mother business is complicated.' My eyes veer back to the photo, as if it possesses some kind of magnetic charge. 'You really might not like what you find.'

His face softens. 'Kate, are you sure you want to carry on with all of this?'

Well, you've changed your tune, I think, but I know that's below the belt.

'No one will judge you if you don't.'

I bite my lip. 'I kind of feel I have to, now I've started … even though it scares the shit out of me.'

Mark nods in that slow, thoughtful way that's a sure sign he disagrees but knows better than to tackle it head on.

'It's easy to jump to conclusions,' I say. 'But it was chaos back then; the pandemic was reaching its height. Who knows what kinds of pressures were brought to bear? I mean, how many other drugs were fast-tracked and failed that we don't even know about? Maybe they were just the ones that got caught.'

The obstinate child in me wants to convince him, even though I'm barely convinced myself. 'And it's still not clear what her role was in all this. She may not even have known about those other trials.' I notice Mary's hands. They're clenched so tightly around her bag that I can see the whites of her knuckles.

Mark looks at his feet. I can guess what he's thinking. I've only known this woman's my mother for a couple of days and already I'm leaping to her defence. But, like so many of our spats, I'm compelled to keep fighting my corner long after I've realised he's right.

'Pharmaplanta folded, didn't it?' He wisely moves the conversation on. 'Was that before his court case or after?'

'After. But I conducted a little research of my own. It went into receivership and was scooped up by one of the big guys. They stripped all the assets and closed it down.' I give him a sideways glance. 'Guess who the raiders were.'

Mark rubs his forehead. 'Go on.'

'The very same company that developed Rackinol.'

Mark's mouth falls open. 'You're kidding?'

'Nope. Makes you wonder, doesn't it?'

Rackinol: the wonder drug, the first new class of antibiotic in over thirty years. It only took a few months for some strains to develop resistance. But at least it actually worked.

Mark slumps down next to me. 'So then. What's the plan of attack?'

'Well, rather unhelpfully, Mary's dropped off the radar. All the usual avenues have drawn blanks.' I sigh. 'So Harry's got two theories. She spent a good chunk of time in Africa. If she died overseas, the death may not have been registered here. She was still in the UK when they closed the borders. But some people with connections still managed to get out.'

Mark frowns. 'Surely customs would know whether she left the country or not? If he can hack into her insurance records I imagine immigration is a walk in the park.'

I take a breath. 'Not necessarily. Harry's contacting the embassies in the countries she used to visit.' Mark's frown deepens. 'I know it's a long shot. But Harry's prepared to give it a try.'

Mark snorts. 'I'll bet he is.' His voice drops to a mutter. 'As long as the meter keeps running.'

I stand up and walk over to the window. I'm beginning to understand why I felt wary.

He clears his throat. 'So – what's the other theory?'

I turn to him. The sticky legs of impatience are crawling all over me. 'She may have changed her name.'

Two pink circles appear on Mark's cheeks. As if they're embarrassed on my behalf.

I clasp my arms. 'Imagine the shit she must have got! All those patients' relatives and friends. Not to mention the press. They turned those guys into pariahs, and who can blame them? Maybe she wanted a fresh start. I mean, look at what happened with the alumni office, twenty years on. People still must be prowling around.'

Mark's tongue probes the back of his mouth as if he's trying to dislodge something from behind a molar. 'OK ... but if she's still in the country, what's the problem? It must be on record somewhere.'

'Jesus, Mark! Because if you change your name by deed poll, it doesn't have to be registered anywhere, OK? It's like searching for a fucking needle in a haystack!'

Mark looks as if I've just slapped him. A distant burst of laughter echoes outside.

I run my hands over my face. 'Sorry. I'm just a bit ... This is difficult for me too, you know? It's been a very long day.'

He blinks. The confusion in his eyes makes me think of Sasha and my heart twists. 'I'm just trying to get my head around it, that's all, Kate.'

I sink down next to him. 'Sorry. I know. Believe me, so am I.'

I decide to navigate to safer ground. 'According to the records, she never married. Not under her birth name, anyway.' I glance at Mark. 'And she didn't have any more children.'

When Harry first told me this, I was glad that she wasn't the matriarch of some new family. Glad that I was the only one. But I feel differently now. Part of me yearns for a brother or sister. Someone I could share this with.

'A career lady, then?' ventures Mark.

'Until it all went belly-up, yes.' I think of the other photo. I'm suddenly not so sure I want to show him. But if I start with secrets now, who knows where it might end?

'Come and look at this.' I sit down at the computer. Mark peers over my shoulder as I load the file. Rows of men and women in evening dress gaze back at us from the screen. 'Check out the third row from the front.'

It takes him less than a second. 'Blimey. Is that her?'

Even amongst all those women, Mary stands out. Her hair is curled into a bun, her body sheathed in a simple blue gown. An ironic smile plays on her lips, Mona Lisa style. But she's not smiling at whoever's taking the photograph. Her gaze is directed at a man in the front row with blond hair and piercing blue eyes who's holding some kind of certificate.

'Harry found it in the news archives. Some trade conference in South Africa.'

Mark edges closer. 'Well, it's easy to see where you get your looks. How long ago was that taken?'

I keep my voice steady. 'Forty-six years.'

Mark's face drops. He lifts a finger and points at the man in the front. 'Hang on, is that...? That's not Piet Bekker?'

The churning in my gut intensifies. 'The one and only.'

Mark lets out a whistle. 'I didn't know they went back *that* far.'

'Me neither. It was just after Pharmaplanta was born. Check these out.'

I open another document and scroll down:

'Local Plant Provides Hope for AIDS Patients...'

'Dodonaea viscosa: Could This Be the Answer to TB...?'

'A couple of these went on to become successful drug brands. Turns out Pharmaplanta weren't always the pariahs they're made out to be.'

Mark frowns. 'I don't get it. How could someone who worked so hard to combat disease end up using it like that, as a weapon?'

'Beats me.' I rub my eyes. 'Sometimes it feels like I'm stuck in one of those computer games. Every time I think I'm getting somewhere, a door opens onto another world – one that I didn't even know exists.'

Mark glances at the door. 'Have you said anything to Sasha yet?'

I shake my head. 'Before I put her through that, I need to know where this is going. It's a lot for her to cope with, particularly so soon after Pen.' I think of our conversation. 'To be honest, I'm not sure how she'll take it.'

'Oh, you never know.' He raises an eyebrow. 'I reckon she's tougher than you or I give her credit for.' He squeezes my shoulder. 'Come on. It's time you called it a day. Let's cheer ourselves up with some Nordic noir.'

I close the files, one by one, until all that's left is the conference picture. I stare at Mary's face until it dissolves in a blur of pixels.

Was there something going on between the two of them? Or am I reading too much into that smile?

I think of the empty box on my birth certificate.

That photo was taken eighteen months before I was born.

CHAPTER 25

LILY

Neither of us speaks.

Margaret glances behind her as though she's considering walking back out. She's taller than I thought, in much better shape than her years suggest. Perhaps I should have left things to Graham after all.

'What are you doing?' Her question fractures the silence.

I cannot answer, fearful of lying and of telling the truth. I clench my frame, as if it can help me. As if it can whisk me away to safety, like Dorothy's shoes.

Tap three times.

Her eyes move behind me, over the furniture and the photos. A slight frown wrinkles her forehead. 'This is my room.' Her words are hesitant, as though they're in doubt. Then her face stiffens. She points her finger at me. '*You.*'

I slide my hand into my pocket and feel the icy touch of the scissors. If only those blades weren't quite so blunt.

'You're the one who kept staring. In the crafts room.'

I remember to breathe. 'That's right.' I force myself to meet her gaze. 'I believe you know who I am.'

Her mouth twitches. 'Do I?' She gives a slight shake of her bob. 'I don't think we've met.'

Either she's really good, or Graham's got this wrong.

I swallow. 'She's very beautiful.' I nod at the gold-framed photo. 'Your daughter.'

Margaret steps closer. She stares at the picture with such tenderness that I have to look away. Strange, how guilt can even trump fear.

'I'm ver—' My voice fails. 'I'm sorry. About what happened.' I squeeze my fingers against the blade, ashamed of the inadequacy of words. 'I don't ... blame you. For being angry.'

Her face screws up. 'I'm not angry. Why are you saying I'm angry?'

The blood pounds in my ears. 'Margaret, I have to ask: was it you that sent me the postcard?' She stares at me blankly. I take a breath. 'Did you ... push me? In the bath?'

She frowns and shakes her head. 'I don't—'

'I won't press charges or anything. God knows, you had cause.' My limbs feel weak and jittery, as if they might give way at any moment. 'I just want to know.'

Her eyes flit around the room like a frightened bird. She starts rubbing her left arm; her hand massages the same spot over and over. 'Are you making fun of me? Is this some kind of joke?'

I step back. 'No! I'm sorry, I just...' I sink my teeth into my lip. 'I thought you might have been sending me things. Because of ... what happened. In South Africa. To your daughter.'

She stops fidgeting. 'You mean Jodie?' She gives a nervous giggle, like a young girl's. 'So *that's* what all this is about.' Her face relaxes. She picks up one of the photo frames and smooths her thumb over the glass. 'She's having a whale of a time over there. Look.' She shows me her daughter's picture, in South Africa. 'She's really taken to it. I think it's the climate.' Margaret smiles and for a fleeting moment I see the resemblance with her daughter. My throat constricts. 'That's her latest fellow: Jack, I think. Or is it James?' She cocks her head. 'It won't last, of course; they never do.' She laughs. 'She's always got them queuing up.'

Margaret gazes at the photo and in that look I recognise the fulcrum of her campaigns: a mother's love that burns so fiercely, anything that obstructs it – drug companies, lawyers, even reason – is incinerated.

'Yes.' I clear my throat. 'Yes, I imagine so. A good-looking girl like that. She must have the pick of the crop.'

Margaret's eyes remain fixed on the photo. I stretch out my hand to touch her but, at the last moment, I pull it away.

'I'm sorry to have bothered you.' I stagger to the door, desperate to get back to my room. I raise my wrist, then I remember. 'Sorry, Margaret. Would you mind?'

She peers round, surprised, as if she's forgotten I'm here. She lifts her arm and the door opens. Before it closes, I catch a last glimpse of her, photo frame in hand. Still smiling.

I shove my frame along the carpet, dragging my heels behind. Tears roll down my face, unstoppable. Like Pandora, she has unlocked them. Those memories I have kept buried for so long.

And now they're coming for me.

Flying up out of the depths.

CHAPTER 26

Twenty-six years pre-Crisis

MARY

'Oh, one last thing—'

'Quick, Piet. I'm nearly out of credit.' A fawn dog with floppy ears sniffs my bag for food then trots off to the next phone kiosk.

There's a suck of air. 'I've made arrangements. For Friday.'

I loop the silver cord tight around my fingers. I imagine his mouth against the handset. His breath vibrating along the wires, all the way to me.

'You mean—?'

'In the morning. I don't have to leave.'

My thumbnail grates over the metal ridges of the cord.

'Did you hear me, Mary?' The display panel flashes zeros. 'I said I can st—'

I clasp the phone to my chest. Squeeze it tight. And breathe.

■ ■ ■

He always leaves early, just as the first streaks of gold colour the sky. That's when the guilt comes knocking. But not tonight.

Tonight, when the heat fades a little, we'll take a stroll down to the waterhole and see what comes to drink. We'll tumble into that rickety old bed and stay there until the hornbills chatter us awake.

We won't get dressed, won't go anywhere.

Tonight, he is all mine.

■ ■ ■

'I have something for you,' he says, the grease shining on his lips. The last couple of *sosaties* sizzle on the fire. Somewhere close by a hyena calls, its lonesome notes rising and falling. He delves into his pack and pulls out a small white box.

I raise an eyebrow, try to smother my delight. 'Didn't we just do my birthday?'

Fire-shadows jump over his face, accentuating the whites of his eyes. My heart is thumping.

It feels like Christmas at Grandma's.

Like I'm four years old and I'm opening my very first present.

Inside the box is a purple velvet pouch. I tug the cord loose and a golden bracelet tips into my palm.

'It's not one of your fancy Western designers,' he says, watching me. 'But it's hand-crafted and each piece is unique.'

I twist it round in my fingers. Spirals of foliage clamber across the gold; each leaf and petal has been meticulously engraved. 'Those were my idea,' he adds, almost bashful. 'Indigenous species only, of course.'

I slip it over my wrist; the cool metal slides against my skin. 'I love it,' I say, eyes stinging. 'It's the most thoughtful gift I've ever had.'

I load the track on my Walkman and we dance barefoot beneath the mopane tree, our headphones connected, as the fire fizzes and spits. When the song ends we keep turning together, in slow circles. Amidst the chorus of crickets and frogs come other cries. The wail of a jackal. The screech of an eagle owl. The whoop of a hyena as it rallies its clan.

The wind picks up, spraying us with dust, and we run inside. We pull off our clothes, laughing at the dirt that falls from our hair. As we move together, the bed creaks and the bushwillows rattle outside. Piet's back arches against my fingers as I probe his neck with my tongue, the charcoal taste of him in my mouth. I lower my hand, circling the vertebrae at the base of his spine. His breathing slows, deepens. The radio crackles; faint voices cut in and out, brusque clips of Afrikaans. I slip my hand into the hollow under his ribs. His caresses become more urgent, pulling me closer, kneading my skin. The receiver splutters: a fuzz of static in the wind. My fingers stretch across his stomach, as light as a butterfly's tongue.

Piet, *is jy daar*?

He freezes. I feel the ebb and flow of breath against my cheek.

Piet?

He pulls away from me and lifts himself up on one elbow. My heart plunges.

He leans across and switches the radio off.

■ ■ ■

The first thing I hear is the hammering on the door. It steals into my dream: the two of us, caught in a cyclone, trees slamming against the hut as we're tossed around like corks. Then comes the shout:

'Piet? Piet, man! Open the bladdy door!'

I open my eyes. Piet sits bolt upright. It sounds like Dani:

one of the rangers he trained with. Piet leaps out of bed and grabs his shorts, stepping into them as he runs. I just manage to get my shirt on before the door hurls open.

Dirt spirals across the floor. '*Ag*, man, where you been?' cries Dani, his eyes screwed tight. 'I've been trying to reach you. Why didn't you pick up?'

I give my jeans a desperate yank. There's a raw thump in the pit of my stomach.

'Sorry, I … I didn't hear…' Piet's voice trails off as Dani brushes past him and stops.

Dani glares at me. '*Yussus*.' He twists his lips as if he's about to spit.

This is the threat that has lurked behind every touch, every kiss. Ready to fall on our love like a guillotine.

Dani makes a noise like a growl. '*Soos die vader, so die seun*.'

Piet balls his hands into fists. The colour rises from the base of his neck all the way up to his cheeks. And I work it out: like father, like son.

'What's happened?' His voice is like sandpaper. Dani doesn't answer. 'For Christ's sake, man, just spit it out!'

Dani's gaze lingers on me a moment longer before he turns to Piet. '*Fokken stropers*. They got one: a female. Could be more. Bastards started a fire, down by the western perimeter. We thought it was more refugees.' Dani shakes his head. 'I sent everyone down there. Left them free rein in the rest of the park.'

Stropers, Afrikaans for poachers. Piet's told me all about them, how more and more are crossing the border. With rhino horn worth as much as gold and Mozambique still in the grip of a bloody civil war, it doesn't matter what defences the parks put in, how closely the game guards patrol their sections. Desperate people will risk everything.

Piet snatches the radio off the table.

'The dogs have picked up the trail,' says Dani. 'I hope the hounds have a bloody good go at them first.'

'What about the rhino?' asks Piet. 'Is she still alive?'

'For now. But it's not looking good.' Dani heaves a sigh. 'She's down on her side, in a gully. She took two darts, we can't move her.' Dani's face stiffens. 'They made a fucking mess of it, Piet.'

Piet strides to the cupboard and pulls out his rifle. Cold flutters of panic race round my belly. I try to catch his eye but I can feel it already, like a wall coming down.

'And now this bloody wind keeps changing,' continues Dani. 'They've set a backburn but the flames are jumping right over it. It's already crossed two firebreaks. We need all the beaters we can get.'

Piet grabs his jacket and the two of them march to the door.

'I can help.' I try to keep the desperation out of my voice.

Piet doesn't look at me, just shakes his head. 'It's too danger—'

'Please, Dani.' Dani looks round. I steel every part of me to meet his gaze. 'Let me come.'

Dani shrugs his shoulders. His lip curls. 'If you think you can make yourself useful.'

I tug on my boots and run after them. The jeep's headlights cast two tunnels of light into the scrub. Spiky clusters of leaves and thorns tumble past my ankles; the wind's high-pitched whine sounds like hunted prey. I cup my hands over my eyes. Through the swirls of dust, I see Piet, locked in conversation with Dani, his hands slicing the air. As I approach, the two men swing into the front and Dani fires up the engine.

We tear through the bush, bouncing over ridges, snapping branches on both sides. I see Piet's profile in silhouette: his jaw is rigid, the anger pulsing off him. He doesn't look round. A speckled bird darts in front of the jeep. It swoops left and right, blinded by the glare, its frenzied wings a blur of motion. Normally Dani would slow down, flick the lights off and on, but not tonight. The small, feathered body smacks into the bumper and bounces off.

'Where did they get in?' Piet has to shout over the engine's roar.

'Not sure yet,' says Dani. 'But they won't get back over the border tonight.'

The jeep twists round another corner and I duck down as more debris flies past. As I clutch the back of Piet's seat my fingers brush his shoulder. He flinches. Just minutes ago I was lying in his arms. I want to scream at him, beat my fists against his back. Anything, to make him look.

The radio sparks. Dani clamps it to one ear. All I can make out are muffled crackles.

'They found a hole in the fence,' he shouts, gripping the steering wheel tight in one hand. 'About forty kilometres north. Looks like they made it out of the park.'

Piet swears and Dani presses his foot down harder. The jeep pitches and rocks until eventually it skids to a stop by a huge termite mound. Two vehicles are already there: one is a park truck, the other doesn't have any markings and looks military. Dani radios ahead to warn them we're coming.

'Only a few minutes,' he says to Piet. 'We're needed elsewhere.' I follow his gaze and am shocked to see a flickering orange tear across the horizon that seems to grow by the second. Even from this distance I can smell it: the acrid stench of torched vegetation. I glance at Piet and see the flames reflected in his eyes.

'Slowly now, no sudden movements,' says Dani. 'She's still heavily sedated, but we don't want to cause her any more trauma.'

As we approach the gully, I see two men bent over a huge grey hulk. It looks more like a carcass. The rhino's head is stained black with blood; a continual stream bubbles out of the gashes in her face where her horns used to be.

'Jesus.' Piet's voice is a whisper.

'They used a *panga*. Cut right into her sinuses,' says one of the men, a ranger. 'She's struggling to breathe.' The guard beside him gently wipes her mouth. 'The vet's on his way, but I don't know how long she'll last.'

There's a pitiful gurgling noise as the rhino tries to take a breath. The bile rises to my throat. I swallow. 'What's a *panga*?'

It's the ranger who answers. 'African knife. Bit like a machete. Not a precise instrument.'

Dani's eyes gleam at me. 'Every gram of horn counts. So they slash as close to the base as possible.'

I've heard the horror stories, but nothing has prepared me for this: a living animal with half its face gouged out. Suffocating in its own blood.

'They must have given her a huge dose,' says Piet as he lowers himself down. 'How far off is the vet? D'you reckon he's got enough antidote?'

'I don't know. At least an hour.' The ranger sighs. 'But if we don't get her up soon, it'll start affecting her circulation. There's a risk she could end up being crushed by her own bodyweight.'

Piet drops to his knees beside her. 'What about this wound? Have you put anything on it?'

The ranger shakes his head. 'I've cleaned it up as best I can, but we need to seal it. She's losing a lot of blood. I need antibiotics, proper dressings. Deep cuts like this turn septic fast.'

'How about a temporary barrier?' Piet nods at the guard. 'Isn't there a local infusion we can use?'

The ranger speaks quickly to the guard in Zulu. The guard says something, nods and picks up his rifle. He scrambles out of the gully and marches off into the dark.

'About two kilometres west of here, there's a sandy area where a creeper grows,' says the ranger. 'He says they use the pulp from its leaves to treat skin infections.' His gaze returns to the rhino. 'I've no idea if it'll work on her. But it's worth a try.'

'What's it called?' I say. All three men turn to me and my cheeks burn. I catch Piet's eye for a second. He immediately looks away.

The ranger frowns. '*Ikhambi-ekhohlisayo*. I'm not familiar with its English name.'

An unearthly roar blasts from Dani's radio. It sounds like a jet engine flying directly overhead. He listens intently, trying to decipher words amidst all the snarls and snaps. I can taste the smoke in the back of my throat. The fire has ripped open the sky: no more stars tonight. I wonder how many creatures have already perished in its jaws.

Dani looks at Piet. 'We have to go.'

Piet strokes the animal's back, as gentle as a lover, and climbs out of the gully.

'Good luck,' he says to the ranger. 'I really hope she makes it.' He keeps his eyes fixed on the rhino. 'You should stay.'

It takes me a second to realise it's me Piet's speaking to. My heart thuds. 'Piet, please. I can help.' I rub the bracelet on my wrist like a talisman, as if it can transport us back to the tender world of constellations and kisses, back before any of this happened.

'It's too dangerous.'

I turn to Dani, my breath erupting in tight little bursts. 'You said you needed more beaters.' His eyes narrow. He doesn't answer.

Finally, Piet looks at me. 'I'm sorry, Mary. It's decided.' His eyes are black coals in the darkness. 'You're better off here.'

It's as if he's just gouged a hole in my body. As though my organs are spilling out onto the red earth and seeping down to the molten core below.

I don't hear from Piet for another three weeks. Not that I need to.

That one look tells me it's over.

CHAPTER 27

LOOK. THINK. TELL.

Have you, or a relative, been offered illegal medication?
Have you noticed any odd behaviour where you live or work?
Do you think your medi-profile might have been hacked?

Drug resistance is only a few mutations away.
If you see ANYTHING suspicious, report it immediately.
Be vigilant. Trust your instincts. Our lives depend on it.

COUNTER INFECTION POLICING.

KATE

'Hi, Mrs Connelly. It's Harry.' His breath gushes down the phone. 'I've got news.' I stiffen. 'It's been a toughie. In fact, one of my toughest. But, as my boss always says, "persistence pays off".'

My pulse goes into overdrive: all gallops and hops, like a child learning to skip.

'We've found her.'

I reach for some words, but they've abandoned me. I grind my nail into the counter and stare at the canvas print of the four of us. Our last holiday with Pen, although we didn't know it. Bright smiles and blue sky, hair blowing wild around our heads.

'Mrs Connelly, are you there?'

'Yes, sorry, I...' I lick my lips. 'Are you certain?'

'One hundred percent. We've tracked down the deed poll.'

Fear scuttles round my belly. I should be jubilant.

'I can tell you, your average person doesn't cover their tracks like that. But then, she wasn't your average person, was she?'

My eyes are still glued to the print. But instead of my family, it's her face I see. Her smile.

'Congratulations, Harry. I know how much work you've put in.' It sounds lame, even to me. And another thought hits: what the hell am I going to tell Sasha?

Harry sweeps on, undeterred. 'So, are you ready?' I close my eyes. I'm about as far from ready as it's possible to be. 'Your birth mother changed her name to Lily Taylor. Turns out Lily was her grandmother's middle name.'

Lily.

Lily Taylor.

If I say it enough times, it might begin to seem real.

'I used to have a great aunt Lily,' Harry continues. 'Sweet old lady. Until she got Alzheimer's.'

Mary Sommers. Lily Taylor. They're just names.

'I've got all the documents; I'll send them over now. Have a look through, and then we can chat about next steps.'

Next steps? Jesus.

'I've traced her to a residential home. Some really high-end joint.'

'What?' It's as if Harry's just pushed me out of my front door and slammed it.

'Don't worry, those places don't take just anyone. She'll be getting top-notch care. Not like the fleapits most of us are destined for.'

'But I...' The words lodge in my throat. 'I didn't realise you had an address already...'

'Oh, yeah. Piece of cake now we've got the name. Actually, it's not that far from you—'

'Harry, I'll call you straight back.'

I press both hands against the wood and breathe. I remember having the same feeling when I discovered I was pregnant. I'd wanted a baby so much, for so long. But, after my initial elation, all the dangers that I'd so convincingly played down reared their ugly heads.

I can kill it right here, if I want to.

I gaze out of the window. An enormous bumblebee crawls out of a purple allium, black legs furred with pollen. Its ponderous body lurches from one sagging flower to the next.

I thought I wanted it, I really did. But now I realise that, deep down, part of me never believed we'd find her.

I remember what the South African in the dispensary told me. He'd actually worked in one of those hospitals they used. When he saw the data in Brotanol's pharmacy file, he tried to object. He couldn't understand how those trials had ever been approved.

I stare at Pen's face, at the laughter lines mapping out from her eyes, and my whole body aches.

You should look...

Did you have any idea what you were starting, Pen?

If you were here, what would you say to me now?

Stick to the facts. Remember why you started this.
Why it's important to carry on.

I drag my eyes away, take a deep breath and pick up the phone.

'Sorry about that, Harry. Someone at the door. You were saying … my mother's in a care home.'

'That's right, Mrs Connelly. Osteoarthritis. I suppose in your line of work you come across it quite a lot.' He coughs. 'Other than that, though, for a lady her age, she's in pretty good shape, according to her profile. No signs of dementia. No cancer or UTIs. None of the usual suspects.'

I wonder what qualify as the usual suspects in Harry's mind.

'If you like, we could send her a mess—'

'No.' I swallow. 'What I mean is, I'd like to think about it.' Ridiculous, really. I've been thinking about nothing else for weeks.

There's a slight hesitation. 'Of course. No rush, no rush,' he says, amenable as ever. 'Just let us know when you're ready.' They must be used to people baulking at the finishing line. 'Or, if you prefer, we can organise an intermediary. To, you know, facilitate things.'

'An intermediary?' That sounds even more formidable. Like some kind of peace treaty negotiation.

'Some families use them. Particularly when circumstances aren't so…' I brace myself for Harry's choice of word. 'Straightforward.'

'Hmm. I'll give it some thought,' I say, trying to rally some enthusiasm. 'Thanks again, Harry. You did a great job.'

I lean back and massage my temples. My head feels as if it's been submerged in a pressure chamber and come up too fast.

I glance at the clock. One hour before Sasha's home.

As I pad into the study, a curious calm settles over me. But when I open my laptop, I see my hand is shaking. Harry's email is already there, loaded with attachments: medical records, deed poll, details about the residential home. God only knows how he got them. I smooth my hair back behind my ears and open a new document. My fingers hover over the keys.

It feels like vertigo. Like my first sponsored abseil. Hands gripping rope, toes clamped to the edge. About to step off.

Honi soit qui mal y pense...

If I'm going to do this, then I'm going to do it myself. The old-fashioned way.

Dear Lily,

Too informal? I press delete. The cursor flashes.

Dear Ms Taylor,

No. That won't do either.

Dear Mother,

Just typing the letters makes my fingers tingle.

Well, that'll certainly get her attention.

Then again, it could frighten her off for good.

CHAPTER 28

Twenty-six years pre-Crisis

MARY

I look at his face, and it still burns, this unbearable longing. I'm frightened to say it, but I must.

'Piet. I'm pregnant.'

There's a huff of breath, as if I've just slugged him. His eyes pinch shut.

I stared at that little white square while the toilet dripped behind me, the stench of bleach making me want to gag. I counted the seconds in my head as my lips murmured a prayer. But no prayer could stop those two red lines from materialising.

He swallows. 'I thought you were on the pill.' Each word spits out, staccato.

'I was.' My voice is thin and reedy; I'm trying so hard not to cry. I tell myself that everything will be OK. That somehow, I'll get through this. But I am two months pregnant. And completely alone.

'Maybe it was that time I got sick. Remember?' I touch his arm.

He snatches it away as if I am contaminated. 'Don't.'

The words roar out before I can stop them. 'You never minded before.'

I hate how I sound. I'm not one of those women, all bitter and needy.

'Look,' I say. 'It's not my fault. I didn't plan for this to happen. Please, Piet. I don't know what to do.'

Piet scrapes his fingers through his hair. He can't even bring himself to look at me. I wonder if things might have been different. Or whether he would always have left me, and I was just too stupid to see.

'OK, OK. Sorry. Let's think about this.' His legs start to jiggle, as if they're itching to run. I want to press my hands on them, make them still.

All of a sudden they stop. His tongue slides over his teeth. 'I can put you in touch with someone,' he says, softly. 'Someone discreet.'

It feels like an icy draft, blowing through me. 'What do you mean?'

His beautiful blue eyes turn to me. There's fire there, but it's not passion. 'Don't play games, Mary. Come on. You know you'll have to get rid of it.'

■ ■ ■

I am standing at a metal gate flanked by two white pillars. An ornate trellised veranda nestles behind a cluster of palms, just visible above the security wall. The grounds are clearly extensive. This house was built with old money. For the 'right' kind of people. This house says: *we have what you want.*

I sense movement at one of the upstairs windows. Black shutters have been pinned back either side, like dead butterflies' wings. I see a girl peering out; she has dark-blonde pigtails and is wearing a red spotted dress with puffed sleeves. For some reason I lift my arm and wave. She doesn't wave back. Just stands there, still, like a photograph. Her head swivels round as a woman appears behind her, with a tight face and short brown hair.

My hand moves over my belly. I turn and walk away.

I have come to Piet's house, to see the lives he favours over this one. The family he's so desperate to protect.

So when it comes to it, I do not waver.

He killed our love. He will not kill our child.

CHAPTER 29

LILY

'There we are, Mrs Taylor. All finished.'

Hailey wraps a fluffy white robe around my shoulders and helps me off the table. 'You sit down there,' she says. 'You've earned a rest.'

She's given my joints the full workout; every part of me is throbbing or on fire. But there's magic in those hands of hers. And it's nice to be touched.

'You did well this morning,' she says, as if I've actually achieved something. 'I should think you're feeling a bit tired.'

I'm exhausted. But that's not the physio. Even if I do manage to drop off at night, I keep starting awake. I'm convinced someone's there, in the room. Like a child, I've taken to keeping a light on.

Hailey squirts the table with disinfectant and gives it a vigorous wipe. As she busies herself dispatching my germs, my eyelids begin to droop. Vivid patterns spiral behind my eyes. It feels safe in this room, in Hailey's capable hands, with her soothing music and exotic oils. No one will come for me here.

'Same time next week, Mrs Taylor?'

Her way of moving me along. I pretend I'm asleep. Through the slits of my eyes I watch her scrubbing her fingers, removing any parts of me that might have seeped in through the gloves.

'Oh, bless! You're dropping off.' She blots her hands on a paper towel. The snap of the bin jolts me back.

'Shall we get you back to your room?'

I do not answer but she helps me up anyway and manoeuvres me into the wheelchair. They're fond of rhetorical questions, the staff here.

Hailey opens the door and a blast of cold air hits my face. As she wheels me down the corridor my eyes move over the walls, darting from one flowery print to the next. I've taken to doing this, scanning each room repeatedly, though what exactly I'm looking for, I'm not sure.

Hailey transfers me into my chair and tucks a blanket over my knees. 'There we are: nice and comfy.' They're fond of first-person plural pronouns, too. 'Warm enough?'

'Yes, thank you.'

'Now, don't forget your exercises, will you? Keep those joints nice and active. I'll see you next week.'

Let's hope so. The door swings shut behind her. I resume my search of the bedroom. I check the windows, my dressing table, the credenza. All seem to be in order. And then I see it. Leaning against the clock on my bedside table. An envelope, written by hand. My heart thuds. It takes three attempts to lever myself up. I shuffle closer.

Mrs Lily Taylor
Liscombe House

Oxford postmark. Neat, disciplined letters.

The thumping in my chest accelerates. It's only a few days until my birthday, but still ... I scan the bushes outside. They might be there, in the garden, watching. Seeing how I react.

Come on, Lily. Just open the damned thing.

I grasp the envelope: it's light – too light for a card. I tug at the corner and slip one finger underneath.

It rips.

Inside is one sheet of paper, typed. I read the first two words. Everything goes black.

■ ■ ■

Nearly fifty years and the grief still burns, sears right to the bone.

Dear Mother

So many memories. Like paper cuts. Cradling her against me, her tiny body all red and wizened from my womb. Eyes dark as coal, blinking back their first light. Golden hair slicked to her scalp with blood and vernix, those delicate fingers reaching out to the world, conducting an orchestra I cannot see.

You'll have to get rid of it.

The anger has dulled with the years. The love for him, gone, congealed into something hard and raw. But not for her. Even now, it still blazes. I was a fool to believe it could ever fade.

She was still in my arms when the nurse told me to get her ready. Because the lady from the agency had arrived. I lifted her up, breathed in her sweet, sweet fragrance, still amazed that something so pure could ever have come from me. I remember uncurling each tiny pink finger, which gripped mine as if her life depended on it. I could still feel the weight of her in my arms after she'd gone. Then came those long, dark days, when the milk swelled in my breasts until they hurt, as if my body was punishing me for what I'd done. I remember pumping it into cold plastic bottles. Sobbing as I tipped it down the sink.

I shuffle my frame over to the wardrobe, bend my head into my clothes and grope around for the box. I balance it on the metal bar, catching my breath, and stagger back to the dressing table. I ease the key into the lock.

It finds me straight away, as if it knows. A small brown packet. I lift the flap and give it a shake.

A lock of the finest baby-blonde hair floats into my palm. The room dissolves in a blur.

'Lily, what is it? Whatever's the matter?'

My hand curls shut. Anne is staring at me, aghast. I slip Kate's letter into my pocket.

'I ... it's nothing.' I cuff my eyes.

'Here, let me get you a tissue.' Anne dives into the bathroom. I feel the itch of hair in my palm and clench my fist tighter. Anne hunkers down beside me and hands me a wad of tissues. 'Oh, Lily. Would it help to talk about it?'

I stare at her broad, kind face and it pulls at me, the temptation to tell. About the letter. About Kate. About everything I've done. These lies, they have a weight to them, that doesn't diminish with time. I imagine opening my mouth and letting the truth fly out, like an exotic caged bird.

Anne pats my arm. 'I'm always here for you. You do know that, don't you?'

Her kindness melts me. She has been good to me, Anne. But this isn't just my decision to make.

I take a breath. 'I do. And I'm grateful.' I sigh. 'It's ... I had a letter. About an old friend. She passed away. Her daughter wrote to let me know.'

'Oh, dear. I'm so sorry. Were you close?'

I have to look away. 'At one time, yes. Although we hadn't seen each other in a long while.' I swallow. 'If you don't mind, I ... I think I just need to be alone for a bit.'

She scans my face, brows pinched together. 'Of course.' She

sucks in her lips. 'Can I get you anything? Cup of tea? Water?' I shake my head. 'Well, just ring if you want anything, won't you? Anything at all.' She gives my arm one final squeeze.

I wait until the door has shut and open my hand. I lift the hair to my cheek. It's still so soft. As soft as the day it was cut.

I stole a pair of surgical scissors from the storage cupboard. I had to wait for hours: we were hardly ever alone. I think that was the policy for mothers like me, in case we changed our minds and made a run for it. I gripped those scissors, terrified to open the blades, in case she suddenly twisted her head. In the end I put her on my breast and let her suckle until her eyes rolled back in sleep. I stroked her hair, soft as silk, watching her eyelids flutter. Then I quickly snipped a twist of hair from the back.

I told the social workers that I couldn't cope with being a single mother; that I had a career to consider. I was depressed. All that was true. I'd sworn I'd be a better mother than my own. But the childhood I'd always dreamed of was out of reach for my daughter, too. Every time I thought about keeping her, I'd remember what I'd lost. To get beyond Piet, I had to let her go, too. Even then, I couldn't escape him. The Crisis pushed us back together. Life's funny like that. It has a way of punishing you for your bad decisions.

I take out Kate's letter and re-read the words of my child. I had never dared to let myself hope. But behind the hope lies fear. I shouldn't rush into this, like some hapless lover. I must consider the risks, not just to me, but to her. She is safe and happy, she has a family of her own. I made a promise that I wouldn't interfere. That I would let her live her own life, innocent of the past. I cut all ties, even though it was like losing her all over again. She says she knows about me, about my work. But she doesn't know everything.

I glance at my calendar. On today's date the number nine is scrawled in black felt-tip pen. I stroke the golden strands of hair and ease them back into the envelope. I fold the flap and press it to my lips.

Outside, the wind is stirring up the branches. I watch the sparrows dart back and forth amongst the leaves. And I wonder if hearts are like bones: they can mend if they break.

But the mending gets harder, and the breaking much easier, with age.

CHAPTER 30

KATE

I stare at the white marble slab. Black letters carved into stone. In the absence of speech my ears fill with other sounds. Aeroplanes. Traffic. The rustle of Sasha's coat. This is the first time she's come. Sasha doesn't do memorials or ceremonies; doesn't do anything, usually, that harks back to the Crisis. Perhaps her being here is some kind of olive branch. These days our rapprochements tend to stem from actions rather than words.

She's been monosyllabic the past couple of days, sequestering herself up in her room. She seemed surprisingly stoic when I told her about Mary, but maybe that was a front. It's either that or her idiot boyfriend has been messing her around again.

In memory of the doctors, nurses and medical staff who worked tirelessly for our country and gave their lives in service during the Crisis.

'They loved not their lives even unto death.'

I remember Pen taking me to the Remembrance Day service when I was much younger than Sasha. I didn't really understand why people were putting paper flowers on a cross, but the posh dress, the clipped conversations all told me it was important. And the silence. Particularly the silence. Trying to stay quiet for one whole minute, while the birds sang and people coughed, desperately afraid that my body would let me down. They all stood the same, those veterans, even the really old ones: shoulders back, feet together, with that sad, distant gaze. Probably the same gaze I have now.

'You OK?' Mark slips his arm into mine.

I feel a wave coming and I swallow it down. Absurd, really. If you can't cry in a place like this, then God knows where. I nod and brush my hand over the stone. Its icy touch sucks the warmth from my fingers.

'So many of them are foreign,' whispers Sasha, squinting at the names. Her hair straggles across her shoulders like the tendrils of some exotic flower.

I take a breath. 'Before the Crisis, lots of doctors and nurses came from overseas to work here. We relied on them. It wasn't like it is now.'

I remember how desperate it got, near the end, even after they'd officially closed the borders. It wasn't just medics. Care workers, undertakers. Coroners and priests. Those poor people had to undergo days of screening for the privilege of working in our death camps.

A pale-lemon butterfly flits over a purple buddleia and settles on the monument, wings twitching. My gaze moves down the polished brass plaque.

The Palace of Auburn Hills
Palau Sant Jordi, Barcelona
The Kombank Arena, Belgrade...

It reads like a tour schedule from the old days. Denim-clad stars hunched over electric guitars, rocking out lyrics to thousands of adoring fans. My eye veers halfway down.

The O2, London...

I see Lucy's face beaming at me, all flushed and sweaty.

Katie, I owe you big time!

This was the moment, the pivotal moment that separated

the before and after. Like 9/11, like London and Manchester, like the stories Pen told me that her mother had told her about the two world wars. Nothing could ever be the same again.

Mark squeezes my arm. 'Do you want to lay the flowers now?'

Flowers? I'd forgotten about the flowers. I'm gripping them so tight I must have throttled the poor things. I kneel on the hard marble; spots of pink pollen spatter the stone. I prop the lilies against the column and tuck the card underneath.

Still missing you, Luce. K. xxx

It was the band's first UK date, fresh from their Asia tour. I scored two seats, right up in the gods: they even came with a vertigo warning. I remember those mad bellows of favourite songs, echoing around the arena like football chants; the breathless lulls in between. All twenty thousand of us, pressed in together. Sucking in the same recycled air.

The first time anyone had an inkling was when the next month's schedule was cancelled. They said 'postponed', although no new dates were forthcoming. The initial Twitter chat suggested the lead singer had succumbed to a niggling chest infection after a punishing few months on tour. He was 'resting up' they said, 'doing fine'. He even posted a picture of himself from his sickbed. I remember thinking how happy he looked in that bright, sunny room.

One week turned into two. The posts said the infection was lingering. Another round of antibiotics commenced. There were rumours of more sinister diagnoses, even other band members falling ill, but the marketing hand of the record label crushed them. No new dates materialised. When it got to four weeks, the tour was officially cancelled. It was around that time that Lucy got ill. Then the news broke. The singer was in an isolation chamber in a high-level infectious disease unit. He had a rare form of TB that wasn't responding to drugs. Two days later, he was dead.

The press went nuclear. Two other band members followed, one fan and then another, until it seemed like every day there was a new case. It would take many more weeks and many more deaths before the world woke up to what was really happening. Before we realised that this was just the start.

A sharp breeze curls into the back of my neck. My eyes protest, sticky with tears, as I hold my own minute's silence. I think of that photo of Bekker, being led up the steps. What is it they say? Evil wears the prettiest face. Three hundred and seventy-five million. That was the official TB count. Some said three times that many died. When the other resistant infections kicked in, the records couldn't keep up. Whatever else my birth mother may have done, at least she helped bring that bastard to justice.

Dear Mother...

I picture her, reading my letter: her eyes widening, the sharp intake of breath. Her hands trembling as she seals it back in its envelope, the bitter residue of shock coating her tongue.

Nearby a blackbird sounds the alarm. I wait another second before pushing myself up. My knees are so stiff that I have to lean on Mark until the blood seeps back into my calves. As I stretch, I see Sasha wandering off across the grass.

'Sasha?'

My daughter either doesn't hear or chooses not to. She scowls at her phone.

'Sasha!'

She peers round. She's got that 'wtf' face on that makes my blood boil.

Mark glances at me. He touches my arm. 'Careful.'

I sigh. 'I'm sick of being careful.'

Sasha ambles back towards us, mobile still clutched in one hand. I turn to Mark and the penny drops. 'It was you,' I say. 'You made her come.'

Mark opens his mouth and closes it.

I fix Sasha with a stare. 'Have you even *looked* at this plaque?'

She stuffs her phone in her pocket. 'Sorry.' It sounds more like an insult than an apology. 'Something just came up.'

I should stop now. Walk away. But I can't.

'You know, Sasha, a lot of the fans were young, like you. Off to see their favourite bands. Or watch a match.' My voice has an edge to it that could cut glass. 'Most of the carriers didn't even know they were infected. After the security report they started calling them *vectors*. I remember having to ask someone what it meant.'

She doesn't say anything. Just frowns, as if it's me that should be apologising, not her.

'We never used to be afraid of coughs. We barely noticed them. That was part of the problem.' My words have distilled themselves into a cold, clinical staccato. 'You see, when someone coughs, jets of air shoot out of their lungs at fifty miles an hour. Those jets can stretch for several feet. And each one contains thousands of microscopic particles.'

Sasha regards me warily. She's heard this voice before.

'Of course, that's nothing compared to sneezes.' Sasha's eyes dart to her dad and back again. 'Forty thousand particles, if I recall. And those boys can blast out at two hundred miles an hour.'

'Kate—'

I shrug him off. 'In TB carriers, each of those particles is packed with bacteria. All looking for a host. Out of sunlight, they can swirl around quite happily for hours.' My fingers illustrate with delicate spirals.

'Kate, please,' Mark tries again. He's too late: it's already barrelling up inside.

'Once they're inhaled, the bacteria travel into the upper respiratory tract, and from there, to the lungs.' I pause. 'That's where they make their home.'

Sasha throws up her hands. 'OK, Mum, OK! I get it!'

'Do you? Do you really?' My cheeks are on fire. 'I appreciate that the world's worst act of terrorism must be an unwelcome distraction from your social life. But was it too much to expect you to show just a *smidgeon* of respect?'

Her lip curls back. 'Jesus! I came, didn't I?'

I give a derisory snort. 'Well, bully for you!'

Sasha shakes her head and stomps off. My voice rises to catch her.

'You know, we had to endure things, really terrible things, to get through this.' I'm jabbing my finger at her now, shrieking, like the worst kind of mother. 'We made sacrifices! Every day. To try and make the world safe again.'

She wheels round with a bitter laugh. 'And whose fault was it that things all went to shit in the first place?' Her eyes bore into me. 'Do you have *any* idea what it's like, growing up in this "safe" world of yours? How fucking suffocating it is? Nothing left to chance, endless checks and scans?' Her pale skin has mottled a deep crimson. 'Remember those stories you told me, about how you and your mates used to jump on a plane and fly off somewhere for the weekend? Or go to some bar to meet guys? I've seen the films: people rolled into bed with complete strangers!' She flaps her hand. 'No body scans. No STD checks. No profile searches.' She glares at me. 'I can't even hug a friend without asking! Wouldn't you say those are sacrifices? How do you think *that* feels?'

It's as if all the air has been pressed out of me. I gaze into her eyes and I see it, I finally see it for what it is: her blasé attitude to all the perils around her, our constant battles over staying safe. She had no choice in any of this. Is it so surprising that she fights against it? It must seem like a golden age, the way things used to be.

I take her wrists and gently uncurl her fingers. Press my skin to hers.

How happy would I have been, growing up in this kind of world?

Perhaps we aren't so different after all.

CHAPTER 31

Fifteen years pre-Crisis

'We stand at the edge of the millennium, facing the spectre of incurable TB.'

WHO Report Estimates 8.4 Million New TB Cases, Exacerbated by HIV Epidemic and Rise of Multidrug-Resistant Strains

The latest global TB report from the World Health Organisation shows a twenty percent increase in TB infections in those countries most affected by HIV, despite efforts to control the disease.

India and China have the greatest number of cases, but Africa is projected to take over from Asia as the region with the highest incidence of TB, responsible for a third of all new cases over the next five years. 'Time is running out,' commented a spokesperson. 'Our surveys show that new, multidrug-resistant strains are proliferating. The worst-affected countries simply don't have the resources to detect or treat this disease effectively.'

■ ■ ■

MARY

A little girl with long fair hair lifts one shoe off the kerb, her hand gripped tightly in her mother's. She skips along the crossing, chattering away, oblivious to her parent's silent preoccupation with her phone. What is she: nine, ten? I study the eagerness in her face, the easy flow of limbs, and my stomach contracts.

Could that be her?

I always get like this around her birthday. One month, two weeks and four days until she turns ten. A whole decade: that's how much of Kate's life I've missed. Would just one gift hurt? One letter? A simple photo of her blowing out her candles or opening her presents? My hunger soars as the day approaches, craving answers to the same questions:

Is she happy? Healthy?

Did I make the right decision?

A horn blasts behind. I pull forward, and my eyes flick up to the mirror. The girl trots along the pavement, her blonde tresses bouncing up and down.

I wonder what they'll get her. A pink Furby with big blue eyes? A Tamagotchi in a purple patterned egg? My chest tightens. Then she can pretend that she has a baby, too.

I accelerate onto the dual carriageway but have to brake as I hit the queue. Oxford traffic: I certainly don't miss that when I'm away. I sigh and turn up the radio.

'...of deaths continues to rise as the Sydney flu epidemic claims more victims, pushing the health service to breaking point. Unofficial reports say the death toll has reached twenty thousand...'

All in all, I'd say the new millennium hasn't got off to the best start. Not only has the Aussie flu been rampaging across the globe, but WHO just flagged multidrug-resistant TB hot zones in all thirty-five countries it surveyed. They now estimate a third of the world's population is infected. As if that wasn't bad enough, in January, a fifty-six-tonne meteorite crashed into

Earth, 257 passengers perished in two separate plane crashes and the last Pyrenean ibex was crushed by a tree.

Just to be clear: none of these events had anything to do with the millennium bug. It still astonishes me how worked up everyone got about a computer glitch that was entirely fixable while the real superbugs were multiplying in our midst. Ten percent of Americans genuinely believed that a Y2K apocalypse was coming. As the clock struck midnight, did any of their dire predictions materialise? OK, so a couple of radiation-monitoring systems went down in Japan, and Russia launched some scud missiles, just for the hell of it, but that was about it. Which just goes to show what $300 billion and a bit of collective focus can achieve. Looks like those millennialist Christians got themselves all tooled up for nothing. If it was tribulation and pestilence they wanted, they should have placed their bets elsewhere. I know my Revelations, my mother made sure of it, and if these microbes keep ploughing through our drug defences, we'll suffer several apocalyptic plagues before they're done.

It takes forty minutes to get round the ring road but eventually I reach the Science Park. I navigate the complex warren of roundabouts and pull into Unit Nine. It's not even eight, and the carpark's already full. I double-park in front of a black BMW and stick a note under its wiper. As I hurry along the raked gravel path I glance at the borders: a striking combination of magenta geraniums and dark-blue salvia. I head left, towards the double doors. The silver towers are blinding in the sun, and I have to cover my eyes.

'Morning, Dr Sommers.' The security guard waves a listless arm towards the barriers.

'Morning, Barry.' I swipe my card. 'Good result, last night?'

I haven't a clue about football, but it pays to keep security on side.

He makes a noise like he's been winded.

'Ah, sorry.' I march past him to the lifts. 'Pretend I never asked.'

Just as the doors are closing, a tanned hand prises them apart. 'Leaving without me again, Mary?' A man steps in with black, curly hair and feline green eyes. He's panting a little; he must have run. A small part of me is pleased.

'Careful, Mike.' I allow a smile. 'Insurance won't cover you if you lose those fingers.' I brace myself for the inevitable question.

'So, what happened to you last night?'

I tuck a strand of hair behind my ear. 'Oh, I bailed … I had a ton of paperwork to get through.'

'Really?' He arches an eyebrow. 'You could at least have said goodbye.'

'Sorry, the bar was rammed … I tried to find you.' We both know I'm lying. 'Was it a good night?'

He holds my gaze and snakes his finger along my throat. 'Not as good as it could have been.'

There's a delicious silence. His lips twitch. Just as I think he might kiss me the lift bounces to a stop.

I shoulder my bag. 'Well. Until the next time.'

'Call me.'

'I will.'

'No.' He shakes his head with a mournful look that almost guilt-trips me. Almost. 'You won't.' The doors slide shut.

I stroll up to the sensor and press my thumb against the screen. There's a click as the lock releases. My nose embraces the familiar tingle: an earthy, astringent odour that most people would find unpleasant. I shrug off my bag and lean against the door. Sunlight floods the lab, illuminating columns of plants trailing from floor to ceiling. On back-lit shelves stand rows of glass bottles and jars, neatly arranged by size. There was a time when I thought I would turn my back on all this. Make a fresh start. Thank God, I came to my senses. I'd lost enough already. I wasn't going to lose my career, too.

I wrestle into my lab coat and pull on goggles and gloves. Seedlings at varying growth stages sprout from tubes, lined up in their racks like soldiers on parade. I select a fleshy, triangular leaf from a plant in an adjacent rack: Carpobrotus edulis. The name comes from the Greek: *karpos*, meaning fruit, and *brotus,* meaning edible; its salty-sweet fruit can be eaten cooked or raw. I roll the leaf between my fingers, as if I'm skinning up, and slice off a tiny section with a razor. Using the tweezers, I place the specimen on a glass slide and add one drop of distilled water. I attach the coverslip and position it under the microscope.

Commonly known as the sour fig, this plant has attracted a lot of attention, and not only in its native South Africa. These leaves are packed with tannins and flavonoids: they're widely used as a remedy. Piet's company, Pharmaplanta, just released results from preclinical HIV-1 trials. My fingers tighten around the focus. Apparently they look very promising. I press my eye to the lens and observe the flat, oblong epidermal cells and the more elongated and spherical mesophyll cells in between. Methanolic extracts of these leaves have, allegedly, inhibited the growth of MRSA, too. My gut twinges. I'll bet Piet's loving it, all those multinationals knocking at his door. But, despite their efforts and investment, they still haven't cracked TB.

I carefully detach a leaf from a different seedling and repeat the procedure. As I slice the section, some of the precious juice oozes down my glove. Carpobrotus falsus, the false fig: the creeper they used on the rhino that fateful night. It's taken me nearly a decade to track it down. Whereas the sour fig spreads like wildfire to the extent that, in some countries, it's considered invasive, its sister plant has a much more limited distribution and is a damn sight harder to grow.

I swap the slides over and adjust the focus. Dazzling, green honeycomb-like structures burst into view, interspersed with tiny air spaces: much more compact than the other leaf's. The varied cell patterns remind me of the scales along a crocodile's back. The pulp from these leaves has been used to treat the wounds of local tribes for generations, and yet hardly anything about this plant has been documented. On my last trip, an elderly grandmother told me the grisly story behind its name. Taken from the Zulu, *ikhambi-ekhohlisayo* means deceptive or false cure. With careful preparation, the leaves are said to cure a range of infections, but the succulent purple fruits are highly toxic. Many children over the years have died, thinking the fruit they ate belonged to its sister plant.

I cut another section and place it on its side underneath a different microscope. As I increase magnification, the stomata become visible: tiny breathing pores in the under-surface of the leaf. They look like eyes, staring back at me. Dotted around them are the bright-green chloroplasts, where photosynthesis takes place. Based on my interviews, and some initial tests, I am hoping this plant could be a contender. I now have over a hundred testimonies that claim drinking the juice from its leaves cured them of TB. The question is, even if these stories are true, can the false fig perform against the latest resistant strains?

TB doesn't announce its presence. Like the best killers, it moves quietly. Catching its victims unawares.

Piet had a point when he lectured me all those years ago. While Aussie flu makes the headlines, a new, lethal strain of TB is silently proliferating, biding its time. Enter the latest challenger: extensively drug-resistant TB. Resistant to the most powerful frontline drugs it's merrily blasting through our second-line defences too, causing even more devastation than previous MDR-TB strains. It's not just TB that's confounding our drug defences either: pan resistance has spread. Respiratory, skin and gut infections. UTIs and STDs. Some strains, like pneumococcus, have developed resistance to new drugs in less than a year. And yet, even though the shelf lives of antibiotics are plummeting, there are still no new classes of drugs in the pipeline. Our arsenal is being depleted. At speed.

So, are the COBRA crisis response meetings in full swing? Are doctors peddling fewer prescriptions? Have farmers stopped pumping healthy animals full of drugs?

The stomata eyes gaze back at me reproachfully. It's like watching a plane crash, in slow motion. Instead of vengeful angels, we have apathy.

Better hope my hunch about these leaves pays off.

CHAPTER 32

LILY

'Oh dear. I thought casserole was one of your favourites?' Natalie regards my plate with something approaching remorse.

'Sorry, I'm not really that hungry. Perhaps it's the heat.'

I feel hollow, all bled out. If they opened me up now there'd be nothing but bones and air. Opposite me, Jean spoons in another mouthful. A line of gravy drips down her chin.

'It's made with real beef, you know: all organic. From certified farms.' Natalie gives me an encouraging smile. 'Not that stuff they grow in the labs.'

I contemplate the glistening chunks of flesh congealing in a sea of gravy. Normally I'd be tucking into seconds. But there is no normal anymore. I dreamt about her again last night. Woke to another wet pillow. All the guilt has returned, all the torturous what-ifs. The thought of actually meeting her consumes me.

'I remember when we used to eat meat every day,' says Jean, still chewing. 'Bangers and mash. Shepherd's pie. Sunday roast.' She nods at me, as if she wants me to join in. 'Those farmers had a lot to answer for.'

My stomach moans, as if in protest. I wonder how many people ended up falling prey to the food they ate. Not exactly a successful business model, killing off your own customers. Quite ironic really. Those poor animals had more antibiotics in their short lives than I'll ever have.

THE WAITING ROOMS **221**

Jean puts down her fork and smears her lips with a napkin. She waits for Natalie to move on and leans closer: 'Do you know what's happened to George?'

The sour meat on her breath mixes with a sickly smell of talcum powder. I wield my own napkin like a shield. 'What do you mean?'

She runs her tongue around her teeth. 'Haven't seen him since yesterday.'

A faint ringing starts in my head, like an alarm that's just been triggered. I sat next to him yesterday, after tea. I scour the grey and white heads in the lunch hall. Most of them are still eating, dentures battling the stringy bits. No one misses a meat lunch unless they're ill or vegetarian. George is no vegetarian.

I scan the room again, my heart skittering. 'Maybe he's got a visitor,' I say. 'Doesn't he have a daughter in Cornwall?'

Jean's mouth puckers. I'm not fooling anyone, least of all myself.

Natalie wheels the trolley over and starts clearing dishes. I signal for her to come closer. 'Where's George?'

She straightens up as if I've said something obscene. Her smile vanishes. She clatters the plates together and stacks them on the trolley.

'Please, Natalie.'

She tips the leftovers into a tub, her gloved fingers blotted with gravy. Just as I think there's no point asking, she bends to my ear: 'I shouldn't be telling you this.' Jean strains towards us, the veins bulging out on her neck. 'But I know you and George were quite close.'

A million electrical impulses fire across my synapses. *Were.* She said *were*. The ringing in my head becomes an intense whine, like the sound of an aircraft engine before take-off.

'It's his leg,' she whispers. 'They don't know for sure, but it looks like cellulitis.'

Cellulitis: NC. I shift in my chair, as relief sours to shame. I liked to sit with George. He wasn't much of a talker but that was fine by me; I took comfort from our quiet companionship. I should have learned by now, surely? Don't get attached. It's a whole lot easier on your own.

Across the table, Jean catches my eye. I shake my head.

'Try not to worry,' says Natalie. 'He's in the San. They're doing everything they can.'

I think of George languishing at the cold mercy of Dr Barrows and tears prick behind my eyes.

Pam thumps a bowl of rice pudding down in front of me. A dollop of jam bloats out from its centre like an angry spot. The cloying smell of milk sparks a memory that takes my breath away. I press my palms against the table and scrape back my chair.

'You OK, Lily?' says Jean, as I scrabble for my walker. I don't trust myself to answer. I clench the bar, let the fire burn through my fingers. Blunt the images with a different kind of pain.

Instead of turning left to Carroll, I head to the activities lounge, torn between the urge to get away from people and the fear of being on my own in my room. The casserole turns in my belly.

'Lily?' Natalie's at the door; I didn't hear her come in. She bustles over and touches my arm. 'I'm so sorry, I wish I hadn't said anything now. I know how upsetting it is, when friends get ill.'

I swallow. 'No, really. I appreciate you telling me. All this secrecy. It only makes it worse.'

Her fawn eyes scurry over my face. 'Please, try not to upset yourself. I know you've been a bit down lately. Anne tells me you had some sad news.'

My heart jolts and then I remember. 'Yes. Yes, I did.' That's the problem with lies, they catch you out. I need to be more careful. I wonder if Anne's told her about the bath incident, too. They probably think it's the start of dementia. Maybe it is. Graham's screened the residents, the staff, even the delivery men. Nothing. He's probably just humouring me and thinks I've made the whole thing up.

Natalie curls her apron around her fingers. 'Is there anything I can do, Lily? I'd like to help.'

Before I can answer, a piercing wail blasts through the room. I clamp my hands over my ears as Natalie yanks out her phone. Her face darkens. She says something but I can't hear her over the alarm. She points to the door and shouts: 'This isn't a drill! You need to get back to your room.'

I wheel into the corridor, panic spiralling in my chest. Residents lurch out of the dining hall with frantic eyes; some still have napkins tucked in their collars. I tell myself it's probably just one of the staff who's tripped the system. But the siren continues to pulse.

'What's going on?' asks a woman with tight grey curls who's grappling with the control on her hearing aid. She blinks at me. 'Is it a fire drill? Should we be assembling outside?' A small part of me wants to laugh.

The shuffling and puffing continue as people press past. I check my watch. Almost three minutes.

Anne rushes up. 'That's it, everyone, nice and orderly. Back to your rooms.' Her voice has that sing-song tone that always gives her away.

Jean spots me and elbows her way through. She hisses in my ear: 'Do you think it's George?'

I picture George staggering out into the bushes, bandages sagging around his weeping legs. 'Perhaps.'

Her eyes sparkle. I manage a stoic smile, put my head down and push on.

I only know of one person who ever made it out of the San. That was before they upped the security. They found her in a matter of minutes, secreted in my little arbour; she didn't even make it past the gates. Maybe she thought she could wait it out, stow away with one of the deliveries. Or sneak out at night, during a change in shift. Not that it would have done her much good. Even back then, residents were all microchipped, like dogs. The only way to get off-grid is by surgically removing it. Which makes me think she wasn't thinking. That it was some unplanned, primordial instinct: fight or flight. Trouble is, by the time you're sent to the San, there's not much fight left.

The carers herd us along as the siren wails. Someone behind mutters something about an alert. My stomach wrenches. It's not someone trying to get out. It's someone trying to get in.

Etiquette vanishes as the more able walkers start shoving past the wheelchairs and the frames. There are squawks of protest as the jostling gathers pace. I try to slide my feet a little quicker.

'Steady now,' Anne calls. 'No need to push.'

They ignore her, as rumours burgeon.

It's the latest convert to EAA.

It's an escaped patient from one of the Waiting Rooms.

It's a pro-lifer, stepping up the campaign.

Or maybe, I think, with a jolt, *it's the shadow in the bathroom.* Sweet Jesus. What if they've come back for me?

I glance at my watch. Seven minutes: that's a record. Pam

bustles past, checking the windows. 'Come on, Lily. Hurry up! This is a lock-down.'

Doors open and close; locks thud across, like silenced bullets. As my door swings shut, I wonder how safe we really are. If someone knew the systems, all this security might work against you. Trap you in with your attacker. In your own room.

I stab the remote. My screen flashes. 'News.'

'ALERT: A seventy-four-year-old man has escaped from Penworth Hospital for the Elderly. Unconfirmed reports suggest he was in quarantine...'

I stand in the middle of the room, unsure what to do. A man dashes past the window in a black uniform and mask, and I freeze. His head swivels towards me and for a terrible moment our eyes meet. But he carries on running.

The siren stops and sounds again: one short blast followed by another. I know that means something, something important, but I can't remember what. I stumble to the window and yank the blinds shut. I stuff my hands over my ears as my blood pounds to the same relentless rhythm. After another two minutes I realise the alarm has stopped.

A silence descends that has a volume all of its own. Echoes of the siren reverberate in my head. I think of the other residents, cowering behind their doors. All those breaths being held. All those dormant infections, awaiting their trigger to wake.

There's a shout outside. A burst of commands and radio static. I glance at the blinds but don't move. I know how this scene plays out, I don't need to see it. The ambulance will already be there, back doors open. Someone will be sedated, strapped down, delivered. Order will be restored, and we will carry on as before.

I don't know how long I stand there, heart drumming against my patch. All I can think of is Kate. That's the trouble with hope. Just when you think you've weaned yourself off it, its devilish little head rears up and sucks you back in.

CHAPTER 33

KATE

Against the background hum of the air-pressure unit, my earpiece relays the staggered sounds of breathing. Behind clear plastic sheets and grey hoses lies a small, white-haired woman, dwarfed by wires and machinery. A pool of sweat is collecting in the hollow at the base of her throat. An image flashes into my mind from that film Pen used to love so much, set in war-torn Egypt. A handsome archaeologist licks the sweat from his lover's suprasternal notch. That's what it's called, that little hollow. My suprasternal notch is overflowing; a continual stream soaks the material under my chin. In fact, my sweat is streaming pretty well everywhere: along my back, between my legs. This bulky yellow suit may save my life, but right now I'm fantasising about shearing it off, sprinting to the antechamber and throwing myself under the shower.

My patient's eyes flutter, and I move closer. She looks so frail, as if she's fading into the bedsheets. I don't remember Pen looking like that, even at the end. Perhaps it's because I saw her the way I knew her to be, without the sickness inside her.

I open the comms port. 'Hello, Mrs Janson, do you remember me? My name is Kate. I'm a nurse. I'm here to look after you.'

There's a tinny echo as my earpiece feeds back my voice. We must look like monsters to them in this get-up. Whether they can hear me or not, I always try to reassure them. She doesn't react; her glazed eyes are fixed on the roof of the tent. I check the monitor. She's reached critical, but these latter stages are so unpredictable; they can last much longer than you think.

The sheet lifts a fraction. Her lips move but no sound comes out. I ask her to repeat it. Her voice is so faint the mic can't pick it up, but we're all taught to lip-read for exactly this reason. I press my face closer. I get it the third time.

'Help me.'

Something inside me sinks. She's on the maximum pain relief I'm allowed to give her. I hate these cases; why don't they sign? For some it's religion. For others it's fear that it might get abused. But for many, it's the pressure of family. Even though they're in agony and there's nothing more to be done, relatives still object. By the time patients end up on a ward like this one, it's too late. Even if they want to, they're no longer deemed capable of changing their minds.

I reach my hand into one of the built-in gloves and stroke her arm. Her skin is an ivory grey. 'Try to sleep,' I say. 'The drugs will help with the pain.'

She squints at me, eyes clouded with fever, and I feel the familiar ache. There's so much death around me. I used to help people live. I wonder if Mary's signed a directive. For all I know, she could be in a hospital like this, fighting for her life.

Mrs Janson clasps my glove. 'Please,' she mouths silently. 'I want it to end.'

My hand stiffens. It still upsets me, when they ask. I trained to be a nurse. I never wanted to play God.

'I'm so sorry,' I whisper, easing out of her grasp. 'I'm doing everything I can.'

Her ashen face crumples, and she turns away.

I look at the poor woman, heaving out each breath. In the

old days, they used to up the morphine. Let patients just slip away. But now everything's monitored, recorded, analysed. No one's allowed to slip anywhere, not unless they've signed. And I remember what that journalist said all those years ago. Before the AD legislation was passed:

'I'm not afraid of being dead. I'm just afraid of what you might have to go through to get there.'

I scan Mrs Janson's records. Seventy-nine. Husband died five years ago. There's a daughter in Scotland, but she elected not to come for a farewell. It's easy to judge, but it's different on the isolation wards. Even if the family do make it, by the time they get here, most patients can't recognise them.

I check the window. Shani's there at the console, watching. But she has four of us to contend with this afternoon. I wait until she's occupied with another chamber, and move to the dispensing unit. I select a vial and collect a fresh bottle of water. After fumbling with the cap, I manage to syringe the contents of the vial in. By the time Shani looks up, the empty vial's in the waste and the water's in the isolator trolley.

'Here you are, Mrs Janson,' I say, wheeling the trolley over to the tent. 'Some lovely cool water.' I say it nice and loud, and push the bottle through the hatch. Mrs Janson doesn't move. I press the switch and the top part of the bed starts to rise. I place my arms into the gloves and step into the half-suit. 'This will make you feel better.'

I grasp the bottle and twist. Even though I've broken the seal, it's not easy: not when you're wearing two sets of gloves. I touch her shoulder. 'It'll help.'

Her eyes swerve past me and gradually focus. I check the console: Shani's got her back to me. 'Small sips,' I say with a slow nod.

The corner of Mrs Janson's mouth twitches. She reaches out a shaky hand. She has to do this, not me. That's the rule I've set myself. She's so weak I'm worried she might drop it. But she takes the bottle and lifts it to her lips.

'That's it,' I say, a fluttering in my chest. 'Gentle now. Just a little at a time.'

I watch her throat contract as she swallows and wonder if anyone ever kissed her there. I hope they did.

It takes a while, but she finishes it. Her head rolls back on the pillow.

'Well done.' I press the button and the bed descends. 'That's it, you rest.'

She mouths two words: *'Thank you,'* her eyes already elsewhere.

I smooth some strands of hair off her forehead and take her hand. 'I'm here with you. Don't be afraid.'

The bottle slips from her fingers. I check the monitor.

When the numbers start to drop I push the water bottle back through the hatch, into the isolator trolley.

I walk round the tent and drop it into hazardous waste.

■ ■ ■

My bag drops to the floor as I slump against the wall. It's all I can do to wrestle out of my coat. Mark's banging pans in the kitchen as if he's taking part in some kind of performance. I wrinkle my nose. Onions. He never shuts that door when he's cooking, no matter how many times I tell him. Right now, though, I couldn't care less.

I wash my hands and stagger to the fridge. Mark looks up, spatula in hand. 'Hi, love.'

'Hi.'

I root out a half-empty bottle of Chardonnay. 'Fancy a glass?'

'Sure.' I fetch the large ones. He eyes me over the pan. 'Tough day?'

'You could say that.' I collapse into a chair.

Mark gives a couple more stirs. 'Well, just make yourself comfy. Your day is about to improve.'

'Oh yeah?' I pour him a glass and slug the rest into mine.

'Firstly, this is an outstanding carbonara.' He dips a spoon in the pan and takes a pantomime slurp. 'Cooked to my very own recipe.'

'What, with extra bacon, you mean?' I lift the glass to my lips. Cold citrus slides across my tongue.

He wags his spoon at me. 'A chef does not reveal his secrets.' He strolls over to the sideboard. 'And secondly, I think you might be interested in this.' He holds an envelope aloft in one hand. The weariness slips off me, like a coat.

I press myself out of the chair. My mouth suddenly feels dry and sticky.

Mark hands me the letter but doesn't quite let go of it. 'Just remember,' he says gently, 'whatever's in there. It doesn't change who you are.'

I stare at the envelope. The address is spidery and lopsided, like the scribbling of a child. Just seeing my name written like that sparks a current. I have no idea whether it's excitement or alarm.

Folded inside are two sheets of good-quality writing paper: the kind Pen used to use. I glance at Mark. He touches my cheek, ever so lightly. I smooth out the pages, resisting the urge to skip to the end. It feels a bit like it did when Janet pulled out my file. Am I to be set adrift once more?

Dear Kate,

Thank you. Thank you so much for writing. I cannot describe how much it means to me. Many years have passed since I held you in my arms. Now, I am an old woman. But I have never forgotten you. You were such a beautiful baby.

I reach for the chair. I feel light, almost giddy. Only now, can I see how heavy it's been. This waiting. This not knowing. I've been carrying it around like a ballast stone for weeks.

'Everything OK?' Mark's voice sounds miles away. I nod but don't lift my eyes from the page.

You must have many questions. About what I did, and why. But the most important thing to understand is that it was not for a lack of love. Giving you up for adoption was one of the hardest decisions I have ever made.

Her words slice me open. Haul out a part of me I didn't even know was there. It's like grieving, for this baby who lost her mother. This baby who was me.

Mark hands me a tissue. As I wipe my eyes I notice the dried black smudges between her words. I think about the paltry records, the request for no contact. Why?

You write that you understand why I changed my name. That you have read about my past. I do not expect you to forgive me. I have done some good things in my life, Kate, and some bad things, things that I regret. You must know that I am far from perfect.

But I did what I thought was best at the time.

All those conversations with Sasha and with Mark. The photos. The countless hours spent trawling articles, as if she were some riddle that could be solved.

You asked about a visit. I would dearly love to see you.

I grab Mark's hand. 'She wants to meet!'

Relief spreads across his face. 'That's great, love. Really great.'

But it is important, for your own safety and mine, that you address me as Lily, not Mary. The other thing I must ask of you is that you do not refer to me as your mother, although I know this must seem strange.

My smile wilts. Can she not face up to what happened, even now? Am I still such an embarrassment?

If, after reading this, you still want to come, I will try to explain. If you do not, I will understand. Just receiving your letter has brought me more happiness than I deserve.

I will wait to hear from you.

With much love, always,

Lily

The papers sail loose from my fingers. I sit back and grind my knuckles into my eyes.

Mark gently takes my hands. 'So?'

I give him a tight smile. My head feels sore, as if I'm coming down with something.

'Take a look.' I hand him the letter.

He shakes his head. 'You really don't have to—'

'I want you to. It's important.' I gaze at his soft, brown eyes, at the cowlick on the top of his forehead and wonder why I needed more.

As he reads, I run over her words again, my hopes rising and falling, buffeted in the storm. She claims she loves me, that she's never forgotten me. She wants a visit.

So why do I feel so let down?

'Wow,' Mark says eventually. He takes a deep breath. 'That was honest.'

'Yeah. That's one word for it.' I flex my palms against the table.

Mark edges closer. 'It seems like she genuinely cares about

you, Kate. I know that last bit must be upsetting. But I suppose with her history and everything … she has to be careful.'

'I guess so.' I sigh. 'She doesn't want me swanning in, blowing her cover.'

The pan simmers away, steam running down the splashback like black tears.

Mark sucks in his lips. 'What exactly do you think she means by "for your own safety and mine"?'

Honi soit qui mal y pense…

My instincts whisper a warning. There's something else. Something she's not saying.

And yet even as I process that thought, another part of my brain is estimating how long it will take for all the visits admin to go through.

'Who knows?' I down my wine and thud the glass on the table. There's a noise like an eggshell cracking; a fracture line appears across the base.

I carve my nail into the cleft until it splinters.

There's absolutely no way I'm stopping now.

CHAPTER 34

Five years pre-Crisis

Government Experts Warn of Tipping Point as Number of Superbugs Spirals

Global actions and investments 'falling way short'

In a report released today, Public Health England (PHE) warned of an impending crisis unless antibiotic resistance is addressed. PHE confirmed that, over the past decade, its labs have identified nineteen resistant superbugs that defy all antibiotic treatment. The report also revealed a worrying trend in the number of cases of multidrug-resistant TB. Until recently, TB was mainly prevalent in Africa and Asia, but the latest figures show the 'white plague' is on its way back in Europe.

Only last week, the director of the National Infection Service launched a scathing attack on the EPA, which approved the spraying of 'last resort' antibiotics in Florida's orange groves: 'Sloppy regulation and poor decision-making can no longer be tolerated,' she said. 'We are facing the most urgent health risk of our time. More than seventy percent of pathogenic bacteria are resistant to most antibiotics on the market, and our last lines of drug defences have been breached. Patients are dying because we can no longer treat them. Do we value oranges more than people?'

MARY

Throngs of dazed, sweaty faces emerge from shop doorways, breath smoking from their mouths. Above them, Christmas trees jut out at precarious angles, bracketed by metal rods. I navigate the bobble-hatted hordes and the slaps from bulging bags as guitars, violins and sleigh bells compete in a festive din. A girl strolls past with a cardboard carton, licking her sugared lips. The burst of caramel makes my mouth water. My eyes swerve to the kerb. Sure enough it's there, like a promise: the honey-roasted nuts stand, steaming trays of sticky-sweet heaven piled behind the glass.

I rummage for my purse and get in line. That's when I notice a convergence on the pavement: an indistinct heap is interrupting the flow. Amidst the rush of legs, slumped against a window, is a body sheathed in a sleeping bag: a man's, I think, refuse sacks on either side. Behind him, fairy lights tinkle over silver and gold baubles, and herds of ghostly reindeer scamper down the glass. His chin has sunk onto his chest, his face obscured by a baseball cap. Raw, gloveless fingers cling to his quilted cocoon. Most people give him a wide berth, averting their feet as well as their eyes. One shopper strays too close and kicks the tin in front of him; it rolls over a scrap of cardboard with words on it that no one reads.

All of a sudden the man jerks and topples forward, as if someone just yanked his strings. He braces his palms against the pavement, his breath steaming out in violent heaves. I reach him just as some blood splatters onto the concrete, glistening under the lights. A woman jumps back and covers her mouth. Some shoppers slow down to stare, their faces twisted in disgust, others studiously ignore him and hurry past.

I march over, squat down and touch his shoulder. 'Hi. My name's Mary.' The man remains hunched, gasping between coughs; his smell triggers a memory: sickness and sweat. I yank out my phone. 'I'm going to get help.'

A ragged blanket moves beside him, and a small, wiry head peeps out. Some kind of terrier. It eyes me warily and nudges the man with his snout. He doesn't respond.

'I'm calling an ambulance. Can you tell me your name?'

The dog nudges him again, more insistent. One quivering hand lifts and clutches its coat. An ashen face peers out from the cap. My chest tightens: he's barely more than a boy.

'Can you understand me?'

His mouth moves but only a wheeze comes out. The dog whines, gazing at him with filmy brown eyes.

'Tomasz.' He explodes in another fit of coughing.

A small crowd has gathered, but no one offers any help. It takes another twenty minutes for the ambulance to arrive. When the paramedics set to work the terrier becomes agitated and one of them asks me to take it. I grope around the bags for a lead, but all I can find is a bit of rope. To my surprise, the dog lets me loop it around its neck.

'Which hospital are you taking him to?' I ask, after they load him in.

'University College.'

'What do you think's wrong?'

The paramedic's eyes narrow. 'You know him, do you?'

I swallow. 'No.' I look at the dog. 'I just want to help.'

The paramedic sighs. 'Where d'you want to start? This is the second time we've picked him up this month.'

I swallow. 'Is it … TB?'

His mouth flattens. 'He was diagnosed weeks ago. But they

can't keep him in hospital for six months, they need the beds.' He shakes his head. 'He needs a dry, warm place to stay, hot meals. Supervised medication. But no shelter will take him, not in that condition. Same as those other poor buggers.' His eyes drift to the blanketed, still bodies huddled beneath spray-frosted windows.

'You come across this a lot, I take it?'

The wrinkles around his eyes deepen. 'It's a major issue on the streets, and it's only getting worse. Especially with the migrants. Even if they're diagnosed and start treatment, most drop out after they're discharged. So they get sick again, we pick them up again and they have to start over.' He rubs his forehead. 'Many are developing resistance to the drugs, and that's a real problem. Not to mention the others they've infected in the meantime.' He glances at me. 'There are no symptoms, not at first. People carry on, not even realising they've got it: going to work, dropping the kids at school.' He shakes his head. 'Talking of which, you should get yourself checked. Better to be safe.'

I follow him round to the back of the ambulance. 'What about you? How are medical staff protected?'

'We're all given the BCG. But that's not much use if it's pulmonary. We should really be wearing masks.'

As the driver turns to shut the doors, Tomasz levers himself up and shouts something. The dog lunges forward, and the rope flies out of my hand. The terrier leaps onto the stretcher; the other paramedic grapples with it, but the dog hunkers down, defying gravity with four paws.

I lean into the back. 'Tomasz, it's OK!' Tomasz lifts his eyes; he looks even frailer under the ambulance's glare: a ghostly white, like the scampering reindeer. 'I'll look after him, don't you worry. Until you come out.'

The dog noses his face. Tomasz burrows his fingers into its ruff and whispers to it. He pats the dog twice and gives it a firm shove. The paramedic catches it and hands the squirming bundle to me. The doors slam shut.

I march to the bus stop, clutching the terrier tight under one arm, in case it makes a dash for it. I don't even know its name. I take a seat by the window, keeping my hand firmly on the rope, and resolve to buy a collar and lead. The dog whines a little, paws up at the window, panting, but eventually it resigns itself to my custody and settles at my feet. It expels a long, deep sigh.

Behind me, someone starts to hack. Instinctively I stiffen. Maybe we should all be wearing masks. So much for progress. Despite the warnings, we've allowed the 'dread disease', as Dickens called it, to flourish. The TB count in this city has doubled over the past decade: London has become the TB capital of Western Europe. Many of those infected, like Tomasz, are homeless or on the breadline. A recent report attributed the increase to poor housing, inadequate ventilation and overcrowding: exactly the same conditions that triggered the Victorian epidemic. Back then there was no vaccination or cure. TB was responsible for a quarter of all deaths in Europe.

As we crawl past Regent's Park my phone buzzes: one new message. I read it and take a sharp breath. The dog opens one eye. I dial her number. It rings five times before she deigns to pick up.

'Ah, Mary. You've seen it, then.'

My irritation spikes. I keep my voice level. '"*Strong South African interest...*" Let me guess...'

'Before you start, I'm really not at liberty to—'

'It's Pharmaplanta, isn't it?' She doesn't say anything and my heart sinks.

'It's just a partnership, Mary.'

'Partnership?' I scoff. 'Didn't you know, Jayne? That's Afrikaans for takeover.'

She sighs. I imagine her drumming the arm of that monstrous, flowery sofa while her effete husband scurries round the AGA baking mince pies.

'OK. I'm only telling you this because we go back a long way.'

I have a fleeting memory of Jayne at Oxford: serious fringe and serious social climber; she short-circuited her twenties and shot straight into middle age.

She clears her throat. 'Carpobrotus falsus. They want access to the data.'

My stomach thuds. That fig certainly lived up to its name. I failed. I tried so hard and still failed: years of work, all come to nothing. The chemical properties we isolated from those leaves did ward off the TB bacilli, even the resistant strains. The trouble was, they warded off a lot of other things too. The agents in the drug were so toxic they caused organ damage. Failure, in some cases. After extensive preclinical tests on mice the trial was abandoned.

'They claim they've got some revolutionary new procedure,' she continues. 'That might neutralise the toxicity. And they're willing to share.' I don't mask a snort. 'You should be pleased, Mary.' Her tongue sharpens. 'A lot of money was invested in that plant. It was your baby, after all.'

My jaw clenches. In the most delicate of movements the dog finds its way onto my lap. I sink my fingers into its fur. 'So what does this make me? The surrogate mother?'

'Don't be dramatic.' She sniffs. 'Think about the possibilities.'

I don't want to think about possibilities. She's opened a page of history I've tried very hard to close.

She changes tack. 'You know how bad things are over there. Eighty percent of South Africans are infected. Over seven hundred thousand new cases a year. And as for the MDR strains ... the estimates are off the scale.'

I don't need telling, I know the stats off by heart. Thank God the majority don't go on to develop the active form of the disease. Even so, TB remains the leading cause of death in South Africa. And now it's back here. Could this be our destiny, too?

'On your head be it,' I say, well aware that the deal's already been done. Before she can think of a snide reply I wish her a merry Christmas and hang up.

The dog snores gently, the heat from its body warming my thighs. Fairy lights blink in silhouetted branches. As the bus inches past queuing traffic, my mind veers to Pharmaplanta. And Piet.

Twenty years. I've worked hard at forgetting. But the scars are still there, albeit faded, like the ones you see on X-rays of TB patients' lungs. And I recall what a radiologist once told me about those X-rays. Assuming the infection isn't active, there are two potential avenues to explore:

Do the scars indicate a past infection that has since been cured?

Or are they an aggressive latent infection that, given the right conditions, might activate at any time?

My fingers curl a little deeper into the dog's fur.

Until I see him, there's no way to be sure.

CHAPTER 35

LILY

'Morning, Lily!'

I keep my eyes screwed shut. I can just see her tiny hands stretching towards me, feel the warmth of her on my breast. I try to hold on to her, but she eludes me, fading with the light.

There's a ripping noise. 'Looks like it's going to be a nice day.'

It's only Natalie, drawing the curtains. I roll over and face the wall. Start counting. Common daisy, English lavender, wood forget-me-not...

'Bad night?' she asks as the bed whines its way upright. I don't answer. I'm consumed by memories: so desperate to see her and so afraid that I won't. What if my pursuer knows about Kate? Is it just coincidence that her letter should arrive now? No one knew, apart from Graham, I made sure of that. I kept my side of the bargain. The question is, did Graham keep his?

Natalie pulls back the covers. 'Here. Let me help.' With some effort we get my legs over the side. 'One, two, three.' She hauls me up. I slot my wrists into the clamps and shuffle to the bathroom.

'We've got a couple of extras this morning,' she says, clinking the bottles. 'On account of your birthday.'

As if I need reminding. Five days until cut-off. I wonder how I'm going to get through them. Since Kate's letter, the hours trudge by even slower, as if they're fearful of moving on. Sunday. She's fixed it for Sunday. I just have to make it till then.

Natalie helps me onto the toilet. 'The good news is, you've had most of your boosters. So it's just the bloods and the flu shot today.' She steps behind the door and waits. 'Let's have a little peek at your EET...'

EET: eyes, ears and teeth. As cut-off approaches they give you the full works, while they still can. From cataracts to cavities, each body part is assessed to ward off likely candidates for infection.

'Eyes all good,' she mutters. 'Ears syringed ... What about the dental review?' She pops her head round. 'No extractions?'

Pre cut-off, the majority of residents have any teeth they've still got removed. Another blessing of age: your mouth, like everything else, starts drying up, so your teeth become even more prone to decay. Most people would prefer not to die from an abscess.

I flash Natalie a wide grin. 'I'm a stickler for oral hygiene. I refuse to hack out the few bits of me left that still function.'

She gives me a wry smile and closes her screen. 'Lily, you're as tough as they come.'

That's where you're wrong, I think. I'm a sitting duck.

Natalie tips the urine into the specimen pot. I wash my hands, drying each finger in turn. She eyes me in the mirror. 'Actually, Lily, there's something I need to tell you.' Her lips tighten. 'I wanted to give you a heads-up. Before the rumour mill kicks in.'

I keep my eyes on my hands.

'It's George.' She pauses and my heart thumps. 'He was doing a little better, but then ... I'm sorry, Lily. There was nothing they could do.'

I blink at her. So. They must have taken him. To the Waiting Rooms.

'Now, please don't upset yourself. The infection advanced so quickly, by the time they came he didn't know a thing about it.' She sighs. 'He'll soon be at peace, God rest his soul.'

I think of George, making that final journey: packaged and processed like a slab of meat. And his daughter, speeding along those Cornish roads, preparing herself for her father's farewell.

'First your friend. Now this.' Natalie sighs. 'Troubles have a way of coming all together, don't they?'

A heavy despair sinks through me. Despite all our vigilance, things still happen. Like George's legs and Vivienne's teacup. And my shadow. No amount of procedures are going to save me from that. I rub the disinfectant gel into my skin and try to think about anything else.

'Do you have children?' The question comes out of nowhere, takes even me by surprise.

Shut up, you fool.

A cloud passes over her face, just for a second. 'Me? No.' She screws the cap on the pot and busies herself with the trolley. 'We wanted them, but you know ... how difficult things became.' She pulls off her gloves and drops them in the bin. 'Especially for women like me.' Her mouth puckers. 'I had PID.'

I feel the blood rush into my cheeks. PID: pelvic inflammatory disease. Often caused by resistant STDs like Chlamydia. 'Oh, I'm sorry,' I stammer. 'I shouldn't have asked.'

'It's OK. I made peace with it a long time ago.'

I fumble for something to say. But I'm caught in that ridiculous tussle between empathy and fear of saying the wrong thing. Chlamydia never used to be considered a big deal: nothing a few tablets couldn't clear up. Once the Crisis hit, all that changed. Resistant to treatment, the infection spread, scarring the uterus and fallopian tubes. Even if women did manage to get pregnant, they were much more likely to miscarry or have stillbirths.

It's Natalie who breaks the silence. 'You're right-handed, aren't you, Lily?' She helps me into the chair.

'Yes.'

She picks up a blue tourniquet. 'In that case, I'll take the bloods from the right arm, and do the flu shot in the left.' She rolls up my sleeve. 'Sometimes it can feel a little sore.'

I watch her face, furrowed in concentration. She tightens the strap around my arm and dabs it with an antiseptic swab. 'I need to take three of them, I'm afraid.' She unwraps the needle and attaches it to the tube. 'Ready?' I nod and look away. I hardly feel the prick.

'How about you?' she says.

'I'm sorry?'

'Children. Do you have any?'

The heat burns in my face. 'No,' I say, like Judas. But it's true. I sacrificed the right to call her daughter. She doesn't belong to me.

'You know, this may sound strange,' Natalie continues, swapping over bottles, 'but in a way I'm glad. Imagine bringing a child into the world back then.' She shakes her head. 'You used to hear some real horror stories. Like our next-door neighbour, Jeanette: lovely girl. Only twenty-five.' She sighs. 'She picked up a vicious RTI. They couldn't do a thing for her.'

I keep my eyes on the tube. RTI: reproductive tract infection. Pre-Crisis, most mothers in the West had never even heard of such a thing. Why would they? Antibiotics saw off any hint of an infection before it took hold. But that was before.

Natalie inhales. 'I remember popping in to take her some

shopping, and there she was, on her knees. Clawing the wall.' Her mouth stiffens. 'They delivered her baby two months early. Poor thing survived but it was totally blind.' She deftly removes the needle. 'Jeanette wasn't so lucky.' She looks away for a second and presses a cotton wool pad over my skin. 'There we are. Just hold that a moment, will you?'

I think of all those women, like Natalie, desperate to conceive. The many others who died during pregnancy or labour. And those poor babies, saddled with infection from the womb.

I gave birth to a perfectly healthy baby who enjoyed all the perks that medicine had to offer.

And I gave her away.

'Whoa, steady on, Lily.' Natalie frowns. 'You're making it bleed.'

I look down. A dark red circle has spread out from the centre of the pad like a flower.

She gives my arm a quick clean and tapes on a plaster. 'Right then, on to the next one. One more jab and we'll be done.' She slips my dressing gown off my shoulder and unwraps another needle. She draws in the vaccine. This time I feel it, just a scrape. 'There we are.' She rubs my skin with a wipe and sticks on a small brown plaster. 'How are you feeling? A bit light-headed? I can fetch you a biscuit, if you like.'

I shake my head. 'I'm fine.'

'Are you sure?'

'Sure.'

She rips off her gloves and drops them in the yellow bin. I think how I can extend our conversation. I feel a need to talk. To do something, anything, to fill this void.

'Natalie?'

'Yes?'

I fiddle with the tie on my dressing gown. 'Did you ever ... consider trying again? You know, after ... after they'd found a cure?'

She squirts more gel onto her fingers. I watch her knead it into her skin. 'We talked about it. Although I was badly scarred. But, in the end, it wasn't to be.' A slight furrow appears on her forehead. 'I lost my husband, you see. Just months before they discovered that new drug.'

'Oh, Natalie. I'm so sorry.' I think again how little we know of people. Even those we see every day. 'Forgive me. I'm really putting my foot in it today.'

'It's OK.' Her mouth twitches. 'He was a furniture restorer. People used to bring him things from all over the county.' She looks down at her hands. 'I always used to nag him about wearing his gloves, but he never did.' I catch the ghost of a smile. 'Said he couldn't feel the wood.'

I sigh. So many tales of loss start this way. Our habits couldn't catch up fast enough with the new reality.

She draws a breath. 'He was working on this antique chair. Beautiful old thing, it was: rosewood, inlaid with mother of pearl.' She swallows. 'He snagged his palm on a nail. It was only a little cut, but...' Her jaw quivers. 'He got MRSA. In three weeks, he was dead.'

Her grief fills the space between us and, like a chain reaction, unlocks something in me. 'I lost someone too,' I blurt.

She nods, as if it's only to be expected. 'Someone close?'

My memories billow up inside. 'We were, once.' Kate has shattered my defences; I'm fearful of what might escape next.

Natalie's voice lowers. 'What took them?'

I swallow. 'TB.'

'Ah.' Her breath comes out in a sigh. 'The white plague.'

My chest tightens. I remember Piet using those words. They called it that because of the anaemia it brought on.

'We all have our stories, don't we?' says Natalie. 'Our share of pain.' She wipes her eyes. 'Goodness, look at us.' She smiles. 'No good crying about the past, is it? Look to the future. That's what I tell myself.'

She's right: we should look to the future. But sometimes the past won't let you go.

She grips the trolley and walks to the door. 'Now, you rest up, Lily. Don't want you keeling over. If that flu jab starts bothering you, I can bring you some paracetamol. Breakfast shouldn't be long.'

As the door shuts, I see an image of the two of us, dancing beneath the mopane tree. How tender he was, then. It changes to the sharp silhouette of his face in the gully. That terrible look. The same look he gave me all those years later.

I solemnly and sincerely declare...

I glare at my lumpy hands. The hands that signed the statement. That took those fruit and cultivated their seeds. I remember the ranger stripping the creeper's leaves, its purple flowers dropping to the ground around his feet like a wreath. Pounding those leaves in a bowl while the poor creature lay there, making that awful gurgling noise. The plant couldn't save her either.

I squeeze my fingers until they burn. Kate doesn't deserve such a mother. I should never have agreed to see her. I've put her in danger too.

I pull out an old, tattered dictionary from the back of my drawer. I press my thumb into the crease, and an envelope sails out onto the carpet. I think of the words I must write, although every inch of my body screams not to.

But as I bend to pick it up, my eyes widen.

The envelope is empty.

Kate's letter has disappeared.

CHAPTER 36

Crisis

Worse To Come, Warns CMO

As the TB death toll tops twenty thousand, the prime minister urges people to obey curfews and remain in their homes.

With increasing numbers of hospitals across the UK being forced to shut their doors, the PM has made a plea for people to remain calm. 'We have some of the best people from industry, academia and the NHS working night and day to find a vaccine and a cure,' he assured reporters yesterday.

But at a press conference, the CMO was less optimistic. 'This is a highly evolved strain. The reality is we're playing catch-up in an arms race that started decades ago and we're barely over the starting line.'

■ ■ ■

MARY

The buzzer punctures the silence. I'm expecting him but my heart still leaps.

Take a breath.

I curl my hair behind my ears. Smooth my skirt. Brace, as if I'm about to launch myself out of a plane.

I open the door.

'Hello, Mary.'

My chest pounds, a pathetic reminder of what used to be.

He takes off his mask and smiles. Reckless: he isn't yet inside.

'You'd better come in.'

His hair's a little thinner than I remember. A few more lines. But still ... skin, lips, fingers. Each part of me has its own memory.

He shrugs off his coat. The room tilts on its axis, shrinks just a little. This is the first time we've been alone together for twenty-five years. But he hasn't come here to sleep with me. He's come because something's wrong.

I concentrate on the wrinkles around his eyes. 'You managed to get through the curfew alright, then.'

He nods. 'Flashed my card. Dropped a couple of names.'

My, how you've gone up in the world, Dr Bekker. WHO Emergency Committee, no less. They only pulled me in because he asked them to.

'Thanks for letting me come, Mary.' He rests one hand on the teak cabinet. His eyes scurry around the room like a restless dog. 'I know it's late.'

I notice the scar on his cheek has faded. Like so many things. A memory ambushes me, and I slam it back.

'Nine bodies, on the way here. Just lying in the street. Two of them looked like they'd been there some time.' His fingers tap the wood as if he is playing the piano: up and down, up and down. 'Why don't they obey the curfew? The army are working shifts but even so...'

'They're desperate, Piet. Can you blame them? It doesn't matter how many alerts are broadcast, how many notices they're sent, they still think if they can make it to a hospital they might stand a chance.'

'If only,' he sighs. 'If the TB doesn't get them then something else will. The crematoriums can't keep up. There's talk of requisitioning more incinerators. But with all the farm stock to get through, they're overrun too.'

Strange, how normal these conversations have become. At least this disaster saves me and Piet from having to contemplate our own.

'You know about the fires, I take it,' I say.

'Which ones?'

'At the detention centres.'

A prominent scientist's tweets about the supposed origins of the pandemic have ignited a racial war. *I'm not a racist*, he wrote, *but it's a fact that the majority of UK immigrants come from high-incidence TB countries such as India, Pakistan, China and Nigeria. Many of them carry a latent form of TB that immigration screening fails to detect. The disease can activate at any time.*

Piet shakes his head. 'As if we don't have enough to worry about. Why do people always need a scapegoat? We're getting it from all sides. Some idiot in the Commons is talking about nationalising the manufacture of antibiotics. For good. As if drug development were as simple as running trains. The industry needs R&D investment and tax incentives, not state ownership. You'd think they'd have learned their lesson from the coal mines.'

I've heard the arguments and I have sympathy with them, even if they aren't practical.

He sighs. 'If they gave it to the NHS, they'd blow what little reserves they have left in under a year.'

I grip the chair. 'Maybe nationalisation isn't the answer. But, as you were always fond of pointing out, putting shareholders' interests over patients' doesn't exactly turn out well.'

He gives me a sharp look. 'Still keeping me in check, I see.' His face relaxes. 'Must be that rebellious streak.' The heat rushes to my cheeks. 'You look well, Mary. How are you? Family keeping safe?'

What family?

The old wound resurfaces: bloodied and raw.

I swallow. 'Why exactly are you here, Piet? I assume it's about the trial.'

He opens his mouth and closes it. 'Yes, and ... no.' His fingers hover, mid-tap. My body tenses. 'The truth is, Mary, I wanted to speak with you. Alone.'

There's a rushing noise. As if I've jumped out of that plane and the air is barrelling past my ears, the ground racing up to crush me.

'We never talk about what happened. I know it was a long time ago, and the whole world's going to hell, but...' His eyes wander up to mine. 'I'm sorry, Mary. For how I behaved. I wasn't ... I didn't handle things well.'

I cannot speak. I'm torn between pressing my hands over his mouth and letting him say the words I've longed to hear.

'I've been thinking about it a lot, lately. I want to settle things between us. Put the past to bed.'

An unfortunate choice of phrase.

He sucks in his lips. 'So we can move on.'

Move on? The anger rolls up through my body like a waking dragon as the age-old recriminations clamour to let rip.

Did you know we had a daughter? That I had to give her away? Did you ever love me or was it always about the sex?

It takes all of my strength to muzzle them; they can't help me now. But I'm damned if I'm going to make it easy for him.

'Tell me about the trial, Piet.' My voice is cold, clinical. There's no absolution to be had here.

'Please, Mary. Can't we at least—?'

'It's not good news, is it? Otherwise you wouldn't have come.'

His eyes burn into me. I recognise that expression. It's the same one he had that night. Things could have been so different.

If the poachers had never come.

If Piet had picked up the radio.

If he had left her for me.

These alternate worlds used to whisper to me, used to beat their wings inside my head. I thought I'd finally managed to dispatch them.

'OK.' He swallows. 'Have it your way.'

My way? It never went my way.

The wall slides back down between us as silence fills the room, like a noxious gas. I move to the window, slowly suffocating.

A convoy of aid trucks rumbles past, sandwiched between two army jeeps. I notice the soldiers have started carrying guns. I wonder how long it will be until the food parcels run out.

'You're right,' he says, eventually. 'About the trial.' He coughs. 'It's not the response we'd predicted.' I grip the windowsill. 'Brotanol did inhibit the growth but ... there were some adverse reactions.'

A bitter taste creeps into my mouth. 'What kind?'

He hesitates. 'Liver and kidney dysfunction.'

I spin round. 'What? But you said they'd reduced toxicity! That the earlier problems had been rectified.'

His eyes flash. 'Drugs react differently in healthy and sick bodies. And the immune systems in this cohort were severely compromised. Most of them, remember, were refugees.'

This cohort ... refugees. Does it help with the guilt, I wonder, if he doesn't call them people?

'How serious is it?'

He takes a deep breath. 'Twelve. Twelve fatalities.'

'Jesus, Piet—'

'If we'd used subjects who were in the earlier stages of the disease, they would have had greater tolerance. Administering antibiotics alongside immunotherapies is a complex process; reactions can vary widely. The dosage parameters must have been off.'

'So you screwed it up, then, is that what you're saying?'

'No, I'm saying we learned a valuable lesson at an unfortunate cost. Another variable might be the level of exposure to different strains. That's something we'll need to test.'

An icy chill washes through me. 'You're going to farm it out again, aren't you?' He doesn't reply. 'Aren't you?'

He looks me straight in the eye. 'The drug can work, Mary, we know it can. We just have to do more studies.' He pauses. 'It's been approved for trials in South Africa.'

And there it is, the unwavering flame of his ambition. Captain Ahab, taking the whole ship down.

'Before you let fly, Mary, hear me out. It'll only be administered to a controlled sample of patients, on compassionate grounds.'

I shake my head. I want to hit him. I want to punch him in the chest as hard as I can.

'We're talking one or two hospitals at most. Informed consent. Entirely voluntary.'

'*Voluntary*? Is that what you told the ethics committee? What option do those patients have? I knew you could be a ruthless bastard, Piet, but I used to think you at least had *some* principles. You can't just ... experiment on people. You have to take it back into the labs.'

He throws his hands in the air. 'We don't have time for that! Every second, dozens more people are infected and we're no closer to a vaccine.'

'This is exploitation, of the most vulnerable! It's against all ethical codes. What did you do? Use your old boys' network to cut some corners? Grease a few palms to push it through?'

His jaw clenches. 'You don't get it, do you?' There's a fire in his voice that used to send me scrabbling for compromise. 'We're at war, Mary! And in war, people have to do things. Things they would never normally do. And we're not just fighting any army, we're fighting a silent army that's evolved to resist anything we throw at it—'

'Don't patronise me, Piet, I know the facts—'

'No, you don't!' He's practically shouting. He checks himself. 'Not all of them. The bacteria are replicating quicker than previous strains. A much higher proportion of people are developing the active form of the disease. You know how transmissible TB is. And with the length of incubation period, well...' He swallows. 'The reproductive number originally varied between four and ten, depending on the country. Now they think in some cities, it's closer to fifteen. That's fifteen new people infected for every one person that gets it.'

Jesus. The same ratio as measles. But a damn sight more deadly.

'This strain is activating TB in carriers where it has lain dormant, and it's reactivating TB in people who've had it before. Which means those two billion carriers out there are sitting ducks.'

As if on cue, I hear a strange whimper outside. On the

pavement, just in front of my flat, a woman is on her knees, rocking slowly back and forth. She throws back her head and howls. That's when I notice the small body lying in her lap. The lacy pink nightdress with blood stains over the bunnies.

He comes up behind me. 'This isn't going to burn itself out, like influenza. This is just the start.' He pauses. 'And now there's intelligence that suggests there may be more to all this than we thought.'

I can't take my eyes off the child. One pale arm hangs loosely over her mother's thigh, palm outstretched, as if she is begging.

Where is our daughter, I wonder? Is she at home, safe with her family? Is she even alive?

Piet pulls me away from the window. 'Are you listening, Mary? There've been reports. At the highest level. Some kind of unholy alliance between man and microbe.'

I stare at him and something shrivels inside. 'Sorry, what? What exactly are you saying?'

'It's quite simple when you think about it. Bacteria are programmed to replicate and survive. They're adept at seeking out new hosts. To accelerate the spread, all someone has to do is ensure that conditions are optimal.'

'Oh, God.' I clutch the back of the chair. I want to pinch myself, and wake up. This is the stuff that happens in books and films, not here, in this sitting room, with John Lewis sofas and Laura Ashley prints.

The blood throbs in my ears. 'Are you saying …? Is some kind of organisation behind this? Is that why it's spreading so fast?'

He nods. 'We expected the disease to thrive on the main transport routes from Africa and Asia, but these other pockets in the West don't make sense. None of the transmission models can explain it. It's not as if there aren't precedents.' He rubs his knuckles into his eyes. 'In the Middle Ages, when the Mongols lay siege to cities, they catapulted the corpses of bubonic plague victims over the walls.'

My stomach roils. 'Who would do such a thing?' I lower my voice. 'Piet: who do they think's responsible?'

He hesitates. 'They're not sure yet.' His gaze shifts to the window. 'Or if they are, they're not telling me. But all it'll take is another couple of mutations and then no amount of isolation chambers or infectious disease units are going to be able to contain this.'

Piet's eyes are blazing, electric. My heart stills. Can it be that part of him is actually enjoying this?

I step away from him. He frowns. 'What is it?'

'You.' My skin pricks. 'You're in your element.'

'Pardon?'

'I'll bet you're loving it, aren't you?'

He screws up his face. 'Sorry, what are you talking about?'

I raise my hands like a preacher. 'Piet Bekker: the wise apostle. The man who predicted this would happen.' My arms drop to my sides. 'You just can't wait to be the man who saves us all.'

He stares at me, bewildered. Like a priest who's just been told that God doesn't exist. 'Don't be absurd. You can't really think that, Mary.'

'Can't I?' Now I've got a reaction I can't stop. 'You've always relished a good crisis. Let's face it, Piet, there's only ever been one true love in your life. And that's Piet Bekker.'

I expect him to defend himself, but he doesn't. As the silence between us grows I think of my mother. Of how like her I have become.

'I should probably go.' He picks up his coat. He looks older.

As if he's aged since he stepped into my flat. He reaches the door and turns. 'Whatever you think of me, consider the facts. Production has to ramp up. You understand the vagaries of that plant better than anyone, and, right now, it's the only weapon we've got.' He touches my arm. 'Please, Mary, I...' His hand falls to his side. 'We need you onside.'

I stare at his fingerprints on the cabinet. Smears in the dust.

Choices, there are always choices.

But sometimes, none of them seems right.

CHAPTER 37

KATE

I tuck in my shirt a little tighter and adjust my skirt. *Stop faffing, girl.* That was one of Pen's favourites. If she could see me now: I'm onto my third outfit and it's only nine o'clock. I've been awake since five. Did she have any inkling where this would lead?

Mark wanders in with a mug of tea. 'You look nice.'

'Nice good, or nice bad?' I smooth my hand over my stomach; it doesn't stop the churning.

He slips his arm around me and nuzzles my neck. 'Definitely nice good.'

'Watch that tea!' I bat him away, laughing. He sits on the bed and takes noisy slurps. I can already sense the words hovering on his lips.

'Why don't you let me drive you?' It's the third time he's offered. 'You hardly slept last night.'

'I'll be fine. It's not exactly far.' I tidy a smudge of eyeliner. 'And if the worst comes to the worst, Sasha can take the wheel. I'll just shut my eyes.'

No one was more surprised than me when Sasha asked if she could come. She still has her reservations, but our little spat at the monument seems to have cleared the air. For now. And Mark didn't object. Even though I know he'd much rather be there himself.

He plucks absently at the duvet. 'You will go easy on her, won't you?'

'Sasha?'

'No! Lily.'

I glance at him in the mirror. 'I thought you were more worried about what *she* had to say, not me.'

He meets my gaze. 'I just want it to go well, that's all. I know you want answers, but I guess it's like any new relationship. You have to ease in gently. It doesn't always click straight away.'

I pencil in the arch of an eyebrow. 'Don't worry, I wasn't planning the Spanish Inquisition.' He smiles. 'I'm steering clear of any drug-related questions. And I'm sure Sasha will intervene if I get carried away.'

'Yeah, that's what worries me.' We both laugh. Mark comes up behind and hugs me, hard. I breathe him in. 'Good luck.' His mouth presses to my ear. 'Remember: you're a brilliant nurse and a wonderful mother.'

I wrap my arms around his. 'You missed out the wife part.' I turn and kiss him gently on the lips. 'I'll be fine.'

I pick my way downstairs, trying not to slip in my heels. Sasha is waiting in the hallway, kitted out in skirt and boots: no ripped jeans or crop tops in sight.

She gives me the once-over. 'Off for an interview?'

'Oh. D'you think it's too—?'

'Joke, Mum!' she trills.

I grip the banister as my nerves take another spin. Maybe I should have let Mark come after all. 'Right. OK, then. Ready?'

'Yup. And you?'

'As I'll ever be.'

As we walk out to the car I give her hand a squeeze. 'Thanks for coming with me, Sasha. You didn't have to.'

'Well, the way I see it, if I've got a notorious criminal for a grannie then I'd better suck up to her from the start.'

I exhale. 'I'll assume that's another joke.'

She smirks. 'After all the shit I've put you through, I figure I owe you.'

I stop and brush my fingers over her cheek. 'Honey, I'm your mother. It doesn't work like that.'

I unlock the car. Sasha swings her long legs into the passenger seat. As we crunch along the drive, I see Mark in the rear-view mirror, waving, and something bittersweet stings inside.

A sense of something passing.

As if our family may never be quite the same again.

■ ■ ■

It's not what I expected.

Manicured hedges line the long driveway, interspersed with ornamental bushes at discreet intervals. The building itself remains hidden until we round the last corner; it rears up in front of us, flanked by majestic beech trees. Wisteria and pink roses clamber across Cotswold stone; rows of windows peer out from underneath. This bears no resemblance to the establishments I've seen. It looks more like a stately home.

'This is a bit smart,' says Sasha, eyes bulging. She elbows me. 'Your mother must be loaded.'

I'm too nervous to play. This reminds me of when Dad and I pulled up at the church, before we went down the aisle. I want to do this, I really do. But I have no idea how things will turn out.

I default to details. 'Make sure you call her Lily, OK? Even if we're alone.' I tug my hair behind my ears. 'The cameras aren't supposed to record the sound. But in these places, you never know.'

Sasha frowns. 'OK, now you're beginning to freak me out. How come you're so calm?'

'Remember, I do calm for a living. You can't see what's going on inside.'

We walk up the path towards the huge oak door. As we get closer, I realise the period look is an illusion. The building is relatively new, no doubt purpose-built: it's been weathered to make it look older. I count three security cameras watching us and exchange glances with Sasha.

I press the buzzer. After a few minutes a short, olive-skinned woman opens the door. 'Hello, can I help you?'

'We're here to see Lily. Lily Taylor.'

A smile breaks out across her face. 'Ah, you must be Kate. Her friend's daughter. It's a pleasure to meet you. So nice for Lily to have visitors. Please, come in.'

As we walk through the vestibule the smell hits me: just like the hospital; chemically fragrant. I put my bag into the tray for the scanner. She indicates a small black box next to the security gate.

'If you could just place your thumb here, please.'

I press my thumb onto the glass and a blue light flashes. The gate opens. 'Well,' I say, in an attempt at a jocular tone, 'at least our thumbs are clean.'

The carer's mouth droops. 'I'm so sorry about all the checks. We have to be so careful. I remember the days when all you had to do was sign your name in a book!'

Obviously hospital humour doesn't work here. 'Please, don't worry, I'm a nurse. I'm used to it. It's good that you take these things seriously.'

We turn left into what must be the visitors' area. She leads us through another door into a room with two white cubicles: smarter-looking versions of the ones we have at work.

'If you'd like to leave your bag here.' She presses a button and the cubicles slide open. 'This won't take long.'

Sasha hesitates and shoots me a look. 'This is just a scanner, right? No radioactive extras?' Sasha's not normally one to baulk at such procedures. She must really be nervous.

The carer interjects. 'No need to worry.' She flashes Sasha a smile. 'It's just the usual smart imaging. We don't use tracers for microbial scans.'

She bustles over to a white filing cabinet and pulls two packets out of a drawer. 'Now, could I ask you both to undo your top buttons? We need a bit of skin for the sensor.' She turns to me. 'You know the drill, I expect.'

I lean across to Sasha. 'It's basically a disposable patch.'

Sasha nods and disappears inside. My cubicle smells of the usual plastic and disinfectant: its familiarity is bizarrely comforting. The carer follows me in and unwraps the sensor. It's no thicker than a sticking plaster.

'There we go,' she says, positioning it over my heart. 'I'll nip next door and do your daughter's.'

The cubicle closes, sealing me in darkness. A violet beam of light moves over my eyes and rotates slowly around my body. Even though I do this every day and I'm positive I'm clear, I'm still relieved when there's a beep and the door on the other side slides open. I walk into a beige room with black leather sofas that feels more like an office reception. After a couple of minutes, Sasha appears.

'Lily knows you're here,' says the carer. 'She's on her way now.' My stomach tightens. 'I'll take you through shortly. Can I get you anything to drink?'

'I'd love a cup of tea. What about you, Sasha?'

'Just a glass of water, please.'

The carer leaves us and I start to pace. A camera swivels round above us.

'They've more security in this place than school,' says Sasha, eyeballing the camera.

'Hardly surprising,' I say. 'These are the shores of the River Styx.'

She looks at me blankly. I don't know why I just said that: it's a sure sign I'm stressed. I start another lap of the room.

'Mum!' Sasha catches my arm. 'Can you stop that? You're like a demented parrot in a cage.' I burst out laughing. It's a welcome release.

The door opens and the laugh freezes on my lips.

'Mrs Connelly, Lily's ready for you. Would you and your daughter like to come through?'

CHAPTER 38

LILY

The little red light on the camera blinks at me like a reptile's eye. I have a sudden urge to go to the toilet, even though I've just been. My head feels too heavy. As if there's a weight on the back of my neck, pressing it down.

She's here. She really is here.

I've barely slept these past few nights. When I do, my dreams consume me. I think I hear her, crying for a feed. Even after I wake.

I remember her warmth as she suckled. The little snuffles and whimpers she made. Each detail was a new miracle. The pink filigree of veins on her eyelids, so fine they were almost transparent. The way her mouth made a perfect 'O' when she slept. The nail on her little finger: no bigger than a buttercup's petal.

I hear voices, and the pounding in my chest intensifies. I cover my hands with my sleeves and fold them in my lap.

The door opens. A handsome woman with light-brown hair walks in and stops. Her pale-blue eyes shimmer like crystals.

'Kate?'

The word emerges from somewhere so buried that I barely recognise it. My baby. My beautiful baby. All grown up.

She doesn't answer, doesn't budge from the doorway, just gazes at me, completely still. A blonde-haired girl behind her whispers something, and the spell is lifted. Kate steps forward, and I scrabble with the arms of my chair. I latch onto her with my ugly claws as my eyes dissolve in tears.

I hear a gravelly voice saying the same thing over and over: 'Sorry. I'm so sorry. Sorry.'

It's mine.

■ ■ ■

KATE

The door presses like a dead weight against my hand. I am frozen, unable to move. It's worse than when I went down the aisle. Because I don't know who's in there waiting for me. This mother that disappeared. Who I can't even call by her real name.

I take one step.

A frail woman with white wisps of hair sits hunched in a chair. She could be one of my patients. I recognise her, just, as the woman in the photo. But the years have taken their toll. She lifts her head. Sallow skin sags beneath pleading eyes.

'Kate?'

Is this her? My mother?

I feel nothing.

'Mum,' whispers Sasha behind me. 'Mum, you need to go in.'

I command my feet to move. As she strains to get up I notice her hands: gnarled and sculpted by arthritis. She clings to me like an injured bird and says something I can't make out. She repeats it, over and over, and I wonder if she does have dementia after all.

There's an almighty crash. I spin round and see the startled face of a carer, hands still outstretched. Teacups roll across the carpet, jettisoning fluid; cake has already toppled off plates. Lily and I are still holding each other, like two dancers who have been interrupted on stage. The woman drops to the floor, muttering apologies, and starts sweeping the china back onto the tray.

'Oh dear. Shall I get a cloth?' I bend down to pick up a glass, grateful for an excuse to let Lily go. The carpet squelches under my feet.

'No, no, please, I'll deal with it,' says the carer, blushing. She collects the remaining crockery and scurries out of the room.

'Well, that's what you call an entrance,' says Sasha.

Nobody smiles. Lily collapses into her seat, eyes circling the floor.

The carer reappears a few seconds later with a tea towel and a bowl. 'I'm so sorry,' she says, mopping the carpet. 'So clumsy of me. This won't take a minute.'

We all watch her in silence, as if we're the audience at a play.

I try to remember what I was going to say to my mother.

But the moment has gone.

■ ■ ■

LILY

Her disappointment rolls across the room, stifling me. She can't even look at me: the wizened remains of the mother she never knew. I want to gather her to me, breathe her in, but there's a wall of years between us. What did I expect? She's a mother, with a daughter of her own. I think of all the photos in Margaret Benn's room, and my chest aches. Those moments in Kate's life: I've missed them all.

'Hello, Lily. I'm Sasha.'

It's the girl. She bends down and touches my arm, like the visiting vicar does sometimes.

'I'm Kate's daughter.'

She has hair the colour of burnished gold. I look up into electric blue eyes.

A keening sound escapes my lips. The eyes, the hair, everything.

Sweet Jesus, it's him.

She pulls away, and I think that's it. But she kneels down in front of my chair and wraps her pale, thin arms around me.

I see Kate watching us from the other side of the room, her mouth contorted, as if in pain.

She brings her palms up to her face and starts to shake.

■ ■ ■

KATE

I don't know how long we've been here. The three of us, in this room. It feels as if time is shifting: speeding up and then slowing down. My body has rebelled; I can't trust it. I have no idea what it might say or do next.

'She's the image of him, you know,' says Lily, nodding.

'I'm sorry?'

'Your father. He was an exceptionally good-looking man.'

Sasha raises her eyebrows. I ignore her. I'm stunned Lily's brought that up.

'You've probably guessed by now that he was married.' She tugs at the sleeves of her cardigan. 'I loved him. Really loved him.' She turns her watery gaze to me. 'But he had his own family. It wasn't to be.'

I see the hurt in her eyes, even now. I wonder if he knew about me. Strange to think that I may have a half-brother or half-sister somewhere who have no idea I exist.

I take a breath. My mind is racing with so many questions that I'm at a loss where to start. 'What happened to him?'

Her gaze shifts to the carpet. 'He died, many years ago. In the Crisis.' She clenches her fingers. 'I'm sorry you never knew him. But perhaps it was for the best.'

The question sticks in my throat, fighting to get out. 'I ... I imagine it must be difficult, having to dig all this up again.' I swallow. 'Please, don't worry about the fact that I ... that you weren't married. That doesn't bother me at all.'

She turns to me and her face crumples. 'I know what you're thinking. There were lots of single mothers my age; why not me?' She shakes her head. 'I wanted you, Kate. I wanted us to be a family, but that just wasn't possible.' Her lips tremble. 'I was so afraid that ... that, after everything that happened ... I wouldn't be enough.'

Her honesty sinks me and I have to look away. Lily reaches for my hand. I let her take it.

'I've thought about you so often, Kate. There have been countless times I regretted my decision. But later, when the Crisis came, I knew I was right.' She cradles my palm in her veined, crooked hand. 'You were loved and brought up by good people. You're a successful woman with your own family now.' She smiles, but it's a painfully sad echo of her Mona Lisa smile. 'I'm glad you never had to endure the blemish of my mistakes.'

I stare at this old lady in her chair. This lady who is my mother.

I don't understand. And I don't necessarily agree.

But I realise that none of that matters, as the distance between us peels away.

CHAPTER 39

Crisis

Shocking Rise in Infant Mortality after Hospital Outbreaks of MRSA

'We are staring down the barrel of an amputation glut,' warns Director of National Infection Service.

A leaked report claims that the TB pandemic has been compounded by an explosion of infections in overcrowded hospitals caused by multidrug-resistant bacteria, including MRSA and E. coli. The number of untreatable infections has rocketed, with a sharp increase in bloodstream, urinary-tract and respiratory-tract infections.

'Infected cuts, surgical wounds or catheters can be fatal, even to healthy adults,' said one doctor we interviewed. 'Children and the elderly are particularly at risk. If infections are allowed to progress, to save lives, we are forced to amputate. The safest thing is to stay at home and avoid infection. Without an effective drug arsenal, doctors are powerless to help.'

■ ■ ■

MARY

I slump back in my seat, eyelids hovering. With my eyes almost shut and mask on, I look as good as dead. Unconscious, at the very least. It's a whole lot safer if they think you're not breathing. Joel has taught me that. I watch the grey strip of track in my wing mirror, the sliver of trees in front. I start to count. If someone's coming for you, they'll make their move before twenty, in case you hit the pedal and go. Joel has taught me that, too.

Six. Seven...

Something erupts from the branches. My eyes snap open. Only a wood pigeon. Lucky: one that got away. It flaps its stubby wings and settles on a distant telegraph pole. As it bobs its head I think of those grey feathers sashaying into a little pile on the kitchen floor. Moons of onion tucked under its pale, nude wings. My stomach claws at me. God, I hope he turns up.

All these decades of overmedicating our livestock have finally caught up with us. As if the food shortages weren't bad enough, we've managed to transmit our human TB strain to our farm animals, who, in turn, are passing it back to us, incubating more and more virulent strains. The vast majority of cattle have been massacred; they say the pigs and sheep are next. Even those farms that managed to avoid infection aren't exempt from the culls, not unless the animals are antibiotic-free. The last thing we need is to keep on transferring resistance. Given that under three percent of animals have been reared organically and all meat imports have stopped, meat, fish and poultry are pretty well off the menu. The Crisis has turned this country vegetarian.

There's a sudden flash in the tree tops, like sun reflecting off glass. I check my mirrors. Nothing.

Sixteen, seventeen...

A gunshot ricochets in the branches. I shunt back my seat and hit the floor. Blood thumps in my ears as I cram my body under the steering wheel. I should never have risked it. Diesel and cars are big bounty. Looters are everywhere.

Twenty-one, twenty-two...

There's a light crunch of feet. Getting closer. My hand creeps into my bag and curls round the pepper spray. Sweat pricks under my arms.

My door rips open. The smell hits me first: blood and earth, and something else: a musky, feral scent. Two wild eyes glare at me, red filigrees of veins straggling out from the pupils. This face is so beaten by the elements that it looks as if it's been roasted.

'Dropped something?' Joel's whiskered mouth twists into a smile, exposing jagged peaks of teeth. Grotesque as they are, I can't help but stare. I don't see many mouths these days. Joel is not one to bother with masks. As he explained to me once, with a tap of his rifle: 'If I don't like the look of someone, they won't get close enough to breathe their germs over me.'

The floppy neck of a bird swings towards me like a pendulum; electric-blue and emerald feathers shimmer above one scarlet-masked eye.

I scramble up onto my seat. 'I ... I heard a shot.'

He sucks in his lips. 'Pigeons. One of God's stupidest creatures.' A waft of sour breath blows in my face. I resist the urge to tighten my mask. 'Don't even have the sense to hide.'

I follow Joel's gaze to the still body lying underneath the telegraph pole and feel a twist of remorse. I'm not a fan of killing wildlife. Or breaking the law. But I'm not a fan of starvation, either.

I pop the boot, anxious to move things along. 'Only enough diesel for two cans, I'm afraid. I'll try to bring more next time.'

He gives a disgruntled snort. 'Might not be a next time.' He scratches his nose leaving a smear of dirt like some tribal marking. 'Woods round here are cleared out. If you're sticking to game, I'm going to have to look further afield.'

There must be hundreds of Joels all over the country, making a fortune from the misfortune of beasts. Paid to cull livestock and game that they're supposed to incinerate, instead they sell the meat on, for commodities or cash. I refuse to take any farm stock, though, no matter what they say. I'm prepared to take my chances with game: they haven't been stuffed with antibiotics; the wildlife culls are mainly a precaution.

Joel lumbers round the back and thuds a bag into the boot. 'Haunch of venison and a brace of pheasants.'

Such culinary delights used to possess a rustic charm. 'That's great, Joel. Thanks.'

The whole car shakes when he slams it shut. 'Make it three next time.'

I hit the accelerator. In my rear-view mirror I see Joel staggering towards the telegraph pole, a jerry can clenched in each hand. He stoops over, pockets the pigeon and disappears back into the trees.

If it wasn't for my Pharmaplanta fuel allowance, my protein levels would be seriously deficient. If I'm careful, and sleep at the lab some nights, I can save enough fuel to trade. The extra e-coupons, though, are as good as useless; there's barely enough food for people to spend the rations they have. The travel permit's handy, though; it gets me through the checkpoints. They even kitted out my car with a purifier. It's in their interests to keep me alive.

I bump along the track, scanning the hedges partitioning each field. Clouds loom overhead, cloaking every leaf and branch in a film of grey. A tractor stands abandoned in a half-ploughed field, waiting for a driver who never returns. In the distance rise the all-too-familiar plumes. The acrid stench of charring flesh permeates the car, too pungent even for the purifier. And I remember what Piet said all those years ago: 'The stench. It never leaves you.'

My mind starts playing tricks on me, imagining bodies folded into hedgerows, looters lurking under trees. The noise of the engine seems unfeasibly loud. I switch the radio on, low volume, more for distraction than news. The road's not far now. Just got to get past the farm.

'...stay in your homes. Only drivers with authorised travel permits will be admitted through checkpoints. Ration packs will continue to be delivered every two weeks; update your order online through the Government Gateway...'

Despite the woeful list of instructions, just hearing that official, sane voice calms me.

'...the latest health advice and to order medication...'

The presenter falters. 'I'm sorry, I...' There's a rustle of paper. 'We've just received some breaking news.' I lunge for the volume button. 'A report released by the security services claims that the UK, the US and several other European countries may have been the victims of bioterrorist attacks.' My heart slams in my chest. 'It's alleged carriers infected with the resistant TB strain were used to spread the disease. A statement by the home secretary is expected shortly...'

It's true, then, what Piet told me. Someone harnessed that disease. We are the architects of our own disaster.

The car thuds over a rock, sending it spinning out to the side. I lift my foot off the accelerator and remember to breathe. Up ahead a pair of rusting metal gates are propped against a green barn with a corrugated iron roof. Ivy straggles over the walls of empty pens. I glance up at the farmhouse; damp cobwebs cling to lichen-coated stones. No face appears at any window.

I skirt round the building onto the cobbled drive that leads down to the road, the news still buzzing in my head. That's when I see him: a small boy, hanging over the gate in front of the cattle grid. He kicks the gatepost with one listless foot, as if it's just another day.

I kill the radio and skid to a stop. I keep the engine running. There's never been anyone at the farm before. The boy looks up. He has hollow cheeks, sunken eyes. No mask. He hesitantly lifts a hand. It's more of a question than a wave. This is no coincidence. He's been waiting for me.

I swallow, trying to get some moisture into my mouth. That gate is the only thing that separates me from home. My instincts tell me to flee, that this is some kind of trap. I imagine a sweat-sodden man barrelling out of the farmhouse, clambering into the car, his phlegmy breath coughing into my face.

The boy's jaw pumps as if it's gearing itself up for something. I keep my foot on the pedal. The gate is flanked by a stone wall on one side and a barbed wire fence on the other. Both look pretty robust. I scan the fields behind. The ground's too soggy; if I try to go round, I could get stuck.

I lower my window an inch. 'Sorry, can I help you?'

His lip trembles. 'My mum...' My heart sinks. I know what's coming. 'Please, can you take her? To the hospital?'

My eyes squeeze shut. 'Listen to me. A hospital is the worst possible place to be right now.'

His eyebrows knit together. 'She's got the sickness. They can help her.'

'No,' I say, softening my voice, 'they can't.'

I think of the newsfeeds. Rows of beds all squished together, people hunched over bowls, slumped on floors. Bandaged stumps of limbs...

'The doctors don't have any medicine that works. And they already have more patients than they can cope with. Your mum's much better off here, in the fresh air, away from—'

'Why?' He thumps his hand against the metal bar. The force of it makes me start. 'Why can't they make her better?' Now the tears come. He cuffs them back. 'That's what doctors are supposed to do, isn't it? Make people better?'

My heart burns. 'I'm so sorry. Right now, the best thing for her is rest.' He glowers at me. 'You know, people do recover.' My platitude sticks in my throat. The survival rate for this TB is forty percent at best. And that's assuming nothing else takes hold.

'What's your name?' I ask gently.

'Peter.'

'How old are you, Peter?'

He juts out his chin. 'Nearly eleven.'

'Is it just you and your mum at the farm?' He hesitates and nods.

The boy looks as skinny as hell, but there are no other indications that the disease is active.

'Do you know how to use the Gateway?'

He frowns. 'Of course.'

'So you understand who to contact if ... if you need help.'

His eyes drop to the ground. He gives the post a violent kick; the gate hurtles back.

'Where's your mask, Peter?' He doesn't answer. 'It's important to wear one. To stop you getting sick.'

He grinds his tooth over his lip. 'Didn't stop her, did it?'

Part of me, the selfish part, wants to hit the accelerator. But I can't just knock this child off the gate and abandon him.

I swallow. 'Maybe not. But if you're going to look after your mum you need to try and stay strong.'

I sneak a quick glance at the farmhouse. All is quiet. I check my mask, take a deep breath and open my door. Peter eyes me warily. I walk round to the boot, the back of my neck tingling. When I flip the lid his eyes widen. But he doesn't let go of the gate.

'It's OK. I'm just getting something.' I haul the deer leg out of the boot, brandishing it with both hands. 'Take this.' He scowls. 'It's venison: deer meat. Very nutritious: packed with protein and iron. That'll help your mum. It's tasty too. But don't overcook it.'

He doesn't budge. 'You're just trying to get me off this gate.'

I can't help but smile. This boy's smart as well as brave. 'Maybe I am. But everything I've told you is true. And when I come again I'll bring you more.'

His head tilts. 'How do I know you'll come back?'

'Because it's a promise.'

He blinks. 'People break promises. All the time.'

It kills me. He's only a child and he's all grown up.

'Well,' I say. 'I'm not one of those people.'

I see the conflict in his freckled brown eyes, the lack of trust. God knows what he's been through. He slides off the gate. His feet scuff towards me, pushing up the dirt. As he gets closer I realise just how scrawny he is; his clothes look as though they belong to an older brother. My heart twists. Maybe they did.

I hand him the dark-red stump of flesh. 'Can you manage?' He staggers a little and nods. I ferret in my bag for a card. 'Any problems, you call this number. There's an email too, in case the lines go down.'

We stand there a moment, unwilling to move. My arms reach

out and pull him close. It's a clumsy gesture but the boy doesn't flinch. I can feel his back rising and falling as he gulps soft, quick breaths. The hunk of deer presses into my ribs, a fleshy bulk between us.

I let him go. I slam the boot and heave myself back into the car. 'Keep your doors locked. Don't hang around outside. Anyone comes apart from me or the food truck, don't answer, OK?'

'OK.'

My window slides up; the purifier whirs discreetly. As the car rattles over the cattle grid, I watch the boy totter back to the farmhouse, clutching the leg.

And, just like that, another slice of my humanity withers.

CHAPTER 40

KATE

'Come on, Mum!'

'Coming, coming.'

I risk another quick scan of the carpark and scurry after her. Sasha strides towards the arched glass doors as if she is leading an invasion. Three teenagers dawdle along behind, heads buried in their phones. A woman in a green headscarf and sunglasses climbs out of a car. My eye lingers on a man in a track jacket and trainers who seems in no hurry to go anywhere. His hands are stuffed in his pockets, his forehead gleams with sweat. He catches me looking and stares right back. I force myself to turn away. It doesn't stop that slow tingle up my spine.

It only takes one.

'Everything OK?' says Sasha, as I glance over my shoulder. The man follows us through the doors and swaggers left down a corridor, his soles squeaking on the tiles.

'Yup.' I clamp my mouth shut before the question makes it onto my tongue. This letting-go business is hard. A few weeks ago this mall was in total lock-down.

Sasha narrows her eyes. 'You were about to ask, weren't you?'

I raise my hands in surrender. 'I didn't, though, did I?'

'Honestly, Mum...'

'I know, I know. It's just ... I'm programmed.' She rolls her eyes but there's a glimpse of a smile. I sigh. 'You wait until you're a mother.'

Her face tightens for a second, and she buries her head in her bag. 'Actually, I ordered myself a new one.' She holds aloft a purple polypropylene mask with the words *KISS MY MASK* in jagged yellow capitals. 'Like it?'

I raise my eyebrows. 'Very droll.' I manage not to ask if it's been produced to a sufficient spec, but make a mental note to check later. I slip my arm into hers. 'Come on, then. Let's hit the shops.'

This trip was my idea. I used to love shopping. I remember going with Pen when I was Sasha's age, trailing round the precinct with a clutch of bags, scooping up bargains. Now it's just another exercise in risk management. But Sasha's always game for a spree, so this is my way of thanking her. And finding out what she really thinks. I still can't believe how good she was with Lily. But something's bothering her, I know it is.

A sudden memory of Lily surfaces, clinging to me. I remember that initial emptiness when I saw her. The hurt in her eyes. And yet, the longer I spent in that room, the more familiar she became. We have no shared history, no binding memories. But, by the end, there was a visceral connection I never expected. Her blood to my blood. Her bones to mine.

Sasha ambles into a shoe boutique. The air sticks to my throat, hot and clammy; the purifier can't be working properly, I ought to report it. She brandishes a brown ankle boot with a platform heel. 'What d'you reckon, Mum? A bit retro?'

'Maybe.' I clear my throat. It really is stuffy in here. 'Isn't there that other shop, Sasha, a bit further down? They normally have a better selection.'

Sasha waves at an assistant. 'I think I'll try them on.'

I sneak a quick peek at the monitor. No alerts. I survey the racks of monoped merchandise and try to drum up some enthusiasm. I inspect a black shoe with a flamboyant gold buckle and kitten heel. As I apply disinfectant gel from the dispenser I notice a woman, about my age, peering through the shop window. She's not looking at shoes, though. Her gaze is fixed on Sasha, her lips drawn tight. It's the lady from the carpark. She looks as if she's just seen a ghost.

'Do you know that woman, Sasha?'

'What woman?' Sasha's head remains bent over her trainers.

'The one at the window. With the headscarf.' By the time Sasha looks up the woman is already walking away. 'She was staring at you. Like she knew you from somewhere.'

Sasha frowns and heaves on a boot. 'She was probably just looking at the display, Mum. This is a shoe shop. You should try it.'

I follow the green headscarf until it disappears into another boutique. I watch for a few seconds, but she doesn't come out. When I turn round, Sasha is wandering around in her socks, picking up one boot after another. Even she seems a bit lacklustre about it all.

'I thought we might try that new brasserie for lunch,' I say. 'It's supposed to be very good. You know, the one Jenny was talking about? It has excellent ratings.'

Sasha gives me a look. 'For food or hygiene?'

I smile. 'Both.'

The assistant arrives with another red box. A pair of faux-fur boots lie nestled in tissue paper like guinea pigs off to be buried.

'I checked out their menu: they do that pasta dish you like. Made with real eggs.' Sasha tugs on a guinea pig and zips it up. 'We probably shouldn't leave it too late, though. Jenny says they get really busy.'

'OK. Sure.'

Two pairs of boots and three boutiques later we finally make it to Keelie's Brasserie. The place is packed. Exhausted mothers shovel spoons into toddlers, their pushchairs waiting patiently by their sides; coiffured ladies huddle over tables, swapping the latest travesties of marriage. With a little negotiation, I score a table by the window. There's a reassuring echo of conversation and tinkling of cutlery against plates. Sasha stares at the menu board, tapping her fingers. She's let her nails go: they're all ragged and chipped. That's not like her.

'Linguine it is.' She exhales. 'So, then.' She lifts her eyes to mine. 'What's the news?'

I smooth the napkin over my knees. 'What do you mean?'

Sasha raises her eyebrows. 'Come on, Mum. You hate shopping.'

'Well, maybe it's my way of saying thanks.' I smile. 'Talking of which, Liscombe House messaged me earlier. We're all set for Sunday.'

'Oh, good. Dad'll be pleased.'

I peer at her over my coffee. 'And you?'

She frowns and takes a couple of noisy sucks on her straw. 'Of course.'

The waitress arrives to take our food order. I scamper through our choices and wait for Sasha to say something. She doesn't.

'So...' I exhale. 'These past few weeks have been a bit of a rollercoaster. How are you feeling about things?'

She inclines her head. '"Things"?'

I lick some froth off my lips. 'You know: me. Lily. The birth-mother business.'

'Ah. I thought that might be it.' She pushes her glass away. 'Can we not have this conversation now? We're supposed to be doing the mum-daughter thing.'

'That's what the mum-daughter thing is, honey. Having conversations. Particularly the tricky ones.'

She makes a snorting sound.

'What does that mean?'

She shakes her head. 'Nothing. Forget it.' She keeps her eyes on the table.

I touch her hand. 'Please, Sasha. I promise I won't jump down your throat.'

She scoffs. 'Well, that'll be a first.' I manage to smile through it. Just.

She looks at me and sighs. 'You really want to know?'

My stomach tightens. She sounds like a doctor from the old days, just before they gave a terminal prognosis. I nod.

'And you won't get upset?'

'No, I won't.' I offer her my little finger, the way she used to, when she was little. 'Pinky promise.'

She reaches over and curls her little finger around mine. 'Pinky promise it is.'

She takes a breath. 'I know this sounds ... It's not going to sound right, but...' Her eyes dart from her hands to me and back again. 'This thing with your birth mother. I get it's important, of course I do. But it's like it's taken over. You said it wouldn't change anything, but it already has.'

I clasp my hands around my cup and squeeze my lips together. In case any words try to fly out.

'I mean, you're always squirrelling yourself away. You don't talk. Not to me, at any rate.' She jabs a finger in her chest. 'I'm the teenager here. I thought that was my gig, not yours.' I attempt a smile. 'And even when you are around, you're so ... uptight.' A flush of red creeps into her cheeks. 'We don't even mention Pen anymore. It feels like, I don't know, like I'm supposed to forget about my real gran, while you scurry round trying to find me a new one.'

Hot shards prick behind my eyes. I blink them back.

She bites her lip. 'You see, this is exactly why I didn't want to do this.' Someone on the table next to us bursts out laughing.

'It's OK, Sasha. Really.' I reach for her hand. 'It's me that should be apologising. I know I haven't...' The words get stuck and I try again. 'When I discovered who my mother actually was ... well, I had some doubts of my own. I suppose I wanted to protect you.' I swallow. 'It became a kind of compulsion. To keep trawling. As if all that information might ...' I hunch my shoulders '...I don't know, prepare me somehow. Explain why she did what she did.' I sigh. 'I haven't forgotten about Pen, though. I promise. Not for one moment. Whatever happens with Lily, she'll never replace your gran.'

I feel the familiar ache, but it's not as raw; it doesn't suck the air out of me as it did those first few weeks.

'I read up about it, you know,' Sasha says quietly. 'About what happened.'

I knew this was coming. I'm surprised it hasn't already.

'She was the one who originally discovered it, wasn't she? That plant.' She grimaces. 'I don't want to sound mean, but this Mary, Lily ... I mean, she *seems* nice. I actually felt sorry for her when we were there. But what kind of person is she, really?'

Now it's my turn to look down. How much do I say when I don't even know myself?

'I know it's difficult, Sasha, but we can't really make judgements until we hear her side of the story. As far as I understand, it wasn't Lily's job to run those drug trials. It was Bekker's.'

Sasha sucks in her cheeks. 'I know, but she worked right

alongside him. She had access to the information.' She frowns. 'People died from that drug, before it was even sent to South Africa. They already knew how toxic it was and they still experimented on them like rats. What kind of people would do that?'

My chest tightens. How long must I wait before Lily gives me some answers?

Sasha lifts her eyes. 'Do you think she had anything to do with the other stuff?' She swallows. 'You know. With EAA?'

So now we're on to the conspiracy theories. Although I can't say the same question hasn't occurred to me. 'I doubt it. After all, she did testify against him. And, as far as I'm aware, there was never any case against her.'

Sasha's mouth slides into a half-smile. 'Yeah, but that was a long time after the attacks. If she suspected, why didn't she come forward earlier?'

I have no answer. I've been around these questions so many times, I'm worn out. And Sasha doesn't know the half of it. I think of that photo of the two of them at the conference and feel the same nagging twist inside. But who am I to criticise? How will history judge what I do for a living?

We're both relieved when the waitress arrives with our order. She deposits our dishes with professional cheer. A tantalising aroma of lemon and garlic wafts up from my plate.

'They never actually convicted him, you know,' I say. 'Bekker died in prison, during the trial. He always swore he was innocent.'

Sasha stabs three ribbons of pasta and lifts them to her lips. 'Yeah, well, from what I've read, the evidence was pretty clear.' I watch Sasha's mouth moving in slow circles.

I pick up my fork and put it back down. 'Look, Sasha, I'm

under no illusions. I know she's no angel. Come to that, nor am I.' I sigh. 'This is your choice. You don't have to see her; you don't have to have anything to do with her, if you don't want to. But I do. Because whatever she may or may not have done, she is my mother. Are you OK with that?'

Sasha brushes her lips with a napkin. There it is again, that tightness in her face. She keeps her eyes on her bowl and nods.

I lift her chin. 'Sasha?' My heart thuds. Her beautiful blue eyes have misted over. 'Oh, love. Look, I'll cancel the visit, make our excuses, we can just—'

'No, Mum, it's not that, it's...' Her gaze wanders desperately around the room.

I knew it. That idiot boy. I say the words as gently as I can: 'Is it Jake?'

She doesn't answer. One solitary tear carves a line down her cheek. I clench the table. You want to take the pain for them, but you can't.

I fold my hands over hers. 'You're a beautiful girl, Sasha. And smart. Never be afraid to walk away from something, if it's making you unhappy.'

A strangled noise comes out of her throat. My worry distils into fear.

'Sasha, what is it?'

She shakes her head. 'Not that smart.' She gulps back a sob. 'I'm two weeks late. God, Mum. What am I going to do?'

CHAPTER 41

LILY

The lights go off, and the fidgeting and murmurs gradually cease. Everyone turns to the doorway, which is festooned with slightly tired bunting and pink balloons. Tongues slide over lips, smudges of lipstick plastering the cracks. Anne processes in as if she's walking down the aisle, and a sickly smell of baking permeates the room. The residents have the same expression I remember seeing on some children's faces at their parties: a heady mixture of excitement and dread.

'Happy Birthday, Lily!'

An enormous Victoria sponge slides perilously close to the edge of her tray. As the cake lands on the table a cloud of icing sugar puffs into the air. All eyes are drawn to the glimmering seven and zero.

Anne turns off the candles and picks up a knife; its steely glint draws me in like a promise. 'Make a wish.'

I think of Kate, her hand tucked into mine, and something wrenches inside. My daughter. My only daughter. There are still so many things I need to tell her. But even as the thought takes shape, I see the envelope floating to the floor. I've searched everywhere for her letter. Maybe I put it down somewhere, somewhere so secret that I've forgotten. Mother used to do things like that all the time. Could this be the start of my own unravelling?

'There you are, Lily.' Anne hands me a thick slice bursting with buttercream. As I reach up to take it I feel a twinge in my arm: that flu jab's still sore. Anne serves up the rest of the cake on floral paper napkins while Natalie passes round beakers of tea. The residents tuck in with appreciative mumbles, fingering the sponge. Beaded necklaces bob up and down on craggy throats like boats on a restless sea.

I force myself to take a bite. Jam explodes on my tongue. They've used the proper stuff, made with real strawberries; I'll bet Anne had to twist Cook's arm for that. The carers make an effort, they always do, but this is a ritual we've outgrown. There's nothing to celebrate about this occasion.

Diane hobbles towards me, one desiccated hand clasped around her stick. She's something of a legend here: twelve years post cut-off.

'Don't think about it,' she says, nodding at the candles. 'That's the key. Enjoy each day God gives you. Or you'll drive yourself mad.'

As if on cue Harriet bursts into a warbling rendition of 'Happy Birthday'. She turns to me and claps her hands.

'Isn't this magical? Can I have a balloon? Please? Just one?'

'Help yourself,' I say. 'Take as many as you like.'

Pam glares at me and escorts Harriet out. Her mewling protests echo down the corridor.

The others take their leave, one by one. Some wish me a happy birthday; others avoid my gaze, unsure, as if I've already contracted an illness that might be catching. I remain in my seat. I'm sticking to the communal rooms, no matter what Graham says. I can't afford to take any chances.

'Well then, birthday girl,' says Anne, sweeping scatters of crumbs into her hand. 'How did you like your cake?'

I pull my face into a smile. 'Delicious. Real strawberries.' I tut and shake my head. 'What would Mrs Downing say?'

Anne snatches up a couple of napkins, bloodied with jam. 'What the eye doesn't see…' She bends over and gives the table a furious wipe.

'Actually, Anne, I wanted to ask you something.' I scan the room. We're the only two left. 'You haven't seen a letter, have you? Addressed to me? Only I seem to have misplaced it.'

She peers round. 'Oh dear. Where did you have it last?'

'In my room.' I clasp my fingers together. 'The cleaners wouldn't throw something like that away, would they?'

She frowns. 'I shouldn't think so.' She deposits a fistful of beakers on the trolley. 'Are you sure you didn't put it down somewhere? Have you checked all your little hidey holes?'

'Anne, I've looked everywhere.'

'Well, try not to fret, I'm sure it'll turn up.' She pats me on the arm. 'Like that card from Elaine, do you remember? Where did we eventually find it? Oh yes, tucked down the back of your chair.'

I carve my nail along the seam of the cushion. *That was different,* I think.

Anne eyes the door. She digs her hand into her pocket and whisks out a small box wrapped in shiny-blue paper. 'For you.' She smiles. 'Just a little something.'

They're not supposed to give us presents; it could be misconstrued. But Anne always gets me something. 'Anne, really. You shouldn't waste your money on me.'

'Get away with you.' She flaps her hand. 'Birthdays are important.'

I tug the bow, and the paper falls away, revealing a pink box with some shop's name printed in black italics. That's Anne for you: considerate to the last; she doesn't use sticking tape because she knows I struggle. I ease the lid open. Nestled in white tissue paper is a small silver brooch in the shape of a rose.

'Oh, it's beautiful.' I hold it up to the light. Silver petals shimmer on a twisting stem, the safety clasp tucked underneath. My throat tightens. 'Thank you. It even looks like a Boscobel.'

She beams. 'As soon as I saw it, I said to myself, "That's the one." Do you want me to put it on for you?'

'Please.'

'Shall I pin it just below your collar?'

'Perfect.'

She pulls the clasp round, pinching it between her thumb and forefinger. 'Keep still now.' She bends forward and I catch a burst of flowery scent.

Pam comes storming up behind her. 'Where's the meds list?'

Anne turns, just for a second.

'Ouch!' I flinch away from her.

Anne gasps. 'Oh Lily, did I catch you?'

A bead of blood swells under my shirt. I cannot speak.

Anne grabs a clean napkin. 'I'm so sorry. Don't worry, it's just a little nick.' She presses the paper against my skin and a red circle soaks into the flowers.

I think of Natalie's husband. It's all I can do not to howl.

Anne swallows. 'Pam, go and get the antiseptic, will you?' She's using that extra-calm voice: the one she has for emergencies.

Pam stares at the box and the wrapping paper then back at Anne. 'All this fuss,' she mutters, shaking her head. 'I told you it would get you into trouble one of these days.' She hurries off towards the kitchen, and I see Anne's lips tighten.

'Please, try not to worry, Lily,' she says, a film of sweat glistening on her forehead. 'The brooch is silver. That's one of the reasons I chose it.'

The paper flowers have disappeared, submerged in a bloody pool. I remind myself that silver is antiseptic and the pin looked clean. That it's a gift, a lovely birthday gift.

Pam slopes in with a first-aid kit. Anne snatches it off her without a word and rips an antiseptic wipe out of its wrapper. She dabs away until all the blood has gone and sticks on a plaster. 'There you are. Good as new.' I manage a tepid smile. Anne's eyes meet mine and she reddens. 'Sorry, Lily. I didn't want to give you cause to fret. Today of all days.'

'It's OK, Anne. Really.' I must sound convincing because her face relaxes a little.

'Right then,' she exhales. 'Where were we? Oh, yes: cards. Back in a jiffy.'

As soon as Anne's out of sight, I slip my fingers under my shirt and gently probe the plaster. It doesn't hurt. I press a little harder. There's a faint throb but no more blood appears. I notice a small, rusty stain on my shirt that looks like a teardrop.

Anne returns and deposits five cards on my tray. 'This one's from all of us,' she says, handing me a large oblong envelope. On the front of the card is a painting of an English cottage garden not dissimilar to Auden's. 'Everyone's signed it.'

I read the birthday greetings as Anne hovers behind. 'Thanks, Anne,' I say. 'You've all gone to so much trouble.'

'Well, I know this day can be difficult. We wanted to make it nice for you.' She squeezes my arm. 'People care, you know, Lily. Not all of them show it, but, well, we're very fond of you.' She gathers up the wrapping paper and places the brooch discreetly in its box. 'Anyway, I'd better get off before I cause even more trouble. Don't worry, we'll keep an eye on that.' She nods at my plaster. 'I'll leave you to read the others in peace.'

I try to ignore the little flutters of panic in my chest and pick up the first envelope. The looping letters give her away: it's from Diane; she sends me one every year. It's a picture of a spring hare; I'm pretty sure she gave me the same card last year. I recognise Mrs Downing's military print on the next one. For some reason she always sends her own card, as if she can't bring herself to mingle with the other staff, even on paper. I push it aside and pick up the next one. My heart thuds. I know that neat, disciplined hand.

On the front is a white, star-shaped flower with six delicate petals and arching leaves. It's a star of Bethlehem: a member of the lily family.

Dear Lily,
I hope you have a lovely day.
Very much looking forward to seeing you.
Kate, Mark & Sasha

I trace my finger over her words. Did Kate understand the significance of the flower? The star of Bethlehem symbolises forgiveness and reconciliation. Or is that just wishful thinking?

I stroke my plaster. Six days till she comes. One hundred and forty-four hours. I just need to hold on till then.

I'm about to push myself up, when I notice the last envelope. The address is typed: black, Times New Roman. The hairs on my neck stand up. Twelve point.

A picture has been cut out and glued on the front. It's the same creature as before, only this one is lying on its side, in a pool of blood. With a gaping wound where its horns should be.

My fingers refuse to move, but the card falls open anyway. A little whimper escapes my lips. The letters have been cut out and stuck on too.

HAPPY BIRTHDAY, MARY.
THIS ONE WILL BE YOUR LAST.

CHAPTER 42

Crisis

'Incontrovertible Evidence' Bioterrorist Group Responsible, Says MI5, as Global Death Toll Reaches 200 Million

The UK's intelligence chief announced today that there was 'incontrovertible evidence' that the terrorist organisation Equality Above All (EAA), was responsible for triggering the TB pandemic. 'EAA planned and executed a deadly series of bioterrorist attacks over a period of months, deliberately infecting huge numbers of people in concert venues around the world with a drug-resistant strain of TB.'

In his statement, the prime minister commented: 'This is the worst terrorist attack in modern history. Two hundred million innocent lives have been lost because of the despicable actions of one organisation. The United Kingdom and our allies, will not rest until these monsters are brought to justice.'

■ ■ ■

MARY

I activate the security shield on the polytunnel and step outside. A dank grey mist smothers the science park, all the chillier after such fertile, moist warmth. The steel-and-glass buildings have been consumed by a dense bank of clouds; the lake at the perimeter is barely visible. I scan the gravel path, the rampant lawns, the straggling ornamental beds, slowly succumbing to weeds. All is still.

I tighten my mask and am about to make a dash for the car when I sense movement, down by the water. I stiffen. Through the mist I can just make out the squat bodies of two ducks, paddling nervously through the reeds. A rare sight these days. Most creatures have been eaten or culled. Wild fowl. Badgers, foxes, deer. Now they've started on the pets. It's not enough for our own species to expire, we have to take the rest of the animal kingdom with us. At least the plants are flourishing.

I watch the ducks until they swim out of sight, and hurry along the path. As I turn left, I spot a black Mercedes I don't recognise in the carpark: the only vehicle apart from mine. It wasn't there when I arrived. I pick up my pace, fishing for my keys.

One tinted rear window whines down. 'Dr Sommers?'

I freeze. Eyes the colour of dirty paintbrush water peer out above a high-grade mask. I glance up at the office windows: a pointless exercise, no one's there.

I swallow. 'Yes?'

'Could I have a word?'

'I'm sorry, do I know you?'

'Not yet.' He flashes his ID. I take one step closer. Commander Graham Parfrey. My eyes are drawn to the badge's crest: a golden-winged lion sporting a fish tail with the words *Regnum Defende* underneath. My stomach thuds.

'Please, Dr Sommers. No need to be alarmed.' He says it with the professional nonchalance of a heart surgeon. 'We just need your assistance with something.' He opens his door. 'It won't take long.'

I look wistfully at my car. I have a powerful urge to make a bolt for it. 'Sorry, what is this about...?'

He pats the seat. 'I think it's safer to have this conversation inside, don't you?'

My tongue grates along my teeth. I grip my bag and climb into the back. The car reeks of leather and disinfectant. As soon as I shut the door, there's a gentle hissing sound.

'Just the purifier.' He nods at me. 'Give it a couple of minutes.'

I thought the filters they gave me were high spec; these make mine look positively Stone Age. As we accelerate over the first roundabout I try to glimpse who's in front, but a tinted partition renders them invisible. Three more roundabouts until the main road.

The man removes his mask. Sharp cheekbones transect a hollow face. 'Feel free,' he says. Reluctantly, I oblige.

'Well, it's a pleasure to meet you at last, Dr Sommers. Your work is absolutely vital.' He smooths his hands over his knees. His fingers are slender and hairless. More like a woman's. 'We have high hopes.'

High hopes. That sounds just like Piet. I haven't heard from him in over a week.

He taps the seat. 'I'm told it won't be long now until the second batch is despatched.' My stomach flutters as the same old doubts wheel round. He knows all about it. Of course he does.

I take a breath. 'That's a lot of pills we're sending over for two hospitals. Do they really need that many?'

'Well, it's hard to predict. As I'm sure you're aware, things out there are pretty serious. The hospitals are totally overwhelmed. As they are here.'

Pretty serious. We British just love our understatement. The population has been decimated.

'The lab propagation looks promising,' he continues. 'Which is just as well, given the challenges you've experienced with traditional cultivation.'

I clench my fingers. He hasn't got me here to discuss growing techniques. 'In vitro propagation isn't really my department. That's Dr Bekker's.'

'Of course.' He flashes a smile, resplendent with veneers.

We pull out onto the main road. Three cars are abandoned on the verge. As we pass a bright-orange Mini I glimpse a woman's body, slumped over the wheel.

He looks on, impervious. 'And how is the talented Dr Bekker?'

I feel a spike of irritation. 'Busy, I expect. Like the rest of us. Sorry, what exactly was it you wanted?'

He inspects a nail. 'How long have you known Piet Bekker, Mary?' His question is casual, as if he's just making conversation. 'Do you mind if I call you Mary?'

I shift in my seat. 'I prefer Dr Sommers.' I feel the weight of his eyes on me. 'We first met when I was in South Africa. Over twenty years ago. I worked for his company for a couple of years. Then I left the country, and we lost contact. Until the Crisis.'

He nods. 'Did he ever speak to you about his ... political opinions?'

An icy finger creeps up my spine. 'It was South Africa in the nineties. Everyone spoke about their political opinions.'

He smiles, humouring me. 'And what were his?'

I frown. 'Well, obviously, Piet – Dr Bekker, I mean – was anti-apartheid.' I swallow. 'He believed in equality. He wanted the violence to end.'

'Equality?' There's a sudden urgency to his voice that triggers an alarm bell. 'Were you aware that Dr Bekker's father was a staunch supporter of de Klerk?'

Old money: that figures. A memory of Piet's house surfaces. I keep my tone neutral. 'From what I understand, Piet and his father were two very different people.'

His lips purse. 'And what about Dr Bekker's views on the West? He had one or two opinions there, didn't he? Particularly about the pharmaceutical industry. "Unscrupulous inaction"; he was rather fond of that phrase as I recall.'

'Well, I can't say I blame him. Apart from HIV, Africa was largely left to fend for itself. So yes, sometimes he'd get ... frustrated.'

'Would you say he was anti-West?'

'Not at all. He disliked the 'club mentality': the West looking after its own. Worshipping at the altar of profit. That doesn't make him anti-West. Just human.'

The car slows. We must be at the first checkpoint. An army vehicle rumbles past. I rummage for my permit.

He stays my arm. 'That won't be necessary.' The soldiers stand aside and we accelerate past the barriers. My pulse quickens: this must really be serious.

'Look, Commander Par—'

He waves his hand. 'Please, call me Graham.'

'Has something happened? You should be asking Dr Bekker these questions, not me.'

'That's the thing, Mary. We can't.' He leans forward; there's a cloying whiff of cologne. 'We're not sure where Dr Bekker is right now.' One eyebrow arches. 'No one is.'

A cold sweat breaks out under my shirt. 'How long has he been missing?' He doesn't answer. 'Piet wouldn't just abandon the trial. It means the world to him. What if he's sick?'

The intelligence officer looks at me. 'We're pretty sure Dr Bekker *wants* to be missing.' My eyes widen. 'When did you last hear from him?'

I hesitate. 'About a week ago.' I frown. 'Sorry, what do you mean, he wants to be miss—'

'Are you aware if Dr Bekker ever had any ... affiliations with certain organisations? Political ones, I mean?' I shake my head. 'Bekker obviously sounded off to you about things. Would you say that his views over the years have become more ... extreme?'

I stare at him. What is this? I feel as if I'm playing a part in a play, but no one's given me the script.

'Has he ever hinted at anything ... seditious? "Payback": that sort of thing?' He leans closer. 'Think, Mary. Tell me anything, even if it seems unimportant.'

I blink at him as my brain tries to catch up. I can sense this man's impatience building.

He changes tack. 'You've presumably heard of an organisation called Equality Above All?'

The hair pricks up on my arms. 'Of course.' I inhale sharply. 'You don't think they've done something to him?'

The officer looks down at his hands and back at me. 'Quite the contrary. I know this may come as a shock, Mary. But it's our belief that Bekker may have been working with them.'

The blood roars in my ears. 'What? No. Absolutely no way. You actually think...? No, that's madness.'

'We have intelligence that suggests Bekker passed on his knowledge of the TB strains to known radicals. So they could harness the disease for their own ends.'

His words stretch and warp, as though I'm hearing them in slow motion.

I shake my head. 'I don't understand ... He would never ... He's spent his whole life fighting disease!'

I bite down on my cheek and remember the conversation Piet and I had in my living room:

It's quite simple when you think about it ... To accelerate the spread, all someone has to do is ensure that conditions are optimal...

I drag my hands over my face. 'I'm sorry, I don't, I can't believe it...'

The officer regards me coolly as the car accelerates onto the motorway.

Jesus, where are they taking me?

'How well do you actually know Piet Bekker, Mary?' His lip curls. 'I mean, these days?'

I run my tongue around my mouth. 'We're colleagues. I hadn't seen him in years before we ... before the Crisis.'

'Precisely.' His eyes flash. 'A lot can happen to a person in twenty-eight years.'

An avalanche of memories crashes through my head: that day we spent on the TB ward; our recent fight at my flat. Piet's blazing blue eyes, angry at me, angry at the world.

Could he...?

I stare desperately out of the window. Smoke billows from the other side of the carriageway: it looks like an enormous bonfire has been dug into a muddy trench, stretching across two fields. It's not logs that are burning though. People in white, hooded suits spray more fuel into the blaze.

'Your testimony is key, Mary. Because, once upon a time, you did know Piet *very* well, didn't you?' My heart thuds. He locks on to me like a cobra about to strike.

I force myself to meet his gaze. 'I'm sorry, I'm not sure what—'

'Enough.' The way he says it cuts me dead. 'You weren't just work colleagues. You were lovers. Until he jilted you, that is.' The saliva dries in my mouth. 'Which must have been very difficult, for a woman of your calibre. Particularly in your ... condition.'

The breath stops in my throat. I think I'm going to be sick.

I wrench the door handle, even though we're going at least eighty, but of course it's locked. I scrabble for the window button. The officer grabs my arms and forces them down by my sides; his wiry frame belies his strength.

'What do you want?' I pant, as all the fight seeps out of me.

'Evidence,' he hisses. His grip tightens. 'You have it, Mary. You may not realise it yet, but you do. Face it, Piet Bekker is no stranger to betrayal.'

Memories tumble. The wind whipping my hair as I study each bone in his face. His lips moving down my neck. That night, of the fire...

'No.' I shake my head. 'I can't do this. I *won't* do this.'

He releases me and exhales a long, slow breath. 'Still protecting him. Even now.' He slides his hand into his pocket and pulls out a phone. 'Have you heard from Kate lately?' My heart stills. 'No?' He stabs the screen. 'Well, the good news is, she's healthy. For now.'

He holds up a photo of a young woman in an ivory wedding dress, standing outside a church. A smiling man, with a kind face, is next to her. Tears swell. I blink them back. She looks radiant.

'Happily married.' He calmly pockets the phone. 'Even contemplating a family of her own.'

My nails dig into the flesh of my palms. *How could they possibly have found out?*

He sighs. 'But, hospitals are such dangerous places...' My head jerks up. 'Oh, didn't you know? She's a nurse. A very competent one, by all accounts. Quite the reputation.'

I clench my jaw. I am harpooned. The anger quivers through me.

I lift my eyes to his. 'Please...' The word comes from somewhere so deep, it accumulates a density all of its own.

His mouth looms closer. I can taste his stale, minty breath. 'There are two ways this can go, Mary. The choice is yours. In both scenarios, Bekker is going down.'

Tears trickle down my face, as I disintegrate, cell by cell.

He reaches over and catches one with his finger. 'Don't let her be a casualty of your misplaced affections. Again.'

CHAPTER 43

KATE

I edge the door open and crane my neck round. She's there, bundled up in her duvet, like a caterpillar in its cocoon. I listen to the soft rhythm of her breathing, watch the flicker of her eyes. I remember those nights kneeling by her bunk when she was little, just watching her. Curling my hand through her hair.

'Hi, Mum,' she croaks. She sounds as if she's had a very big night. Except I know she hasn't.

'Hi, love. Sorry, I thought you were asleep. Did you get much rest?'

'Not really.'

I manage a bleary smile. 'Me neither.'

It kills me that she's been holding this all by herself. I should have noticed; all the signs were there.

She presses the heels of her hands into her eyes. 'Has Dad gone?'

'Yes, don't worry.'

I hate keeping secrets from Mark, but she made me swear. Strange, how petrified she was about what her dad might think. Their relationship has weathered the teenage years much more smoothly than ours.

I draw the curtains, and a pallid light seeps into the room. Sasha levers herself up and wraps her arms around her knees. She looks so pale. I want to scoop her up and kiss where it hurts. Make it better.

She takes a breath. 'So. Have you got it?'

I hold up the white paper bag with the green cross that's been lurking in my drawer. She eyes it, as if there's a snake coiled inside.

'Good job your dad didn't find it; I'd have had some serious explaining to do.' I ham it up a little. 'Seeing as he's had the snip.'

She stretches her mouth into a smile, for my benefit.

I swallow. 'Fancy a cuppa?'

She shakes her head. 'It was torture enough having to wait this long. I just want to get it over with.'

After the initial shock when she told me, my next response was relief. That, despite everything, she'd confided in me. I didn't shout at her or call Jake an irresponsible idiot. Didn't lecture her about unprotected sex or whisk her off to the nearest clinic. I just wanted to help. Prove worthy of her trust.

She throws off the covers and swings her legs out. She pads past me, her satin nightdress hugging her curves. I feel a nostalgic ache. My little caterpillar has transformed into a young woman. With a body ready to have children of its own.

She reaches the bathroom door and stops, like a horse refusing a jump.

'Everything OK?'

'Shit, Mum.' Her voice sounds very small. 'What am I going to do if it's positive?'

I squeeze her shoulder. 'Let's just take things one step at a time.'

Wise words, Kate. That exact question's been bouncing around my head all night. University. Career. Marriage. Wasn't that the path we'd imagined for her? She hasn't even left school. The only positive I can summon is that at least she knows she can conceive. And with that thought sidles in another. What if things change? What if the bacteria steal another march on us? Now, Sasha could give birth safely, with proper medical care. Who knows how easy it will be in ten years' time?

I open the packet and pull out a shiny foil pouch. There's a waft of lavender and disinfectant as Sasha lifts the toilet lid. I tear along the strip and take out a white plastic stick. Even though I know what to do, I read the instructions anyway.

'There you go, love,' I say gently. My stomach loops, as if it's me that's taking the test, not her. She looks at me as if I'm handing her a weapon. 'You need to keep the tip in the stream for at least ten seconds.' I lay a strip of toilet paper on top of the cabinet. 'When you're done, pop it on there.'

She eyes the little pictures on the box. She wanted to do this the old-fashioned way: no pregnancy app, no record on her profile. I try to keep my voice normal. 'The lines will appear in that little window.'

Her gaze darts to mine. '*Line*, Mum. That's all I want. Just one, single line.'

'Yes, of course.' The blood rushes to my face. 'I meant the one in the control panel too.'

I remember staring at a little white stick, praying for two lines, not one. It took me four tests to get them.

There's a rustle as she hikes up her nightie. Then just the sound of our breathing.

'Remember, aim for the strip. I'll tell you when to stop.' I turn away to give her a bit of privacy. Although I'm desperate to check she's doing it right.

I hear a faltering stream and start to count. I wonder if my birth mother used a test like this. Did she count her ten seconds with longing or with dread?

'Uugh, disgusting!' Sasha pulls a face.

'What's wrong?'

'Some of it went over my hand!'

'Don't worry, just keep going. You're nearly there ... And ... stop.'

Sasha drops the stick on the cabinet and thrusts her hands in the sink. She soaps her fingers over and over. 'How long?'

'Just two minutes,' I say. What I don't say is that those two minutes stretch to infinity. That they are like time travelling through space while the seconds, hours and days battle past in this room.

Sasha peers at the stick.

'Try not to look, honey,' I say, fighting the urge to check myself. 'I know it's hard. Wait until it's time.'

I listen to her raggedy breathing and focus on my reflection, beside hers, in the mirror. *Fourteen, fifteen, sixteen...*

As she pushes back her hair I notice the arrow-shaped nick above her eyebrow from when she fell off her scooter. My hands clench. I want to throttle that scrawny bastard.

'It was my idea, Mum.'

For a moment I wonder if I said it out loud.

'It was just the one time, honest. Normally we're careful.' She grips the basin as if it's the only thing holding her up. 'I suppose I wanted to be ... impulsive, for once. No pills for this, skins for that.' Her head sags. 'Just live. In the moment. Like they did in those films.' My throat constricts. 'I know it sounds stupid, but—'

'No, Sasha.' I gently run my fingers through her hair. 'It doesn't sound stupid at all.'

I remember the thrill of the unknown, that collision of stars. When all that mattered was the heat of skin on skin and the heavy pull of desire.

I glance at the stick. There's a very faint blue patch, like a wash of paint. I make myself look away. One minute fifteen seconds to go.

Her body tenses. 'How long now?' The hollowness in her voice sinks me.

'About a minute.'

I count each second: breath after breath.

'Mum, when you were young, did you ever, you know ... get caught out?'

I curl a lock of her hair around my finger. 'No. That's not to say I was always careful. Before, I mean. I was just lucky, I guess.' I pause. 'But I knew someone your age that wasn't.'

Maria Hallows. Her name rises up like a ghost. Skinny girl with long legs. Pale-green eyes.

Sasha takes a breath, and I know what's coming. 'What did she do?'

I remember the gossip that day Maria didn't come to class. She hadn't said anything, but we all knew. I don't think she ever told her parents.

'This was before the Crisis, remember.' Our eyes meet. My tongue tests the word against the roof of my mouth. 'She had an abortion.' Just saying it feels dangerous. 'No one had any idea that ... how things would change. How difficult having a baby would become.'

'So she didn't consider adoption, then?'

'I don't know. Maybe. But that wasn't what she did.'

And it strikes me how hard a decision adoption must have been. Perhaps even harder than the alternative. To carry a child for nine months, knowing you were going to give it up. Could Sasha put herself through that? Could I stand by and watch my daughter give her baby away? Neither Sasha nor I would be here if my birth mother had made a different choice.

Seconds stretch and contract, heady with their own power.

'Is it time?'

'Nearly, love. Ten seconds.'

Sasha's shoulders slump. 'I don't know what I'll do if ... I'm not sure I could, you know...'

I wrap my arms around her. 'Shhh, it's going to be OK.'

I wish I could save her from such a choice. I wish I could glide in with my sparkly wand and make it all go away. What advice will I give her, if two lines appear, not one?

The second hand finally thuds round.

'OK, darling. It's time.'

We both turn.

Sasha throws her arms around me and bursts into tears.

CHAPTER 44

LILY

The bee crawls across the pink velvety folds towards the stamens, fur glistening with pollen as it fills its sacs. Pollination. Fertilisation. Germination. The cycle of life. This tiny square of garden is all the nature I have left. I'd so wanted to show Kate, next time she came.

A sudden twinge rockets up my arm. Another wave comes, blurring the pinks of the Boscobels into black. When I got dressed this morning, there was a pale pink rash like sunburn stretching from my collar bone to my shoulder. I managed to get my shirt over it before Pam saw. Damned brooch, I knew that wouldn't be the end of it. Was it just bad luck? Or did whoever sent me that card tamper with it? Who knows? It's no use fretting about that now.

Tears roll down my cheeks. They're a constant stream, as if my eyes can no longer hold them. The throbbing in my arm is insistent, no matter how many painkillers I take. God knows how I got through the bloods this morning. Afterwards, I just sat there, waiting for Dr Barrows to come. Should I tell Kate? I circle round and round this question. Our relationship is like a flower that's only just starting to bud: extremely fragile and vulnerable to attack. What if she thought that was the only reason I'd agreed to see her? To try and beg favours, get access to the drugs? She'd be risking her job and her reputation. After everything I've done, what would be the point of that?

Something flashes past, a glimpse of iridescent green. I grasp for the word through the fog. Dragonfly, that's it: supposed to be good luck if one lands on you. Their short lives only span a few months. Some don't even get that.

It darts back towards me, its emerald body sparkling in the sun.

'Lily?'

My heart thumps. Is that Pam? The dragonfly disappears. Perhaps the blood test has caught up with me after all.

'Lily, are you out here?'

My hand moves to my patch. Is Dr Barrows with her? Is there an ambulance outside, waiting for me?

My breath rations itself to small gasps. I could just throw myself at her mercy. Anne's partly responsible, after all. If Anne could prove it, maybe she could…

Footsteps.

My courage deserts me. I stay silent. Start conjuring names.

Catmint. Columbine. Coral bells.

A jingle of keys.

Daisy. Delphinium. Foxglove.

Breathing. Getting closer.

Geranium. Hollyhock…

'Here you are!' Natalie pushes through an arch of leaves.

So. The arbour has betrayed me too.

'I've been calling you for ages! Didn't you hear?' She mops her brow and stabs my frame in front of me. 'Come on, then. Up you get. I've got another three to do after you.'

I stare at her as the blood screams in my ears.

'You've forgotten what day it is, haven't you?' She smiles. 'Wednesday. Time for your rub.'

My body sags against the bench, but my relief is short-lived.

'Oh, sorry, yes. It's just that ... Well, my hands ... they're quite a bit worse today.' I realise I'm panting. 'Maybe we should give it a miss?'

She frowns. 'That wouldn't make much sense now, Lily, would it? The balm's supposed to help with the pain. Don't worry, I'll be gentle on those joints.'

She hauls me up, and I swallow a cry. I shuffle along the path in front of her as the burning radiates down my arm. I have to think of something. Anything. But my mind is at a loss, frazzled by the pain.

Just as we reach the ramp I remember. 'Where's Anne? I haven't seen her.'

'She went home yesterday, after lunch,' Natalie breezes. 'Nothing serious; probably something she ate. But you know how it is in this place. Can't take any chances!'

It's as if all the air has been pressed out of my body. I pitch forward over my frame.

'Careful, Lily! Are you OK? It's sweltering out here. Let's get you inside.'

Cold waves of panic roll through me. Anne won't be allowed back for at least forty-eight hours. Maybe longer. What am I going to do?

Eventually we make it back to my room, and Natalie helps lower me into the chair. My blouse is soaking and I reek of sweat; she must have noticed.

Her mouth puckers. 'Are you overdoing it, Lily? Not so far next time, I think.'

I watch her push up my right sleeve, trying not to tense. She unscrews the lid and a sickly-sweet smell pervades the room. There's a sucking sound as she smooths the honey over my fingers and a treacly warmth seeps into my bones. Normally I enjoy it. But all I can think about is how much the other arm is going to hurt.

'How's that?' she asks.

I have to take a couple of breaths just to keep my voice steady. 'Good.' I don't take my eyes off her hands. 'Actually, it's helping.' I run my tongue over the sweat on my lip. 'Look, I've made you late already. We could just focus on this one?'

She moves round to the base of my thumb. 'Oh, I wouldn't want to short-change you.' She smiles. 'Don't worry. The others can wait.'

As she rolls up my left sleeve the saliva builds in my mouth. The cloth tightens above my elbow and I wince.

'They're really giving you some jip today, aren't they?' She tuts. 'Those tablets not helping? I'll have a word with Dr Barrows. See if we can get you something a bit stronger.'

She starts kneading my fingers. The heat sparks up my wrist and keeps going, like an electric current. I can sense it already, how bad it's going to be, as if the pain receptors have fired off their impulses and my brain is sounding the alarm. I clench my jaw. Any moment now. Any moment.

She squeezes my wrist. I yelp and jerk it away. A wave of nausea sweeps through me.

'Goodness, is it really that bad? Look at you, Lily, you're dripping!'

I shrink back in my chair. 'Please, Natalie.' Hot tears press behind my eyes. 'Can we just leave it?'

She clamps her hands on her hips. 'OK, Lily. What's going on? Have you taken another fall?'

'No, I...' I nurse my arm in my lap. 'It just hurts. I must have bumped it or something.'

She gives me an indulgent smile. 'Lily Taylor. Do you think I was born yesterday? Come on. Let's take a look.'

The blood drains from my face as she slips the blouse off my shoulder.

'Oh.' The way she says it isn't good. Like the worst kind of surprise. 'It's quite inflamed.'

She pulls on a fresh set of gloves and gently presses her fingers around the hard red lump. The breath hisses between my teeth.

'Try to keep still, Lily.' She probes under my arm. I flinch. 'Is that tender?' I grimace. 'Hmm. Your lymph nodes are a bit swollen. Odd. Nothing's shown up on your profile.'

She looks up. The smiles have gone. 'I'm sorry, Lily. But that's definitely infected.'

And there it is: the death knell. It sinks me, even though I've known, all along.

She frowns. 'How long has it been like this?'

I hesitate. 'Two or three days.'

Her mouth gapes. 'What? Why on earth didn't you say something? You of all people know how important it is to act straight away.' She hunkers down on her haunches. 'Lily, what's going on? Why didn't you tell someone?'

A sob catches in my throat. Just thinking of Kate unravels me, like a loose spool of wool. 'If I reported it, they'd cancel my visit.'

'Your visit?' Her eyes widen. 'Oh, Lily. You can always postpone a visit. You can't delay an infection.' She sighs. 'Do you know what might have caused it? Did you catch yourself on something? In the garden, perhaps?'

I swallow. How much should I say?

Natalie's lips tighten. 'I can't help you if you don't talk to me, Lily.'

I slump back in the chair. 'I ... I think it was the brooch.'

'What brooch?'

'It was a birthday present. From Anne.' The blood rushes to my cheeks. 'The pin nicked me when she put it on.'

Natalie glares at me. 'Anne *knew* about this? I didn't see anything in the incident log.'

My words trip over each other in their rush to get out. 'It was an accident. Please. I don't want her getting into trouble. It was just a tiny prick. She cleaned it thoroughly.'

The breath shoots out of Natalie's mouth. 'Obviously not thoroughly enough.'

And just like that, doubt creeps into my mind. What if it's no coincidence that Anne's off? My chest squeezes. It's always those dearest to you who betray you in the end.

She stands up and takes a deep breath. 'I hate to say it, Lily, but...'

I clamp my hands over my ears.

I will not listen. I will not hear her say it.

'...we're going to have to take you to the San.'

The walls swoop in. Voices explode in my head: protests, wails, pleas. I see that woman's face lolling towards me. Her body, entombed behind the doors.

'Please, Natalie. There must be something you can—'

'You know the rules. Apart from anything else, it could be contagious.'

I cannot breathe. I think of Kate taking the call from Mrs Downing. Her face changing, the initial shock. Would she care, after a life without me? Would she really notice, if I was gone?

'I can't go to that place,' I whisper. 'Not now. I'll never see her again.'

Natalie fixes me with a stare. 'Who?'

'My friend's daughter,' I stammer. 'The woman who came the other day.'

Natalie's brow furrows. And I realise, she is my only hope.

I wet my lips. 'Actually, Natalie, that's not quite true.' I swallow. 'She isn't my friend's daughter.' I prise the words out of my mouth. 'She's mine.'

Natalie steps back. 'But you said ... I thought you said you didn't have any children?'

I lift my eyes to hers. 'I had to give her up for adoption. After she was born. That visit was the first time I'd seen her, since, since...' I grab Natalie's hand and another spike of pain sears up my arm. 'Please, Natalie. I have to see her again. I need to make things right. There's still so much I have to say.'

Natalie gently pulls away from me. 'A daughter,' she whispers. 'Such a precious thing.'

The room fills with silence. Spots of light spark behind my eyes.

'You know, just a few days earlier, you wouldn't have had a problem.' She shakes her head. 'It's not right. I've never agreed with that Act.'

My voice erupts. 'I'll do anything, Natalie. Anything at all.' The pounding in my shoulder intensifies. 'I have money.' Her face stiffens. 'For the drugs, I mean. For whatever it takes.'

She glances at the door. 'What you're suggesting is illegal, Lily.'

'I know—'

'It would be extremely dangerous. For me and for you.'

I scan the map of her face as the blood judders through my veins. 'You can trust me, Natalie. I'm good at secrets. I won't ever tell.'

She stares at me for the longest time. She has lost so much in her life. Why should she help me?

'Alright. I'll see what I can do.'

My body folds in on itself, as if someone's just filleted out my spine. 'Thank you. Thank you so—'

She holds up a hand. 'No guarantees. And if anyone asks I'll deny it.'

I want to jump up and hug her. Kiss this woman's feet.

'You're not to say a word, Lily, you hear?'

'Of course. I won't tell a soul.' I steel myself as she dabs antiseptic on my arm, determined not to make any fuss.

'You need to keep your head down. Stay in your room as much as possible.' She uncoils a bandage and wraps it tenderly around my shoulder. 'Keep this covered at all times, OK? And no fiddling. I may be able to jiggle the rota a bit while Anne's off, but I won't be able to look after you all of the time.'

I gulp a couple of breaths. 'How will you get hold of the—?'

'There are people who make that their business.' She shoots me a look. 'Not that I've ever had dealings with them myself. But I know some that have.'

'What about the patch? Won't things start to show?'

'Frankly, I'm amazed it hasn't triggered an alert already. I'll take a look at your profile, see what I can do with the data feed. But as for the bloods...' She tapes the bandage. 'That's going to be trickier.' She tips her head to one side. 'Although, there may be a way...'

I gaze up at her, willing her to go on.

'Remember those bloods we took, before your birthday?'

I nod.

'They always keep some back, in case they have to run more tests. That might just buy us a few days' grace while the drugs kick in.'

The relief is so intense I feel giddy. 'I ... I don't know what to say, Natalie...'

'Say nothing, Lily Taylor.' She gives me a tight smile. 'Nothing at all.'

I have a sudden urge to confess everything, to tell her about the cards and all the things I've done.

'I need to get going now, Lily.' She pulls off her gloves and drops them in the bin. 'The others will be wondering where I am.' She walks to the door and turns. 'Remember, stay in your room. I'll bring you more pain relief later. If all goes well, I'll have something stronger for you by morning.'

I ease my shirtsleeve over the bandage, sink back and shut my eyes.

So close. So terribly close to becoming another day-tripper.

CHAPTER 45

Crisis

Security Tightened at Old Bailey as Trial of 'Plague Doctor' Continues

Bekker, who faces mass murder
and terrorism charges, refuses
video link and will be present
in court.

■ ■ ■

MARY

I step into the antiquated wooden box, gripping the ledge so tight that my knuckles blanch. The purifiers hiss from the ceiling like an audience at a pantomime when the villain appears on stage. I straighten my back, stare at the oak-panelled wall and breathe. I feel naked, under everyone's gaze. Their prejudices already circling.

Don't look up...

The usher clears his throat. 'Repeat after me. I do solemnly, sincerely and truly declare and affirm...'

My mouth opens but only breath creeps out. I know he's there, watching me; the only thing that separates us is a panel of bulletproof glass. Four months in custody; it's a wonder Piet's still alive.

I swallow and try again. 'I do solemnly, sincerely and truly declare and affirm...'

I'm taking the affirmation, not the oath. There is no Almighty God here.

'...that the evidence I shall give...'

'...that the evidence I shall give...'

'...shall be the truth, the whole truth and nothing but the truth.'

My tongue flicks over my lips. I think of the statues I saw above the entrance. A bare-breasted Truth gazes at her reflection in a mirror. She has weathered much worse than the others: her nose has gone and much of her hands. Her pitted, scarred body bears testament to the travesties that take place.

'...shall be the truth, the whole truth and nothing but the truth.'

There's a tapping of fingers on keys. Charlotte Tanner QC stands and gives me her snake-charmer smile, her chestnut hair coiled neatly beneath the wig. 'For the benefit of the court, please state your name.'

'Mary Kate Sommers.'

'And your age.'

'Fifty.'

'Can I ask you to speak clearly into the microphone and address your answers to the jury, not to me?'

I glance round. Five men and three women stare back at me, as if I'm the one in the dock. A reduced jury: they had to pass a law for that, just to keep things going. For this trial, they'd have had no problem getting the full complement.

She tugs her black gown forward over her shoulders. 'Dr Sommers, you are a master of science and a doctor of philosophy, is that correct?'

First, establish credibility...

'Yes. I graduated from Oxford University with a first-class honours degree in biology and went on to complete a doctorate in plant science.'

'And what is it that you do now?'

'I investigate the properties of plants to ascertain their use, principally for medicinal purposes.'

A couple of men at the front are furiously typing away. My heart skitters even though I know the court has imposed reporting restrictions. I've been assured that no details of my testimony can be published while I'm alive.

She checks her screen. 'Does your work necessitate a lot of travel?'

'It used to, yes. Before they closed the borders.'

'Where did your work take you?'

'All over, really. Africa. Asia. Europe.'

'Did that include South Africa?'

My heart is pounding so hard I'm worried the microphone will pick it up. 'Yes.'

'And when did you first visit?'

'Twenty-eight years ago. I went there to do field research. For my PhD.'

Miss Tanner drags a painted black nail over the cuticle of her thumb. 'And was it during this research that you first met the defendant?'

My teeth clench. *The defendant.*

'Yes.'

'Can you tell us a little about how you met?'

My eye veers to the gallery, which is almost empty. Pre-Crisis, this courtroom would have been packed, but now only family or people directly connected with the trial are admitted, due to the risks of infection. I search for Piet's wife. Thank God, she's not there.

'I was in Astofele: one of the national parks. Collecting data. I had an encounter with a rhino. Dr Bekker came to my aid.'

'I see. And what happened after that?'

'We went our separate ways. But a couple of weeks later, I bumped into him at one of the camps. That's when I realised we shared an interest in botany. Albeit in different fields.'

'And what was his particular field?'

'Bioprospecting. He was searching for plants with medicinal value for the development of new drugs.'

The defence counsel is bent over his screen, fingers flying across the keys; a fold of chin spills over his stiff wing collar.

'And did the defendant mention TB at this point?'

'Yes. I hadn't realised how big an issue it was in South Africa. But when Dr Bekker took me to a local hospital, I saw for myself how serious the situation was.'

'Dr Bekker took you to a hospital?'

'Yes. To show me the TB wards.'

'And what was your impression?'

I take a deep breath. 'Well, to be honest, I was shocked. The hospital was crammed; they were completely overwhelmed. The HIV epidemic had exacerbated the spread of TB. Drug resistance was already rampant.' I wipe my hands on my skirt and resume my grip on the ledge. 'We're used to seeing scenes like that now, in this country, but not back then...'

Out of the corner of my eye I see the judge highlight something on one of his papers.

'And so, after your trip to the hospital, Dr Bekker asked you to come and work for him, is that correct?'

'That's right. As part of his new venture.'

'And what was the job he offered?'

'He wanted me to help set up a new screening programme. In South Africa. For native plants that showed medicinal potential. South Africa is rich in diversity and has a long history of traditional medicine.'

'Did you accept?'

'Yes.'

'Even though, if I understand correctly, you had been working in a different area of research?'

'Yes. But my skills were relevant to both areas.'

'So, would it be fair to say that Dr Bekker changed your mind?'

'I suppose he did, yes.'

She shuffles her papers and nods. Her eyes glitter. We're moving out of the safe zone. 'Can you remind the court how old you were at this time?'

I pretend to think about it. 'Twenty-three.'

'Twenty-three. And the defendant would have been...' she checks her notes '...thirty.'

I inhale. 'Perhaps, I ... don't really recall.'

She purses her lips. 'After Piet Bekker recruited you, did you see much of him?'

'Not at first. I was mainly working out in the field. He travelled a lot, too.'

'You said "at first". Did things change?'

Cramp needles my fingers. 'Two, maybe three months in, there was a big company dinner. To celebrate a breakthrough with HIV. After the meal we got talking.'

'And what did you discuss?'

A man in a grey wool coat sidles into the gallery and takes a seat. My heart lurches. Commander Graham Parfrey.

'Sorry, I ... Could you repeat the question?'

'What kinds of things did you and Dr Bekker discuss, after the meal?'

'He asked me how I was enjoying the job. We discussed the latest riots ... what might happen with the government, that kind of thing.'

She arches her fingers and carves each nail into the pad of her thumb like a cat sharpening its claws. 'And what happened next?'

I keep my breath steady. 'He asked me if I'd like to visit the northern section of the park. He said he rented a hut there.'

'A hut?'

'Yes. An old ranger's hut.'

'I see. Was it just you he invited? Or were other people going to be there?'

'Just me.'

She raises an eyebrow. 'Didn't you think that a little strange?'

I grip the ledge. They've rehearsed this with me so many times, but my body still rejects it, like a toxic implant. 'What do you mean?'

'Well, that a director of the firm, a married man in his thirties, with a six-year-old daughter, should ask a twenty-three-year-old employee to "visit his hut"? Alone?'

The defence counsel looks up at the judge and frowns. My jaw stiffens. I know what I'm supposed to say. That I was afraid of offending him, that it might hurt my career, that I felt pressured into it because I was young and naïve.

I focus on the intersection of the QC's hair with her wig's tight grey curls. 'I ... I didn't really see it that way.'

Her mouth twitches. 'Did you go to the hut, Dr Sommers?' Her tone is sterner.

'Yes.' I think of the bushwillows tapping the windows.

'And what happened?'

I summon the first lie. It catches in my teeth, like sweetcorn, but it doesn't taste like sweetcorn, it tastes like milk that has soured, fruit on the turn. 'He seduced me.'

Such a poisonous word: 'seduce'. Parfrey chose it specially. All the implications of rape without the charge.

The defence counsel leaps up. 'Objection! Your Honour, this is clearly "bad character" evidence, highly prejudicial and of no relevance to the case.'

Charlotte Tanner gives the barrister a tight smile and turns her sights on Judge Wheeler. 'Your Honour, this evidence is a vital part of the prosecution case.' The judge peers down at her, adjusting his glasses. 'Establishing the nature and history of the relationship between the defendant and this witness is important explanatory evidence, given the significance of her testimony. As such, it should be presented before the jury.'

It's not enough for them to unpick the fabric of Piet's professional reputation, they have to smash his personal integrity too. Cheapening what we had, laying the moral transgression at his door so the jury don't see me for the brazen sinner I am.

The judge rolls his pen through his fingers. 'I am minded to agree with you, Miss Tanner. But perhaps you could establish it a little faster?'

'Thank you, Your Honour,' she says, with a slight bow. 'I just need to ask a couple more questions, Dr Sommers, before we move on.' She clears her throat. 'When you say Dr Bekker seduced you, did he actually force himself on you?'

'No!' We didn't rehearse that. 'That's not what happened.'

'What did happen, then?'

My eyes swerve up to the dock before I can stop them. It's as if I've been winded.

Piet sits hunched in the wooden box, flanked by three prison officers. They've made him wear a mask, despite the purifier. Is that normal? The smart black suit cannot disguise it: he must weigh half what he did. His hair reminds me of the judge's wig: a yellowing grey. His eyes are the only bit of him I recognise.

'Dr Sommers, could you answer the question, please?' Miss Tanner draws me back. She told me, repeatedly, not to look.

I press my palms into the sharp wooden corners and try to breathe. 'We had sex.' There's a rustle from the jury's bench.

'Consensual sex?'

I swallow. 'Yes.' I feel Parfrey's laser stare. That bastard better hold true to his promise.

'Dr Sommers, did you and the defendant meet again, after this occasion?'

Take a breath...

'Yes.'

'How frequently?'

'Maybe four, five times a month.'

'And how long did this affair go on for?'

'About a year.'

'During that time, would you say that you were close? Your relationship, I mean?'

Another memory ambushes me. 'We became close.'

'What kinds of things did you talk about?'

'The job. Wildlife. Politics.'

'Politics?' She scrolls down her screen. 'Could you tell us a little more about the defendant's views at the time?'

I take a deep breath. 'He felt the government should stop dragging things out. He wanted the violence to end.'

'So he was against apartheid?'

'Yes.' I hesitate. 'He believed in equality.'

'Equality?'

'Yes. For all people. No matter what their colour or background.'

She turns to the jury. '"Equality for all people".' She holds up both hands, as if those four words seal the case. 'Were those the exact words he used?'

I swallow. 'Yes.'

She pauses, ostensibly checking her notes while the jury continues to stir. And I think of what Piet said about bush fires. How they had to sacrifice some animals to save the others.

She tugs her gown. 'What about Dr Bekker's views on the West? Did he discuss those too?'

'Sometimes.'

'Can you recall what he said?'

An unbearable tiredness sweeps through me. I try to remember my script. 'He thought Western countries should be doing more to address diseases like TB. Diseases with high mortality rates that afflicted mainly developing nations.'

'But, hadn't his firm already received a number of quite substantial research grants from Western institutions?'

'Those were mainly focussed on HIV. Antibiotics weren't considered a priority. Especially not for TB.'

'I see. And how did Dr Bekker feel about that?'

'Well, obviously he was frustrated. The way he saw it, Western pharmaceutical companies were only interested in making drugs that gave their shareholders a decent return, and meeting sales quotas in countries that could afford them. Investment decisions were based on profit, not need.'

'You say he was frustrated. Would you go as far as saying he was angry?'

'Sometimes. Millions of people were dying.'

'Angry enough to do something about it?'

The defence counsel jumps up. 'Objection!'

'Sustained.' The judge leans forward. 'Miss Tanner, tread carefully.'

'Yes, your Honour.' She bows her head. 'My apologies.' She turns back to me. 'Let's move on. Dr Sommers, after your relationship ended, did you continue working at Pharmaplanta?'

'Only for a short while. I did a bit of travelling, then I returned to the UK, to write up my PhD.'

'And did you and Dr Bekker stay in touch?'

'No.'

'You were aware of his work, though?'

'Yes. We worked in the same industry.'

She nods. 'In your opinion, Dr Sommers, is Dr Bekker an expert in TB?'

'Well, he's not qualified in pathology, but he's worked in the healthcare and pharmaceutical sectors, and witnessed its mutations over several decades first hand.'

'So, would you say that he's knowledgeable about the disease?'

'Yes. Extremely. Particularly from a pharmacological perspective.'

'I see. And when did you next have direct contact with Dr Bekker?'

'After my research was taken over by Pharmaplanta.'

'And when was that?'

'Approximately six years ago.'

'And was your relationship at that point purely on professional terms?'

'Absolutely.'

'But you saw each other through work?'

'He had a whole new team working for him by then. We only saw each other at occasional meetings.'

'Were you ever alone together?'

I steel myself. 'Only once.'

'Can you remember the occasion?'

As if I'd forget.

'Yes.' I swallow. 'He came to my flat. In February last year.'

'Dr Sommers, can you recall the exact date of that meeting?'

'I believe it was the twenty-second of February.'

'The twenty-second of February?'

'Yes.'

'Are you sure?'

'Yes. I'm sure.'

She rubs her chin. 'Can you tell the court what happened, please?'

A buzzing starts in my ears. 'Dr Bekker came after work, that evening.' I glance at the dock. For a second, our eyes meet. The back of my neck tingles. It's like staring into a void. 'He wanted to give me a heads-up about the results of the latest drug trial. For Brotanol.'

Fingers scurry over keys.

Miss Tanner turns to the benches. 'Ladies and gentleman of the jury, it's my duty to remind you that it is not the role of this court to make any judgements concerning the Brotanol trials. The ethics and legality of those are the subject of an entirely separate investigation.'

That woman has no shame. By pretending to ensure the jury remains impartial she flags the allegations and prejudices them even more.

'And how did Dr Bekker seem, when he arrived?'

'He was fairly agitated.'

'Why do you think he was agitated?'

'Well, at first I assumed it was about the trial.'

She cocks her head. 'You said "at first"?'

There's a cough from the gallery. I daren't look up, in case it's Parfrey.

'After he told me what had happened, I was very upset. I told him I didn't want to have anything more to do with it.' I keep my eyes on the wall, just above the jury's heads. 'But then he started talking about the TB strain. Saying that I didn't understand how bad it was. That it was only going to get worse.'

'Did he explain what he meant by that?'

A dull pain throbs at the base of my skull. 'He said there was more to the Crisis than people thought. He said something about ... about how we were at war.'

'"At war"?' She stares at me, brow furrowed.

I wet my lips. 'Yes. And that, in war, people had to do things. Things they would never normally do.'

She gives the court a minute to digest this. 'And who were we supposed to be at war with? Did he say?'

I try to swallow but all the lies have wedged in my throat. I think of that picture of Kate on her wedding day and spit out another: 'He mentioned an alliance.'

'An alliance?'

'Yes.' My voice is suddenly very quiet, as if it would prefer to shrink away entirely.

'Speak up, please, Dr Sommers. What sort of alliance?'

'He said it was an alliance "between man and microbe".'

The courtroom swells. My skin is sticky with the heat of everyone's gaze.

'Did he mention a name?'

'No.'

'Did he tell you what this alliance was supposed to have done?'

'He said...' I cringe as an image of Graham Parfrey surfaces, relentlessly editing my words. 'He said that they'd deliberately spread the TB strain. Through targeted attacks in big city venues.'

There are murmurs in the jury. Someone knocks over a glass; I flinch.

'"Targeted attacks"? Did he provide any further details?'

'He said...' Everything inside me teeters. 'He said: "It's simple when you think about it. Bacteria are programmed to replicate and survive. They're adept at seeking out new hosts. To accelerate the spread, all someone has to do is ensure that conditions are optimal."'

I hear a sound, like a hiss of tyres. I look up. Piet sinks forward until his forehead knocks against the panel. The judge leans over and whispers something to the clerk.

The QC presses on. 'Just to be clear, Dr Sommers, the defendant told you this when he visited your flat?'

'Yes.'

'On February the twenty-second last year?'

'Yes.'

'Did he give you any idea where he had procured this information?'

I make myself look at Parfrey. He gazes back at me, without expression. And I think of that quote: *Betrayal is the only truth that sticks.*

'No.'

She brandishes a wedge of papers, cheeks flushed, chin high:

ready for the kill. 'I would like to refer the jury to the testimony we heard last week from the intelligence officer on behalf of the security services. You should all have a copy in your jury bundle.' I notice the page at the front is highlighted with green stripes. 'Can I ask you all to turn to page five, paragraph three.' She pauses while the jury members shuffle through their stacks.

Her voice rises. 'The first intelligence reports about the city attacks weren't released until the twenty-fourth of April last year.' She slaps the file down. 'That information was classified. So, given that the defendant was not himself a member of the intelligence service, how could he possibly know all those details?'

Bile stings my throat. 'I ... I don't know.'

'Nor do I, Dr Sommers.' She eyes Piet. 'Not unless the defendant had prior knowledge of those attacks. From a different source altogether.' She slides her tongue over her teeth as I garner myself for the plunge. 'Did Dr Bekker mention anything else? For example, did he indicate whether this ... "alliance" might strike again?'

My chest tightens. I think of Lady Justice, frowning above me on the way in: sword thrust into the clouds, scales held ready.

'He said...' My words disintegrate. I force them out. 'He said, all it would take is another couple of mutations. And then no amount of isolation chambers or infectious disease units would be able to contain it.'

A woman in the gallery shouts something, and the defence leaps up.

It's unfathomable, the things we are capable of.

Piet lifts his cuffed wrists, palms pressed together, as if in prayer, and slams them against the glass.

CHAPTER 46

LILY

A dark-yellow stain oozes through the bandage like an oil slick. The flesh bulges out either side, a deep crimson, as if it has burned in the sun. The throbbing is persistent, unlike any pain I have felt before: I haven't slept, I can't eat, I can't think. The infection has spread, marching down my veins in angry red lines. I glance again at my watch as my head pounds; the numbers snake in and out of view. Natalie must be on shift by now, surely? Why is it taking her so long?

Nightmare scenarios flit through my mind: Natalie at the dispensary, Natalie at the scanner. Bulky security officers fishing through her bag and leading her away.

If any of the other carers come, I'm done for. She has to be here. I can't abandon Kate, again.

I tentatively touch the bandage and wince. It's no good; I have to look. I pull off the tape and unwind the gauze, sucking air through my teeth. My hand trembles with every loop. The final layers have stuck to my skin, and I howl as I pull them off.

A fetid odour spills into the room. My brain wheels, unable to reconcile this putrid imposter with the arm that existed before. My shoulder has been consumed by a fiery orange ring. A pimple of mustard pus glowers at its centre like a crocodile's eye. I have an overwhelming urge to hack it off.

I fumble for the bandage and try to twist it back round. I

tug too hard and the bile rushes to my throat. Two days ago, this was just a small red lump.

I lever myself up with my right arm and fall forward, onto my frame. My head reels as I clutch the bar with my other hand triggering another excruciating wave. I stagger to the basin, run the tap as hot as it will go and furiously soap my hands. I imagine Dr Barrows' black boots striding over from the San. Her wan lips reciting their verdict, implacable as a machine.

I lurch back into the bedroom. Everything's off kilter: the furniture's sliding to the left. My whole body aches; sweat oozes from every pore. Just as I make it to the chair there's a metallic snap. I hold my breath. The door opens.

It's her.

'Good morning, Lily.'

I open my mouth but nothing comes out.

'How are you? You look a little flushed.'

I realise I'm panting. 'The pain.' I swallow. 'It's much worse.'

'Oh dear.' Natalie's forehead creases in a frown. 'Those tablets I gave you not helping?' I blink at her as another swell knocks the breath out of me. She pulls on some gloves. 'Right, then. We'd better take a look.'

She slips the dressing gown from my shoulder. Her mouth puckers. 'Have you been messing with that bandage?'

'I ... I just had a quick look.' I try not to tense as she starts to unravel it. 'Have you got them?' My question blurts out. I cannot contain it any longer.

I wait for her to say something, to reassure me. She unwinds the gauze, round and round. As she peels back the last layer, even she draws back. She pinches the putrid cloth between her thumb and index finger and drops it into the waste.

Her eyes meet mine. 'The infection has progressed.' She nods at the boil of pus as if I have done well, as if I have excelled in my field. She rips off her gloves and reaches for the sanitising gel. She rubs it into her smooth, pink skin, one finger at a time.

Any minute now, she's going to tell me. She's going to whisk out those tablets and everything will be fine.

'By the look of it, I'd say that's Staphylococcus aureus.'

The sibilants echo around my head, summoning a distant memory of an old nursery song. A staph infection. That's not good. Not good at all.

She gives me a brittle smile. 'No wonder it's painful.'

I have to ask her something. Something important.

'Did you get them?' My words sound slurred, as if I've been drinking.

'What, you mean these?' She produces a steel tube from her pocket. It rattles as if there are bullets inside. 'Oh yes, I got them.'

I slump forward. The roaring in my ears gets louder.

'But they won't help you.'

Something's off-beam here, her voice is too light, too ... happy. 'But ... I thought that ... Why not?'

'Because they're not antibiotics. They're painkillers.'

Painkillers?

'Oh, Mary, you still don't get it, do you?'

My name cuts through the haze, jagged and sharp. I feel a surge of adrenaline, as if I've just tripped and every nerve and sinew are rallying to stop me crashing to the floor.

'Why do you think the infection advanced this quickly?' Natalie looms closer, her breath cool against my cheek. 'Because it entered the bloodstream directly.'

And I hear it: that twang, the one I spotted by the fountain. Wherever she said she was from, she was lying.

She strolls to my dressing table and lifts out the tin. 'You don't recognise me, do you?' She finds my box in the wardrobe and slots in the key. 'You recognise this, though.'

She rifles through the papers and thrusts the cutting in my face. I flinch.

Kill not Cure...

'He tried to stop this. He did everything he possibly could to expose them.' Her voice is raw. 'Why did you do it? Why did you tell those lies?'

I stare at her like a cornered child. 'Please, you don't understand, they—'

'It destroyed him!' She screws the clipping up and tosses it on the floor. 'Everything he'd worked for, his reputation, all ruined.'

'I...' My words splinter. I try again. 'I had no choice, they made me—'

'He died, because of you!' Spit bubbles between her teeth. 'My father.'

It hits me with the force of a punch: *My father*.

'You're a liar and a slut. Every time I've had to touch your gnarled, deformed body I've thought: it's God's punishment. God's punishment on you.' Her chest heaves. 'My mother was a good woman. A loyal wife. She didn't deserve that. She didn't deserve any of it.' A tear bleeds down her cheek. She cuffs it away. 'You even had the nerve to come to our home. I didn't know who you were, but she did.'

The girl at the window. Pigtails and puffed sleeves. I reach for her name. It floats towards me, just out of reach.

'It was me that found her, you know. She couldn't bear it. She lost everything, not just him.' Her lips tremble and she turns away.

Cara. Piet's daughter, Cara.

'I'm so sorry. I never wanted any of it to happen.' I swallow. 'I loved him too.'

Her face twists as if something unspeakable just crept out of my mouth. Her voice thuds into the room. 'He wasn't yours to love.'

She snaps on a fresh pair of gloves and grabs my left wrist. I crumple. 'That's why you did it, isn't it? Because he was the one thing you couldn't have.' She tightens her grip and I howl. 'Well, now it's your turn.'

She stabs my thumb with the lancet. 'It took me a long time to find you.' Her voice is calmer now, more controlled. 'But I never gave up.' She watches my blood seep into the tube. 'Remember George?' I see an image of George, dozing off in his armchair, glasses sliding down his nose. 'Consider it a little leaving present from him.'

I grope for a connection as the blood whines in my ears. Legs. Something to do with his legs...

Natalie screws on the lid. 'That was no ordinary flu jab.'

Her words percolate my brain and I remember: the cold scrape of the needle, the push of fluid into my vein. And I see them – all those bacteria swarming through me; thousands of rods dividing, multiplying, consuming my cells one by one. I pitch forward and retch.

'The others,' I gasp, sharp stabs of panic mingling with the pain. 'My profile. They'll know.'

She sticks a label on the tube. 'Oh, I took care of that days ago. I had a little play with the feeds. But now it's time to let the real data do the talking.' She slots the tube back into the rack with the others. 'By the time they've analysed this you'll be dribbling into your nightie.'

Something deep inside me stirs. I spot my tablet on the bedside table and try to lever myself up with one arm. Before I can get my balance, Natalie darts in front of me and whisks it away.

'I suppose you'd like a word with your long-lost daughter.'

A different kind of fear coils through me. Scissors. Where did I leave those scissors?

Her lip quivers. 'Did he know about her?'

I hold Natalie's gaze as my hand creeps towards the dressing table. Slowly, slowly. 'No, he...' I ease the drawer open. 'He never knew.'

She marches over and slams the drawer shut.

I grab her hand. 'Please ... please don't hurt her. She's your family too.'

Natalie yanks her hand away. Her fawn eyes bore into me. 'I have no family.'

Tears roll down my cheeks. I feel as if I am drowning. As if I am back in that bath tub, the warm, minty water filling my lungs.

She reaches the door and turns. 'Oh, one last thing, Mary. I've made a little adjustment to your forms.' The vein in her neck pulses. 'You can forget about your directive. You'll die alone and in pain. Like they did.'

As the lock thuds across I lunge at the wardrobe. I cling onto my clothes and sweep my hand along the ledge. There's nothing there. Jackets and shirts strain against their hangers and ping off, one by one. I pitch sideways and my shoulder slams into the wood, making me heave.

And that's when I realise. The metal tube in Natalie's hand. It was my stash of painkillers she had all along.

CHAPTER 47

KATE

I pad across the tiles to my locker and pull on my shirt. My body feels leaden, compressed, as if gravity has increased; every nerve and muscle clamours for sleep. I wonder how Sasha's getting on. When I dropped her off she looked done in. At least her pale, freckled face had a smile on it.

One line. One single, blue line. I never thought I'd be so pleased to see one of those.

I tug on my trainers and ferret in my bag for my phone. One missed call and one voicemail: both Liscombe House. My heart sinks. I'll bet it's Mark's medi-profile. If his sniffle costs us the visit I'll be seriously pissed; I promised Lily we'd all be there.

I shoulder my bag and clamp my mobile to one ear.

'Hello, Mrs Connelly, this is Mrs Downing. I'm calling to let you know that unfortunately Lily has been taken ill.' I stop in my tracks. My eyes widen. 'As Lily doesn't have any next of kin, we thought we should inform you. She's currently in our sanatorium, but her situation is quite serious. Please do give us a call as soon as you are able.'

Quite serious. I know what that means.

I hit 'call back' and march towards the exit. Angie holds up her hand to wave but drops it when she sees my face. I shake my head at her and keep walking. Damn. They're engaged. I dash through the doors and spot a cab just pulling up at the rank. I sprint to the head of the queue and, before anyone has time to protest, stick my medi-profile up against the driver's window.

'Liscombe House, please,' I say into the microphone. 'It's an emergency. As fast as you can.'

The lock thuds back, and I clamber in. I dial Mark. It rings four times before he answers. 'Hi, love—'

'Lily's ill and it's serious. I'm on my way to Liscombe House now.'

'Oh God, what's happened?'

'I don't know, I literally just picked up the message.' I swallow. 'But it doesn't sound good.'

'Kate, I'm so sorry. Shall I head back? I could meet you there, bring the car.'

The thought of having Mark with me is suddenly very tempting. I hesitate. 'I should probably see what the score is first. Assuming she's still there.'

'Are you sure?'

I'm not sure about anything. I take a deep breath. 'I'll ring when I know more.'

'Alright. If there's anything you need, just call me, OK? Anything at all.'

'Will do. Love you.'

His voice softens. 'You too.'

I try Liscombe House again. Still engaged. They must have more than one line, surely? I grip the phone, willing the traffic to go faster. A column of cars crawls along in front of us, like a colourful cortege. The driver mutters something and starts punching buttons on his sat nav. I stick my head through the hatch. 'What's going on?'

'They've shut the bypass. Must be another demo. So now they're sending all the traffic this way.'

Christ. 'How long, d'you reckon?'

He shrugs. 'Fifteen minutes. Maybe twenty.'

I grit my teeth. A lot can happen in twenty minutes.

I listen to the message again. Mrs Downing said 'taken ill' which rules out accidents or falls. I run through the usual contenders: UTI, heart attack, stroke. I'll bet it's a UTI; care homes are notorious for them. Although, with their state-of-the-art monitoring, Liscombe House ought to be catching things early. Before they progress.

I try calling again. No answer. At least the traffic begins to move. Hedgerows and roads converge in twisting tunnels of grey and green until, eventually, we pull into the gravel drive. My guts spiral as the austere building looms towards us.

I pay the driver and haul myself out. I ignore the cameras above the entrance and slam my hand on the bell. I'm about to ring it again when the door opens. It's one of the carers I met before.

'Hello, Mrs Connelly. Please, come in.' She keeps it professional but her doleful green eyes give her away. The hairs on my neck prickle. 'Mrs Downing knows you're here.'

I'll bet she does. 'Take me straight to Lily, please.'

She sucks in her lips and hovers in front of me, uncertain. 'Oh. You ... you didn't get the message?'

'I've been trying to call you back for the best part of an hour. What's the diagnosis?'

Her mouth opens and closes. 'I'm sorry, I ... I'm not permitted to go into details.' Now I see it on her face: not just worry. Fear, too. 'Please. Follow me.'

She leads me through security. We pass the first gate but instead of turning left after the scanners she heads right through a different door. We go down another carpeted corridor with rooms on either side. I stick one pace behind her, trying not to step on her heels.

She stops outside a wood-panelled door.

'What's going on?' My tone is harsher. 'This isn't the sanatorium. I'm a qualified nurse, I'm entitled to see her.'

She gives me a desperate look. 'Would you mind just waiting here? Please ... just for a moment.'

She knocks once and disappears inside. I hear hushed voices. The door opens and a woman who I assume is Mrs Downing appears, all collars and glasses.

'Mrs Connelly,' she says, with practised calm. 'Do come in.'

I don't move. 'Where's Lily?'

She blinks once then turns to the carer. 'Anne, would you please bring us some tea? And ask Dr Barrows to come to my office.' Her gaze swivels back to me: shrewd, brown eyes magnified by her spectacles. 'Mrs Connelly?' She waves her arm towards a chair. 'I think you should sit down.'

Those six words, they're such a cliché. But they hold a terrifying power.

I move an inch over the threshold. 'I'm a ward sister, Mrs Downing. Cut to the chase.'

She appraises me with her owlish eyes and takes a breath. 'After I rang you this morning, I'm afraid Lily's condition deteriorated.' Now my fear is real, I can taste it, bitter on my tongue. 'She had an abscess. On her arm. We drained it, but the infection was already advanced.'

My forehead throbs. 'She's not here, is she?'

She hesitates. 'No.'

My eyes squeeze shut. I think of Lily strapped down in one of those death wagons, making the journey alone. I want to beat my fists on the floor. Not now. Not when we've only just found each other.

'Why didn't you call the hospital? They could have paged me. You've got all my details, there are least three other numbers!'

'Mrs Connelly, your mobile was your preferred contact number. I assumed that you would pick up your voice—'

'I was working on isolation! I can't exactly answer the bloody phone!'

Her face tightens. 'I'm very sorry, Mrs Connelly, but you have to understand that, legally, we're only obliged to inform next of kin. We called you out of kindness, and you've Anne to thank for that. She told us how close your mother was to Lily.'

There's a knock at the door. A middle-aged woman in a white coat appears like a spectre. Mrs Downing looks visibly relieved.

'Ah, Dr Barrows. I was just telling Mrs Connelly about Lily's ... condition. She's understandably very upset.'

Dr Barrows' face is grave, with a veneer of empathy. I know it well. It's the face of a professional who deals with death for a living.

Mrs Downing swallows. 'As you're aware, Mrs Connelly also works in the medical profession. Perhaps you could explain to her in a little more detail what happened?'

'Certainly.' Dr Barrows folds her hands in her lap. I note the red lines around her wrists: marks of the trade. 'When we tested Lily's bloods this morning, the platelet count was significantly lower than usual. She was also exhibiting a high temperature and abnormal heart and respiratory rates.' She pauses. 'On examination we found an abscess on her left shoulder. It seems she had been hiding it for at least three days, possibly longer. Which explains why the infection had already advanced into her bloodstream.'

'Three days?' I'm incredulous. 'How on earth could she have concealed something like that? Apart from anything else, it must have been incredibly painful. I thought you people were supposed to provide round-the-clock care?'

Mrs Downing rushes in. 'Mrs Connelly, I appreciate you're upset, but I can assure you, Liscombe House provides the highest standards of care. Nothing on Lily's profile prior to that point had given any cause for concern.'

Dr Barrows glances at Mrs Downing. She clears her throat. 'Shall I continue?' Mrs Downing nods. 'We administered fluids and oxygen, but, by mid-afternoon, Lily's breathing had become even more irregular and her mental state severely compromised. We had to make a judgement based on the level of infection. I'm sorry, but the rules are very strict about that. She was taken to a hospital for the elderly just under an hour ago.'

I sit forward. 'Hang on, why didn't anything present on her profile earlier? That level of infection doesn't just happen overnight.'

The doctor hesitates, and I glimpse a tiny chip in her veneer. 'We are investigating that.' She arches her fingers. 'But, according to the data, there were no substantial changes to any of the vital signs until this morning.'

I rub my forehead. There's definitely something not right here. 'What about a directive?' My throat constricts. 'I assume she's signed?'

They exchange looks. 'She did.' Mrs Downing's hesitation stills my breath. 'But she changed her mind.'

'What? When?'

'Just before her birthday.' She pauses. 'It happens quite a lot.' The rehearsed way she says it makes me want to hit her.

Dr Barrows takes over. 'Once people reach cut-off the procedure becomes a lot more real.' She swallows. 'They worry about decisions being made prematurely. Or that, later on, they may not be judged fit to change their minds. So they rescind their directive.' She looks at Mrs Downing. 'It's my understanding that Lily rescinded hers a couple of weeks ago.'

Whatever fight's left in me fizzles out. So this is how it is. For those countless relatives I've had to deal with. This is how it feels, the other side of the fence.

'Which one is it?' I ask, already moving to the door.

'I beg your pardon?'

'Which hospital have they sent her to?'

Dr Barrows hesitates. 'Penworth.'

My face falls. '*Penworth?* But she isn't high risk!'

She just manages to meet my gaze. 'I'm very sorry. It was the only one that had any beds.'

I hurl the door open and clatter straight into the carer. I push past her, and race down the corridor.

Thirty minutes. With that traffic, forty. I can't be sure Lily's even got that.

I grab my phone to call ahead. Penworth. Why did it have to be fucking Penworth?

I'm almost at security; I can see the gates.

'Mrs Connelly? Mrs Connelly, please, wait!'

I turn. A woman is running towards me. It's the other carer, from last time. The one who dropped the tray.

I hold up my hand. 'I'm sorry, I haven't got—'

'Please, it's important. It's about Lily.'

There's something in her face that halts me, even though I know every minute counts. 'What is it?'

She glances behind her and ushers me away from the gates. 'There are things you need to know,' she whispers. 'About her past. But we can't talk here.'

I step away from her and shake my head. 'I don't know who you are, but I don't have time for this.'

She comes closer. 'We both know Lily's not her real name. But I'll bet she hasn't told you everything.' Her lips tighten. 'Like who your father is, for example.'

Our eyes meet. And, with a jolt, I recognise her: it's the woman from the shoe shop. The one who was staring at Sasha.

My blood chills. 'Who are you?'

'I'll explain everything. It won't take long.'

I stare at the gates. I should leave. Now. I know I should.

She follows my gaze. 'If you care about your family, you'll want to listen.'

My pulse goes into overdrive. 'What is this? Some kind of threat?'

She doesn't answer.

I swallow. 'Five minutes, that's all. And I mean it.

CHAPTER 48

Miraclu-skin™: say goodbye to cuts and bruises!

We all understand the perils of ageing. As the years go by, our
skin becomes more delicate and prone to injury.
A simple scratch or bump can easily develop
into something much more treacherous.

Miraclu-skin™ undergarments clothe your body in a protective
shield, saving you from life-threatening cuts, tears and bruises.
Our special lightweight mesh technology provides the extra
strength and protection elderly skin needs, whilst maximising
air circulation and comfort. The soft, porous fabric will keep you
warm in winter and cool in summer, with built-in UV protection
so you don't need to worry about sunburn either.

Why take unnecessary risks? Enjoy life!
Order Miraclu-skin™ today!

Available in ten tasteful designs for men and women.
All sizes available, from extra small to extra large.

LILY

There's that ringing noise again. Is it one of them? They aren't human. I don't know what they are. They look like beekeepers. Or spacemen. They don't speak, just check your tubes and they're gone. Maybe they're machines. They always said that would happen. They've got me stuck in here, for their little experiments. Nowhere to hide now.

Where am I? It's not the San. I remember those men coming. Dr Barrows, she was there. She smiled at me. She never smiles. She spiked my arm and it slid through my veins like a snake, ice cool. I tried to fight it, even though the pain was making me weep. Then they strapped me down and put me in that box. Is that the right word, box? No, something else. A wild white face. He knew it. That poet.

The wailing. I can't bear it. It just goes on and on. I can't stay here. Bad things happen.

I stretch my fingers across the sheet, try to lever myself up. My arms are clamped to my sides as though they've wedged me in the mortuary rack already. That woman must have done it. Strapped me down, like a lunatic.

'Take them off! Please, someone!'

I dig my elbows into the mattress and arch my back. Oh, God! The pain. Like a thousand cuts. They're butchering me alive. Darkness swoops. I can't c—

■ ■ ■

There's that sound again: metallic grating. Those poor children; their coughing never stops. There are hundreds of them. Hacking and spitting. I hear them crying for their mothers. They never come.

'Is that you, Kate?'

Skin all pink and wrinkly. Tiny fingers, curling up to mine.

'Where are you? Have they taken you already?'

Please. Let me hold her. One last time.

'I'm sorry! I'm sorry I couldn't save you. I couldn't help any of you. Please, just let me go...'

I pray for death to come.

It's close now, I can feel it.

Stalking through my body. Claiming me bit by bit.

CHAPTER 49

KATE

She leads me down a corridor that smells of detergent, filled with the rumble and rinse of machines. We pass through what must be a drying room. I peel off my coat and fumble my way through steam into another room peppered with ironing boards.

'That's it. I'm not going any further.' I stop and wipe my forehead.

She closes the door behind me and leans against it, sweat sheening her face. 'I couldn't see it at first,' she says, studying me. 'But now I can. It's the eyes.'

'Look, I told you, I only have a—'

'They're not the right colour. But they're the same shape.'

The breath spills out of me. 'That's it, I'm leav—'

She raises a hand. 'Wait, *sister*.' My mind swerves. 'Well, half-sister, to be precise.'

I stare at her blondish-brown hair. Her fawn eyes.

'It was a shock to me, too.' Her mouth twitches. 'She managed to keep it a secret from everyone. Including the father.'

'You mean ... you mean, you're Lily's—'

'Your mother fucked my dad.' The expletive stings like a slap. 'While he was married. To my mum.'

It's like an icy breeze. Of course. The family I never knew. Sweat slicks down my neck.

'I used to hear Mum sobbing, night after night, when she thought I was asleep. I was six years old. Only later I figured it out.' She wets her lips. 'She knew that whore was trying to steal him...'

I cringe. 'Please, don't call her—'

'But he wouldn't leave. He would never leave us, not by choice.'

Her voice cracks and it's as if a fissure has opened up. Behind shines molten lava.

'How does that saying go? "Stronger than lover's love is lover's hate"?' Her eyes glitter. 'Twenty-eight years she waited. Well, I waited too.'

A high-pitched whine drills through my head. I scan the room for another way out. There isn't one.

'I was there, you know. At the trial.' Her lips tremble. 'They called him "the plague doctor". My father! A man who devoted his life to curing people!' She steps closer. 'Without *her* evidence they'd never have had a case.'

Her breath blows in my face. 'Have you worked it out yet, Kate?' I bring my hands up, as if they can protect me. 'Your father was Piet Bekker.'

It all spins loose: photos, articles, conversations collide in the vortex. I stagger to a sink and grip the cold porcelain with both hands.

'They refused him bail, sent him straight down. Do you know what the death rate was back then, in prisons?' She punches out each word. 'Eighty percent.'

She is building to something. Something terrible. I want to hurtle past her, to safety, but I am paralysed, like a rattlesnake's prey.

'They never proved it was him, but nobody cared. He died

before he was sentenced. From the disease he'd worked so hard to cure.'

I have done some good things in my life, Kate, and some bad things. Things that I regret...

She looms over me. 'She's not a nice person, your mother. Your father was a good man, a brilliant man. But Mary—'

'What did you do to her?' The words creep out of my mouth like mice: small and frightened.

She regards me with lacklustre eyes. 'Nothing she hadn't already done herself.'

My panic spirals. I edge away from her. 'Better to confess now. Let them try to save her.' I swallow. 'They'll charge you with murder.'

A shadow flickers over her face. 'Let me tell you about murder.' She lunges forward and grabs my wrists. 'An innocent man, destroyed.' She drags her nails across my veins. 'A wife so wretched she slits her wrists.'

I wrestle free. 'I ... I'm sorry, I didn't know—'

'Just leave her,' she hisses. 'Like she left you.'

I see the hatred in her eyes, like a force between us. I meet her gaze. 'I can't.'

Something like a sigh escapes her lips. Her hand slides into her pocket.

My body tenses. 'Please. Don't.'

She smiles as her hand closes round something I cannot see.

I charge at her; we crash into the ironing boards. I yank her arm up hard, behind her back, as I've been taught. She claws at me with her other hand, but I manage to swivel her round and pin her against the wall. I press my body tight against hers and reach into her pocket.

My fingers touch plastic and cool metal. 'What is it?'

She doesn't reply.

'What's in the syringe?'

She swallows. 'Just a sedative.'

I yank the sheath off the needle and press it against her skin. 'You'd better say now if it isn't.'

Her throat makes a clicking noise. 'Be my guest.'

I inject her in the median cubital vein. Her body stiffens and relaxes. Her head lolls back, and she slurs something that I can't quite hear. It sounds like 'save the trouble'.

Her eyes haze over. She slides down the wall to the floor.

I bring her left arm and knee up and roll her onto her side. My hands are shaking. But as I rest her head on her other arm I realise something's wrong. Her breathing's slowed. I'd expect that.

It's too slow.

I put my fingers to her neck. The pulse is already faint.

I bend my cheek to her mouth.

She has stopped breathing.

I pull her onto her back and check her airway. My hands run over her sternum and find the spot. I press the heel of one hand to her chest and start pumping. I count to thirty as my own pulse thunders in my veins.

No response.

I yank out my key ring and pull on a face shield. I tilt her head up and pinch her nose then clamp my mouth over hers. I breathe into her once, twice and check again. Nothing. I feel for a pulse and start the chest compressions again.

I keep going, the sweat running down my face. I don't know how many cycles. Eventually my arms cramp up and my knees go numb. I drop back on my heels, panting.

She stares at me, unseeing. Her eyes are a different colour, but she was right about the shape. I brush my fingers over her eyelids and feel their warmth, not yet ebbing away.

A part of me collapses. I brace my hands against the floor. As if they can stop my fall.

I had a sister. A half-sister.

And I realise. What she actually said.

It wasn't 'Save the trouble'. It was 'Save *me* the trouble'.

That needle was never meant for me.

It was meant for her.

CHAPTER 50

LILY

Something moves in front of my eyes. Is it a hand? I'm not sure. I can't stop shivering. Like those others. Glazed eyes, sodden in sweat, they shiver from their beds to their graves.

'Lily?'

Too bright. A fierce white light, like ... What's it called? That metal? All the sparks fly out when it burns. Mags ... magsenium. Is that it? You have to wear goggles, though. Or you'll hurt your eyes.

'Lily, it's Kate.'

I dreamt they were here. We were all together. I tried to tell her the things I need to say.

But this whining drowns everything.

Like crickets.

They used to go all night, in the savannah. The night orchestra. Who called them that? Was it him? I think it was.

'I'm right here.'

'Kate?' Even in my dreams she comforts me. I try again. 'Sorry ... I'm so sorry, I had to protect you...'

They sound like the husks of words. Like words that have rotted, buried for too long.

'It's OK, Lily. None of that matters now.'

I love you.

I would have liked to say that, one more time.

Words, letters fail.

She cannot hear me. No one can.

...

KATE

I know what to expect, but it crushes me. Tears spring to my eyes and I furiously blink them back. She looks so small. A child in an adult's bed. Fiery tracks criss-cross her skin like bloody rivers, mapped with angry red spots. Her left arm's so badly swollen; it must have been agony. I grip the chair I lifted from the nurse's station. There's none to be found here.

I unbuckle the straps and ease off the cuffs. Despite the padding, I can see the marks on her wrists where they've chafed her. A deep-purple bruise flowers her skin where they put in the cannula. I temper my breathing and take her right hand. It hangs cold and limp in my palm.

'Lily, it's Kate.'

I hope she can still hear me. Hearing is the last sense to go. People forget that; they talk as if the patients aren't there. Sometimes they say terrible things.

I stroke her hand. 'I'm right here.'

'Kate?' Her voice is like sandpaper.

I bend closer. 'Yes, it's Kate.'

Her body judders with fever. As much as I want to believe otherwise, I don't think she knows I'm here.

She says sorry, over and over. 'I had to protect you...'

'It's OK, Lily. None of that matters now. I'm here.' I pull up the blanket and try to piece her words together, like a jigsaw. Her language is already compromised. My chest tightens. Won't be long.

The nurses said she went berserk when she came to. That it took three of them to restrain her, and even then she managed to yank out the IV line and the feeding tube. I find that hard to believe. But then, things are different at Penworth; they work to their own agenda here. I doubt they'll do another PEG after this one. They should just let her pull the damn thing out.

'She hasn't signed, you know,' said one of them when I arrived. A small woman, sounded Asian, but it's hard to tell in the suits. 'We have to log you're here.'

It was her way of being kind. I know I can't do anything; I'm in enough trouble already.

I think of my sister, sprawled on the floor, and despair swells through me.

I used to help people live.

I should have come straight away.

I mop Lily's face with a wipe. The skin is stretched over her bones like papyrus. I moisten a swab with fresh water and dab it around her lips. They're already parched; soon they will crack. I take another swab and gently work my way inside her mouth, careful not to wet it too much in case she chokes.

'Help! Please, someone. Help me.'

There she goes again, that poor woman by the window. She keeps wailing, but nobody comes. She's not my responsibility, none of them are, but it's hard to block out the cries of the dying. I get up and draw the curtains, but I still hear them. The whimpers and groans. The mutterings. Someone – a man, I think – is weeping. The rest are either asleep or unconscious. The lucky ones.

Lily moans and starts scrabbling at the sheets. I pull out the kit, ready.

'There's something on me!' She tugs the feeding tube. I fill the syringe: 5mg of haloperidol. What they've given her isn't enough, not now.

'It's crawling across my stomach! Get it off!'

'It's OK, Lily.' I lift her wrist and inject it into the cannula port. She screams and her other arm flails round, catching my ear.

'It's bitten me!'

'It's OK. It's just a sedative. To help you sleep.' I lean across her, let her beat her fists against my back. They're like a toddler's, drumming slower and slower until eventually they drop back on the bed.

I lift her hand. Her fingers are bent, locked into her palm, like crooked bicycle spokes. I rummage in my bag for some cream. I uncurl each finger and gently rub it in.

■ ■ ■

LILY

'Piet? It's me, Mary. Piet?'

He doesn't answer. Why won't he look at me? He's lying in that gully, with his face in the dirt. If I could just touch him ... maybe he would listen. But my hands are frozen, unable to move.

'Piet!' I slip down beside him. His arms are splayed, feet angled into the red earth, as if he's about to burrow his way down. Blood fans out around his head like a blanket.

He turns; there's a gurgling sound, like river water running over stones.

I stagger back and scream but no sound comes out.

There's a gaping hole where his face should be. Splintered bone. Tatters of skin and sinew.

'I'm sorry,' I whisper. 'I'm so sorry.'

The only things left are his eyes. His beautiful eyes.
The colour of a monsoon sky. Before the rain falls.

■ ■ ■

KATE

She says his name, over and over. My father's name.

I smooth the sheets and whisper: 'It's OK, Lily, it's OK.' I daren't give her any more Haldol. 'Don't worry about the past. Try to rest.'

Gradually, her breathing slows, but it's still too fast, as if she's running a race only she can see. I brush her hair off her forehead. It feels like wet strands of silk.

A new noise chimes above the mutterings. I peer round the curtain at the rows of faces. An eerie silence descends, as if they know. The chimes are coming from the bed at the end, by the window. For her sake, I hope it's that woman. Or the weeping man.

I check on Lily, but she's somewhere far away, resting at last. Those chimes used to be a warning; they used to bring nurses running. Not any longer. When it gets to ten minutes I stand up and start to pace. All this technology and they still can't get it right.

After fifteen minutes, I hear footsteps. I move behind the curtain to watch. A nurse strolls along the ward, pushing a trolley: casual, unhurried. Based on the height I'd say it's a man, but it's hard to tell. The wheels rattle across the tiles like chattering teeth and come to a halt by the bed. He checks one of the patient's arms, then the other and punches some buttons on the monitor.

Draw the bloody curtains! I think. *You know the procedure!*

His fingers drum the rail as the flashing-red seconds count down. After 180, the chiming stops.

Life is extinct.

He tears off the Velcro straps and yanks back the bedclothes. I see now it is the woman; her hospital gown has ridden up, exposing emaciated thighs. He strips off her gown and dumps it into the waste; the lid clangs shut. There's a ripping noise as he pulls off the electrode pads. Raw patches of skin glisten underneath.

I check the adjacent bed, praying whoever's in there is unconscious. Above the sheets I see a waxen face – a man's, I think. His eyes are open. He watches the nurse disconnect the drip and remove the cannula; sees the blood dribble out onto the sheets. The nurse grabs the feeding tube and pulls; there's a smacking sound as he tugs it out. When he parts the woman's legs to cut the catheter valve, the man turns away and starts to sob.

I creep back to the bed and take Lily's hand, trying not to squeeze too hard. She moans softly in her sleep.

A couple of minutes later, I hear the bed wheel past. I think of those refrigerated shelves in the basement, the black numbers on square metal doors. At least her stay there will be brief, unless there's some hiccup with the admin.

They like to burn the bodies within three days.

■ ■ ■

LILY

Tired.
So tired.
Her. Here.
Fading.

Yes.

Yes.

...

KATE

She takes four rapid breaths. I count the seconds on my watch. I get to thirty before she takes her next one.

I stroke her face. 'I'm right here, Lily. Your daughter: Kate.' My voice catches. 'No need to be afraid.'

I notice the purple blotch on her arm where the blood is collecting. I check her wrist: barely a pulse. She is so still. Like a photograph. Like the ones Victorians used to take of their relatives after they'd died.

I swallow. 'I'm sorry we didn't meet sooner. That we didn't get the chance to know each other...' My words stumble as I think of Lily, in that room, with my sister. 'I'm sorry I couldn't protect you...'

Her eyes open, and it is as if the film has lifted. She looks so young all of a sudden; the years have melted away.

She tries to say something. Too faint. I read her lips.

Love...

My tears spill onto her face. I press my lips to her cheek. 'Goodbye.'

A tiny flutter of her hand in mine. Like a butterfly.

It's enough.

...

LILY

The African sun beats down on my shoulders. Two hornbills cackle as they hop from branch to branch.

My baby gazes up at me and curls her fingers tight around mine. She smells as sweet as a meadow. As fresh as the newly cut grass.

A droplet of rain kisses my cheek. I turn to him and smile.

He takes my hand.

My hand.

Fingers straight and slender.

Oval nails with little white moons.

CHAPTER 51

KATE

There's a light rain. Not enough for an umbrella, but enough to make the leaves glisten and the damp creep into my shoes. Flowers weave between the grassy mounds, a carpet of pink, yellow and white. Behind us are dense patches of woodland: the sole survivors of an ancient forest that once stretched for miles. Beyond the fence green and gold fields spread over hills to the horizon, like a giant patchwork quilt. I wonder how many people have stared at this view. How many lie buried under our feet. I inhale the smell of wet earth and try to rally my senses.

'They're stunning, aren't they? The wildflowers,' says Anne. She looks smaller somehow, wrapped up in her navy raincoat.

I nod. 'It's the perfect resting place.' This natural burial ground was Anne's suggestion. The bodies still have to be cremated first, but it's better than some sterile plot sandwiched between a thousand others. 'I think Lily would approve.'

A slight breeze rustles the branches above us, loosening wet beads onto our heads. Sasha grimaces and gives her hair a shake. I smile. It's been hard these past few weeks. On all of us. But it's brought us closer. Perhaps that's Lily's legacy. The only one she could leave.

'One of her friends is over there, by the wall,' says Anne. I glance up, half expecting to see someone, but there's only a wooden owl and a wicker wreath. It's curious, the things people leave, these intimate glimpses into past lives. Gold-sprayed pine cones and metal dragonflies. Ceramic hedgehogs and sleeping cats. I wonder what Sasha will leave for me.

'Lovely lady, Elaine. Wasn't she, Pam?' Anne continues. 'It's nice to think of the two of them, back together.'

There's something comforting about the way Anne talks, as if the dead are still here, we just can't see them.

I look at our select few, huddled around the grave: just my family and the two carers. To my relief, Mrs Downing hasn't shown up. We had a fraught few weeks during the investigation. Mrs Downing's efforts to protect her reputation nearly landed me in jail. I thought I was going to be charged with Cara's murder. My lawyers convinced them to drop the case, citing self-defence. It doesn't change the facts, though: I killed my only sister. I'll have to live with that.

I check my watch and glance at Mark. 'Do you think we should wait?'

'Up to you. There's no rush, is there?' He touches my cheek. 'Give it a few more minutes. He may have got lost.'

A buzzard's mournful cry echoes above the clouds. My gaze returns to the pages I'm clutching. This reading took me a long time to choose. It's not easy finding the right words for someone so close, who you knew so little.

Mark nudges me and everyone looks round. A figure shuffles towards us, leaning heavily on a stick. Graham was the only one who responded to my carefully worded announcement. Despite my brief, he is dressed formally: the black wool coat and felt hat are from another era. As he hobbles closer, his face stretches into a grin.

'Kate,' he says. 'You are your mother's image.' He lifts a bird-like claw. A waft of cologne drifts between us.

'Thank you for coming, Graham.' I tentatively raise my hand. Despite his infirmity, something about him puts me on edge.

'I'm not late, am I?' His grey eyes flash.

'Not at all.'

He takes his place in the circle, and a gradual hush descends. I try to ignore the skips in my chest and focus on the urn at my feet.

'Thank you all for being here today. We chose this burial ground because, from what I understand, my mother was not a religious woman. As a botanist, she believed in the creed of science and the natural order of life. So it seemed fitting that she should come to rest here.' My eyes wander to the hole. I take a breath. 'During her career she accomplished many remarkable things, for conservation and humanity. But, as with many, the Crisis took its toll.'

I look up. All eyes are on the grave apart from Graham's; his are fixed upon me.

'I have heard some wonderful stories about Lily, from those who cared for her.' Anne gives an emphatic nod. 'It is a great sadness to me that I did not know her better. But then I remind myself that at least we got the chance to meet again. To learn a little about each other.' I swallow. 'Although our time together was brief, there is comfort in that.'

Those last moments. That flutter of her hand. Other than birth, that's about as close to someone as you can get.

'I have chosen a reading that some of you may know. It still resonates across the centuries.' The pages quiver and I try to still my hands.

Fear no more the heat o' the sun
Nor the furious winter's rages;

Thou, thy worldly task hast done,
Home and gone and ta'en thy wages;
Golden lads and girls all must,
As chimney sweepers, come to dust.'

I hear whispering. It's Graham. He's reciting the verses with me.

'Fear no more the frown o' the great,
Thou art past the tyrants' stroke;
Care no more to clothe and eat,
To thee the reed is as the oak;
The sceptre, learning, physic, must
All follow this and come to dust.'

There's a muffled sob: I think it's Anne. I block it out. I have to get through this.

'Fear no more the lightning-flash,
Nor all the dreaded thunder-stone;
Fear not slander, censure rash;
Thou hast finished joy and moan;
All lovers young, all lovers must
Consign to thee and come to dust.'

I fold the paper and slide it into my pocket. Mark leans over and kisses my cheek.

I kneel on the grass. The wet blades soak through my dress. I clasp the urn and unscrew the lid.

Her ashes are silky and cool against my fingers. I scoop some into my palm.

I release them. They fall, dusting the earth like snow.

We stand in silence, watching each person take their turn. This ritual, with such intimacy, feels outdated. We're not prepared to touch the hands of the living, but we'll sink our fingers into the remains of the dead.

When Graham hobbles forward, Mark offers an arm. Graham ignores it and lowers himself painstakingly down. He slips his hand into the urn. As he rubs the ash through his fingers he mutters something I can't quite hear.

I tip the rest of her ashes into the grave. A powdery cloud rises, which the breeze catches, taking a small part of her elsewhere. Mark shovels a thin layer of earth on top, and, together, we lift the wild cherry in. As we pack the soil around its roots, some cherries patter to the ground, like red tears. I squeeze my hands into the earth. I thought it wouldn't hurt as much as Pen, but it's a different kind of grief. For the days not had, the moments missed. The tenderness that couldn't be shared.

Sasha gives me a fierce hug. 'You did great, Mum,' she whispers. I hold on to her. Unable to let go.

'You head off with your father,' I say eventually. 'I'll follow in a little while.'

'You're sure?'

'Sure.'

I watch her walk across the burial ground with Mark. The two carers follow. Only Graham remains.

'That reading you chose,' he says. '*Cymbeline*. Perfect.'

'Thank you.'

I wait for him to give his condolences and leave. He does neither. I notice some flecks of ash on my sleeve. I go to wipe them off and change my mind.

'She loved you very much, you know. Your mother.'

I stare at him. 'You knew?' A slow smile carves into his face. 'I thought she kept it a secret?'

'She did.'

I frown.

'Everyone has secrets, Kate. That's a universal rule. Some people's job is to discover them.'

My jaw stiffens. He's either some kind of hack or one of those disreputable search agents; that entry in the obits was a stupid idea. 'So. You weren't a colleague.'

He purses his lips. 'Not exactly.'

I clench my hands. 'You lied to me.'

'Well, it would have been a little complicated to explain over the phone.'

I scan the burial ground, but everyone's gone. I hesitate. 'Who do you really work for?'

Veined eyelids hover over his eyes. 'The government. Intelligence, to be precise. At least, I used to.'

Intelligence? Jesus. I slip my hand into my pocket. If I hit 'redial', Mark should pick up.

Graham glances at me. 'Don't worry, Kate, there's not much I'm capable of these days.' He sighs. 'If I were you, I'd listen to what I have to say. We don't have much time.'

He dabs his forehead with an immaculate white handkerchief. And that's when I clock it: the sheen of sweat, his gaunt pallor.

'What is it?' I say. 'Cancer?'

He grins. 'Seen quite a few like me, I suppose.' His shiny veneers look obscene in his mouth. 'Shall we head over to that bench?'

He limps off, not bothering to see if I follow. I quickly message Mark. Graham eases himself down slowly, but I see him wince as he touches the seat.

He folds both hands over his stick. 'I assume you know about Brotanol. And Dr Bekker.'

I run my tongue around my mouth. 'What I've read and what I've heard are two very different stories.'

He nods. 'Indeed. Did your mother speak to you about it?'

'Not really. We never got the chance.' I pause. 'Cara did, though.'

He gazes past me, to the fields. 'Ah yes, Cara.' His lip curls. 'We underestimated her.'

I think of Cara, lying on the floor, and my anger sparks. I'm tempted to just walk away. Leave him to rot with his cancer.

'Did Lily know? How toxic it was?'

He taps his stick with one desiccated finger. 'By the time she was briefed, decisions had already been made. There was nothing she could do.'

'He knew, though, didn't he?'

Graham doesn't respond.

A blackbird hops down in front of us and starts foraging. It scurries from grave to grave, prodding the soil for grubs.

'So,' he says, 'what did Cara tell you?'

I meet his gaze. 'That our father was innocent. That he'd been set up and the whole thing was a lie.'

His expression doesn't waver. 'You know, there never would have been a problem if your father hadn't let his emotions get the better of him.' He sighs. '"A sacrifice of the few to save the masses." Even Bekker conceded the logic on that one. Where we differed was on what constituted "the few".'

I frown. 'What do you mean?'

'Bekker initially agreed to the trial. But when he found out how many hospitals were going to be used in South Africa he kicked up the most almighty stink. Threatened to leak it to the press and Lord only knows what else.'

My eyes widen. 'He tried to *stop* the drug being used?' Was Cara telling the truth, then?

The blackbird unearths a worm. The worm flails and writhes,

trying to bury itself back in the ground. The bird spears it with one foot and pecks at it, tearing off one piece after another.

Graham takes a breath. 'We didn't have the luxury of time. It was a question of national security. We needed to ramp up.'

'But you *knew* how dangerous that drug was.'

'Come on, Kate, you remember how dire things got. All those riots and fires. WHO had been predicting an antibiotic apocalypse for years! And, as the history books will tell you, things have a tendency to turn ugly when deaths rack up on that kind of scale. "*Vive la Révolution*" and all that...' He leans closer and I smell an acrid cocktail of antiseptic and cologne. 'Your father became a liability. One that had to be contained.'

The saliva dries in my mouth. 'So you did set it up. His involvement ... The terrorist links...'

'Well, it's a lot easier if you can fixate the loathing of the masses on one common enemy. Preferably a human one.'

All that's left of the worm are a few bloody segments. The dismembered remains slide away across the grass.

'Rumours were already circulating about bioterrorist plots, although nothing had been officially confirmed. The data was all over the place, so it didn't take much to fan those flames. Lots of groups wanted to steal the glory, but we needed something plausible that could be controlled. A network of our own.'

I blink at him. 'What ... what are you saying? Are you implying that ... that EAA weren't responsible?'

Graham barks a laugh. 'That bunch of hippies? They couldn't organise their way out of a bus shelter.'

My mind spirals. 'But ... what about the arenas? And the vectors? I was at one of those concerts, for God's sake; I worked in a hospital. I saw them with my own eyes!'

'Ah yes, the vectors. An artful packaging of a disaster waiting to happen.' He lifts his eyes to mine. 'Of course there were carriers. But they weren't orchestrated by EAA. Or by anyone else, for that matter. EAA was, put simply, a marketing exercise. The perfect scapegoat for the woeful failures of a system that allowed the Crisis to unfold.'

I see the concert hall and Lucy's face. The panic in the hospitals and the headlines. And I think of Lily on her deathbed, apologising over and over. Saying his name.

'You're wondering why your mother testified against him, aren't you?' Graham rakes his stick along the gravel. 'So now we come to the nub of it.'

I stare at the cherry tree I just planted. Dark thoughts crowd in, each vying for attention.

'I'd never understood why such a handsome woman hadn't ever married or settled down. She'd taken the occasional lover, but nothing serious; she could have had her pick.' He pauses. 'We already knew Bekker had certain political leanings from his apartheid days. It took a bit more work to uncover the rest. Which was when I discovered that he and your mother knew each other much better than we'd realised.'

I think of the press articles, the conference photo. That Mona Lisa smile.

'Then I hit the jackpot.' Graham's eyes flash. 'You.'

I edge away from him. It feels as if I am sinking. Down, beneath the grass, with all the others. Into the soft, wet graves.

'Imagine how much fun the papers would have had,' Graham continues. '"Love Child of Killer-Drug Duo Discovered". "Unmasked: Secret Daughter of a Terrorist". Not the best introduction to your birth parents, is it? You see, unlike your father, Mary applied her head over her heart. She understood what she had to do. I saw first-hand what it cost her.'

The pieces rearrange themselves and finally I see it. My mother, having to choose between her lover and her child. Choosing me, after all.

I dig my nails into the bench. I want to grab him by his saggy throat and squeeze.

'Why are you telling me this now? Is it some sort of confession? A shedding of guilt before the end?'

He gazes at me, but his eyes are distant. 'Believe it or not, I actually became quite fond of your mother. She loathed me, of course.' He sighs. 'I thought you should know what lengths she went to, to keep you safe. As she never got the chance to tell you herself.'

I jump up. 'You've got some nerve. She died because of you! They all did. My father, his wife. Even Cara. Where does it end?'

Graham looks at me as if I'm a child. 'Death comes to us all sooner or later, Kate. You know that better than most.' He swallows. 'You've a right to be angry; I'm not here to defend myself. But at least now you know the truth.' He mops his brow. 'And on that note, I really must be going.' He pockets his handkerchief and starts to lever himself up.

'What's to stop me taking all this to the press? Finish what my father started? I'm sure the papers would love to hear your story.'

He steadies himself against the bench. 'Absolutely nothing. But if they want to interview me, they'd better be quick. I'm booked into the Peace Clinic tomorrow.'

He tips his hat. I glimpse a lattice of thin grey strands. 'Goodbye, Kate. I'm sorry about your mother. She was an exceptional woman. But I'm glad I finally got to meet you.'

I watch him hobble down the path: a hunched black spectre. It's a relief when he turns the corner and disappears.

I walk to the cherry tree and run my hand over its leaves. 'He was wrong about you,' I whisper. 'They all were. Everything you did came from the heart.'

CHAPTER 52

New Hope Dawns in War against Infection: Trials of Bacterial 'Gene-Shredder' Show Promise

With no signs of the antibiotic restrictions being lifted or shelf lives improving, new gene-editing technology may bring the long-awaited boost to healthcare we need. Volunteers from five hospitals for the elderly have signed up to trials for a radical new procedure being developed by bioscience start-up, Prosper. Specific DNA strands are targeted in disease-causing bacteria, which contain critical genes required by the pathogen to function.

'There's a certain irony here,' comments CEO of Prosper, Dr Rich Hendren. 'By using these tools, we've effectively turned the bacteria's own defence mechanism against them. The beauty of this treatment is that we avoid the opportunity for bacteria to develop resistance because we target multiple genes in one go.'

Initial results look promising. Three months after being treated for an extensively drug-resistant infection, seventy-five percent of the volunteers are still alive.

KATE

Sunlight streams through the window, illuminating floating columns of dust. The room looks bigger now the furniture has gone. Ready for its next tenant. Lily spent years in this room, but now only the ghosts of her things remain, commemorated by bright silhouettes on the wallpaper, the odd dent in the carpet. At least her flowers are still here. Daisies, lavender, roses. I'm not so sure about the blue ones. She would have told me.

I sit with my back to the wall and rest the wooden box on my knees. I drum the lid with my fingers, afraid to open it. There was so little of her in everything else we went through. Clothes, pictures, books. The odd piece of jewellery. But there's evidence in here, I know. My lawyer told me.

The door swings open and Anne sticks her head round. 'Goodness, what are you doing down there, Kate? Let me bring you a chair.'

'I'm fine, honestly.' I smile. 'I like floors.'

Her eyes drop to the box. 'You've got it, then. Lord only knows why they sent it back here.'

'I know. Still, it's a chance to see her room again. One last time.'

Anne's lips tighten. 'Doesn't seem right, Lily not being here. I keep expecting to see her in her chair.' She tugs at her apron and sighs. 'I still can't believe everything that went on. You think you know people...'

They found the puncture wound on Lily's left arm. The coroner said that was why the sepsis came on so fast. It's still not entirely clear how Cara duped the monitoring systems. So now Mrs Downing has her own investigation to contend with.

Anne lifts her eyes to mine. 'Even now, I can't stop thinking about it. I should have listened. Lily tried to talk to me, you know, but I—'

'Anne, please, this isn't your fault. It went way back. I'm not sure any of us could have stopped it.'

We lapse into silence. I'm thinking about Cara. About how much of a victim she was, too.

Anne takes a breath. 'You mustn't blame yourself either, Kate.' I look up. 'I'm talking about Natalie. Or whatever her real name was.' She sighs. 'It wasn't your fault, what happened. How were you to know?' Anne shakes her head. 'None of us had any idea what she was capable of.'

Anne means well. But the truth is, if I had acted differently, at least one death might have been prevented. Those were dark days, after my arrest. I knew I was innocent, but I still didn't have the full picture. After hours of questions, I began to doubt myself. And Lily.

Anne squeezes my shoulder. 'Can I at least bring you a drink?'

'Got any gin?'

She smiles. 'I'm not sure our nutritional regime stretches to that. Will tea do?'

'Sure.'

I wait for the door to close and smooth my thumbs over the wood. What other secrets does Lily have in store?

I lift the lid. A faint scent stirs, like some kind of spice. Nestled inside is a bundle of envelopes and papers squeezed together with an elastic band. I release them; they flutter into my lap like felled birds.

I sift through until I spot a yellow, crinkled newspaper cutting.

Kill Not Cure

Hundreds of TB patients suffer agonising deaths after taking unlicensed, experimental drug.

The Brotanol children. Bones stick out of pinched faces beneath the sunken hollows of their eyes. This is the picture that triggered a public outcry. I think of Graham and my heart pounds. All those years, she carried that guilt.

I fold the cutting and put it back. Amidst the pile I notice a small, bulging envelope with a single letter on the front: *K*. Inside is a tiny plastic wristband. The band's been cut but the white button-lock still holds the two pieces together. A strip of pink paper is encased in the middle with words in blue biro:

Baby of Mary Sommers

I curl the ends together to make a circle. It's hard to imagine my wrist ever fitting something so small. And it comes again, that yearning, like a small, burrowing creature. For the mother I didn't know. For the baby I was. A mourning for what might have been.

I sort through more papers. I discover a photograph, sandwiched between two envelopes: one of those old-fashioned prints that must have been developed from film.

A man lies naked on a bed, eyes closed, sheets tangled around his legs. One arm is outstretched, sprawled across an empty pillow. I note the tanned, muscular body, the high cheekbones, the shock of fair hair. Behind him, a table-lamp throws shadows over the room.

I imagine her watching him, waiting until he'd fallen asleep. Slipping out from under the sheets and tip-toeing across the floor.

He looks so peaceful. My father.

On the back, in faint pencil, is the name of a game park that sounds familiar. And a date.

The picture was taken the year before I was born.

CHAPTER 53

KATE

The dawn chill makes the hairs on my arms stand up as we rattle along the road. The jeep throws arcs of light across the scrub, transforming grey silhouettes into bushes. Fiery streaks emerge in a cobalt sky, surpassing the crescent moon. I inhale the musky scents of unknown creatures as the first tentative notes of birdsong start to trill.

'I could get used to this,' I say. 'Where's everyone else? We haven't seen one other car.'

'Perhaps they're taking the morning off, having a lie-in.' Sasha grins. 'Had a few too many beers. Like someone else we know.'

My daughter never ceases to surprise me. At home, I have to virtually drag her out of bed, but here, a 5.30 start poses no problem. But then it's not every day you see a lion stride out in front of you or a troop of baboons cross the road. We have been so lucky. I can understand why Lily fell in love with this place.

'Shall we take this left loop?' Sasha points at the map. 'I don't think we've done that one yet. There's a water pan in about five K's.'

I glance at her and nod. Over the last week her porcelain skin has darkened to a light olive. It suits her. I like seeing her without make-up: I can glimpse the young girl she used to be.

We turn onto a gravel road, sending a pair of hornbills chattering up into the air. A gold spiral dances around the car. It's the sun, reflecting off Lily's bracelet.

I hope you're happy I came.

We slow to admire three vultures, hunched like chilly old men in a dead tree.

'Shouldn't be far now,' says Sasha, squinting up the road. 'So take it easy.'

'OK.'

A herd of impala look up from the grass and freeze, gazing at us with impossibly pretty eyes. As we get closer, they bounce off behind the bushes, their dainty legs kicking out behind them.

I round the next corner and slam my foot on the brake; gravel spins out from the wheels.

'What the...?'

Right in front of us, twenty metres up ahead, is a rhino. Its plated body spans the entire width of the road. The animal starts to its feet and turns, displaying two magnificent horns. I grip Sasha's arm as she just about suppresses a squeal: this is our first one. In our haste to grab the camera, we almost miss the smaller shape hiding behind.

'Mum, look!' whispers Sasha. 'A baby!'

I feel a rush of adrenaline. I'm not sure if it's fear or excitement, or both. I signal Sasha to stop scrabbling. The mother trots forward a few steps and her baby presses in underneath.

'OK,' I say, my mouth all sticky. 'Time to retreat.'

I put the car into reverse and crawl back, metre by metre, eyes glued to the windscreen. The mother stands her ground. Her conical ears are constantly swivelling, pinpointing exactly where we are. When we reach what I hope is an acceptable distance, I slow to a stop; the engine idles at the ready. She gives a couple of snorts that makes my heart leap but she doesn't come any closer.

'Switch it off,' whispers Sasha.

'What?'

'The engine. Switch it off.'

I glare at her. 'Are you crazy?'

'The noise is probably what's freaking her out. Rhinos have poor eyesight but very acute hearing.' Sasha appears to have assumed the role of game ranger. 'As long as we keep our distance, I reckon we're fine.'

'Try telling that to the insurance company when she totals this jeep!'

'Shhh!' Sasha scowls at me. 'Mum, will you just go with it? You're in Africa now. You don't possess the high ground on hazards.'

'OK, OK.' I exhale. 'But we're out of here the moment she stirs.'

I turn off the engine and the sounds of Africa flood in. Two exotic birds I don't recognise make strange hoops and trills. A dung beetle buzzes past, its body tipped precariously like a plane about to crash. A baboon's bark makes both Sasha and me jump. The rhino continues her vigil, whipping at flies with her tail. The baby peeks its head out from between its mother's legs, curious to see us too. Its horns are tiny: two little stumps like teeth, either side of its nose.

Eventually the mother relaxes and wanders over to the grass. The two of them begin to graze. I take silent gulps of air while Sasha leans out of the window, clicking away. Every so often, the mother lifts her head to check on us, and my hand flies to the ignition. Each time she resumes her feed. The baby never leaves her side.

We sit there, together, watching, until they amble off into the bush.

Despite their size, within seconds, both mother and baby have disappeared.

ACKNOWLEDGEMENTS

There are many people to whom I owe thanks for helping me get this book into the hands of readers. As a debut writer, the journey is as much about persistence as it is about skill, and for that you need the unwavering love and support of family and friends. I had that. You know who you are.

I must thank my agent, Harry Illingworth, at DHH, who was the first agent who really 'got' the book and took a bet on me, patiently answering my rookie questions. And I also want to thank the wonderful team at Orenda Books, particularly Karen Sullivan, whose super-human energy and passion breathed new ideas into the novel, and to whom I am permanently indebted for bringing this book to life.

This journey started with an innocent subscription to a creative-writing group: the Chippie Writers, led by a wise playwright: Alan Pollock. His encouragement and that of the other writers was pivotal, and I will always be grateful.

Special mention must go to my alpha reader: Bill Hudson. His thoughtful edits and ruthless murdering of inadequate characters has been, and continues to be, priceless. Thank you. I must also thank Rob Way for his assiduous help with all the medical bits, Nessa for the South Africa checks, Jo Copestick and Clare Litt for their publishing insights and support, and my industry mentor, Jonathan Eyers, who not only gave me excellent technical advice, but also hope, during bleaker moments. The Bridport Prize judges also warrant my thanks. The shortlisting of *The Waiting Rooms* strengthened my belief in the novel and helped me along the path to representation.

My final and sincere thanks go to my long-suffering husband, Dave, and to my daughters, Nuala and Aaron. It's really down to them, in the end. Only a family can keep persuading you you're doing the right thing, when it makes no logical sense whatsoever. Thank you. This book would never have been written without you.

THE INSPIRATION BEHIND
The Waiting Rooms

When I tell people I've written a novel about an antibiotic crisis, I get some funny looks. *Why the hell has she done that*, I see them thinking, *can't she write about romance or serial killers: something a little more jolly?* Well, I can't. Sorry. For me, it has to be dark issues or dark science: the things that keep me up at night. Things that I hope keep you up, too.

I had the idea for *The Waiting Rooms* after I read some scary facts about antibiotic resistance. Those facts became the foundation of my pre-Crisis chapters and you can read more of them on my website. I did a lot of research. Believe me: the slide towards an antibiotic crisis is real. What happens next: the size and scope of the crisis, the diseases that flourish, and the choices society and governments make, is not. Yet. Those details were mine.

Which brings me on to the premise of the book: no one over seventy is allowed antibiotics, in a last-ditch attempt to keep resistance at bay. A little extreme, you may think. But consider this: antibiotic use by age group is a U-shaped graph. The highest number of prescriptions to stave off infections go to the young and the old. In the UK, the over-seventy-fives account for a quarter of all antibiotic prescriptions. The over-sixty-fives account for a third.

The global population is ageing. Virtually every country in the world is experiencing growth in the number and proportion of its elderly, with the over-sixty-fives growing faster than all other age groups. The global population of the over-eighties is expected to more than triple between 2015 and 2050; in some Latin American and Asian countries it will quadruple. By 2050, one in four people in the US and Europe will be over 65. But how well is our society coping with this change?

A recent report by the Royal Society for Public Health claims that ageism is the most commonly experienced form of prejudice and discrimination in the UK and Europe. Compounding this, we have social-care systems and health services already in crisis, and needs are only going to increase.

Put all this together and you have the perfect storm.

For those readers who are interested in scaring themselves further about these and other issues in the book, I've assembled more facts and links on my website.

But a warning.

The deeper you delve, the less speculative and more probable the world of *The Waiting Rooms* becomes.

Enjoy.

www.evesmithauthor.com
@evecsmith